"Dranoff does a good job of building a world in which supernaturals exist, but not everyone knows it, or they choose not to believe. This first book in the Mark of the Moon series is a good start to what could be a great paranormal romance/urban fantasy."

—*Library Journal*

"*Mark of the Moon* is a one-of-a-kind paranormal erotic story. The plot is original, and Dranoff introduces truly authentic creatures.... Dana is a very complex, unpredictable character."

—*RT Book Reviews*

"Beth Dranoff does a great job with her storytelling... I look forward to reading more from her."

—*Alpha Book Club* on *Mark of the Moon*

"The author has a talent for creating rich descriptions and crafting an intriguing plot with lots of action."

—*The Novel Lady* on *Mark of the Moon*

Coming soon from Beth Dranoff and Carina Press

Betrayed by Blood
Shifting Loyalties

BETH DRANOFF

MARK OF THE MOON

Recycling programs for this product may not exist in your area.

ISBN-13: 978-1-335-88615-6

Mark of the Moon

This edition published by arrangement with Harlequin Books S.A.

www.CarinaPress.com

Printed in U.S.A.

For Zak.

MARK OF THE MOON

ONE

THE SKIN AT my wrists chafed, steel buffered by satin and faux fur—although clearly not buffered enough. My back was crisscrossed by strips of black leather buckled into place around two-by-two-inch breast patches.

I'd call it a bra, but if we're being honest it's more of a barely-there colored napkin than anything in the utilitarian undergarment family.

Then again, seeing as I was chained from the ceiling in a matching leather thong and five-inch platform Baby Jane shoes so red they matched the Cherie Cherry color of my lips right down to the shine, perhaps utilitarianism could be seen to have more than one interpretation at this point.

How did I get here? Let's call him Jon. For the purposes of this particular game, we'll even call him *Master*. I had allowed him to cover my eyes, blackness fastened with a quick-release knot. I could feel his breath along the length of my neck; his tongue tracing a line along my skin to the lobe of my ear. With just a tip of incisor, applying pressure *there*, just *so*.

The guy was definitely full-body tingle-worthy. Six foot two inches tall, wavy honey-gold shoulder-length hair, green eyes, black brows. Muscles honed into stomach flatness; arms, butt and thighs rounded nicely in a non-steroid kind of way; full, blood-red lips.

The sound of his voice had me craving him, needing to reach out and touch, be touched.

Irresistible. Kissable. A delicious Mr. Right Now.

I could feel Mr. Right Now behind me, blowing raised heat along my left ear and down my neck with a throaty chuckle. His fingertips tracing the beauty mark tattoos scattered across my back. An icy breeze drifting in through a February frost-edged window raised goose bumps in surprising places as he lifted my dark curly hair up just a bit to nuzzle, then bite, that spot where neck meets shoulder. Again I felt the imprint of his teeth on my skin, this time pressing against muscle. Bruising. Marking me as his.

Jon was sporting his own leather gear, something involving laces and iron rings and not much else. I could feel the chilled O of the ring holding all those laces together as Jon pressed against me from behind. The contrast of hot and cold made me shiver, a delicious tingle from my toes up to where he was nestled, hard as a rock. And then higher still, until my scalp prickled with an energy that needed release.

There was pounding.

For a moment I thought it was my heart through the thickness of my throat. Then I realized it might be the sound of knuckles on wood, someone wanting to be *here* rather than *there*.

"Are you going to get that?" I tried for neutral and almost nailed it.

Jon stood in front of me, so close that the hairs on his chest and legs tickled. Then the blindfold was off.

We kissed like nobody was waiting to break through the door on the other side of this moment.

I almost didn't hear the knocks anymore as Jon touched me right *there*, his finger coming away wet, then wetter still as he dipped the glistening digit into his own mouth, watching my face, finishing the gesture with a soft *pop*.

"Open the fucking door!" The voice growled—there was definite male with a hint of something else. "I can smell you two! Freaks. Open the fucking door now or I'm breaking it!"

"Give us a minute!" I figured if the guy could smell us, he could also hear me. "Shit," I muttered. "At least help me out of these." I shook at the chains.

Jon stepped forward and laid a feather-light hand on my wrist as the door flew off its hinges and a shifter, halfway through his change, charged through to leap past me and onto Jon. With angry whiskers twitching and claws outstretched, the feline grazed my calf with a razor-sharp nail as he knocked Jon over.

"You shit," the man growled as he straddled Jon. "I wasn't enough for you? You had to take yourself on a mortal? *Girl?*"

Jon shrugged, and his smile held a faint apology even as he reached up to scratch behind the other man's fuzz-covered ears.

"Hello, standing right here?" I didn't really want to intrude, but my leg was starting to throb. I should probably get some antiseptic on that, once I got free from my bindings. Then the pain kicked in.

"Dana?" Jon's voice was suddenly in my ear. "Are you okay?"

No.

Not okay at all.

My last thought before the world turned black.

FALLING.

Searing pain.

Blinding headache; blades of fire in my gut.

I can't move, but I can feel.

All I can *do* is feel. My entire body is sensation.

Skin prickling, hair standing on end; surrounded by shadows. How many are there? One? Two? Ten? I have no idea. Could be one hundred, one thousand, more—all they are to me is shades of light and dark.

There, a flare of light. *There*, another one.

I reach out to touch the brightness and come away with clumps of soft fur in my hand. Blackness washes over me again, velvet on satin, a feeling so pure it hurts.

And then there's nothing.

TWO

I WOKE UP slowly and realized I was alive.

I was sore. My muscles screamed from overuse, although I couldn't remember doing much more than hallucinating. Memories of pain, flashes of recollection.

Memories making me want to sit up, fast. Except I couldn't. I couldn't move my arms or legs.

I squeezed my eyelids shut before opening them again to flex outwards. Left, right, up then down. Visual stretches. *Sure.*

My breath ran ragged, fear hitching a ride as I looked around, unable to move more than my eyes, toes and fingers. I realized I was strapped to the kind of hospital-style bed normally found in a mental institution. The padded restraints were old-style nut-brown leather lined with faded grey-tinged flannel that you *knew* used to be white. I didn't want to think about what might have gotten them old and dirty. Stainless-steel buckles were firmly fastened. The work was professional; definitely not intended for recreational use.

Black walls and white leather furniture came into stark view as I scanned beyond my prone position. A small cut crystal vase on the cherry wood nightstand was filled with dead pink roses, shriveled into perfect immobility either by neglect or purposeful patience. Beyond that was a thick pile carpet, black with streaks and swirls of blood red and pumpkin orange.

Drawing awareness back into myself, I realized that my left foot was warmer than the rest of me. Curious, I peered along my black tank top—encased torso, down across the expanse of starched hospital sheet, following the outline of my legs to where my captivity attached itself to steel bars at the end of the bed.

There.

A long-haired cat, all brown and black stripes like a small raccoon, was curled up against my ankle watching me with glowing green eyes that didn't blink. As I stared, it crooked a paw to its mouth and licked at the pink skin of its pads, then rubbed the moisture up against its face. I was ignored during the ablutions.

ONE DAY, a while back, this wild-looking woman with a head of matted white dreadlocks came up to me on Bloor Street. She put out her hand, wizened lips puckered in a skin-peeling O, and looked *not* at me with crazy-ass brown eyes fading to grey. No, she looked above my head and around me.

"Here, kitty kitty kitty," she said, and cackled, her toothless grin giving way to a single remaining incisor that winked at me like a lone ice floe in a murky swamp of putrescence.

I saw her three times in seven days. Always on Bloor, that east-west corridor bisecting central Toronto into north and south. Once it was outside the Bloor Cinema. Another time it was as I passed by the Borden Avenue laneway, piled high with trashcans of fresh refuse from nearby restaurants.

Each time, the same response.

Here, kitty kitty kitty. Parched lips cackling sound in my general direction.

Each time, I ignored her.

The third time she was sitting outside the Tranzac Club, a few doors south of Bloor on Brunswick Avenue, waiting for me. No idea how that was possible—my being there had been a last-minute thing.

As before, I pretended she didn't exist, the way us big-city inhabitants learn to do.

This time, she was having none of it. Reaching out to touch my arm as I passed and leaving flesh imprints of white behind. She was stronger than she looked.

Squinting at me, her eyes were suddenly lucid as she angled her body towards me. A conspiratorial gesture. Smelling of urine and mothballs and diesel fuel and other things I chose not to lay name to.

"You don't know who you are?"

I shook my head; denial, avoidance even. Who could blame me, standing on the sidewalk, talking to a woman with eyes so wild and breath so rank? I couldn't look directly at her; I focused instead on her fluorescent green and blue frog puppet winter boots—was that a toe sticking out?—refusing to acknowledge my part in this street-side exchange.

She narrowed her bleary stare and waved the flats of her grooved palms towards me. *Wax on, wax off* came unbidden to mind.

"I can see clearer now." Her voice was a power drill boring through the softened butter of my awareness before the connection was abruptly broken.

"Money for a crazy old lady," she wheedled, lucidity gone as quickly as it had appeared. "Kind kitty got some milk money for an old lady?"

I dug into my pocket and found some change, dropping coins into her grime-encrusted hands before turning back to continue down the street. Her laughter followed.

"HEY, KITTY KITTY KITTY." My voice was a hoarse croak, remembered echoes of the crazy street lady. But was it from lack of use—or from screaming?

No answers, only questions as I tracked the only other living thing in this room. I noticed the streak of orange on the cat's forehead, a thumbprint of baked squash with brown sugar, its eyes now like green olives with a pimento in the middle. The cat's lips were twisted as though it had taken a bite of that pimento and found it wanting.

"My name," it said in a blend of purr and snarl, "is Jun."

Pardon?

I looked closer: whiskers, pink tongue, wide eyes, attitude oozing from every fur-clogged pore. Definitely a cat, but was it real? Inhaling deeply, I made a conscious decision to breathe; on the exhale, I released my incredulity. The key to every good buzz is to go with it—at least that's the theory.

"Jun," I echoed, my voice now surprisingly unwavering. "Like the month?"

Its stare was disdain wrapped in fur.

"No." It shook its head and flicked a bead of moisture off its whiskers. "Like truth."

"Truth," I echoed again. My mind was stupid with the effort of keeping up with our conversation. I was feeling very Alice down the rabbit hole, and wondered again if this was a hallucination. "Truth? What is truth?"

"What's it look like?" Jun replied. "Do I have a fortune cookie sticking out of my ass?"

My turn to stare and raise an eyebrow. At least I could do that. Make the most of whatever small bit of movement I could manage.

Jun ignored my attempt at attitude, opting instead to jump off the bed and pad towards a swinging door I hadn't realized existed. "Later," it said, pushing the door open with its head and scooting the rest of its body through without pause.

I STARED AFTER the cat so long my vision wavered. No choice. I closed my eyes.

And noticed that portions of the darkness were lighter than others.

Huh?

I opened my eyes and looked around.

Light, coming from a large window to my right, glinting off the buckles still fastening me to the bed. Edges of white bleeding around heavy, brocade drapes of red velvet trimmed with black sateen cord. I took the leap of faith necessary: it must be day.

But which day? Which week? Which month, even?

How long had I been *here*, wherever *here* was?

I HAD ANOTHER VISITOR: the first human I'd seen since regaining consciousness. Female. Her straight blond hair was pulled back and pinned into place by matching steel clips that tucked under a starched white cap with candy-cane red stripes. Her outfit could have been part of a matching nurse ensemble or some kind of white latex sex kitten costume. 1950s Doris Day or maybe Sally Field as Gidget or possibly a Tim Burton movie getup replica. *The Nightmare Before the Day That Followed* That *Night.* I stifled a giggle, somewhere between reality and hysteria.

She did the normal medical things nurses do—temperature, blood pressure, listening to my heartbeat and tracking my breath going in and out by watching the rise/fall of my chest. She even took my pulse and made notes of her findings with a number two pencil on what might have been my medical chart.

"What's your name?" Conversation of any kind had to be better than this silence.

"Gwen," she replied, her smile starching wide.

"Well hi, Gwen, it's nice to meet you," I said, polite, carefully keeping my face blank. I wasn't sure yet exactly how nice it was to meet her, but I figured I'd try the honey versus the bees approach. "Any idea when I can go home?"

Oops, wrong thing to say. Her perky veneer dropped momentarily. Blankness, and was that a flicker of hostility I caught before she schooled her face back to cheerful?

"Soon, soon," Gwen replied, re-attaching the clipboard to the end of my bed as she avoided my eyes and fixed the sheet on her way out. "Don't forget, if you need anything, just press the button in your wrist restraint."

She pointed to a heretofore-unnoticed button on my right wrist cuff. *Nifty.* And left me to my thoughts.

Great. Just what I always wanted. I closed my eyes.

I'M TIED DOWN. It's then and it's now and it's happening all over again in my head. So many years ago. "How big you've gotten, dear," he says, coming too close. "What size bra do you wear now?" His questions, his nearness, creeping along my skin like slime. "Tell me, do you masturbate?" The questions, the proximity. Holding my arms behind me in the alleyway, grinding himself into me. I can't move, I can't stop him although I know I should.

Can't.

Move.

The past made present once more.

My mind feels like it's about to snap. Sweat beads my upper lip, no pleasure now; nails poking into my palms, fingers curled tightly into fists. But there's nothing to punch. Nothing I can do but lie here.

With my emotional buttons, you'd think I'd avoid situations like the one I found myself most recently in with Jon.

So then, why?

Titillation perhaps. Confronting my fears. What happened to me before wasn't my choice but this—whatever I make of it, whatever I take from it—is mine. I reclaim my ability, my right, to decide who does what with my body.

At least until now.

As I lie here, powerless to do anything but bite back a scream of frustration.

No choice. Not right now.

And so I wait.

How did I get here? I try to remember. Jon. Friend. Vampire. Also, as I recall, a whiskered man who was clearly on intimate terms with that vampire. *Huh.* Go figure.

I did remember ending up at Jon's place after work. It wasn't the first time.

I've been a bartender at the Swan Song for about three years now—a pit-stop job that took out an extended lease on my life, even though I still preferred to think of myself as a month-to-month-type employee. I also did a little freelance writing on the side, which was how Jon and I met.

Goth Libertines, a local magazine covering dark happenings across Southern Ontario, had hired me to do a piece on a local Toronto artist who was rumored to be of the sunlight-deprived variety. All pumped up, I'd dropped by his Parkdale-area gallery on Queen Street West one bright Tuesday afternoon. The black blinds were down and the front door was locked.

Frustrated, I'd gone next door to grab a cup of coffee—black, one sugar. I asked the blue-haired woman with the clashing caramel-brown, stenciled-in widow's-peak eyebrows about the cafe's supposedly mysterious neighbor.

"Oh *him*," she said, motioning at the concrete wall. "He's an odd one." She nodded, sagely, unconsciously fondling the small gold-chiseled cross she'd fished out from the crevice of her ample bosom. "Won't see him before the sun goes down."

"Why's that?" I kept my voice even, neutral with a hint of bored superiority.

Except that she wasn't as dumb as she looked.

"You know," she said, leaning forward conspiratorially, "he's one of *those*."

"One of what?" I bit back on my desire to shake the woman.

"One of those hippie types." She waved a French-manicured hand, nails like dipped liquid-paper-soaked claws, for emphasis. Or maybe it was to ward off a fruit fly. "You know, the kind that spend all day in bed with other hippie types, doing drugs and," she lowered her voice to a stage whisper, "all kinds of *other* immoral activities."

Maybe she really *was* that dumb after all.

I thanked her for her advice and left the diner. Three hours and twenty minutes until sundown, three hours until my shift started. I'd have to leave a note. Which I did, folding the paper up as neatly as possible and shoving it through the gallery's mail slot. The prickling-hair sensation of being watched followed me as I walked to my truck.

I got off work about eight hours later and, on a whim, headed back towards the gallery.

The usual neighborhood residents—drifters, hookers and dealers—were scattered in and out of the shadows cast by flickering overhead streetlights. Storefronts were a mix of festive colors flanked by dark interiors. Two thirty a.m. on a Wednesday wasn't a big time for shopping, even in downtown Toronto. I passed blocks of darkened shops.

Traffic was nonexistent, unless you counted the potential johns trawling for a date. Nobody honked as I eased my truck to a stop across from the gallery.

The dark drapes were still drawn but I could see yellow highlighting the edges in flickers, as though people were moving around on the other side. I cracked the frost-stiffened window of my truck open. Even from this distance, I could hear music and tinkling glasses and the murmurs of blended conversations.

A party in the middle of the night in the middle of the week? Was it an after-hours bar? Or could it be a hangout for those who preferred moonlight to sunlight?

Maybe I should leave.

My cell phone buzzed, *unknown name unknown number* flashing on the call display. Very helpful.

"Hello?"

"Will you be sitting out there all night or do you plan to come in and join the party?" The voice was male: deep, rich, throaty. The drapes were pulled back to frame a man, his head surrounded by what looked like a wavering halo. It was a trick of the lighting; I knew this, consciously. But it still freaked me out. *An angelic vampire. Right.*

Even from here, I could see the man was beautiful.

I'd thought about my shots, calculating the span of time between now and my last booster. Checked to make sure the tattoo (Hebrew for "life") was still brightly emblazoned on my ankle, even as I touched my right ear to confirm that the tiny Celtic silver cross still dangled from its hoop of matching silver. What can I say—I'm equal opportunity when it comes to religion-based self-protection. One last move to settle the stake in the front pocket of my jacket, the dagger to the right of my tailbone, and one more tucked into the side of my boot.

"Everything good to go?"

"Fine." It may have come out a bit sharper than necessary. Another breath to cover my overreaction. "You *are* Jon Grizendorfer, the owner of this gallery, right?"

"Of course I am," he said with a voice like fingertips trailing through sand. He was waving now. Somehow he made it feel elegant, sexual.

"Okay." Forced calmness. I could do this. "Let me park and I'll be right in."

"See you soon." His voice descended to somewhere

just above a whisper, gravelly yet smooth, pebbles on satin.

"Soon," I replied automatically, disconnecting the line and tossing the phone onto the passenger seat. I put the truck in gear and did a quick U-turn to park in front of the gallery. Parallel parking had never been so difficult.

I HEARD A door I couldn't see *swoosh* open and then swing shut to my left. The hospital gauze-white curtain beside my bed was pushed aside by a new hand—ebony, fleshy, solid.

But still not one I recognized. The muscular arm gave way to an equally muscular chest, obscured only vaguely by olive-green scrubs and a white lab coat.

As the mystery man turned around to close the curtains, bending down to scoop something off a nearby chair, I couldn't help but check out his ass.

Nice. Even covered by baggy hospital-wear, it was clear he had no reason to hide it.

The man turned back again and my reaction time must have been a little slow. His eyes were on mine before I managed to pull them up to meet his, missing the option of feigned indifference by a few seconds. *Whoops.*

He grinned.

"Caught you looking," he said.

I shrugged, going for casual. "And?" Oh yeah, I was good. Okay, so as good as you can be while attached to a bed, unable to move anything except for your eyes, eyebrows and mouth, but still. I cocked an eyebrow at him and waited. Patience being a virtue and all that. If it's a virtue, it must be hard, right?

Well, something was hard all right. His gaze. Taking me all in.

Normally, I might be pissed. Strange guy, looking me up and down, and me in no position to do anything about it. Then again, normally I wouldn't be strapped to a bed, unable to do anything but waggle my eyebrows menacingly.

Right.

"So, Dana," Dr. Not-Yet-Known said. "My name is Anshell Williams, and I'm the resident on call tonight." He examined my chart, all business now. "Your friend, Jon no-last-name-no-fixed-address, was concerned and brought you in."

"Is he here?" Hope, slim, wanting a familiar face in a strange environment. Even if that face was one of a vampire and a casual. . .*friend.* Playmate? Lover was a bit much. What was the politically correct term for a fuck buddy these days?

"No," Dr. Williams said, gauging my reaction. "But he did send flowers." He motioned to the dead roses. Ah. Ironic symbolism made clear.

Plus, daylight. Jon's absence was becoming increasingly logical.

"So," I said, striving to sort through the weirdness. *Don't freak out don't freak out don't freak out.*

"Why am I here? What's this so-called 'medical condition' that requires such extreme treatment in a facility that's clearly not a government-run operation?"

Dr. Williams stopped fussing with the tube he'd been playing with. He looked directly at me; I felt a cold stone of fear reach its long, grey fingers around my stomach and squeeze.

"You may have been scratched by a were-cat," he

said. "So you may also have been exposed to the virus that causes felinthropy. Do you know what that is?"

I nodded. "It's what causes a person to turn into a cat. Right?"

"More or less," he said. "I see, according to your records, that you've been immunized against this through a broad-spectrum therianthropic vaccine you got about eight years ago. It's possible that what you have is a mild case of the virus and the effects won't be permanent. But you're definitely showing symptoms."

"Effects?" My mouth strained to form word-shaped sounds. "Symptoms?"

"Your changes."

"Changes." My lips were numb and I wondered if this was what shock felt like. "I changed?"

What are the words for a reality that makes no sense?

APPARENTLY, YES, I'D CHANGED. Into something involving fur and whiskers and pointed teeth. Nothing I could control, or even replicate on demand; the restraints there to protect me from myself, and stop me from harming those around me. But I was past the worst of it. Or so Dr. Williams thought. A few more hours of observation and then maybe I could go home.

There were implications. If the effects wore off I could go back to my normal life. Had this ever happened? No, but there was always a first time. *Oh.* The medic was making a funny. Ha. So I was stuck like this. A shifter. One of those things I'd been trained to hunt, teachings I'd abandoned when I'd quit the Agency four years ago.

I didn't have to do this alone. Anshell Williams said

the words without being explicit about details. There were others. Of course—I knew this. But did I want to belong to a club that would only now be interested in having me as a member?

Too much to process. Williams left me to check on another patient, although I suspected it was more to leave me with my thoughts.

I did the only thing I could. Closed my eyes and let my mind drift backwards in time while I waited.

JON'S PARTY HAD been an illusion. When I'd walked through the front door all those months ago, it had been into an empty gallery. Instinct had my hand reaching up to toy with my Star of David earring, protection by touch, before dropping down again. *Don't leave home without it.* The walls were filled with strange gothic imagery, bold reds and oranges, streaks of black and inlays of purple. I could almost taste the salty-sweet sin and debauchery they depicted. The artist had shielded his subjects behind strategically placed lace handkerchiefs, latticed fans and entangled limbs—artistic license taken so the works might be shown in public.

Her voice in my head, years past. The slapping of her calf leather gloves, Coke-red to match her thinned-to-disapproving lips, as she smacked the edge of her podium for effect or maybe to wake us up. *Madame des Vérités Cachées.* Loosely translated: Mrs. Hidden Truths. A pseudonym, of course.

Madame had been my Agency training officer in Covert Preternatural Operations, a mandatory seminar-level course for a graduate degree the University of Toronto doesn't advertise on its website. "*Watch for detail,*" she'd say. "*Art reveals. And always wear protection. It doesn't have to be a cross to work; it just has to be some form of religious or superstitious artifact you believe in.*"

One voice out of the many I'd left behind.

Shook my head to focus back on where I was now as the collection of protection charms dangling from my neck pinged against each other. Listened. To the music, the background noises, glasses clinking with ice cubes and voices that swelled and receded, piped in through speakers bolted into the exposed red and yellow and brown brickwork throughout the room.

So. I was alone with this beautiful and potentially dangerous man.

The article. Right. What was my angle again? I fished around for some paper as I fiddled with my pen, capping and uncapping it between my thumb and fore-finger, using everyday movements to focus my mind.

Jon led me to two high-backed wing chairs, upholstered in blood-red velvet trimmed with black satin. A mahogany side table with rounded corners sat between the two seats. A bottle of red wine had been placed on a silver tray with two cut-crystal glasses, their bases upturned to protect from dust.

Jon's appearance contrasted starkly with the room's decor—faded jeans, grey T-shirt under an untucked pale blue button-down denim shirt that framed his narrow hips, a worn black leather belt peeking through as he walked. His jeans were frayed at the cuffs, giving way to steel-toed, well-scuffed black suede cowboy boots. The overall effect heightened the blue-green swirls of his eyes, warmed the tone of his pale skin, and even his style—despite being a little too early '90s for me—still managed to work for him.

The chairs, the table, the color scheme—even Jon's

wardrobe. *Oh.* I let out a breath I'd forgotten I was holding. "So, you're going for the full treatment, eh?" I couldn't help it.

Jon's acknowledgement flashed in his eyes, even as they widened in mock-innocence. I tried to focus on his lips instead. The taste of red wine rolling around on my tongue. Yeah. That was *so* much better.

"You came here looking for a vampire," he said. "I wouldn't want you to leave disappointed."

"I came here to do an interview with you," I replied. Smiling even as I shook my head at him. "Are you up for it?"

It all started that night. The drinks, the interview, the jokes and easy banter. From there we started meeting for coffee, more drinks and casual conversation. Always after dark. There was no question we got along—a lot of the time we spent together was spent laughing. But there was always a distance. We stayed away from sharing too many personal details. Which made the whole thing easier—on me, at least, if not maybe for him as well.

Although it might have been useful to find out about his other lovers, hmm?

Even in my head, my tone was sarcastic.

GWEN, THE SEXY not-quite-night nurse, was back. This time she was in a white PVC getup with matching platform loafer-type shoes.

Relief.

At least until I saw the foot-long hypodermic needle she was carrying.

Shit!

I struggled to move away from the syringe, but it

was pointless—I couldn't do a damned thing. I was growling my helplessness as the opaque serum was shot into my primed and waiting vein.

Finally, she began to set me free.

Gwen explained, while bending over to unbuckle my various restraints, that I'd been under observation for the last forty-eight hours. She also confirmed what Anshell Williams had told me—based on the severity of my convulsions, if I hadn't been restrained, I would have caused damage to both myself and to those trying to help me.

I rubbed my wrists and used the arms of the bed to propel myself upright. "What did you shoot me with?"

She just watched as I folded backwards onto the pillows and the world went dark again.

THREE

I WOKE UP in my own bed.

Layers of patchouli, mandarin, lavender and "fresh rain"–scented laundry soap rolled over me. The feel—my top pillow indented just *so*; the position—on my stomach, one arm tucked between the pillows under my head. Comfortable.

No restraints.

My cat, asleep on my head, purring.

Home.

Home?

Since when did I get a cat?

I was afraid to open my eyes. Experiments with bondage, time in a hospital, blacking out in pain—no way was that real. I couldn't allow it to be.

Please let me have dreamed it.

I forced my eyes open and looked up. No cat. Another trippy mind blip apparently.

Idly, I flexed my back and extended my arms and legs as far as they could go. I rolled onto my back and got into Little Boat pose, legs curled to my chest with arms clasped around bent legs, rocking from side to side. Losing my mind? Maybe. But impending befuddlement was no excuse to slack off on my yoga training.

Holding my calves, I actively chose to focus on my breathing instead of my brain. Inhale, hold, count to five, exhale. Repeat. Roll over onto my front again and into Child's Pose, legs bent beneath me with palms and arms outstretched past my head on the bed. I felt as though I'd grown about five extra vertebrae, and my lower back had lost its customary stiffness. Odd.

Cat pose next. My back definitely felt like there was more of an arch happening. No tail yet though. I was poking at my sanity with a sharp stick. Moving into Dog pose. This one, strangely, felt harder than usual—my legs didn't want to flex as dramatically as they had yesterday. Was it only yesterday? Thinking anything else would be…crazy. Which I'm not. *Yet.*

Time to start my Sun Salutations.

I ran through the various poses in sequence. Easier to focus on my body and the flow of muscle and bone than on the thoughts running through my mind.

Breathing. Stretching.

Still too much energy.

I shook out my hands, wrists, legs; drew circles with my ankles and shoulders to loosen them up even more. Standing in one place, my feet shoulder-width apart, practicing my punches in front of a mirror. Then my kicks. Up and down the length of the room, focusing on keeping power behind the ball of my foot as it made contact with an invisible foe over and over and over again. Front kick. Side kick. Spinning roundhouse kick.

I did sit-ups. Then push-ups. Then knuckle push-ups. Debated going for a jog but opted for skipping rope instead. Anything to work off that frenetic need to *move*, the antithetic effects of immobility pouring out of me as I sweated out my demons.

I'd feel it tomorrow. Or in a couple of hours.

Either way I knew had to stop eventually and relax.

Relaxation meant sinking into the old-style, claw-legged bathtub with sides so high I didn't have to expose any of my naked bits to potential air-chilled breezes. A range of soap selections completed the experience, either herbal or fruity undertones tinged with drops of purified essential oils.

Normally, breathing deeply while surrounded by water would have eased both my mind and my body. Today was a bad day. My hands shook as I poured frothy gel under the running water, and the scents jabbed at my temples with a throbbing staccato of pain. I rushed through what would normally be my favorite part of the day.

Weird.

I couldn't get out of that bathroom fast enough. I left colorful towels behind in a pile on the floor as I put distance between myself and the smells and thoughts that wrapped their vise-like tendrils around my brain.

I retreated to my bedroom on a hunt for clean underwear and something to wear to work. Butt floss or cotton comfort? Red, floral, white or black? Too many choices. I opted for cotton comfort, black. Keeping my options open.

Eh, what the hell. I reached for a matching black cotton/lycra blend stretch sports halter bra. Shrugged into a black T-shirt. Completed the I-can't-be-bothered-trying-to-match-all-my-clothes-today outfit with black jeans. Black socks. Black combat boots with purple laces. Yeah. That worked.

Wait, how did I know I had to work today?

The phone beside my bed was flickering red; someone had tried to reach me. Three people actually—the ones who would notice if I went missing. The first message was from my best friend Lynna, confirming lunch for Thursday. The next: my mother wanting to know about brunch over the weekend. And finally my boss, Sandor, hoping my great aunt—*great aunt?*—had recovered from her operation enough that I'd be able to make it into work today for my 4:00 p.m. shift. Today being Wednesday.

Wednesday? What happened to Sunday, Monday and Tuesday?

I started to feel anxious again.

Focus.

Normality. Being with the here and now. I could do normal. Or at least normal for me.

The clock beside the phone read 3:30 p.m.

Hi ho, hi ho, it's off to work I go?

Apparently so.

FOUR

WORK WAS A three-story warehouse that functioned as a bar/meeting place/conference facility where mortal and otherness met. It's called the Swan Song. Don't ask me why.

It's located in a weird part of town. The old warehouse, complete with rippled aluminum and snot-green siding, is down close by Lake Ontario in an area called the East Bayfront. Known for derelict factories and squatters, most of the area is actually quite pretty in the spring and summer. City planners had scattered wildflower seeds over the garbage, turning a former landfill site into an overgrown nature trail. There's even a community garden. It's the perfect hiking spot for city people who want to pretend their hometown isn't as stinky and contaminated as it really is.

By day, families on bicycles and hand-holding couples stroll through. But when night bleeds the light, things change. Even the darkness teems with life—and not just horny couples making out on the beach.

I'm the bartender at the Swan Song. What other job lets you dress in combat boots without also making you wear military fatigues and sign away the next three years of your life?

Okay, so sure, I'd spent my last three years here. I'd meant to move on. Never quite got around to it. Hadn't figured out a better application of my extensive education yet. So here I am, and there you go.

Next?

The Song was pretty empty and I was getting bored. Until I noticed this Goth guy, very dressed-in-black in a 1980s retro-Bauhaus kind of way. Not unlike myself, actually. And not so hard on the eyes either. *Hmm.*

Worth a closer look. With practiced casualness, wiping down the counter with a grimy rag, I snuck peeks in his direction through hair that just *happened* to fall forward over my face as I rubbed invisible moisture rings from the scarred surface.

The guy did not look happy. He was nursing a Bloody Bloody Mary and staring at a pack of Du Maurier Lights that an earlier patron had left behind. I watched him pick up the box, turn it over in his hand and run his fingers along the sides. Then he did the same with a matchbook that blared the Swan Song's logo—red lettering on a black background with something white and winged that seemed to flutter the longer you stared at it.

Was he a former smoker? Manic depressive? Clairvoyant trying to pick up vibes?

One of my favorite parts of this job is making up pieces of other people's lives. Doesn't matter if it's true—it's almost more fun when it isn't.

The cover band playing this early dark hour blared angsty musical stylings remade into pastel blandness. An artistically revisionist blast from a 1980s past—four guys and a dark-eyed, waif-like androgynous lead singer, all dressed in various shades of dark. Young. They reeked of innocence.

I take your hand / You let mine go / Oh baby baby / I love you so / Come back to me / And be my girl / I'll love you forever / You are my pearl / Don't get scared / The pain won't last / Throughout eternity / We'll have a blast...

I rolled my eyes and noticed a woman farther along the bar do the same. We shared a laugh.

She flicked a glance at Mr. Morose and snaked the tip of her tongue along the edge of her teeth. I nodded and gave her a lopsided grin. *Yup, he's hot. But what's his trauma?*

One of the waitresses, Janey, was trying to get my attention at the other end of the bar so I turned and headed down to get her order. Two lager drafts, a Screwdriver, a Gimlet and Giblet double double on the rocks (gin and innards, shaken not stirred, on ice), a Massive Attack (ground glass, O positive blood, a shot of grenadine, served chilled with a slice of lime), and a shot of *Cusanjo Rojo* mescal with extra worms. *Mmm, yummy.*

You have to develop a strong stomach working here. I mean, those giblets are slimy buggers and you can't think about where they came from or you might lose what little food you ate before your shift.

The blood came from a cow who was meeting a timely death anyway, and this way, all parts of the animal were being used. Or maybe a goat, same proviso. You don't allow yourself to think anything else. You throw the glass chunks along with the contents of the blood bank bag into the blender, add the grenadine and crushed ice, replace the lid and blend on "high" for about a minute until everything froths together. Pour into a glass. Repeat as needed.

The term "finger food" takes on a whole new meaning at the Swan Song. Sure, we've got the usual deep-fried mozzarella sticks, zucchini strips, French fries and onion rings. But you'll also find things like baby bottom flapjacks, frog tongues in a cornflake batter, goreal demon eggs scrambled with grasshoppers topped with a delicate blood and blue-butter sauce, whale blubber on toast, and more—a gourmet cornucopia of oddities and tastes from across the dimensions.

Not that I necessarily believed in other dimensions. But I've seen some weird shit here over the last few years, stuff I couldn't explain, so I'm going to have to declare myself "undecided" on the whole are-we-alone-in-the-universe question, with an option to believe or disbelieve as the evidence presents itself.

In the meantime, my spidey sense was tingling, hairs tickling the back of my neck sending shivers along my spine and up around the edges of my shoulder blades. My co-conspirator was watching *me* now. Up and down. A little too long on the down for my taste.

I believe in that old cliché, to each his (or her) own. But your own doesn't necessarily mean it's my own. And—truly unfortunately sometimes—I just wasn't attracted to women that way. Tried it. Might even try it again sometime. But not tonight, and not with her. Something was off. Question was what.

I tried to get a better look using my peripheral vision. Instead I started sweating, tiny beads of liquid endorphin formed on my upper lip, and an answering heat somewhere lower. Unexpected. I tried to remember to breathe. Her body curved and straightened with a selective fullness. Her cherry-red gloss-covered lips glinted off her glass, and I wanted to know whether the shiny balm was strawberry or bubblegum flavor. Instead, I bit into the coppery salt of my own bottom lip. I'd almost missed the tips of what was barely hidden in the wild curls of her blue-black hair.

Horns.

Demon alert.

Being able to name the source helped me regain control over my cravings. Was I losing my touch? Usually I can spot—and avoid—a trawling demon.

Refills anyone?

But Broody Boy was looking past me towards the arched entranceway to the club. His eyes narrowed as his nostrils flared, anger replacing melancholy. He sat a little straighter and his gaze hardened as a solid-looking man walked in.

Broody seemed to grow—somehow bigger, stronger, more alpha.

Weird.

I followed his gaze and stepped back so fast the corner of the counter behind me slammed into my hip.

Anshell.

Fuck.

The room started spinning and I felt like I was about to faint. I've never actually fainted before, but I figured if I was going to, this is how it would feel. Demon woman was behind the bar now at my elbow, catching me in her arms before I could hit the floor. On the other side of me was some guy I'd never seen before. A flash of shoulder-length hair, not mine, brushed a bare spot on my shoulder as he cushioned one-half of my fall. They eased me onto a nearby stool.

When, exactly, is a dream not a dream?

Cute-but-broody wasn't paying any attention to me at this point. But my boss Sandor was. Moments later he was beside me, edging the patrons away and thanking them for their help.

You don't say no to Sandor, especially if he's being polite. At six foot five inches tall, Sandor towered over most of his clientele. Nothing pretty by human standards, he had three eyes stacked over two rows in a drunken pyramid, pylon-orange tusks curving up and around from just under his cheekbones, warted tree frog—green skin and a tail lined with slabs the size of my palms trailing out behind him. I'd seen him use a combination rear sweep and smack maneuver more than once to clear out a crew of rowdy drunks.

I liked Sandor. He was a good guy for a demon; understanding as a boss, invaluable as a friend. One thing you could always say about him—he stood by his people. He kept the place fairly violence-free, and didn't allow the patrons to hassle us no matter who we were or where we'd come from.

Sure, I'm used to having my own back. Being ex-Agency with a dead father who was a scientist with that same Agency will do that. But I'm also a norm working an intersectional, inter-species bar in a city that only sees what it wants to see, serving patrons who've either taken a beat-down from one of my former associates or know someone who has. So I don't share. Safer that way.

Sandor was the reason I'd stayed at the Swan as long as I had. He would also be the first to encourage me to move on when I felt I was ready.

Right now, Sandor was watching me watch Anshell. He lifted his snout and sniffed, then looked at me, hard.

"Dana, is there something I should know about?"

I shook my head, then nodded, then shrugged.

"He seems to recognize you," Sandor commented. "Don't look up if you don't want to engage."

"Shit," I muttered.

"He's heading this way," continued my boss. "Want me to get rid of him?"

But no immediate need. Mr. Melancholy stepped into the mix, unwittingly blocking Anshell's path to me.

"I told you to stay away from me," Mr. Getting-Less-Melancholy-All-The-Time hissed.

"I'm not here for you," said Anshell.

"But you're here now, and so am I. Get gone."

Anshell stared the other man down. "Get *yourself* gone," he said. Anshell's voice was quiet, a polite incline to his head, but there was force behind those words.

"You can't tell me what to do," Goth Guy spit out through gritted teeth. "Not anymore. I'm not yours."

Anshell smiled thinly.

"If we have no connection, then why are you wasting your time talking to me?" Anshell kept his voice level, pitched low, but for some reason I could hear him as well as the other guy could and they were standing maybe two feet apart—and at least twenty feet from me. "If I were you," he continued, "I would finish my drink and leave now. My business here is not with you."

Anshell's head swiveled so that his eyes met mine.

Damn.

Broody Guy glared at me, then at Anshell. He balled his hands into fists and shoved them into his pockets.

"Fuck this shit," I muttered. "I don't need this."

I pushed myself back to my feet and forced the sludge from my brain. *There. Standing.* Right, that's it. I could stand on my own. No problem.

"I'm going to take my break now, 'kay, Sand?"

Sandor nodded.

I headed straight for the women's bathroom. Pushed open the knife-scored, black-painted worn wood to one of the stalls, lowered the lid and sat. Tried to remember how to breathe. The room was tilting.

I leaned forward and put my head between my knees. Then pulled it out again. No idea why people tell you to do that—it always makes things worse in my experience. Instead I found a pockmark in the door and fixated on that. *Focus. Focus on breathing. The earth beneath the floor beneath my feet. Blood pumping through my veins. The air surrounding me, pressing in on me, me pressing out on it. Inhale, exhale.* My hands were shaking again. I closed them into fists, flexing my fingers and palms outward. Forcing them steady, pushing all other thoughts out of my head. Fist and flex. Fist and flex.

Trick of the light, or were my nails longer, more pointed?

Fist and flex again.

I raised my arms straight out at my sides, bending them at the elbow all the way back so I could touch my earlobes with my index fingers. Stretched my arms upward, gliding my rib cage right and then left again. I was working out the kinks in my body, increasing the oxygen flow to my brain. At least that was the theory.

It was also possible that I was killing time so I wouldn't have to go back out there and face a new personal demon that seemed to have become real and present.

Deep breaths. I could do this.

I flushed the toilet to appear as though I'd done more than just hide in the stall. Ran cold water over my hands, my arms, my face, the back of my neck, until the world seemed more solid. Icy moisture trickled down my spine and puddled on the hilt of the knife I still kept tucked against my tailbone. I stared at myself in the mirror: my face with green-blue eyes and high cheekbones, framed by curly shoulder-length hair, arm muscles hardened by yoga and hauling countless cases of bottles.

Be cool. Face the fear.

I straightened my shoulders, shook the hair off my face, pushed through the bathroom door and back to the bar.

Anshell was sitting by himself now, sipping a virgin orange juice. Don't ask me how I knew that. Or I'd be forced to tell you I could smell it, and that doesn't make any sense at all. Right?

Broody Guy seemed to have left. Sandor was chatting with Anshell, and he didn't seem particularly tense so maybe Anshell was okay. *Good people*—isn't that how they say it?

I ducked behind the counter and picked up the discarded rag to start wiping my way along the bar again. Anshell and Sandor's conversation trailed off as they watched me. Demon girl had now fixated on someone else so yay there.

I could do this.

I nodded at Sandor to let him know that it was safe to leave me alone.

"So," I said, my voice cooling the moment Sandor's tail vanished around the corner. "Drugged anyone good lately?"

Anshell sighed. "Better than the alternative."

"And yet here I am, both walking and talking," I said. "Amazing, isn't it?"

He shook his head and took another sip of his drink. "How are you feeling?"

"Fine." I scooped ice and slammed it down into a clean glass which I then filled with cranberry juice. The night was trippy enough without any help. "The fact that you're sitting here in front of me and we're having this conversation means we've met before. That whole—" I couldn't bring myself to say strapped-to-the-bed "—hospital scene was real."

"Real," Anshell said. "Yes, it was real." He stared into his glass as though the perfect sequence of words might be found at the bottom if he looked hard enough. "There's a lot you don't know," he said finally. "That will probably change by the next full moon."

"Yeah? When is that?" I tried to keep the bitter out of my voice. "It's not like I'm in the habit of checking the moon."

"Four days," Anshell said. "Saturday night. The closer it gets, the harder it will be for you to control your changes. That's how you'll know."

"Know that I'm turning into a pussy?" I regretted the words as soon as they left my mouth.

"Call me," he said, and handed me an orange card on rough cardstock with lettering embossed in red and black ink. Stylized, edgy; the kind of introduction that said art director or creative advertising type. "I can help."

Anshell Williams, Small Business Consultant for the Arts. A phone number. An address on Roxborough Street. As far as covers go, that one was pretty good—irregular hours would be expected, and it was the opposite of what you were actually spending your nights doing.

Okay then. We'll give it a half-point in the always-trust-your-instincts camp.

"Let me help," he repeated. "No strings."

I laughed; short, sharp.

"Yeah," I said. "Sure." Life always came with strings, even if they looked like pretty party favor decorations. I turned my back to him and walked away, leaving the card lying on the counter.

Then, guilty, I turned around. It wasn't his fault I got scratched.

But it was too late. Anshell Williams was gone. Only his soggy card, melting into the cracked faux marble surface next to his half-full glass of orange juice, proved that he'd ever been there.

All that bravado for nothing.

I eased my way over, picked up the card and blotted as much water off it as I could before slipping it into my front pocket.

Couldn't hurt, right?

That's my story and I'm sticking to it.

FIVE

THE REST OF my shift passed pretty uneventfully. Maybe the fates figured I'd had enough excitement for one night.

I poked my head into the back office to say goodnight—or rather morning—to Sandor before heading out. He was busy adding up the night's take into piles of bills, and nudged one of the stacks my way. I nodded my thanks but didn't count it. Instead I fished out my butt-ugly mustard and puke green print *muy grande* change purse, shoving the money into it and burying it back at the bottom of my oversized bag.

"Want to talk about it?" Sandor's voice was low-key, but I knew he was curious as hell. The more interested he is in something, the more neutral his voice gets.

"*Want* to talk about it? No," I said. "*Should* I talk about it? Maybe."

Sandor waited for me to continue.

I frowned as I leaned against the door frame, my arms crossed over my chest.

"I was scratched by a shifter the other night," I said, finally. "I was playing this scene with a guy and I'm guessing it was his shifter boyfriend who got pissed and scratched me when he caught us together. All I know is one minute I'm standing there, and the next… *blank*.

"I ended up in this Goth hospital, strapped to a bed,

and that guy who showed up tonight was a medic there. Or so he said. So I'm thinking I've lost it, whatever *it* is, but instead I wake up this morning in my own bed. It was so freaking crazy I figured it was all some kind of really bad flashback, you know?"

Sandor nodded. He'd had his own experiences with drug residuals and morning-after confusions.

"So I do my thing," I continued, "come to work, everything is right in the world and it was all a bad dream. You know?"

"Except your bad dream showed up and ordered a drink, eh?" Sandor's voice was wry.

"Pretty much. So...what the fuck?"

"What the fuck indeed," he said. "Have you shifted yet?"

"I don't know," I said. "I can't remember." I spread my hands helplessly, palms up, as I shrugged. "According to medic boy, I did. That's why they strapped me down. Or so he said."

"Or so he said," Sandor echoed.

"Your thoughts?"

Sandor tilted his oversized, wart-covered green head to the side and scratched his hairy nose with a thick, brown, scaly nail. He grunted. Then, apparently satisfied with his train of thought, Sandor responded.

"Sounds to me like you might have been infected, and you might be getting furry real soon." He gave me a serious look. "I've heard about that shifter hospital."

"You have?"

"Well." He shrugged. "You hear about things in this business. We can't just walk into Toronto General, slap down our health card and expect to get treated. Demons and others like us—we take care of our own. Us against them. That kind of thing."

"So how come I never heard about it before?" I shifted my weight, leaned against the other side of the door frame.

"You never needed to before," he replied. "Anshell Williams is big in shifter circles. Even runs a pack, the Moon with Seven Faces. His rep is strong but fair. Mostly. And that clan—they're not a bad bunch to run with. For shifters, at least."

"Clan? Like tribal chiefs with headgear and ceremonial swagger?"

"What they do on their personal time is their business," said Sandor. "It's like a social club. Except it's species-specific and you have to be able to control your power—or in your case, your shift." Sandor angled his head to one side. "Can you?"

I shook my head. "Not yet. So then what does Williams want with me?" I was afraid I already knew the answer.

"My guess," said Sandor, "is that Williams is waiting to see if you shift again for real. And if you do, he's such a do-gooder that he'll probably help you."

"You mean recruit me, don't you?" I didn't know much about pack life, but I hadn't left one paramilitary organization to join up with another.

"Probably," Sandor replied. "But if you're shifting anyway, you're better off as part of a group. Really. I know you're not much of a team player—but if he makes you an offer, you should seriously think about it. For your own protection, and for everyone else's safety too. Be glad it's him with the offer and not one of those other pack leads. At least he'll let you choose."

I was beginning to feel like someone who had gone on a first date but ended up drunk at a wedding chapel in Vegas.

"Is there something else you're not telling me?" I looked him straight in his three eyes. He did me the great honor of looking back.

"A random shifter is dangerous," he said. "If you are one, you'll need to learn how to control your shifts."

"What happens if I don't?"

"You'll need to be put down," Sandor said.

Silence. He let the gravity of the situation sink in.

"Great," I finally said. "But no danger of that tonight?"

Sandor shook his head. "I doubt it. If you were that much of a risk, Mr. Williams probably wouldn't have left here so easily."

I straightened up, slinging my bag over my head and across my body to push off from the entryway.

"So as long as we're sure I'm safe for tonight, I'm gonna split," I said. "'Kay?"

"I never said you were safe," he said, grinning. "Only that it's unlikely you'll do any major shifting between now and when the sun rises."

"Yeah yeah, semantics," I retorted, smiling to soften the sting a bit. "Later, Sand."

"Later, sweetie."

"That's Ms. Sweetie to you, babe."

I could hear Sandor's answering chuckle all the way down the hall until I pulled the door shut behind me.

SIX

BECAUSE I WORK for Sandor, and especially because he let it be known that I'm under his protection, nobody really bothers me. Which is pretty damned useful considering the creepy crawly population around here.

The desolation out by the Swan can be oppressive. Tall grass swishing and whispering in summer, hulking piles of grey-tinged snow in the winter. Only the occasional dangling bulb from a still-active factory or the light from a passing vehicle has the power to pierce the shadows.

My skin was prickling as I made my way along the stomped-down path carved between two walls of snow to where my truck waited. Shadows pressed in around me, the air like a vacuum. My nose twitched, itchy, and there was a sour taste on my tongue.

On the outer edges of my peripheral vision, *there*, to the left, a quick shadow darted even farther left and away. Wild animal, or something more dangerous?

Cold winter had given way to a sudden thaw and steam was rising off the tunnel of snow. Moisture from Lake Ontario only added to the unexpectedly warm mist. The drift, like smoke, could be tricking my senses.

Maybe.

I waited a moment, trying to pick up a scent on the

wind. Nothing more unusual than, well, usual. Ignoring the part where I'd just scented the wind for clues.

Another step. *There.* That smell. Metal? I stuck out my tongue, confirming the taste on the wind, rolling the droplets around in my mouth. Another step, cautious, the smell stronger. Five steps, each taking me closer to the end of the snowy walkway, my heart smashing against the cage of my ribs. Five more steps, almost there now, my blood singing.

Deep breath.

I stepped into the parking lot, scanning the area. There, not far from where I'd parked, were rusted barrels of what was probably toxic waste piled high and lashed together with chains.

And spread-eagled, held in place by daggers along and through his arms and legs and torso: a man.

Broody Goth Guy.

Shit.

On either side of him was a vampire, feeding. Blood trickled down Goth Guy's neck from two symmetrical puncture wounds below each side of his rounded jaw. Blood poured from the twenty or so other holes in his body that the daggers had made. I couldn't tell if he was alive or dead.

I concentrated a moment on his chest. Rising, falling. *Okay. Alive.*

I ducked behind a pile of snow. Now what? Back to the Swan? No guarantee Sandor would hear me kicking at the door before the vamps behind me did. But forward took me into the Feed, and one step closer to my own unexpectedly precarious mortality.

There, again, a shadow in the periphery of my vision. What *was* that? Wind whistled in my ear, past my ear, too fast for my senses to catch as anything more than a flicker, a whisper, a touch, light, then gone.

Vertigo. Suddenly blind, I reached out an unexpectedly sweaty palm and slapped it on the wall of snow for support, then spewed the limited contents of my stomach. I was seeing stars, floaters; tiny balls of light bouncing in and out of my vision.

Dampness bound with frost held my hand in place. I dug my fingers into the wall for purchase. Except my nails were going farther than I could ever remember them going.

A deep voice whispered in my ear, barely audible, definitely masculine.

"Are you okay?"

But everything was spinning, tilting, and without meaning to I leaned backwards and landed on my butt. Somehow, I managed to fall away from the puke. Small miracles. I raised my right hand to pull the hair away from my face, wiped the drool from my mouth.

My palm felt rough, like coarse-grained sandpaper. I scratched my head and nicked myself, inhaling sharply and feeling moisture on my digits. I looked down at my hand. Always important to assess the extent of the blood loss.

My hand.

My paw.

My hand?

My paw?

What the fuck?

There was a large paw in front of me, with golden fur and curving claws, droplets of blood tingeing the third and fourth digits. *My* blood. *My* paw.

I inhaled, reflexively breathing into the exhale and

the beginnings of a scream when a hand—human, warm, and not my own this time—clamped down over my mouth. A face I didn't recognize, green eyes made tight with urgency, staring into mine.

There was meaning in his look, intent, eyebrows raised in question. What was the question? He bent forward, chestnut hair tickling my cheek, and I had a weird sense of déjà vu. His lips brushed up against my ear, and again the feeling was familiar. But the words were not.

"If I take my hand off your mouth, you can't scream."

I nodded, although I arched one eyebrow to make it clear this was my decision and not his. Because I understood. Okay, well, not *understood* exactly but accepted. For now. With a proviso to change my mind if the opportunity and desire presented itself.

Slowly, he took his hand away from my mouth. I licked my lips and tasted cinnamon with an after-bite of vanilla. Pure Madagascar vanilla, not the imitation crap you get in the supermarket. Don't ask me how I knew. I just did.

I looked from the stranger to what used to be my hand. From my elbow to my former fingertips, I had shifted.

I flexed, watching my claws extend and retract. It would be cool if it wasn't so damned freaky.

The guy I didn't know was watching my former hand with interest.

"Is that new?"

I shrugged. "Maybe," I said, my words more air than sound. "Depends on who you believe."

My companion chose not to follow the red herring, especially when I didn't say more. Instead:

"Do you know how to fight?" His softly rounded lips brushed against my ear once more, breath hot, words urgent. Vampires have very good hearing, and we did *not* want them to hear us. The only reason they hadn't figured out we were here yet was probably because they were too engrossed in their *ménage-à-sang* to pay attention. But how long before they were sated and ready to hunt again?

You'd think I'd know more about the habits of vampires, given my association with Jon. But no. Some things we didn't discuss much. Actually, we didn't talk much period. I lost my words when I was around him; melting beneath his fingertips, his mouth, his lips on mine.

Damn. So *not* the time to be distracted by sex right now.

My new companion was watching me and I hoped he couldn't read my mind. But how could he? With a half-smile that could have meant anything, he reached out and touched my arm. My hand.

It was a hand again.

I couldn't help it. I jumped. Startled. The man in front of me leaned forward and breathed his earlier question into my ear again.

"Can you fight?"

This time, I dragged my eyes up and away from my newly re-established hand and nodded. I wasn't totally confident—I don't go looking for fights, at least not anymore—but it's not like I couldn't hold my own.

The bar was dark behind us. The night felt like it was buzzing, squeezing the air from my lungs. My vision started to sway again and the man's hand gripped my shoulder. I shook my head and took a deep breath, then another, and another.

"My truck is over there," I mouthed, motioning to the battered 1996 rust-pocked vehicle parked about fifty feet from where we stood. "Do you have any weapons?"

He shrugged. I lifted the hem of one pant leg and flashed him the hilt of my silver cross-covered dagger. Then I lifted my T-shirt, just enough for the moonlight to glint off the handle of another silver dagger. Pulled down the neck of my T-shirt to show my necklace, a match for the tattoo on my ankle; a bit more to the left exposed the thumbprint-sized *hamsah*, a Middle Eastern ward against the evil eye, tattooed over my heart.

I raised my eyebrows at him.

My companion grinned now, his lips twitching mischief. He reached behind his back and pulled out a chiseled wooden stake from a concealed holster, then replaced it just as smoothly. He opened his leather jacket and displayed several blades, sewn into the lining of his coat. Another blade against his tailbone. Another one in his boot.

This guy was packing.

I couldn't help but laugh, although I tried to keep it quiet. Between the two of us, the odds of our survival had just gotten a lot better.

Kaynahorah. Knock on wood. I muttered the words in my head, just in case.

Quietly, we hatched our escape plan. It was brilliant, really. On the count of three, we would make a run for the truck. Okay, so maybe it lacked complexity and layers of strategy. But hey, points for being direct and goal-oriented, right?

The only loose thread was the man having his life force drained from him even as we stood. Hopefully that thread wouldn't turn into a rope that twisted around our necks to hang us. Because we couldn't leave him behind.

Humans, or at least us human-like beings, needed to take care of each other. Damned if I didn't feel responsible for the guy. Do unto others and all that I guess. I mean, if I was daggered and being fed on by some less domesticated vamps, I think I would want to be saved. Right?

I touched the shoulder of my partner in flight. His eyes, shocking blue now and glowing in the reflected light of an overhead bulb, turned to me. Waving my hand—surprisingly smooth and human-seeming again, thankfully—I pointed to slumped Goth Guy. Even from here, I could see his chest continuing to faintly rise and fall.

"Any ideas on how to get this guy out?" His whispered breath, my chest, a straight line of heat. Man, what was with me tonight?

I leaned into his personal space to whisper back.

"I'll distract them, while you sneak around and start loosening the daggers. If you can, get the guy into my truck and I'll be there as soon as I can. Or," I paused, "you could always help take them on *with* me." I waggled my eyebrows. "Two on two—we can take 'em, right?"

He shrugged and gave me a half-grin.

"What the fuck," he responded. "Ready?"

One...two...

I touched his arm to stop him before he took off.

"Wait," I said. "In case anything happens to either one of us. What's your name?"

He smiled down at me, full lips curling back over large, evenly formed white teeth.

"Nothing is going to happen to me," he replied. "Or to you, if I can help it."

"Full of yourself much?"

He snorted quietly.

"Samuel. Sam. Call me Sam." He gave me a small, mock bow. "And you are?"

"Dana," I replied. "Okay. Now that we know what to put on each other's gravestones, are you ready to go?"

He nodded assent. Leaned forward to whisper in my ear, his lips a caress as his words promised more. "Nobody is dying here tonight," Sam said in a low growl. "Except vampires. Let's do this."

One...two...three...

"Hey!"

Okay, so maybe yelling wasn't the smartest thing to do. But I couldn't think of anything else right then. And it did get the vamps to stop feeding.

Unfortunately, I was fresher and—alone, relatively unarmed—I was a walking stereotypical girl target. And I'd just let the nice vamps know that dessert had arrived.

Great. Just great. A good little distraction...assuming I didn't get killed or vamped first...

But my maneuver served its purpose. They released their grip on the limp human. Point for me. Problem was, they were now slinking towards me, the picture of a B horror movie tag-team effort.

Were there this many vampires before? The duo had multiplied exponentially.

One dropped and exploded into dust, Sam's stake driving a hole through its back. Now was no time for a fair fight. Another went down in a matter of seconds. Stake, move on. Stake, move on. Watching Sam in action was like watching a macabre dancer, each move a part of a complex *pas de deux*.

But I didn't have time to watch him for long because those not collapsing into a pile of ash were getting closer.

The first vamp, a hard-bodied woman who looked about twenty years old, attacked. I reached down to grab my stake, thrusting upwards and out in a clean motion just as the vamp was about to land.

An explosion of glittering dust shivered around me. But instead of littering the ground, the ashes seemed to hover in the air, floating lightly on a nonexistent breeze.

No time to watch the show, though, because the rest of the group attacked. Kick, feint, punch, roundhouse kick to the head, stake. Solar plexus slam, uppercut to the chin, stake. Head butt to the vamp holding me from behind, double kick to the vamp bearing down on me from the front. Double stake as both rushed me in tandem.

Quick mental calculation: five down, ten to go.

Sam was holding his own. He'd nailed four to my five and had just smashed two more heads together before staking one and tossing the other to me to stake.

That put our collective count to eleven. We were fighting back-to-back now, punching and kicking and staking the odds more into our favor.

There. One vampire left. It was almost too easy.

Sam and I moved forward, fully expecting the vamp

to run away. Nobody likes to lose, and dying is even worse than losing—especially if you're practically immortal.

But the vamp wasn't running. Instead it was looking over to the area where most of its former buddies should have been dust bunnies in the wind. And started to cackle.

I couldn't help myself. I looked over too. And saw a glowing, swirling spiral of sparkling green and yellow particles. The vamp rushed at me, shouting, "*Behold the glory of Alina! She who walks will slay the righteous and reunite us all! Behold that which is to come! Be...*" And with that, Sam skewered her with a satisfying *thud* and then a *poof* as the dust exploded.

"Don't suppose she might have told us something useful," I said. "Do you?"

Sam shrugged, wiping the sweat from his forehead. "Theatrics got boring," he said. Then he cocked his head towards the ash pile. "What's that?"

I turned to look.

The last vampire had exploded into dust. I'd seen it myself. But instead of scattering on the ground, the ashes floated a moment and then started to swirl around in an increasingly glowing vortex of light and dust. Sam and I watched the molecules dancing closer and closer together. Each centrifugal *swoosh* seemed to strengthen the force's pattern and the particles began to glow an eerie neon green.

"Nice light show," I said, my voice pitched low. "Seen anything like it before?"

Sam shook his head without taking his eyes off the spectacle, which was morphing into a green-smoke version of the vampire staked just moments before.

"*Dust to dust, ashes to ashes,*" the ethereal presence said. "*It has already begun. All is turning to dust, to ashes. She will open her mouth to suck everyone into her hell on earth. We will rule the surface again.*"

"So you're, what, Toronto's version of a preternatural dust-buster?"

"*You dare to mock?*" the mist whispered indignantly. "*Mock not.*"

"The way I look at it," I commented, "why put off until later what you can mock now?"

Beside me, Sam snickered.

The pile of dust drifted closer and, if you can believe it, looked me in the eye. Don't ask me how that was possible because I don't know. What I do know is that I was looking at a floating pile of dust, and that pile of dust was staring straight back at me.

"*We will meet again, sooner than you think,*" it hissed, moving in closer until we were almost touching noses. I started feeling that nasal tickle that presages a big sneeze. The transparent arms rose, reaching out to give me a great big powdery hug.

Aaaatchoo!

It was a good one. Big glob of snot, right in its ephemeral eye.

Thwaaaaakk!

It exploded on contact.

Sam whistled in astonishment. "Way to go," he said.

I shrugged. *It was planned. Really. Inspired phlegm.*

"Let's get that guy and get gone," I replied.

Sam nodded and together we walked over to the Goth Guy's body. He was still breathing, but only just. Between us, we were able to pull out the knives. Dried blood flaked loose as we worked the blades free from both the barrels and his limbs.

Time to divide and conquer. I found some clean snow and rubbed it on the various re-opened, oozing holes.

Sam was cleaning the knives in a different snowbank while I did this. When he was finished, he put them into a leather bag I hadn't noticed before; guess I'd missed it in all the dusty carnage.

Our respective jobs complete, we switched. I got the bag of sharp, pointy objects and Sam got the dead weight. Screw equality; I was fine with Sam doing some heavy lifting. And why not? He was taller than me by about a foot, all his limbs were longer which gave him better leverage, and he was clearly strong enough to handle it.

I opened the passenger door to the truck, flipping the front seat forward so Sam could lean in and roll our rescuee into the back. Together we covered the guy with a blanket. Sam then flipped the seat back and got in, pulling the door shut beside him.

I did the same. We waited in silence as the truck warmed up and the defrost cleared enough of the fog for me to see through both my windshield and rear window. Then I shifted into gear and pulled out of the lot into the waning night.

SEVEN

WHILE I DROVE, Sam made himself useful.

First he watched me fumble for my cell phone. No, that's not the useful part. That came once he realized what I was trying to do, and instead he fished out his own phone from a hidden pocket inside the lining of his jacket.

I shifted my weight and raised my hips up off the cracked vinyl seat, making it easier for me to wedge my free hand into the pocket of my pants.

Out came the crumpled, still slightly sodden business card. Anshell Williams. He'd said he'd help me, and he obviously knew our victim.

I handed it to Sam.

He scanned the card quickly, his face neutral. Then punched in the number while looking out the window.

Either he had a photographic memory, or Sam knew Anshell.

Everything clicked into place.

Of course Sam knew Anshell. They'd walked into the bar together. Sam had also been the random guy who caught me when I'd been surprised into a near-faint by Anshell's arrival.

Which meant…?

For the first time, I looked at Sam. Really looked.

His profile lay in shadow, hollows highlighted by

the street lamps that flickered as we sped by. Friend? Or was I now in more danger?

Sam had fought beside me. If not for his help, I'd probably be dead now. Which meant that if Sam was danger, it probably wasn't of the immediate kind. So maybe being with him was a good thing. Wait and see, that's what I was thinking.

Sam was off the phone now. I hadn't even listened to what he said. Damn. Getting sloppy already.

"Go to the address on Roxborough Street," he said. "The one on the card. Mr. Williams says he'll take care of things from there."

"You trust him," I said. Statement more than question, but my voice raised a note on the word *him* all the same.

"Don't you?" His question was pointed. "You're the one who handed me the card."

"You knew the number without my help," I answered. "I'm Dana. Bartender at the Swan Song. And you are?"

Sam was silent for a full minute. I know. I counted.

"I'm a friend," he said. "That's all I can tell you. But you can trust me."

I snorted. "Not big on the whole trust thing," I said. "Sorry to disappoint."

"I hear you," said Sam. So, I was possibly *not* the only person in the car with trust issues. Good to know.

Then he smiled. His teeth seemed to glow, reflecting the lights of the night.

"It's the best I can do, Dana," he said. "If Williams promised to help you, he's good for it. And I don't want to walk into the nearest human hospital with this guy and try to explain what happened. Too much damage for them not to call the cops. And telling the truth to the cops? Not something I'm gonna do. Those extra-natural guys tend to guard their privacy with your blood, know what I mean?"

I sighed my frustration. "Is your name even Sam?"

"Yes. Wanna find out more about the guy in back? I know I do," he said, flashing me a grin that could only be described as shit-eating.

Sam twisted around and reached backwards to fumble in the limp guy's pockets before coming back to face front with a battered black leather wallet. He rifled through its contents.

"Joseph Dalton Morgenlark," Sam said. "Age 23. 45 Windermere Drive. Probably lives in his parents' basement and listens to the Cure and Marilyn Manson and Rasputina on his headphones while the folks eat dinner upstairs, wondering when he's going to come out of his dark phase, get a job and make something of himself."

I smirked.

"The question," I said, "is what the hell put him at the Swan tonight? More to the point, was what happened to him a chance thing, or was he the intended target for some reason?"

Sam shrugged and looked out the window.

"Was that an *I-don't-know* shrug or an *I'm-not-going-to-share* shrug?"

Sam cocked me a half-smile and shrugged again. This time, though, he was teasing, watching for my reaction.

He was rewarded pretty quickly as I growled frustration and directed my attention back to driving. Hard work, driving, when there's nobody else on the road. *Right.* Speaking of right, oh look, the exit for Yonge

Street. I signaled my intentions to the nonexistent traffic, then exited and started heading north. Since I had no way to know where on Roxborough Street we were going, I figured I'd stick with the closest thoroughfare and assess direction when we got there.

Yonge Street is weird at any time of day but especially in the middle of the night. Down where Lakeshore exits into the north-south city bisector, you've got the questionable shadows of Union Station. From there, it's the hotels and glass towers of the financial district. Past Adelaide the semi-grunginess starts—across from the south end of the Eaton Centre you've got jewelry markets and fast-food restaurants and the beginnings of large big-box store chains.

All this changes at Dundas. Past there, the neon flashing lights flicker over the faces of hustlers, street kids, homeless people and late-night partying stragglers. Then you've got the businessmen in town for some convention or meeting, drunk out of their gourds, stumbling out of one of the many strip joints that litter the street.

Interspersed with all of this seediness is the City's attempted clean-up job on the area. Massive Jumbotrons beam out news and ads to potential consumers. Oversized name brand chain-store locations occupy prize corner spots, and cardboard posters of emaciated, bored models look out at pedestrians.

Annoying? Hell yeah.

Sam seemed to be catching up on his window shopping as we cruised north. The stores gave way to a more upscale environment past College Street, and as I stopped at the lights just south of Bloor at Charles

Street, even I had the urge to hop out and do a bit of shopping. Go figure.

Yonge Street narrowed north of Bloor, signaling the outer edges of Rosedale. One of the old money parts of town. Big brownstones, big lots, big property tax bills, big enough incomes to cover it all. I periodically wondered what all of those people did for a living that they could afford multi-million-dollar homes in the middle of the city. Were they born with it? Did they work their way up to it? What kind of people were they?

So far, I'd never gotten the chance to find out. Apparently today would be my lucky day. There it was—Roxborough Street. I slowed down, signaled left. Just a guess. Sam didn't comment, so apparently I'd guessed right.

The driveway was dark. A latticed wood archway connecting to a similarly patterned fence divided the lane from its neighbor, and the large-leafed vines draped and woven through the slats looked like grapes. Tasty privacy. The motion-sensor-triggered light flared as I pulled up, only to be extinguished an eye blink later. Unexpected; I jumped, checking in the rearview mirror. A reflex against the dark.

Anshell had the front door open the second I killed my headlights. Four people, a woman and three guys, rushed past him and around to the truck. Human? I squinted, trying to trick myself into seeing something that wasn't there. Instead, a streak of trailing orange energy as Sam opened his door and jumped out, pulling the seat forward behind him. In a spin too quick for the others to notice, Sam flipped Joseph's wallet on top of him. A quick conspiratorial grin at me before stepping aside to let the others do their work.

Anshell Williams melted into my periphery. One moment I was leaning against the side of my truck watching his people and their efficiency, separate from the action, and the next I had company.

"Hey," he said. "Thanks for this."

I nodded. Maybe Goth Boy didn't want to deal with Williams and the Pack, but they sure still had feelings for him.

"You doing okay?" His question was nonchalant, but when I glanced over Anshell was watching my face for the words I maybe didn't plan to say aloud. "Anything…change?"

"Not yet," I said. Then I remembered. "Not altogether."

"She did a partial," said Sam, suddenly there and full of the helpful. I glared at him.

"Shut up," I said.

"Takes power to do that," Anshell commented. "Years of practice." He turned to Sam. "You're certain? A partial shift?"

Sam nodded.

"Huh," said Anshell.

"What?" I wanted less cryptic and more information.

But then Morgenlark was strapped into the gurney and the unmarked white van was ready to go and maybe we could continue this conversation some other time.

Anshell climbed into the passenger seat with a parting chin bob, tossing Sam the keys; he caught them without looking. Clearly a reflex. *Shifter?*

Sam glanced at Anshell, then at me.

"I have to go," Sam said.

"So I see." Yup, casual. That's me. Do I ask for

his number? What was the protocol for defying death through shared battling of baddies?

"Okay. Well." He held out his hand and shook mine solidly. "Nice meeting you then."

"Right," I drawled back at him, giving him my best lazy grin. "Next time I need a good fight, I'll give you a call."

Sam laughed. It was a nice laugh.

"Yeah, you do that."

"Okay then," I said.

He hesitated once more. "Be careful out there."

"You too."

As I watched him hop into the van and take off, I was tempted to follow, if only to find out where this mystery hospital was. But now, sitting on the now-empty street with my engine idling, all of the post-fight adrenaline started to ebb and I realized how damned tired I actually was.

And hungry, for that matter.

Enough street fighting for one night. I was going home to crash.

EIGHT

I MANAGED TO get home without further incident. No cops, no accidents. The only thing I stopped for was a bacon cheeseburger with a side order of poutine from an all-night diner. I was famished.

Poutine, my favorite French-Canadian import: fries, plus cheese curds, plus gravy. Mmmm, yummy cholesterol goodness. Short-term gain for long-term…ah hell, who knows what's even going to happen tomorrow? Might as well enjoy myself in the now.

I dragged myself and my steaming paper bag of dinner up the twenty-five concrete stairs leading to the door of my studio. Not the coolest of neighborhoods, but given that the entire strip is overshadowed by an uninhabited hulking castle, it's not bad either.

Casa Loma is a Toronto oddity. Local lore holds that it was built by a rich financier who lost much of his money in a bad business deal. Unfortunately for him, it was one of the assets he had to sell off to become solvent again. Now it's a bus-clogged tourist spot, a frequently used movie set, and a popular place to throw fancy black-tie parties.

"Dana."

Speaking of shadows…

"I'm tired. It's been a hell of a night. What do you want?"

"What do you mean, what do I want? I want to

know," Jon said, stepping out of the darkness of my stoop, "if you're all right." He seemed to waver a moment under the incandescent glow of the street lamp's beam, then solidify. A trick of the light. Really.

I sighed.

One look at Jon and it was clear that sleep wasn't in my immediate future tonight. Oh yeah, sure, I have control over my own environment and I can stand up for myself, but I was tired and I didn't feel like fighting and having some company would be nice.

So I shrugged instead of arguing, clicked open the lock and went inside, leaving the front door open. An off-handed invitation, hardly direct, but it's as good as he was going to get.

After a moment's hesitation, Jon came in and closed the heavy metal door behind him. He set the deadbolt firmly in place before turning around, coming up behind me. He put his arms around my waist and buried his mouth at my neck. A hug, not a bite.

I tensed, surprised, then relaxed into his embrace.

"I was worried about you," he breathed into my ear. "The hospital. But then I heard you were okay. At work." He paused. "Why are you home so late?"

"You know," I said, resting my head on his shoulder. "Work stuff."

Jon nuzzled my neck a moment longer, then stepped back and inhaled deeply. He looked at my bag of food, then at me.

"Something *did* happen tonight," he said, letting go of my waist and walking around in front of me so he could look into my eyes. "A plain burger, that's hunger. A cheeseburger, you're close to your period and craving calcium. A bacon cheeseburger plus poutine...something happened tonight to seriously upset you. What?"

I rolled my eyes and walked over to the bag of food. Grabbed it and started towards the couch, trailing shoes and extraneous clothing as I went. I plopped down, put up my feet, pulled the food out and started eating. Jon watched me, patient, waiting for me to start talking.

Which, after about five minutes of concerted chewing, I did.

By the time I was done, Jon was sitting across from me in my overstuffed winged armchair, his jacket off, scratching the diamond stud in his left earlobe absently.

"Shit, Dana, I'm sorry," he said.

Talk about understatement.

"Are you really a shifter now?"

"No idea," I replied. "But the evidence seems to point to yes. Thoughts?"

Jon shook his head. "This is nuts," he said. "You were immunized, weren't you? A small scratch shouldn't be turning you furry."

"Tell that to my claw hand," I replied, spearing a chunk of greasy yumminess. "Maybe I should look into the expiry date of those vaccines I got."

I forked another piece of gravy-soaked potato and cheese curd goop, and chewed thoughtfully.

"What kills me is that I'm so hungry," I continued, growling my frustration. "If I didn't know about the whole shape-changer probability, I'd swear I was pregnant."

Jon jumped at this, looking at me, hard. No smile now. "Are you?"

I laughed, once; short, sharp.

"No chance," I replied. "You're the only one I'm

sleeping with right now, and we both know that vampires can't procreate."

Jon leaned back in the chair, tense shoulders relaxing a bit again, and began to smile proprietarily at me.

I threw a French fry at him.

"Don't go getting any ideas," I admonished. "Just because I haven't had time to sleep with anyone else doesn't mean we're exclusive. Your furry friend proved that."

"He's an old friend of mine," Jon replied, quietly. "We were together. We're not now." He shrugged. "And if his jealousy caused this to happen to you—Dana, I'm so sorry."

"Me too," I said. "What do *you* think is going on here?"

Jon chose his words carefully. "What you walked in on, in the parking lot, that sounds like a ritual thing."

"A ritual."

"Yes."

"A dust-floating ritual?" Maybe there was a better way to describe it, but I couldn't think of any right now.

"Not exactly," he said. "I'll ask around." He glanced at the window. "I've got to go—it'll be light in a couple of hours."

"So go," I said. Trying not to feel hurt, let down.

I didn't even feel the air move and Jon was kneeling in front of me. He gently extricated the poutine container from my hands and moved between my legs. Kissed the inside of my left knee. Then looked up at me through long lashes, eyes flickering in the light.

"I don't have to go just yet if you don't want me to," he said.

I leaned forward to cup his face in my hands, his

lips meeting mine. Then he pulled back and waited for me to say the words.

"Stay," I said.

Jon's smile turned predatory then, his hands running up the sides of my body to my armpits, shoulders, neck, then back down again. He stopped midway, running his long fingers under the waistband of my jeans. The logical part of my brain had already clicked off by the time the top button was undone, the zipper lowered, and everything was being peeled off. I lifted my ass off the couch to help, just a bit. Pants gone, underwear gone, I was naked from my belly button to the tops of my socks.

Sex and socks—a Canadian tradition.

Jon licked his lips and looked up at me. The glint in his eyes was positively wicked, and I knew he wasn't done yet. He pushed my black T-shirt up, sucking at my nipples through my bra, bringing first one to a point with his teeth, then the other.

I was writhing now, squirming on the couch. Frustrated, I pulled the shirt off over my head. Jon unfastened my bra as I did this, drawing it down along my arms.

He was still fully dressed. There was something so hot about that. In sex, domination, submission, smell, touch, sound...it's all bestial, all animal. Power and vulnerability. Jon had my thighs parted, my feet resting on his shoulders. His mouth was fastened to my core, drinking me in as I moaned my consent.

Oh. My. *God.* The things he could do with his tongue. And teeth. And fingers. Where were his fingers? Was it a finger? Did I care?

I shuddered through an orgasm, no doubt the first of the night.

Jon looked up at me, mouth glistening, and licked his lips. No, he actually slurped my juices off his lips. It would have been gross if he hadn't done it with such relish. Hunger. His hunger—for me.

Not for the first time, I wished my lover was human.

And then it was too late. Good thing no condoms were needed with the undead; no risk of pregnancy or disease. I was tearing his clothes off, too much between us, needing skin on skin. He flipped me over so that he was on the couch and I was on top, straddling him. Wrapping his arms around my waist; my arms around his neck. A momentary kiss, a pause, and then he thrust up into me, I thrust down, and we both went over the edge.

No more thinking. Furry boyfriends. Strangers and daggers and feeding vampires. None of it mattered. Not in that moment.

We made animal sounds as our flesh slapped together, frequency building. Just when I thought I couldn't get much higher, Jon's eyes snapped open and his teeth clamped down on my left nipple. I arched and screamed through my orgasm. The taste of my blood flipped a switch in Jon, and he flooded me with his release.

NINE

IN THE PRE-DAWN LIGHT, I woke up alone.

The pillow beside my head still bore the imprint of him. He'd covered me with a blanket before he left. So considerate.

But of course he'd left. Couldn't expect him to become a big pile of dust just for me.

It was still early, the short midwinter days making 7:30 a.m. seem like 6:00 a.m., with sunlight starting to cast its beams across my bed in defiance of the wicker blinds I pretended were an effective block against the light. The pattern on the bed looked like a mesh net, and its heat melted against me—and my growling stomach.

Hungry again. Awesome.

It was still too early to willingly relinquish my semi-somnolescent state. Coffee might be nice, but sleep was nicer. My stomach rumbled its protest. I ignored it. But rich Arabica, oiled and ground and roasted, infiltrated my senses. I inhaled deeply, eyes still closed. Definitely coffee.

The coffeemaker was at least twenty to thirty feet away from where I lay, and I hadn't turned it on. So how could I smell coffee?

Ah, screw it. I let my mind drift, floating in that space between sleep and wakefulness.

My dreams were weird. Blood and pentacles and fur

and whiskers and claws. Climbing up a mountain of cheese curds that kept crumbling beneath me. A marching band of instruments making ringing sounds. Since when do musical instruments make ringing sounds anyway?

I cracked open an eyelid. My cell was ringing and voice mail wasn't kicking in fast enough. *Damn.* I answered without looking at the screen, belatedly hoping it wasn't a telemarketer.

"Hello." My voice was more of a croak as I closed my eyes again.

"Did I call at a bad time?" Lynna.

I groaned. "Late night. What's up?"

"I called to see if you wanted to go for lunch," she said. "Or would that be breakfast for you? I don't know how you manage working those hours you work."

Lynna worked freelance as a grip on various films and MOWs—movies of the week—shooting in and around Toronto. So really, her hours weren't any different than mine. But since her job was more glamorous—on paper, anyway—she liked to rib me. It's a game we play but I was too tired for it this morning.

"I manage fine if nobody calls me at the ungodly hour of," I checked the clock on the far wall, "10:45 in the morning."

"Fine," Lynna said. "Want to hit Hermano's Hideaway for lunch? I've got a craving for nachos and I'm looking to partner up on the fix."

I tried to think. Lack of caffeine can be a dangerous thing.

"I'm fried," I said. "But I'm also hungry. Noon?"

"You're not going to roll over and forget this conversation as soon as we hang up, are you?"

I grunted, closing my eyes. Mumbled something about "no."

"Dana!"

I jumped. "What? You don't have to yell," I said grumpily.

"Dana, sit up now."

I sat. Or, more accurately, dragged myself into an upright position.

"Open your eyes."

I opened my eyes.

"Now look towards the coffeemaker. See it?"

I grunted in the affirmative.

"Okay, now walk over to it."

I did so, trying to avoid sharp corners. Then focused. There was a note propped up against the coffeemaker.

Dana—

I figured you'd be tired after last night.

Coffee is ready to go—flip the switch when you get up.

Sorry I can't be there to share it with you.

—Jon

I sighed, turned the machine on, and sat down to watch the holy elixir of wakefulness drip through. Lynna kept up her stream of chatter, specifically designed—in my opinion—to wake me up by annoying me.

Which wasn't really fair. Lynna Ghapoor is one of my best friends, and close female friends that stand by you just don't come along that often. Especially those that honor and respect you—never mind supporting you—through questionable relationships, stalled career paths and periodic black spots. Sure, we all get them, but Lynna was sunshine to my impending hurricane of gloom; cutting through the crap by making everything lighter.

I glanced at the sparklingly clear pot of coffee, willing it to drip faster. No such luck. But the relative cleanliness of the glass made me realize that it had actually been cleaned with soap recently, and not by me.

Damn, another considerate thing.

Hello ambivalence, have you met my friend Jon?

"What?"

I'd forgotten that Lynna was on the other end of the line.

"Was it something I said?"

"No." I retrieved my chipped mug—the bowl-sized one with pale green stripes—from the drain. "Jon washed my coffeepot when he put on coffee. All I had to do was turn on the machine."

"Now *that's* devotion," she said. "What, no blood prints on the handle?"

I sighed. Lynna was less than fully enamored of my dalliance, no matter how many pots of coffee he might leave for me or how hot he makes them—or me.

But who could blame her? I wasn't so thrilled with it myself. Especially if now it meant I'd caught the shifter virus through my association with him. I was in no rush to have *that* conversation with Lynna.

"Can I assume that since I hear movement and the sound of you thinking loudly, it's safe for me to hang up and jump in the shower? You're up for real now?"

"I'm up," I said. "See you at noon?"

"Noon," she agreed before hanging up.

I was free to stare at my brewing coffee once more. Finally, the *beep.*

Aaaah.

I felt the world start to come into clearer focus again. Sex is great, but sometimes the pleasure I get from that first cup in the morning—especially when I'm tired—is simpler. Less complicated. I may obsess about my relationship with coffee, but I never wonder where that relationship is going or whether or not it's a suitable substance to spend my first waking hours with.

I took my obsession back to the couch with me and carefully sank into the pillows, cupping the mug in one hand and supporting it with my thigh. I let my mind drift as the steam floated around my face with each sip. Man, even the smell was like liquid ecstasy right now.

Speaking of. How could I turn furry if I'd been vaccinated against the therianthrope virus? It was illogical. I remembered the shots, remembered when I got them. Eight years ago. I shouldn't have been at risk.

Shifters are either born that way, or they're scratched that way. Even so, not everyone is susceptible to the virus—you have to be extra lucky, apparently, to catch it like I did. Which is odd, considering how similar shifter and human DNA is. Only 0.002 of the immunized population could be scratched and still have the change punch its way through. Okay, maybe that's not the exact number—it's been a few years since I signed the consent form. But there aren't many. I remember that much.

Reality is that nobody knows the stats for sure. That's because only a small portion of the non-afflicted population even realizes something beyond the norm exists. Where do you think all those toe-curling fairy tales come from—someone's imagination? Right, sure, some of them probably do. But a more likely explanation is that someone saw something sometime and couldn't explain it away, so instead they turned it into a bedtime story to scare children.

I've learned that people see what they expect to see. Their minds fill in the cracks for what's left. The rest of us? We get graduate degrees in the Preternatural Sciences and end up working for the Agency.

I called Lynna back and left a message, pushing our lunch by half an hour so I could make a stop on the way.

There was something I had to do first.

TEN

HALF AN HOUR LATER, I was showered and caffeinated and ready to go. Too tired to think about matching clothes, I opted for the whole black on black on black theme again. Different black items, same dark effect.

Jewelry. That's what it needed. I fumbled around in my underwear drawer until I found what I was looking for: a Celtic shield knot woven into a circle and overlaid with silver gilt leaves, hanging on a black leather cord that turned invisible in the dark. I figured the Wiccan talisman of protection might help with unwanted supernatural advances as well. Plus, it looked good. So on it went along with a collection of silver bangles, a thick silver band for my index finger and another one for the opposite thumb.

I surveyed myself in the mirror. I looked like a hipster mortician.

Oh well.

PROFESSOR EZRA GERBRECHT'S office looked just the way I remembered it. Overflowing wastebasket nudged up against an extra-large, weathered cherrywood desk littered with old cardboard coffee cups, file folders and stacks of papers. *IN* basket piled high; *OUT* basket nearly empty. The message light flashing insistently on the call-display speaker phone to the right of his antiquated PC desktop computer. Did Ezra ever pick up his messages? I wondered if there was a statute of limitations on voice mail storage, or whether the system automatically deleted them after a certain point.

Ezra's official title was Professor and Faculty Chair of the Department of Preternatural Studies. An obscure, government-funded department assumed to be part of Classics or Philosophy and housed in one of the older wings of a complex most people avoided. Might have been the "sick building" label slapped on it by the Steelworkers' union, or maybe it was the whispers of haunted pain howling their way along the corridors after dark when things moved that shouldn't. Sense memories of things best forgotten.

Ezra's other, lesser-known job title? Senior Director of Special Projects, Covert Division with the Agency.

Even with the professor's back to me, I could tell it was him by the tufts of wild, white hair that spiked and corkscrewed up over the top edge of his high-backed, battered red leather chair. If I squinted just right, I could almost see my father in that chair instead of Ezra. From before he died. Back when he and Ezra were coworkers. Friends.

I swallowed the lump that clogged my throat, blinking back tears that should have dried up long ago. Forcing myself to focus on the now.

The door was open, but I knocked anyway.

The chair spun around. Ezra leapt out of his chair to pull me into a bear hug, and I was stunned by how much he hadn't aged. Sure, the pigment-deprived hair made it difficult to judge his years. But his face was *less* lined, smoother, fuller. Either he had gone on the Hollywood wrinkle reduction plan, or the man was getting younger.

I hugged Ezra back, keeping my observations to myself. Well, mostly.

"Hey, Professor Ezra, you're looking good! You been dipping into the Botox lately?"

Oh yeah, that's me—the queen of diplomacy.

Fortunately, Ezra laughed.

"That's the girl I remember," he replied, eyes crinkling up into a warm smile. "Calls-'em-like-she-sees-'em. How have you been?"

"Fine," I said. "You?"

"Fine fine," he replied absently. "Some things change, some don't. Did you just get back into town?"

I looked away for a moment, shrugged off the words I was about to say. "I've been back for about three years now."

There's no way Ezra could have known about my bad days. The ones where I remembered what it was like to work on those quasi-preternatural experiments. The staring, pleading eyes of those still alive; alive enough to scream through snouts, trunks, tusks—whatever. The yellows of their eyes clouding over from one too many injections, prods from a pain stick, or having just been disemboweled.

There had to be a better way to study the parallels and splits between shifter and human DNA.

I shoved my hands in the pockets of my jeans to hide the shaking and forced myself to remember how to breathe.

"I thought I'd heard you were working down east, somewhere in Newfoundland—making waves," he said, grinning at his own joke. Oblivious.

I rolled my eyes and groaned on cue.

"All these jokes," he continued, "you'd think I was fishing for a compliment, eh?"

Professor Gerbrecht chortled and looked at me expectantly.

If you can't beat 'em, join 'em.

"If you're *fin*-ished," I said, "not to make you feel *gill*-ty or anything, but on a *scale* of one to ten…not to speak out of *school*…could we possibly change the subject?"

Ezra whooped in appreciation. I'd thought I'd be rusty from lack of practice, but apparently I still had it.

Not that telling jokes was the reason I'd come by.

"Listen, Ezra," I said. "I was wondering about those vaccines we got during the program."

Professor Gerbrecht raised his tufted, white eyebrows at me.

"What about them?"

"I was wondering how long they last," I said. "Do we need to get boosters? Are they good for lifetime use?"

"Depends on how long your lifetime is," he replied dryly. "No, seriously, they're good for about ten years. How long ago did you have your last one?"

"Eight years ago."

"So you should be fine. Why do you ask?"

"The formulas themselves," I continued, ignoring his last question. "Do they protect against all strains of vampirism and therianthropy, or are there some kinds of vampires or shifters where the vaccines might not work?"

That got his attention. Ezra's blue eyes cleared and fixed sharply on mine. "Such as?"

Whatever else Ezra might have said was interrupted as a woman poked her head around the corner, smiling full lips over slightly pointed incisors. Her curly black hair fell to her muscular shoulders, and her fitted burgundy T-shirt poured into a pair of skinny black jeans. There were black combat-style boots completing the look. Her pout coaxed the professor's attention away from me. She reminded me of someone, but who?

I narrowed my eyes at the interruption, flipping through images in my head to try to match one up with her face. But all I could draw was a complete blank. *Damn.*

"Cybele, this is one of my former star pupils, Dana," Ezra was saying to the woman. She smiled up at me with a look that said we shared some kind of wonderful secret.

I give good blank stare. Especially when it's for real.

She held out her hand to shake mine, holding it for a few heartbeats longer than was comfortable. Was that a fingernail trailing along the inside of my wrist? A *green* fingernail? I had a sudden urge to grab her, push her shoulders against the wall, and shove my tongue into her mouth. Hold her by the back of her neck. Touch her as she touches…

Abruptly, the thoughts cut off. I looked down and realized my hand was back in my possession again.

"Pleased to meet you," she said, green eyes winking at me. "Although I have a feeling we've met before."

I nodded absently. The eyes. That hair. *Those thoughts...*

It hit me, bricks to the head.

Demon Chick from the bar.

Working for Ezra in the Preternatural Studies Department of the University of Toronto?

Odd.

Coincidence?

Maybe not.

And how did she manage to do that to me? I'd never thought of myself as bi before. I gave a mental shrug and filed that question away for later contemplation.

Whatever her dealings with Ezra were, they were wrapping up. He was ushering her to the door, his hand on the small of her back, gently propelling her out of his office with one hand as he grabbed a clipboard and stack of files with the other. Wait. He was leaving?

"Ezra?"

He seemed surprised to see me still leaning against the wall, arms crossed with a question mark in my eyes. Demon Chick certainly was good at distraction.

"Dana? I'm sorry, I forgot you were here," he said. "Listen, it sounds like you've got some questions and I'm happy to talk about them further with you, but I have to go teach a class now. As Cybele so considerately reminded me. Leave your number with my secretary, and we'll get together, okay?"

I nodded as I watched his sporty, khaki-clad butt wiggle out the door after his demonic sexpot assistant. Succubus maybe? The Ezra I used to know would have been able to spot her a mile off. And now?

Hmm.

Maybe he's ensorcelled. Maybe she's his midlife crisis. Maybe…

Maybe it was time to stop worrying about how other people lived their lives if it didn't directly affect me.

My stomach was growling again, noisily demanding my as-immediate-as-possible attention. Considering the time, I decided to follow its cue and make my lunch date.

ON MY WAY around King's College Circle to the underpass out of the university grounds, I ran into the wild street woman who'd called me *Kitty*. It was a day of weirdness I guess.

Except that the woman's marbles seemed to have shaken themselves a little looser since last we ran into each other. Today she saw me coming, widened her bleary eyes, pulled her lips back over her teeth and hissed before swatting at me. Looking for all the world like a cat with retractable claws outstretched.

I squinted, trying to focus on her hands. Hands that swished again past my nose. Yes, they were hands. Not paws with claws. But I could have sworn I was almost scratched on the nose by a bag lady with cat claws and furry orange paws.

Only one thing to do. Back away. Slowly.

I was across the street at Queen's Park Crescent before I finally looked over my shoulder at the old woman. Orange glowing eyes watched me from the gloom under the bridge. I closed my eyes, opened them, then looked a second time. This time, darkness wrapped its shawl around the woman and I saw only the wildness of her hair, a white flame in the dark, her face turned away from me.

Sigh.

The cosmos was getting a bit obvious for my tastes. Apparently someone wanted me to think I was, or was about to become, a cat. Except that it wasn't possible because my shots were up to date.

Right?

If I wish for something really really hard, can I make it so?

Like the little engine that could, I think I can keep from turning into a cat... *I think I can keep from turning into a cat... I think I can I think I can...*

ELEVEN

A WOMAN LOOKING rather messianic walks into a bar, slaps down three nails, and says: "Can you put me up for the night?"

Okay, so not really. What I actually asked for was a shot of Patrón tequila with a Corona beer chaser. Amazingly enough, I was early so I had time to slug both back before Lynna arrived and had the opportunity to comment on my uncharacteristic pre-noon alcohol consumption.

A bartender who doesn't (usually) drink. Go figure. Just call me one of life's little ironies.

The bar-slash-restaurant was pretty busy for a midweek, lunchtime crowd. The counter in front of the bar was filled with guys in casual office wear and a smattering of baseball caps. I was guessing tourists or guys playing hooky for the afternoon from one of the many Bay Street offices guarding the city's financial empires. Off in another corner was a group of women opening presents and downing margaritas. The rest of the place was a mix of university students, couples and casual friends kicking back over beer and nachos.

"Been waiting long?"

Lynna cheerfully plopped down onto the unoccupied bench in the booth, tossing a sunshine-orange synthetic nylon bag into the corner beside her. I smiled back with lips now salty and slightly numb.

Lynna has a very bright, somewhat exotic—at least by polite Canadian standards—fashion sense. Vivid colors are a staple, and the bolder the statement the happier she tends to be with her outfit. Today was no exception. She'd paired purple velvet stretch pants with a wide black belt and a flowing rust-colored crushed velvet top, which technically laced up the front but was really just an excuse to flash a little of her ample cleavage. I paused for a moment to admire her fire-engine-red patent leather platform shoes.

Basically, Lynna's taste in bodily attire was the antithesis of mine.

The waiter brought me another tequila shot and put the full glass down next to the two empties. So much for worrying about what Lynna might think.

"Can I take those for you?"

I nodded as I plastered a bright smile on my face and thanked him politely for doing what, really, he was being paid minimum wage plus tips to do anyway. But there's a kind of solidarity among those of us who work in the food and beverage service industry, so no being rude to a *compadre*.

The tequila was definitely warming my mood.

Lynna had her brown eyes fixed on me during the exchange, red painted fingernails tapping unconsciously on the scratched, varnished wood tabletop.

"Stop thinking so loud," I said.

"So stop being so cheerful," she replied. "It's creepy."

"Creepy? I was being nice—at least, I thought I was," I said. "Wasn't I? It's been a while I guess. Maybe I've forgotten how."

"No, you seem to have managed it just fine," she

said. "What's going on? You're wired, drinking tequila shots, and the most unnerving thing of all—you're being polite to Rick the Dick. You can't stand him. You barely speak to him. So, spill."

I can't stand him? Glancing over at the plexiglass window between the dining area and the back kitchen, I realized that Lynna was right. Rick was the waiter with capital *A* attitude, the starving artist/actor/cooler-than-thou guy who always gave me service with a sneer. Might have been because I slept with him that once and snuck out without leaving him my number. Did I mention he was a lousy lay? All slobber and quick thrusts. Spent most of the time watching himself in the mirror rather than reciprocating my efforts with anything fun. And here I was, being polite to the selfish snoot. Well. Enough of that.

So I spilled, as requested. The scene, the scratch, the was-it-or-wasn't-it hospital visit, the post-bar incident. Lynna listened to it all, her mouth hanging open. Metaphorically speaking. If she'd really had her mouth open all that time, I'm sure actual drool would have pooled on her crushed velvet top and spoiled the fabric.

At some point, Lynna caught Rick the Dick's attention and ordered us some killer nachos and a couple of frozen margaritas. Extra sour cream, extra guacamole. Can't have too much dip. Especially in the middle of a crisis. As for the margaritas, well, I might have been in a tequila shooter kind of mood but margaritas just plain taste better. So yay Lynna.

The drinks arrived at the table and were met by silence. We both clinked, gulped fast, then smacked our glasses back onto the tabletop. Finally:

"So," I said, "what do you think?"

"Was he cute?"

"Who, Ezra?"

"No," Lynna replied, laughing a bit. "Sam, did you say his name was?"

"Yeah, Sam." I conjured his face in my mind, shadowed by the previous night's events. Grasping at hollows and angles and darkness for a clear image. "I don't know. Maybe. Sort of. He was a good fighter, that's for sure."

"Not a total loss then."

"I guess," I said, with a fleeting attempt at a smile. Then, I blurted out before my self-controlled bravado could filter the rawness of my question: "Lynna, do you think I'm going to turn into a cat?"

She signaled Rick the Dick.

"We're going to need another round of drinks."

TWELVE

It was 2:30 in the afternoon when I dragged myself away from Hermano's Hideaway. Any sun from earlier had fled behind grey, low-hanging clouds. I started walking towards my truck only to remember, belatedly, that I'd had a few too many to drink and shouldn't be getting behind the wheel. Remembered even more belatedly that I hadn't actually driven.

I wasn't due at work for another three hours. Not quite enough time for the alcohol to wear off and too much time to head directly there by cab or public transit. Sparks of energy danced along my skin; too restless to check myself into a café with a book.

I walked.

The lake appeared faster than expected and I shifted my awareness east in the direction of the Swan. At the split in the road around Cherry Beach, I veered off the grime-encrusted sludge of Lakeshore Boulevard, south past the small bridge that spans the Don River, and headed into the warehouse district.

By this time I was re-thinking my decision not to drive. My head had cleared and I realized that I'd be finishing work at 2:30 a.m.—not the best time to grab a cab in the middle of nowhere. I fished around for my cell phone, hoping to catch Lynna before she turned her mobile to silent for the shoot.

The call went straight to voice mail; I left a message asking her to come by and pick me up after she got off work if she could. If Lynna didn't check in time, I might be bunking down in the storage room for the night. Awesome. Remind me again not to drink in the middle of the afternoon on a workday.

I stared blankly at my phone, willing it to ring while I pictured what bedding—if any—was currently tucked into those shelves in the back of the Swan, when I noticed that I had no signal. Odd considering I was about two blocks from a cache of satellite dishes, the space rented out by one or more of the major telecommunications companies with offices in the city.

Chilled, I realized I was absolutely and completely alone. No cars had turned down the lane in more than a few minutes, no gravel crunched under tires, and any rushing traffic noises off the Lakeshore were notably absent. The only sounds I heard were the stones beneath my feet as I tromped, more softly now, along the road. It was my imagination. I knew that. But the air around me felt thicker, spongy, closing in on me and wrapping me in a marshmallow blanket. It was harder and harder to move. And there was a buzzing in my head, like one of those electronic mosquito zappers that used to hang outside my grandparents' cottage.

I looked up and the sky was dark; the sun had set without me noticing.

There, on the periphery. Shadowy figures. Shuffling. Towards me.

Forget dignity. I broke into a sprint, making for the Swan. I was blocks away still. Too far for Sandor to hear me if I screamed, but so close I could see the bar's hulking shape and barbed wire—encircled roof beckoning to me above the bare trees and barren buildings.

The shadowy shapes lumbered ever closer as I jolted forward. Gooey air grasped at my legs. I could see the door. A burst of adrenaline and I was there, banging on the peeling façade. The shadows were behind me now, and I scented their putrescence on the wind. Seconds felt like hours. It was still early—maybe Sandor wasn't in yet?

Then the hanging metal light clicked on and I heard the sound of deadbolts sliding. The door opened and a green, spotted hand reached out and pulled me in, slamming the heavy door behind me. I was gasping, panting, staring at Sandor as we heard the thudding sounds of bodies throwing themselves at the exterior.

Sandor was looking at me, his hair still rumpled from sleep, a wart-encrusted eyebrow cocked in my direction.

"What, you thought maybe it would be a nice afternoon to go for a walk?"

"What were those things?" I was having trouble catching my breath.

"Nuisances," Sandor replied. He walked over to a switch beside the door and flicked it on. Immediately, I heard a hissing sound from outside; shrieks and groans and more thuds before silence. "Gotta remember to spray the place. Best I can do without calling in a team of exterminators."

"Exterminators?"

"AAA Zombie Exterminifactors, really. There's a nest out there. Scares off the clientele. Got to be managed. Speaking of which, how exactly did you draw their attention? They usually ignore the norms in these parts."

I hesitated.

"I, um, might not be entirely norm at this point," I said. "Remember?"

"Oh. Yeah," he replied. He scratched the inner cleft of his left nostril ponderously, curved yellow claw surprisingly gentle, and made a sound suspiciously like "hmph."

"Weird," he said finally.

Understatement.

"It's not your first exposure, but I've never gotten anything other than norm off you up until the last few days. You haven't gotten into any of those injectable drugs all the kids are trying out, have you?"

I narrowed my eyes to look witheringly at my boss. The big green demon was, of course, unfazed.

"No," I said, when pointy looks didn't make the question disappear. "I don't do needles."

"Hmph," Sandor said again. "And that long-fanged one you've been hanging out with, that artist guy. Has he been sinking his teeth into you at all?"

Sandor had me there, and I nodded, a flush burning my ears as I avoided his many eyes for a moment in sheepish unease. "Sometimes," I said. "It's a sex thing. You know how it is."

Sandor gave me a lopsided grin and nodded. Letting me know with his own eye-flick, down and to the left, that we'd all done things in the heat of the now.

"But nothing out of the ordinary there," I continued. "We've been at it for quite a while already. If anything was going to show up in my blood, you'd have smelled it before this, wouldn't you?"

"Probably," he admitted. "Besides, I don't get vampire off you. Whatever it is, there's fur involved."

"Awesome," I replied. "Just what a girl wants to hear."

"I'll ask around," Sandor said, ignoring my last comment. "See if I can find out anything that might be useful to your current situation. In the meantime," he continued, "do you have a ride home tonight? I'm thinking that a long walk might not be in the best interests of your continued good health, if you know what I mean."

"I left a message for Lynna but haven't heard back yet."

"You might want to get the fangy one to come get you then," he said. "More muscle wouldn't be the worst idea."

I shrugged, embarrassed. I hated to call up Jon for small things, especially given our current state of relationship ambivalence.

"Suck it up," Sandor advised, noting my hesitation. "No sense in having pride if you're too dead to enjoy it."

THIRTEEN

Jon showed up not long before closing.

I felt him before I saw him, goose bumps dimpling my arms, a cold that burned at the back of my neck as I wiped down the bar and filled orders before last call. *There.* He sat, lanky frame nursing a stein of dark liquid, looking across the bobbing heads to meet my eyes. Smoldering heat.

I walked over to him, my gait as casual as I could make it. Leaned over, close, so close my hair brushed his smooth cheek.

"Cut it out," I murmured. To anyone else, a lover whispering sweet nothings in her beloved's ear. "Save the glamour for some other time and place. Preferably one with fewer people around."

Jon leaned back, grinning. His smile was still predatory, just a hint of pointed fang, but there was an impish edge to it now. A boy pushing his luck, testing the limits, seeing how far he could get without having his hand slapped.

"Milady's wish is mine to obey," he replied. Like he was fooling anyone.

I returned to my tasks and wrapped up my shift. Finally it was time to go. I did so reluctantly, knowing that leaving the bar meant putting myself in direct orbit of Jon. Which meant temptation.

I couldn't help looking over my shoulder as I got

into his car, a two-door sporty restored something or other, black exterior, red plush interior (cliché much?). I shivered, static pricks of electricity at the back of my neck. I knew I was being watched. Invisible eyes in the dark, soundless except for the *slap slap slap* of the waves off Lake Ontario. Jon seemed to sense it too, scanning the snowy nothingness with narrowed eyes, nostrils flared to catch a scent that didn't seem to exist. He closed the door behind me, shutting off the outside beyond tinted windows. I hoped it would be enough.

Jon blasted the heat. Its toasty warmth eased around me in an airy hug, dulling just a bit of my tension as the metal beast shifted into gear, spewing gravel in its wake. I tried not to notice Jon's chivalry. I didn't want to depend on him. This relationship, this tryst; I knew it couldn't last.

And yet.

The drive passed in relative silence. Too much to say. Jon seemed to accept my reticence, steering the conversation—when he bothered to say anything—onto safer ground: lack of traffic, the weather, other drivers, upcoming gallery exhibits. Why point to the pink elephant in the room when you're not even at the zoo? Finally, when the conversation trailed off yet again, I spoke.

"Thanks for coming down to pick me up," I said. "You know I wouldn't have asked you if…"

"If you didn't really need it," he replied. "I know. You don't want to take anything from me. I get it."

"Yeah," I said.

"You know that's your choice, not mine."

"Look, we both know that this can't go anywhere," I said, my words heavy. "We're not even exclusive—

Mr. Cat Scratch Fever pretty much made that clear. As if I needed it spelled out." I muttered that last part.

Jon let it slide in an awkward pause. We stopped at a red light.

Then: "Claude and I, we're not together like that anymore, Dana," he said. "I don't know what I can say to convince you. You believe what you want. I've got nothing but time to wait for you to come around."

"Or not," I said, just a bit of an edge, skating the bloody tip of the knife.

He didn't take the bait.

"Or not," he said, instead.

I turned in the passenger seat to look at him. Closely. Watching the expressions that crossed his eyes, his face, the telltale twitching at the corner of his mouth.

"I'm it for you? Seriously? Nobody else—no blood buddy, furry leg warmer or fangy friend shares your bed these days?"

Jon stared fixedly forward, hands tightening ever so slightly on the steering wheel.

"What do you want me to say?" His voice was almost as tight as his grip. "You know what I am. Who I am. You knew this going in. Some rules can't be changed."

"True," I said. "I did know. But maybe we should face reality and not make this more than it is. Friends."

"With benefits?" The imp was back.

I laughed, mirthless.

"Oh yeah. There are definitely benefits."

THERE WAS SOMETHING off when we pulled up to my place. And not just the aftereffects of our capital *R* relationship talk. I didn't recall leaving the outside light on. Twitchy. I hesitated with my hand on the on the armrest.

"I can come up with you," Jon offered.

Discomfort over reason. I chose to go it alone.

"No, it's okay. Thanks anyway."

Jon didn't say anything as I got out of the car and slammed the door shut. Walking up those twenty-five stairs to my apartment, I could feel him at my back, even from the car, engine humming. Having him there, so close and yet far, made me feel a little safer. Just a bit though.

I was regretting not asking him in already. My front door opened too easily, the hallway too dark, as I flicked on the hall light and it hit me. That smell. Copper mixed with sulphur. Mixed with *gas*?

I turned to look out the door, light spilling across the stairs, and sprinted, racing back down to Jon's car even as he reversed out of the spot. He didn't notice until I was banging on the window. He unlocked the door and I dove in, screaming.

As the world turned orange.

FOURTEEN

I WOKE UP in a hospital bed. Strangely familiar. Black carpet, red drapes, dried roses on the night table.

At least this time I wasn't in restraints.

I glanced over at the lounge chair to my right, in front of the darkened window, following the line of long legs to the man slouched there, snoring lightly.

Not Jon.

Sam.

I cleared my throat in a not-so-subtle attempt to see if he would wake up. He did, blue-green eyes coming into view as his eyelids peeled open. This guy was muscle in repose, shaggy light brown hair peppered with grey, but aside from his coif there was nothing aged about him. Sam saw me looking at him and his tired features cracked into a smile.

"What happened?"

Sam gave a shrug and I knew what was coming next wasn't going to be good.

"Your kitchen blew up."

"My kitchen," I said. "Um. Was anyone hurt?"

"Fortunately no. It was a localized explosion."

"Okay. Why exactly did my kitchen blow up? It's not like I use it much."

"It looks like there might have been a gas leak. A gas leak that may have been helped along by forces unknown."

"A gas leak," I repeated. "Interesting, but again, *why*?"

"I was hoping you might have some ideas," he said. "Piss anyone off lately?"

"No more than usual," I replied. There was something I was missing. What was it? "What are you doing here, anyway?"

"I've been asked to investigate this matter."

"By?"

"Pack business." Code for Anshell Williams. "You're starting to draw a lot of attention to yourself, and we'd like to know why."

"Well, there's that friendly feeding festival you and I interrupted the other night. Random Goth Guy and the vamp cabal. What about them?"

"Maybe," Sam said, slowly, drawing out the syllables as he turned the idea over in his head. "Anything else? Anyone else?"

Who *had* I seen over the last few days? Who had I spoken with? Only one other name came to mind.

"Do you know anything about a guy named Professor Ezra Gerbrecht?"

Sam's face went thoughtful.

"Gerbrecht. Ezra Gerbrecht." Sam drew out that last word, pronouncing the name surprisingly accurately, the *ch* rolling around in the back of his throat like he had a piece of popcorn caught there. "Yes, I've heard of him. Scientist guy studying the DNA of shifters and other human-based beings. He's looking for the common gene. Right?"

"You sure do know him," I commented. "So, what do you know?"

"Better yet," Sam said, "what do *you* know? That's a pretty random name to pull out of the air."

I told Sam about going to visit Ezra, how I'd taken some graduate-level courses in preternatural bio-science under the man, and about the professor's strangely absentminded behavior. I left out the bits about the Agency. Ezra had been responsible for administering my preventative vaccines as well, or at least had been the medical professional overseeing the project, and I shared with Sam my concern that the vaccines might no longer be effective. Sam had already seen me partially shift, so no point in glossing over that reality.

"But still," I concluded, "I can't think of any reason why he would want to blow up my apartment. I was one of his star pupils. Okay, so I was also one of his biggest disappointments—he thought I was wasting my life working at a bar instead of committing my life to what I studied—but still. This whole thing feels a bit extreme for Ezra."

Sam nodded. "You're right, it doesn't make much sense. But we have to consider all possible options here. Can you think of anyone else who has been acting strangely?"

I debated whether or not I really wanted to open up the can of decomposing worms that was my relationship with Jon. Not really. But what if there was something relevant there?

"There might be one other—for lack of a better word, *person*—who is probably not my biggest fan."

Sam looked at me expectantly.

"The other night I was with my, um, well I was with this guy. And this other guy barges in, pissed and jealous. Seems the guy I was with swings in more than one direction, and the guy who, uh, broke down the door was not too thrilled with my being there. He's the one who scratched me. Not on purpose, at least I don't think so, but still."

"Hmm," Sam replied thoughtfully. "Do we have a name for this cat *person*?"

"I think his name is Claude," I said, increasingly tired. "Ask Jon."

Sam didn't ask who Jon was. Or Claude. My guess was that Jon had been the one to bring me here. Again. But Claude? There *was* more than one pack in this city, right?

I shut my eyes. Too many coincidences, too few alternate explanations. I wanted to sleep; I needed to figure out what was going on. Who wanted to kill me. Why.

The air shifted as I felt Sam stand up and tuck the blanket under my chin, his hand lingering a moment longer than necessary on my shoulder before withdrawing.

"I'm sorry," I heard him say, as though speaking through a hollow tube a great distance away. "You're tired. Rest. You're safe here."

But I knew the truth. Safety was relative.

My father had taught me that. Before the accident. Before the men in suits came to break news that my mother and I would have preferred stay in bad dreams. He should have been okay, my father, in that government lab with his good friend Ezra Gerbrecht.

And yet.

I WAS ALONE NOW, and hungry, and still I couldn't sleep. Light peeked through the edges of the curtains shrouding the windows. I stretched, rolling my head along the pillow, working out the kinks before carefully sitting up. Sore, but I'd live. At least I hoped so. I just needed to get home and take a shower and…wait, no home.

My apartment blew up.

Damn.

I lay back and tried to remember the name of my insurance company. AAA something. Sandor had recommended them, so he would probably know who to call. AAA Insurance? Indemnity? Ishkibibble? Anything more than AAA and I was drawing a blank.

Okay, let's think logically here. Needed to find a place to live. Needed to find a place to stay. Needed to call the insurance company. Get new clothes. Figure out who is trying to kill me. And why. Oh yeah, and food. I could really go for some food right about now.

I had to start with the basics. Find phone. I looked around and noticed a locker in the corner of the room. Carefully, I pushed myself up to a sitting position and tested out my balance by placing one foot then the other onto the pile rug. Okay. Standing was a bit of a challenge, but after a moment the vertigo passed and I was able to slowly make my way over to the locker.

There, my purse. Some singed clothes. Boots.

I scooped up my bag and hobbled back to the stability of the bed. Fished around; found my phone. A folded piece of paper torn from the back of an envelope fell out as I flipped open the case.

It was from Jon. Of course.

Dana,
Give me a call when you wake up. You can stay with me if you need to.
Jon

Ignoring the flashing message light, I thrust Jon's note deep into my bag and instead dialed Lynna. Voice mail again. I hung up without leaving a message. Again.

Fine. I leaned back into my pile of pillows and dialed into my voice mail.

First message: a telemarketer trying to sell me a cable TV package. *Delete.*

Second, third and fourth messages: hang-ups.

The fifth message was from a breathless Lynna. "Dana, I've got this bad feeling. Need you to tell me I'm wrong—or look under my car and kill the spider for me. I'm heading over to the Swan to meet you after work tonight. Please wait for me, okay?"

Sandor's gravelly voice was next. "Dana girl, you coming in tonight? I got a message from your vamp friend that you might be out sick, but I wanted to check to make sure you're okay and to see what's the what. Give me a call when you get this."

The seventh message made my heart go cold. There was a chill emanating from the phone. I swear I could feel a sheen of icy hoar frosting over the earpiece.

"We have your friend. You will meet us." The voice described an area not far from Cherry Beach. "We will talk. And then you will die."

I dropped the phone.

Okay so it wasn't my imagination; there was ice puddling on the bed, searing the top layer of blanket—heat against all logic. Grabbing the edge of the sheet, I lifted it up and flung it as far away from me as possible with a very high-pitched, girly shriek.

Footsteps pounded along the hallway outside my door as Anshell raced, white coat flapping, into the room. Wordlessly, I pointed to the phone, which was melting through the shag to whatever lay beneath it.

Muttering under his breath, Anshell leapt across the room to the fire extinguisher, released the clasps and sprayed the phone until it stopped sizzling and popping. He pulled some thick rubber gloves from his back pocket and put them on before scooping up the mobile communication device, which had now clearly seen better days.

He let out a low whistle as he turned the piece over in his hands. "Girl, you sure do know how to liven up a place," he said.

"Understatement much?" My voice raspy through a chest made suddenly tight.

Anshell hit a spot on the wall and a cabinet I hadn't noticed before opened up. Out came a thick leather rectangle with a zipper on top; in went the melted phone; down went the bag.

He sank into the lounge chair with a squelch, leaned back, and looked at me expectantly.

"Why don't you tell me what's going on here. From the beginning."

WHEN I WAS DONE, he let out another one of his what I suspected were characteristic long, low whistles.

"Starting from the beginning," he said, "which friend do you think is in trouble here?"

"I've only got so many," I replied. "Could be Jon. Could be Sandor. Could maybe even be Sam, although I don't know that we know each other well enough yet. But I'm pretty sure they can all take care of themselves just fine." I gulped, not wanting to force out the words

I knew I had to say next. "I think it's Lynna. Whoever is out there, I think they have Lynna."

I WANTED TO go right away. Anshell made me wait a few minutes to have The Talk.

No, it had nothing to do with safe sex. Besides, let's be serious—that ship had sailed, sunk and set sail again more times than it was worth counting. This Talk had to do with the Pack. Joining. What that meant. Protection, but also a set of responsibilities that maybe I wasn't ready to deal with.

Of course, it all depended on whether or not I was truly a shifter now. Signs pointed to yes, but until I could control and replicate it…

Either way, Anshell was firm on the whole not-letting-me-walk-into-danger, especially not without backup. The way my week was going, I was inclined to agree. I wasn't keen on danger to begin with, frankly, but it didn't look like my life at present was going to make the avoidance of danger an option. I allowed myself a moment of weakness and acquiesced to his offer.

Backup, apparently, came in the form of Sam. Also Jon. Awesome. Two males, one female, and a homicidal poison gas arsonist on the loose. This just kept getting better and better.

FIFTEEN

THE PLAN WENT something like this. I would head, ostensibly alone, to the place the scary melty ice voice directed me to go. Lurking in the background, with a more complex strategy, I was hoping, would be Sam and a team of Anshell's making. Think of me as bait, but armed in places I didn't think possible. Here's hoping it didn't occur to the chilled voice to melt my body armor the way it had done so effectively to my cell phone.

Get in, scope the scene, get Lynna, get out. Cause as much damage as possible. Hope that Sam would be enough to back me up in case Anshell's team didn't come through. Not that they wouldn't come through. Right? Positive thinking there, Dana. Come on. You can do it.

Definitely don't think about your friend, who might be an image master extraordinaire on a film set but was completely unprepared to defend herself. No self-defense classes (Lynna had tried one or two but spent most of the time hiding out in the back of the gym gossiping with the hunky caretaker), and no preternatural vaccinations (what's the point, she said—I lead a very different life from you and I hate needles). Taking a shower and working sixteen-hour shifts was about as much exercise as Lynna was interested in. Pushing herself to her limits meant work, possibly play, but definitely no physical exertion. She'd wait for a big strong man to rescue her.

Not that Lynna would ever admit to the whole dominant male fantasy thing, but it was clear there was something more than sheer laziness behind her apparently limitless ability to sabotage anything that might make a male perceive her as a physical equal.

Not me. I expected my men to keep up with me, and if they couldn't—well, that was their issue, not mine.

What choosing a vampire as one of my lovers demonstrated about my commitment issues, however, was something perhaps I would leave aside for now.

One of my lovers. *Riiiight*. Because I had them lined up around the block. Because I was seeing so many males at the same time. Because I wasn't exclusive with Jon. Because I certainly didn't feel like there might be life (or unlife) beyond the play. No. Of course not.

Denial. It's more than just a river in Egypt.

There *was* Sam. Did I have the energy to start something up with a guy who wasn't preternaturally inaccessible? Mr. Nice Guy With Weapons? No wonder pop psychologists have devoted so much time to the whys and wherefores of our attraction to the bad boys. Rough, dangerous, but of course soft and squishy in the middle when it came to us. Rescue fantasies go both ways, right?

Speaking of rescue, it was time. I drove my truck, scanned and cleared of all magical and mundane traps, to the spot. Turned off the engine with a *rat-a-rat-rat-a-thud*. Note to self: get engine serviced soon. Sat. Drummed my fingers on the steering wheel. Waited some more while scanning the desolate area, waves slapping the shore and breaking against the ice with sharp snaps of sound. Ice + ice demon. Go figure.

Ten minutes passed. Fifteen. Twenty. By twenty-five, I was examining my fingertips for hangnails. At thirty my hair became the subject of some scrutiny, as I began the Great Split End Hunt. Forty had me scrounging around for receipts and organizing them into neat piles on the ripped passenger seat. That kept me busy for at least another ten to fifteen, at which point I realized I'd been there an hour. That would be fifty minutes past the time the swap was supposed to happen. *So* not good.

The disposable cell phone Anshell had given me buzzed against my hip, scaring me out of my skin just a bit. I checked the display: Sam.

"Yes?"

"Keep it cool," he said. "I'm seeing something from behind your vehicle, a ways off but heading towards you."

"From the lake?"

"No, the road."

"So, ice demon. Not much for that lake effect mist, huh?"

Sam chuckled.

"Remember—we're right here behind you," he said. "Keep your head, watch your back and focus on your friend."

"Roger roger," I replied, cutting off the connection and putting the phone in my pocket.

All too soon the fog was there. My windows were sealed shut against the condensation, heart hammering, upper lip prickling with frozen sweat droplets. I couldn't see the end of my hood.

I glanced over my shoulder, not trusting the rear-view mirror. Grey goo. I looked to the front again and almost left my skin behind as I jerked backwards and away. Lynna's cheek was pressed against the windshield of the truck, the rest of her body sprawled at awkward angles. I would have thought she was dead if not for the frantic darting motion of her eyes. She was being held in place by a single taloned hand, turkey claws on the end of stubby marbled orange digits. I couldn't see the arm to which those fingers were attached.

Suddenly the hand rolled away from Lynna with a bloody thud as it hit the windshield wiper blades, severed from its source by a single wickedly curved blade that seemed to whistle even through the partial sound barrier of the glass. I saw a blur of green as what I assumed was the arm and the body behind it was hauled away from the truck. Gelatinous green glop smeared a finger-paint pattern, Rorschach drawings, dripping along Lynna's shoulder. I saw Sam's face, felt him smack the hood of the truck, (was that the severed arm he was using?) as the mist seemed to start clearing. The signal to grab Lynna and go.

In a flash, I had the driver's door open and was hauling my friend's relatively inert form into the truck, pushing her past the steering wheel and onto the pile of receipts. My accountant was *so* going to fire my ass when he got the blurry, smeared, stuck-together stacks this year. Lynna was curled into a fetal ball on the seat. I pushed her feet down and reached across to grab the seat belt. Once I was satisfied that she was securely fastened, I opened the truck door again—my side, not hers—and stepped out.

I had to check things out for myself. Because sometimes I'm an idiot.

Thick silence greeted me. No fighting. Nobody but me, the truck, and Lynna inside.

This made no sense.

And then I wasn't alone anymore. In front of me, there was a blur of motion; a being of pale aquamarine blue with crystalline warts that twinkled in the moonlight appeared. A hand on my shoulder before I could move. Cold numbness where it touched, trickling ice into my veins. I could feel my heart start to pump slower. Sharp fear clawed at my chest. I was powerless in its grip. Not enough air. Too much pressure.

I couldn't let it happen. I narrowed my concentration with the air I had left, and channeled that pressure. The edges of my fingertips started to tingle. I pushed aside disbelief, doubt; my wonder at what my body was trying to do. Claws, nubbly tips starting to lengthen and reshape. But slowly. Too slowly.

Time. I needed more time.

And, clearly, more practice. Instead I settled for distraction, forced through numb lips shaping a single word: "Why?"

"It's not personal," it said. "Someone wants you dead. I'm just the messenger."

"Who?" A gasp. If I was going to die, at least I could find out who would do this to me.

It opened its mouth to answer and fell towards me, green blood blooming on its chest. Like a wall of sound exploding, I was abruptly surrounded by noises of fighting, slashing, screaming and dying as I gulped in breaths of precious air. I looked around and found Sam, dancing to my left in the fray, swinging his sword. Anshell was somewhere to my right, cracking necks. The battle had a feral grace, blood flowing as the players swirled in a killing two-step.

And then it was over. Mist flowed outward and away from the gore, and we were left, standing, dripping green and red, with the carnage that remained.

Except for the blue ice assassin. He was not happy at all. He was, in fact, spitting bits of frozen aquamarine chips tinged with his own green blood as he sat, fuming, swaddled in sparking cords of some kind. The killing blow to his chest was already knitting back together, although the healing was absorbing some of the fabric of his shirt along with the blue flesh. That would be a bitch to get out.

Jon was sitting opposite Demon Blue, fangs out, the laugh lines around his eyes pulled tight in anger. He leaned on a wicked sword, sharp and multi-layered, its handle solid black and covered with runes I didn't recognize. I couldn't make out what Jon was saying to the demon, but from the way the demon was responding (leaning away, looking down, trying to appear as nonthreatening as possible) I could only guess what Jon was impressing upon the would-be assassin. I'd always seen Jon as more of a lover than a fighter, but from his practiced stance and the ease with which he wielded the hefty sword, it was clear that Jon had yet another dimension to add to the picture I kept layering in my head.

He pointed the tip of his cutting edge at the throat of Demon Blue, leaning in just enough to cause a few drops of green blood to drip along the length of the blade. In a flash, Anshell and Sam were flanking the prisoner. Anshell laid his hand on Jon's arm and cleared his throat.

"Be cool," Anshell said. "If you kill him or tear out his throat, he can't tell us anything."

Jon growled in frustration, but withdrew his sword from Demon Blue's version of an Adam's apple. The look Jon threw Blue's way, though, left no doubt that had looks been weapons, Demon Blue would have been very dead. Anshell leaned into Demon Blue as Jon backed off, Good Cop to Jon's Bad Cop. You'd think they had planned it, it came off so smoothly. Sam stood in the shadows, a ways behind Anshell, flanking him and guarding his back. Not for the first time I wondered what, exactly, the relationship was between Anshell and Sam. Commander and bodyguard? Friends? More than friends?

"What did you want with our girl over there?" Anshell asked, nodding in my general direction. "You know she is under our protection?" Okay, we hadn't dotted and crossed any special letters or anything, but it was nice of him to say anyway.

"Like I told the girl," Demon Blue replied, "it's nothing personal. Just a contract."

"Who hired you?" Anshell's voice was level.

"You know I don't know that," Demon Blue said. "It's always brokered though a Shadow Wraith."

"What's this Shadow Wraith's name?"

Demon Blue gave a short, sharp laugh at that question.

"You seem like a guy who knows what's what around here, so I'm going to give it to you straight. I can't tell you her name. Either you're going to kill me or you won't, but with her there is no guessing—I reveal her identity, I'm dead. And dying by her pleasure will, I'm sure, be lengthy and excruciatingly painful because that's how she rolls. So how about we skip that part and get to what's really important here. The details."

"I thought you couldn't tell me anything," Anshell said, after a pause.

"You have to ask the right questions," Demon Blue responded. "And if you rough me up a little, leave a few marks where they won't heal instantaneously, it won't seem like I rolled so easily. But don't kid yourself. I'm not giving up the Shadow Wraith."

Anshell looked at Jon, who didn't need to be looked at twice. He reached out and sliced off a piece of Demon Blue's ear. Then licked his lips. *Blech.* I thought vampires only went for human blood. Apparently not. *Double blech.* I looked away to see Sam watching me with a smirk. Apparently the nature of this particular delicacy was not lost on him, nor was it any kind of surprise. Awesome.

In the meantime, I found myself short on patience. I took a series of deliberate steps forward until I was nose to nose with the creature who had just tried to end my existence. Nothing personal, my ass. My life was very personal—to me.

"Cut the crap," I said. "Tell me who wants me dead."

The demon laughed in my face.

"Listen, lady, you and I both know that if it weren't for your posse of friends here you would be dead. This attitude you're pulling with me? You're bluffing. Get you and me alone again? You'll die with my cold hot self as the last thing you see before you exit this mortal coil."

My dagger was unsheathed and buried in his throat

before he could utter another word. Blue sanguinity bubbled out of the corners of his mouth, and his cerulean eyes started to cloud over in a frozen sheen. I glanced up at Anshell, who was shaking his head.

"What? Can't this guy repair himself indefinitely?"

Sam answered. "Ice demons have two weaknesses: their throats and silver. Unless someone draws out the poison now, this guy is done."

"Oops," I muttered, not very convincingly.

Sam peered over my shoulder to assess the damage. "Dead guys as a rule generally can't tell you anything useful. Not without an exorcist or a psychic, and even then the results can be a little dodgy."

I grunted my response as I yanked the dagger out. Anshell found a towel from who-knows-where and pressed it against the burbling, bloody gash to staunch the flow. Demon Blue took on a few gulps of suddenly precious air as his throat tried to knit itself back together.

Satisfied that Blue Boy wasn't going anywhere for the moment, I bent down to wipe the bloody goo from my knife in the snowbank. It was extra sparkly in the moonlight.

I called over my shoulder to the group. "Any ideas about these diamonds? Like, for instance, do they do anything special?"

"Wouldn't you like to know, bitch," Demon Blue gurgled. Jon kicked him, steel-toed boot to gut, in response.

"Manners," Jon said. "Apologize to the lady."

"I don't see no ladies here," Blue coughed. Jon raised his foot once more, lightning-quick, stopping mere millimeters from the previous point of contact between boot and gut. Blue held up his hands. "But let's pretend that one over there," nodding in my general direction, "is somewhat resembling a lady. In which case, let me express my most sincere apologies for referring to you as a female dog. If you were a dog, you would most certainly be the alpha male—which I guess would make these boys here your bitches, hmm? My mistake."

This time the boot made contact. Who knew that Jon had this kind of controlled violence in him? Not me. But it certainly was coming in handy right about now. If only he could keep from killing Blue out of a sense of misplaced chivalry, we might be able to actually find out what was going on and why I seemed to be at the center of it all. And yes, given that I had just skewered that same Blue's throat moments earlier, I was getting the irony here. Maybe Jon and I had more in common than I realized. Anger issues. Now there's a tie-that-binds kind of shared quality you want in an impermanent relationship.

SIXTEEN

YOU'RE PROBABLY WONDERING where I learned to fight. There's a complicated answer to such a seemingly simple question. Ezra Gerbrecht was at the center of it. My professor, my mentor; the punster with an edge of burnished steel hidden beneath a mad-scientist façade.

I've always had some aggression issues. Lack of patience, quick to snap, not so much with the frou-frou girly-girl ways. Gerbrecht simply honed what was already there.

As part of my Psych 100 elective in first-year university, I was required to participate in one or more focus group sessions—ostensibly to teach us about group dynamics and how people react to certain stimuli. Depending on how you did, you might be asked to participate in more of these collective emotional button-pushing sessions. The carrot dangled was that if you reached a certain level in the selection process, you would become eligible for some kind of cash prize.

I'd thought the whole thing was stupid. I wasn't sure what I wanted to major in yet, but I was pretty certain that Marketing Manipulation wouldn't rank high on my personal list of life goals.

Unfortunately, I couldn't afford to sabotage the effort. Not on a scholarship. So I did just enough to keep me ahead of the interviewer's game, just enough to keep me in the game itself so I could get a good mark.

What I didn't know was that I was a lab rat, we were all lab rats, and with each rung surpassed we narrowed the pool of potential candidates to the inner circle.

Ezra Gerbrecht was covering for the usual professor, Jasmine Anuk, who had taken a leave of absence around the middle of the year. Gerbrecht's easy laugh and ever-present sense of humor had us giggling in class despite our best efforts to project cool detachment.

The focus group exercise was his idea.

An innovation in teaching and learning. That was the spin. And really, anything that had us sitting around and talking rather than writing essays or taking exams was good with us. We were soon part of a select group. Down to ten. Then down to five. And then, finally, the core: James Sanderson, Cora Pescatori and me.

It was all very cloak and dagger from that point on. We played it as though it was a big joke. Come to such and such a place, come alone, bring paper and something to write with, turn your cell phones off once you pass a certain point. As if. I'd seen the horror movies. You know, the ones where that hapless female decides it's a good idea to go for a walk by herself in the woods or down that dark alley. No good comes of it.

So no. I came on my own, but I didn't leave my stuff at home and I did let my roommate know where I was going. My one concession to the game was that I switched my phone to silent.

There. Who says I can't be somewhat accommodating?

The meet went down in the basement of Hart House. The men's washroom across from the Arbor Room. Knock twice. Hold your breath. (What is it with men's washrooms anyway? Stand and aim. Accurately. How hard can that be?) Last stall on your right. Flush three times in succession.

Normally this bathroom got a lot of action. But after midnight on a Sunday, I wasn't too concerned about running into anyone. Other than a security guard, and last I checked he was doing his rounds on the main floor heading towards the Great Hall. Away from me being the key point.

I wasn't sure what flushing would do; apparently nothing save a slight improvement in the overall smell of the place. I was about to flush a fourth time when I felt a hot breath in my ear.

"Mmmm," it moaned, chills along my back. "Fresh meat. Precioussssssss."

It sniffed under my earlobe.

I didn't think. My right hand slapped the wall for balance and my left elbow jabbed, delivering a direct hit just above the solar plexus. I followed with a *one-two-three* maneuver. BAM—left heel to kneecap and down. BAM—back of my left fist, plowing backwards into that snuffling nose. And finally I twisted slightly to my left and with my right hand grabbed at what hair I could grasp while my left hand reached behind the neck of the ear hisser, propelling its skull into the wall with a satisfying *thud*.

It went down. Nice bump forming on its… I was going to go with "head" for lack of a better term. Though its second head hissed at me in warning.

Warning of what?

Plop. Plop thud. Thuditty plop. Sssssssssssssssssssssssss.

Snakes.

The hell with this, I thought, trampling the writhing buggers I couldn't avoid on my way to the door.

Locked. Perfect.

I had my cell phone in hand, ready to dial 911, when I noticed the pipe running across the ceiling to the old-style window, which was slightly ajar. Using the vertical portion of the pipe, I propelled myself first onto the sink and then grabbed hold of the pipe running across the top of the room. It groaned slightly with my weight but held. Hand over hand, I made my way towards the locked door and, more importantly, the open window above it. A quick glance below at the writhing floor was motivation enough to keep going.

Once I reached the exit I started swinging backwards and forwards to build up a pendulum-like momentum. I pushed off the wall behind me with both feet, swung back, and planted a double-foot front kick into that window over the main door. Glass shattered. Swinging back one last time, I planted one foot on the ledge, one leg out the door, and carefully edged out and into the thankfully snake-free hallway.

Followed by the sound of two hands clapping.

Ezra Gerbrecht stepped out of the shadows. I nearly left my skin behind I jumped so hard.

"You did good," he said. "I'd like to talk to you about a job."

AH, MEMORIES. PERHAPS NOT the best time to reminisce. But I couldn't help being drawn in by the parallels. Working with a crew. Loading a demon into the back of a truck bound for shackles and torture-for-information opportunities.

Wrapped in silver manacles and gagged, Demon

Blue landed in my truck bed with a thud. The lid slammed down hard and closed him off from continued view. Yay.

I stood beside the truck bed, tapping restlessly on the stainless-steel edge as I watched Anshell issuing orders to the cleanup crew. Lynna was safely buckled into the passenger seat, twitching slightly but being talked down by Sam's casual charm as he leaned in to joke with her through the now-open window. The copper taste of blood hung in the air, but I didn't sense any of it coming from Sam. Or Lynna. So that was good.

"Dana?"

I looked over at Jon, a silent apparition made suddenly solid beside me. He took my hand in his, stroking back and forth with the edge of his thumb, soothing. His coolness was gentle against my edgy heat, and he raised my hand up so I could look.

I gasped at the sight. My hand was more of a paw with elongated digits: part feline, part human. I wanted to slap a hand across my mouth to cover the shock but in the last second pulled back, realizing I could seriously scratch myself that way. Jon followed my emotions with only a slight narrowing of his eyes, but he didn't let go. I choked out a sob.

"Dana, it's okay."

"I'm horrible. Oh. My. God."

Sam appeared on the other side of me, my other newly sprouted paw in his hand, holding it up to get a better view in the moonlight. He whistled in appreciation.

"Now *that* is cool," he said with a grin. "Think you could do it again?"

I gave him a look.

"If I could, would I be wasting my time cleaning blood off my weapons by moonlight when all I'd need is a good manicure?"

Sam turned partially towards me, his profile silhouetted by the moon. He lifted up my paw to the light, then traced the underside where wrist meets palm, so delicately. I shivered, my eyes closing momentarily.

"No," Sam growled. "Open your eyes."

I did.

Sam's paw was larger than mine with shaggy red fur that hung in streaks. Large claws. But not so much more so than mine.

More to the point, holy electricity, Batman. The touch of the heel of his palm to mine felt like the inexorable pull of a magnet. My breath caught in my throat, my heart was pounding. I knew Jon was on the other side of me, cold to Sam's heat, but the chill was lost in the fires of Sam's partial change.

Jon gave a growl of his own. Reminding me he was there, warning off his partially furred competition.

Gently, I extracted my paws from the grasps of both men and reached my arms up to the light still glowing in the sky, reflecting off my striped orange and black fur. I arched my back and gave a big yawn, tasting the salt and blood and sweat still hanging in frozen droplets on the air. Sweet and salty mixed with copper-sulfur. I took an extra swipe with my tongue around my lips while I was at it, feeling the texture and pointy pleasure-pain of my slightly elongated teeth. Man, what a rush. My blood was singing in my veins, begging me to turn into something else, something more. I could ride it. *Be* it. But then there would be no going back on that thing I'd been trained to fear.

Present and future warring with a past I kept trying to push behind me. *Couldn't.*

So instead I took that sensation, that flood, and thought about a dam, logs building on either side, channeling that energy forward and away. I heard Sam suck in a breath, felt Jon take a step back, sensed Anshell and some of the other fighters drawing closer, moths to my burning, chilling flame.

And then I pulled that energy back, inhaled it deep into my chest. Pushed it down and sucked it back, taking what I had just shared back into my own core. Sun Salutation to the moon. Focusing on my breathing, my paws, the shape of my hands.

It tickled as fur insinuated itself back into my pores, collapsing like a weight-flattened spring. Nails deflating and suctioned back into my skin. It felt like when you take a small wooden nail pick and clean grit out from underneath your nails—except that my nails were remarkably clean for post-brawl, despite my urge to scratch beneath the surface of the pads. *Eww.* My wrists were a little stiff as the bones re-knit themselves into the smaller proportions of the me I recognized, but it wasn't the gut-wrenching pain I'd been led to think that shifting could be.

And just like that, my paws were hands again. Smooth with no blood and no bruising from the fight. *Mine.*

Sam's paws were hands now too. But my scent was in the wind and now he circled me, slinking, man-form flowing to animal and back once more. An eye blink and Jon was there, standing in his way. Sam took a step forward, a threat in his throat, and Jon stared him down silently. Anshell appeared beside Sam, a hand on his forearm, focusing attention away from a confrontation that didn't need to happen.

"Sam," Anshell said. "Back away from this one. Now is not the time." He caught Sam's eye and held it.

Sam gave another grunt, softer now, and backed down and away. I took a proprietorial sniff. Like me but not. Another deep breath in and...

"Dana, you need to cut it out too," Anshell said. "Both of you now. Back off. It's the moon, the fight. Enough."

Something about the timbre, the force behind Anshell's voice pulled me back. It felt like he gripped my skull between his hands, holding it in place, and yet I could see him standing there almost five feet away from me.

What. The. Fuck.

Jon's arm snaked around my waist, an anathema to the life force Sam and I shared. I gripped him back, anchoring myself to the moment.

"Well, that was fun," Sam drawled, all mischievous grin now.

"Indeed," deadpanned Anshell. "If you three are quite done, we have a captive to question. Sam, you're coming with me. Jon, if you would escort Dana back to the house?" Anshell waited for Jon's curt nod, Sam's slower inclination of his head, before continuing. Funny how Anshell didn't give anyone directions, and nobody asked for them either. Jon and I were going to have yet another talk very, very soon.

SEVENTEEN

THE ROOM WAS thick with viscous juices. Seeping diamond-studded green goo covered the darkened walls. I saw the ooze dripping, the sheen as it caught the light from a single bulb swinging from the ceiling. A scene from the nightmares I relived almost every night. I clasped my hands behind my back to hide my tremors as I struggled with flashbacks to another time, another room; a scene I'd hoped never to relive.

"Fuck you and the bitch you rode in on," snarled Demon Blue. His head was thrown back and partially twisted at an angle that wouldn't have been survivable had he been human.

Sam smiled an evil grin and leaned forward, his paw a single digit now—the middle one of course, what else?—and carved a shallow line of blood down the demon's cheek.

"Oh come now," he replied, drawing the claw across the demon's distended lower lip. "Let's keep our fantasies in check, shall we? Maybe a little later on we can discuss who gets to ride whom. But until then, let's focus."

"Focus on *this,* asswipe." Demon Blue spat a great gob of mellifluous blue saliva at Sam. It would have hit Sam just below his left eye, except that he was no longer in range. How could I have missed that *otherness* of Sam before?

Jon edged forward, a streak of light on shadow. He looked human, but only just. I was surprised not to see wings arcing from his back like some vengeful angel on a mission. Demon Blue paled slightly at his approach. Interesting.

"Name," said Jon.

Demon Blue just laughed. "I ain't taking orders from a bitch-slapped, pussy-whipped vampire lapdog."

"Oh?" Jon raised an eyebrow, remarkable in his restraint. Based on his earlier performance, I would have thought something involving pain was forthcoming. Instead, Jon laid hands on each of the captive's shoulders and gripped. Hard. Nose to nose. Blue was forming more spittle to spray on my erstwhile compadre; I could see his throat working up enough residual moisture to pull it off. I opened my mouth to warn Jon when he suddenly smacked Blue on the side of the face, stepping back smoothly before the spray had a chance to lay even a drop on his remarkably goop-free self.

"Again," Jon said. "Name."

"Fuck you twice, cold boy. And I know that's how you like it. You keep playing like you're this girl's great defender, the perfect lover. She doesn't even know what you are."

And then it was the Anshell show. He didn't need to shift to command the attention of everyone in the room. Jon stepped back and Anshell stepped forward, taking the demon's chin in his hand and holding it. Forcing Demon Blue to look into his eyes. Blue fought it, trying to rip the chair out of the sockets where it was bolted to the floor, but no luck. Not for the first time, I wondered which flavor of supe Anshell was, exactly, and what his powers were.

"Speak," Anshell said.

"You know how it is." Was Demon Blue stammering? Seriously? "Like the song says, ain't no rest for the wicked. My services were purchased. The Shadow Wraith did a conjuring, handed me a transparency with the girl's primal deets on it, signed my contract and then dissolved the circle. I don't know more than that."

"Terms of the contract? Method of payment?"

"C'mon," Demon Blue said. "You know it's all electronic bank transfers these days. I have a few set up in some different dimensions—easier to keep curious government cats out of my business. Easy in, easy out."

Anshell raised an eyebrow.

"Any clues in the contract about who ordered the hit?"

"No way. Doesn't matter to me. Not usually." Demon Blue muttered that last bit.

"And this time?" Anshell prompted.

"This time I wish to hell I had a clue who ordered it, because the last thing I need is more of this shit from you and yours."

Anshell gave him one long last look, then nodded to Jon. Who stepped up behind Demon Blue and snapped his neck.

"Oowwwww! What the hell? I told you everything I know!" Demon Blue was howling now as his neck dangled even more precariously over the back edge of the scarred chair.

"I think you need some more motivation," Anshell said. "Sam? Would you mind doing the honors?"

"No problem," Sam replied, lifting up a remote control from the windowsill and pointing it at the wall, causing a large flat-screen TV—65 inches at least—

to descend into view. One click turned it on, a second click activated the *Sponge Bob Square Pants* marathon playing on an infinite loop. The horror. I swear, I'd talk.

By the screech of sheer terror and pain he let out as soon as the opening song started—"*Who lives in a pineapple under the sea / Sponge Bob Square Pants!...*"—I was thinking he was going to cave soon.

I didn't know how parents could stand it...those sounds, that music... I was *so* out of there.

Fortunately, I had a good excuse: work. I couldn't keep wearing the same set of clothes indefinitely. I thought for a moment about dropping by my apartment for a change of clothes, then remembered it had been condemned. The insurance adjuster had called me back this morning with the grim news. No, it wasn't safe for me to go back. Yes, my policy covered standard damages and acts of God. It may or may not cover vandalism. Either way, it was a pretty good bet I'd kissed my security deposit goodbye.

While the adjuster assured me he would do his best to get the paperwork processed as quickly as possible, it didn't change my immediate reality: I had no clothes other than the ones I was wearing, and no money to replace much of anything until that insurance check came in. I sighed. Much as I might want to lounge the rest of the day, I needed to earn money to pay for the replacement of my worldly goods. I needed to go somewhere with a change of clothes, individuals I could trust and a room where I could sleep.

WORK WASN'T BUSY enough to adequately distract me. Not the early shift anyway. Tonight's Snack and Sip special wasn't drawing in the hoped-for crowds, even though by 11:00 p.m. we'd marked it down to half off. Odd really. We're talking smidgelets on toothpicks, rolled in a chipotle-sweet cornflower batter and deep fried before being basted in a cheek-sucking sauce of scraped malaquo intestinal wall juice, chili peppers and blood oranges.

Okay, no, I hadn't actually tried it. But apparently they went great with a Steeping Gash (Blue Curacao, black tea and chocolate-liqueur-soaked sour cherries on ice covered with death-soaked morgue gauze).

Still. We're talking sweet, salty, savory and rank in a single on-special order. Maybe we should have waited for the Thursday 2:00 a.m. crowd to try it out.

"*Babybabybabybabybabybabybaby.*" A guy—two heads, two necks that spindled into double-wide shoulders, with grease-streaked comb-overs that did nothing to hide the triple circlets of teeth which might otherwise be twin bald spots—had apparently been trying to get my attention.

I swiveled my neck to look at him without making a full-body commitment to the conversation. The key was to focus on that spot, approximately level with the tops of his ears but between the double-headed split, where a single-headed individual's eyes might reside. Trick of the trade.

"Yes?" See? I could be polite.

"*Babybabybabybabybabe?*" Both of his lower lips were quivering, although one was coated in a lascivious sheen of saliva while the other set was red and scaly from the cold. You know—winter in Toronto.

"Yes?" Maybe he hadn't heard me the first time. Even though all four of his eyes were staring at my chest. "Hey!" I snapped my fingers up high to divert his attention. "Up here, sir," I said. "What can I get you?"

The babe-babbler stopped speaking and pointed at the chalkboard off to the left of where he was sitting. I tried to ignore the brown beneath his fingernails that ran more to red than earthy.

Oh. He wanted to order the special. Cool—Sandor would have less to throw out now. Smidgelets didn't keep more than a few hours after they'd been thawed.

Lynna called as I was returning from the kitchen with the tray of nip and nibbles. Babe-babbler and I shared the nod, the one that says "hey I see you" and sometimes "thanks, buddy" before I drifted farther from earshot to answer.

She was safely ensconced in one of Anshell's upper bedrooms, waiting for things to cool down on the streets, and feeling chatty. She'd even found someone to cover for her at work for a few days so I knew she was taking this seriously. Calmer, although I suspected Anshell had slipped a little something into her tea to help with that. It even sounded like she was surfing a little white-knight-white-horse crush on everyone's favorite medic-slash-warrior. I warned her to take it slow but by the distracted *uh huh uh huhs* she gave me, I wasn't holding on to much hope that she would listen.

The next call, surprisingly, came from my mother. I'd forgotten all about our dinner arrangement for Friday night. She'd forgotten that the best way to reach me was on my cell phone. Instead she'd tried me at the apartment and had gotten the out of service message. Called my cell next but it kept going to voice mail. Finally she remembered where I worked, called directory assistance for the number and tracked me down here.

Got to give her props for persistence and ingenuity. But I wasn't ready to worry her yet, so I downplayed and distracted her from the obvious (something weird going on) and agreed to meet her at the bagel place uptown at 7:00 p.m. the following night. Sure, it was possible I'd go all furry before then, but life goes on and it waits for no one—especially a dinner with my mum.

I loved my mum. She was one cool lady with a backbone of steel and a serious protective streak. She raised me on her own after Dad died, without much help from anyone. But she was getting older now, and I didn't want to burden her with the latest happenings. I also didn't want a bull's-eye target on her back. So we had to get whatever was going on here resolved by tomorrow night. Otherwise I was going to have to spill, and I *really* didn't want to have to do that.

EIGHTEEN

SLEEP TOOK TOO LONG. I was restless in the Swan's storage room; despite my overwhelming exhaustion, I couldn't turn my mind off enough to let it all go. Legs twitchy. Pillow too hard, mattress too soft, blanket scratchy in all the wrong places. I knew I was safe—okay, hoped I was—but I was on my own in this big warehouse of a place. None of the guys had popped by. Which didn't mean anything, right? I'd managed just fine without the trio before my life turned to shit.

And then there was a rapping at the door and the hairs on the back of my neck stood on end.

"Knock knock," he said.

My breath hitched. I looked around for something to throw, something I could use as a weapon. Cans of newt balls. Jars of goreal pinkie jam. A pillow. I picked up one of my steel-toed combat boots instead.

"I can hear you breathing," he said. "Let me in. We need to talk."

I said nothing. Because talking. *Right.* That's what we needed to do. Because what had happened between us earlier wasn't freaking me out at all.

"Dana, let me in."

I let a full minute go by, weighing the possibilities before finally saying those two words: "Come in."

Sam pushed the door open. Firm. Not aggressive, but not backing down either. He could have entered at any time—the door hadn't been locked. He filled the space with his energy, his bulk, the light behind him framing his hair with an edge of wildness, hiding that spark I knew was in his eyes, the quirk of his mouth. Those lips.

"Demon Blue broke," Sam said. "His name is Gus 'The Diamond' Lazzuri. Hit man. Big surprise there. He said he was hired to kill you because of what we saw, what we stopped."

"You were there too." I was standing now, leaning against the wall, pressing myself away from the heat that was Sam. "Why not both of us?"

"Maybe there's a contract out on me too." He shrugged. "Doubt it though. People don't generally fuck with me because of Anshell."

I seized the opening. "Yeah, Anshell. What's the deal with him anyway? Is he some kind of supernatural warlord?"

Sam shook his head. "Anshell's a good person to call a friend. Leave it at that."

He took a step forward. Paused.

"Anshell asked me to find you, to keep you safe for the night," Sam said.

I snorted. Even with the magnetic pull I felt sucking me towards Sam, I still had my bullshit filter in full working order. Good to know.

A wry grin from Sam. "That's not the only reason I'm here."

"But. Jon…" I said.

"The vampire who exposed you to the shifter virus because he was also sleeping with a jealous he-pussy?" Sam shook his head.

"We have a thing," I started again. "There's no commitment."

"No commitment," Sam echoed. "You were saying how we're *not* possible because of your *not*-commitment with your *non*-exclusive vampire?"

I opened my mouth, closed it. Opened. Closed. "Okay, I'm out," I said. "That was all I had."

Sam took another step forward. He smiled, but there was a dark shadow in his eyes that hadn't been there before. I could faintly hear the *slap slap slap* of the waves against the icy shores of Lake Ontario. A car driving away, muffler dragging on the gravel road, sputtering out exhaust. I took it all in, but it was distant compared to the awareness of Sam standing in front of me. Waiting.

His hand reached out to cup my jaw, traced the edge ever so lightly. The closer Sam got to me the more I felt my skin stretch, yearning, needing his touch. Fearing his touch. A strange tickling sensation just below my skin, fur rubbing from the inside as he went lower, the tips of his fingers starting as flesh and ending as curved points on a furred pad. Changing back to skin and softness once more as he trailed his digits down the side of my neck.

God. Goddess. What a feeling.

Sam tilted his head slightly to the left and leaned in, his tongue tracing heat from the crook of my neck to just below my ear. He was making the sounds of someone enjoying a fine wine.

That small part of my brain, the one that was still barely coherent, was jumping up and down trying to get my attention. Bad idea. Dangerous man.

My nostrils filled with the cinnamon musk of him; I inhaled his heat, an answering quiver deep within.

Bad idea. Bad bad idea. Take a step back, Dana. Back back back.

My back was against the wall, and Sam was in front of me, pressed against me pressed against the wall. His hardness left no questions. I gasped, the last protest. I couldn't do this shouldn't do this can't do this won't do this God Goddess I wanted this.

I reached up and grabbed the back of his head, pulling him to me, opening my mouth, opening my mind, letting all resistance go.

We clawed at each other's clothes, ripping buttons and shirts. Buckles came free, pants came off and he grabbed me by my ass and lifted me up and onto him, pausing only to unsheathe and roll on a condom. No foreplay; none needed. I was wet from his proximity. I reached down to guide him in. One long, languorous thrust and I felt his contained power. He teased me with his length, slowly, then leaned back to grab my right nipple between his teeth. There would be marks tomorrow. I didn't care. I arched my back. He chuckled, my breast shaking with his amusement. He looked up at me from that angle and I shifted slightly…*there*.

Sam's eyes unfocused and he groaned. Growled. My legs gripping his hips, my arms draped across his shoulders, fingers buried in his hair. Soft, soft hair smelling vaguely of cinnamon and vanilla and cold days with warm fires and cider. His broad hands slapped against the wall behind me, on either side of my head.

The wall shuddered behind us with each thrust, jars of otherworldly delicacies jumping on their shelves.

More. I fastened my teeth on Sam's neck. No fear of infection—we were both shifters now. No danger of changing into something we weren't already.

Just.

Oh.

I WOKE SOMETIME between night and dawn to the sound of something breaking. Sam was curled up behind me, arms draped around me in a loose hug. His soft snores purred. But that other sound—that was not a sound that was supposed to happen after closing.

I shifted slightly and listened. A soft swish of fabric, padding footsteps, careful to be silent, not silent enough. I twisted around to meet Sam's eyes. Open now. He'd heard it too.

He inclined his head to indicate the door, then he was on his feet with his T-shirt in one hand and pants in the other. Sam was sliding his gun into the back of his pants and had a knife in his hand while I was still fishing around for my shirt and jeans. Together, we edged towards the door of the storage room and into the gloom of the hallway beyond.

Another crash, this one from the kitchen. We drifted closer. No light, only sound and adrenaline pumping. My fingers itched with the need to sprout claws. Fight or flee. My head said flee but every other instinct I had said fight. I was on a high from the sex and the near-full moon. And now we were hunting. Sam flashed me a grin. He could feel it too.

We formulated a quick plan without using words. I would surprise the intruder. He would circle around to corner whatever or whoever was now rooting through the cutlery drawers. *One...two...three...*

"Is there something specific you're looking for? Maybe," I said, "I can help you find it."

It was the wild woman from the street. Her mouth was open, a puckered O of surprise. She recovered quickly, though, grabbing the nearest cleaver and throwing it at my head. I dodged, but only just. Out of the corner of my eye I could see the blade, still quivering, embedded in the steel covering the far wall by the grill.

"Shit! What the hell?"

"Kind kitty wanted to hunt poor little me," she said. "Celandra does not want to be hunted. Celandra is not a mouse, not a rodent, not vermin for kitty cats to grab between their jaws and shake until they're dead." She cackled. "Or playing dead. Celandra is very good at playing dead." She muttered something under her breath but I couldn't hear it.

"What are you doing here?"

"Celandra was looking for her kitten. Kitten is in danger. Then Celandra noticed all the fine fine food. Celandra is hungry. Kitten's bowl of milk not good enough."

"If you're hungry, hang on—I'll make you something," I said. "But no more throwing knives, okay?"

Celandra bobbed her head in agreement, grey ringlets between the matted clumps springing up and down with the motion.

"Kitten is kind. Celandra thanks kitten for her hospitality. Once Celandra's belly is full, she will tell kitty everything she knows about the danger." She waved shriveled fingers, broken nails hanging askew, hangnails edged with dried blood. "And please call off your hunter cat. I'm fine, you're fine, and his services will not be required for the hunt this fine night."

Celandra's switches between reality and fantasy were unnerving. I looked for Sam in the shadows but saw nothing. Maybe he was hanging back, waiting to make sure there was no danger. If that was the case, I thought I'd play along as well.

"Sandwich okay? You want normal food, right? Nothing slimy or squirmy?"

The faintest puff of wind and she was peering over my shoulder at the stainless-steel countertop, around and into the storage shelves where all the specialty items were stored.

"D'you have any of those rat tails in vinegar and onion? Maybe with a bit of Sandor's special bread-crumby newt ballsack pâté? And turkey. Sliced turkey with mustard."

I stared at her a moment, processing. This was not the first time she'd been here, and she knew Sandor. *Okay.*

I pulled down the bag of bread from on top of the fridge and started making her freakadelic sandwich as requested. Arguing with a crazy, periodically cleaver-wielding woman who wanted special food à la demonic mode just didn't seem worth the effort.

Speaking of effort, where was Sam? I sniffed the air, casually, but nothing. His scent was gone except for whatever still clung to me.

Celandra, in the meantime, was enjoying her food with gustatory relish. She moaned in pleasure, then cocked her head to the side as if listening to sounds unknown and muttered over her shoulder.

At my frown of concern, she tilted her head in the

opposite direction and did that listening thing again. Nodding as if someone or something had spoken in her ear.

"Your hunter has become the hunted. Celandra will help. Bring knives."

And with that she hopped off the stool, yanked the cleaver from the wall and started drifting towards the swinging doors leading from the kitchen to the main bar area. I stared a moment, then shoved down all those feelings that said "help" and "no" and "no way" and "oh crap, not again, could this night get any weirder?" No point. Instead I grabbed a shorter, sharper knife with one hand, a meat-tenderizing mallet in the other, and followed.

Celandra had a glow about her that she immediately tamped down when she noticed me looking. At least that's what I thought her motivation was—it was hard to tell why she did anything right about now. Maybe she just didn't want to draw attention to herself. Although, logical, but perhaps not Celandra logic.

I paused to scent the air once more. Nothing. No, wait. Over there, past the pool tables, more towards the back where the stage area was. A whiff of fur wet with coppery blood. Another scent of—of what?—silver and salt and more blood. Sam's blood.

My blood, as I bit through my bottom lip.

Celandra turned to me, eyes remarkably lucid, and held me back with the palm of her hand. Her touch was gentle but she was stronger than she let on. Once she was sure I'd understood, she turned again and crept forward, closer to the smell. I hung back, waiting for her sign. *Sam was fine had to be fine would be fine.*

Just before she rounded the far side of the bar, my domain, she motioned me forward.

White translucent smoke swirled and eddied around a large mass. Like a glacier, like the mounds of snow outside that had been molded and shaped by the waves, so close, smooth rounded edges sloping down like frostbitten wax drippings. The ridges ran pink with diluted blood, preserved on the hardened shell.

What I had thought was smoke was actually alive. Cloud-like drifts with eyes and mouths and teeth breathing frost, dropping the temperature in the room and hardening the mass with another layer of ice as they danced around it.

And their sculpted masterpiece?

Sam. Partially changed, a paw sticking out of the ice floe, claws extended but barely moving. Or was it just a trick of the light and smoke? No. I refused to believe he was dead. He couldn't be. C'mon, Dana, *focus.*

Okay. Not a trick. Those digits were definitely in motion.

Dizziness making the floor beneath me uneven as I stumbled, a gasped remembrance to breathe. *Sam was still alive.* There was hope.

As I watched, Celandra glided through the circle, waving her arms and hands like Don Quixote tilting at windmills. Her arms were turbines, sluicing through the demonic gaseous entities, daring them to re-form. Which they did, of course—if it was as simple as waving your arms, surely Sam would have escaped by now. She was chanting and crooning under her breath, and the cleaver glinted in the reflected moonlight from the open entranceway to the Swan.

Sandor was going to be so pissed that his security

system had failed. Some death whisperer (for some reason, they made the best security technicians) was going to get another year or more added to their life over this when Sandor was through with them.

The mist figures were already reforming, their mouths elongating to reveal rows upon rows of teeth, nestling into each other like Russian stacking dolls—although maybe, upon reflection, not quite as child-friendly. Celandra kept muttering and weaving, lifting her arms and dropping them again. Getting longer, shinier. Her mouth seemed larger, and she showed off some pretty impressive pointy teeth of her own.

From over her partially shifted shoulder, she looked directly at me and beckoned me closer. Then looked at my weapons. Sure, right, weapons—use them. Okay. Any ideas on how? I watched Celandra, the misty ice demons, and Sam, who wasn't going anywhere at the moment. *Don't think about that. Alive. Had to be.* Swallowing down that lump in my throat, counting backwards from ten, reminding myself to slow my breathing and feel the linoleum beneath my feet while focusing on the immediate need. Fire, for instance.

Wait. What exactly was Celandra shifting into anyway? Was that a...?

I knew exactly what I had to do next.

NINETEEN

I SHRIEKED LIKE a banshee, diving into the fray and waving around my mallet with crazed glee—every bit the manic nut bar that Celandra was playing at. My dancing and waving broke up the smoke for a moment, even though it was drifting farther out and trying to re-form just out of reach. I didn't care. I was a loon with a mission.

While I was distracting the bad guys, Celandra was progressing further into her shift. It felt like it was taking forever, scales rolling over her whole body in groups of five to ten at a time. At this rate, it was going to be a very long night.

"Hey Celandra," I muttered as I danced past her ear, "do you think maybe you could speed it up a bit?"

I wasn't sure she'd heard me, but she gave a little shake and then her back arched and rolled, popping with exfoliate and spiny plates. Her mouth extended even as a long tail sprouted and trailed out the back of her layers of clothing. She was shimmering, blue-green scales catching on the starlight that shone through the high windows of the Swan's interior.

Meanwhile, the watchful mists were tracking me. Not a great feeling. But still I shook and shimmied, waving around my arms and my hammer, dancing in and out of range of the smoky ice demons. They were dissolving and reforming at an ever-faster rate.

I glanced back at Celandra. She was more scales than skin at this point, which was a good sign as far as I was concerned.

But I shouldn't have looked away. A large mouth of toothy layers gaped at me, a hairsbreadth in front of my nose. I jumped back and whacked it on the head with my mallet.

Nothing happened. Fortunately, I was now at least a foot or more away from that particular set of teeth. But then another set snapped at my left ear. *Shit.* This was going nowhere good fast. I snatched the knife from the back of my pants and slashed down at the ear sniffer, making sure the blade ran the cross-section of the thing's head and through its throat. It was a good knife, but I wouldn't have expected it to cut through bone as easily as it did. Or was it bone?

The blade came away easily, edged with bumps of frosty hoar, a bit of translucent green goo streaked across the flat of the shiny metal. The toothy bastard looked at me, dead-on, and gave me a slow wink and a grin.

Uh oh.

I had these snaky freaks writhing around me from all sides. No matter where I dodged, no matter where I waved and weaved, there was another asshole there to replace the previous one. Taunting, tickling, snapping at me.

"Celandra!" I yelled, hoping that she hadn't changed her mind, leaving me to this frosty creeping fate. I couldn't see beyond the opaque mist that surrounded me now, but there was no question the temperature was dropping. That now-familiar tingle in the tips of my fingers started, as claws sprouted and fur rippled up my arms to my shoulders, layering me against the chill and buying me another few precious moments of fight. Which there was no question I was going to lose if Celandra didn't do something, and quick.

Behind me there was a roar and a blast of heat. The mist around me shimmered for a moment before reforming, although maybe it was a bit thinner than before. I tested it out with a swat of my paw and saw the scarred surface of the bar's countertop come into clearer view. Neat.

I began to dance and bob and slash with renewed vigor. Hoping. Hopeful. I'd lost both mallet and knife during the paw shift, but I took a precious second or two of a strategic time-out to locate the knife, scooping it back up to hold it, blade forward, between my teeth. I writhed some more, periodically poking at an ephemeral attacker with a combination head butt, chin tilt then a jab forward with the teeth-clenched blade. It didn't change the odds particularly but it did buy me a bit more space to move around.

Another roar, another wall of heat, stronger than the last. I slipped and almost fell on my ass as the heel of my boot found a puddle that hadn't been there before. The demons were definitely starting to smell now, a mix of salt and char, and their attention shifted abruptly away from me and towards the source of the blast. Scorching flames this time, as crispy bits of smoke made flesh started to rain around me in blackened chunks. They plopped down in water that was turning more into a small stream than a puddle at this point. My vision cleared and I saw flaming shards all around me, snuffed by the water rising now to mid-calf. I heard screams and sizzles and pops. The smell clogged my nose. All I could do was stand there and sneeze, five times in succession.

Then, silence.

Thank you, Celandra.

Let's hear it for friendly dragons. An appreciation the frost demons might have gained had Celandra not just flamed them into melted puddles of gelatinous mush.

I looked around, trying to locate the chunk of ice that was Sam. *There.* The berg was almost completely melted. Celandra the dragon sat there, gently blowing puffs of heat. Forgetting my partially changed form, I bounded over to the chunk of ice and started clawing at it desperately. I could see Sam, wide-eyed and wriggling. I couldn't breathe. I couldn't get to him. *No.* I had to get to him.

"Celandra!" I shrieked out her name. I didn't know what he was to me yet but I knew I didn't want him to die. She looked over at me and nodded her big head, the size of a small minivan now, then raised a bejeweled paw and whacked the top of the ice chunk, once, shattering it.

Sam sat there partially naked, mostly blue, with icy dandruff hanging off his hair and covering his chest. Shivering. I jumped into his arms and wrapped my warmth around him. After a moment, he lifted his arms to wrap them around me right back. Dragon Celandra just sat there, picking her teeth with an orange claw, watching us. I looked up, briefly, catching her eye and hoping there was more human in there than beast right now.

"Celandra, thank you," I said. She nodded. "Sam?

We need to get you warm. Then we have to let Anshell know what happened here tonight."

His voice was hoarse and it took a couple of tries but finally, gravelly, he said, "Okay."

AFTER A WARM shower for both of us, another change of clothes and phone calls to Sandor and Anshell, we found ourselves back in the kitchen—this time boiling water. I was literally at the end of my clothing stash, and I'd had to find some old sweats and a promotional T-shirt that read "Swan Song Saturdays: because there ain't no rest for the wicked" in slashes of red lettering on a black background for Sam. I wasn't sure who the sweats had belonged to, and everything smelled like grease and kitchen fryer, but at least it was warmer than bare, recently frozen skin.

Sandor showed up first. His warty mouth pressed into a thin line as he took in the evidence of the breach in his supposedly impassable security. Sandor had a pad of paper and a well-chewed pencil and was listing out all of the things that needed to be fixed before the Swan could re-open for business. Water damage to the floor—check. Solid steel magicked door blessed by the most holy of the undead—check. Rewiring the security system to make it functional—check. Finding out how this happened and resetting the wards so they actually worked? Priceless. His gaze settled on me a moment before it flitted over to Sam, and then Sam's T-shirt.

"That'll be 20 bucks," Sandor said.

"Put it on my tab," Sam replied, deadpan. Sandor grunted and moved off to start rummaging in the fridge.

Celandra came padding in next, rheumy-eyed, her hair even wilder than before. Thankfully, she was dressed. Naked Celandra was not a vision I wanted lodged in my consciousness anytime soon. She looked at Sandor and nodded; after a moment, he smiled and nodded back.

"Hey Celandra," he said. "How's it shaking?"

She laughed, a girlish innocent laugh like a three-year-old who'd just had a great time splashing in the wading pool with her friends. It was jarring coming from the weathered face of someone who now seemed older than time.

"Celandra and the kitty cats had a great time playing with the fire and smoke and teeth. Celandra tried to drink up all the bad bad water for Sandor so he wouldn't have to clean so much, but Celandra couldn't drink up all the blood. Ice demon blood tastes bad and Celandra couldn't do it, even for her old friend Sandor of the yummy yummy food."

"Don't worry about it," said Sandor, grinning at the dragon lady with an affection that said they shared a bucket of steamed fish heads and marmalade now and again. "I just appreciate you showing up and helping out my friend Dana here."

"Ah yes, the newest kitty in the brood." She nodded. "You have to take better care of your pets, Sandor," she said. "Bad men want to come and play with her," at this she nodded to Sam who just stared at her, "and bad *bad* ones want to make her cry before she begs for mercy and then dies. You can't be letting her go out and play in the streets by herself, you know. Not now."

"I kind of figured that," said Sandor. "But *this* bad man didn't come to hurt her. Right?" Sandor leveled a steely gaze at Sam now. Sam grunted in acknowledgement. "He's a playmate of hers." This time Sandor raised an eyebrow at me for confirmation. I nodded.

Perfect timing. In strode Anshell, followed by a couple of giant-sized flunkies, followed by Jon. *Jon.* Oh *shit.* I kept forgetting Anshell and Jon knew each other.

If Jon noticed something was up between me and Sam, he didn't say anything. Not immediately, anyway. Jon was behind me and in front of me and around me, all at once, a smudge of cool where he touched. Edgy. Worried about me. My guilt flashed in my eyes and a moment later Jon's nostrils flared. He looked at me then Sam, then back to me again. Well. Shit on a stick.

"You were going to protect her," Jon said. To Anshell. "And this place was supposed to be safe." This time to Sandor. Jon certainly knew how to smear the guilt around, softened butter on the toast of Celandra-charred responsibility. *Speaking of...*

"Thank you," he said to the dragon in human form.

"Pretty kitty helped take care of her pretty kitty self," Celandra replied, her mouth full of food and lips stretching into something that could have been a smile. A glob of something blue and veiny landed on her chin, wobbling in gelatinous opalescence before leaving a line of thinning mucus that trailed even lower. *Ick.*

"She has claws so sharp that when she dances, she shreds the air." Celandra's voice went higher, a singsong of words vaguely based in some alternate form of reality. "*Kitty the key / that no one can see / because so pretty / she makes you pity.*"

"Celandra..." Sandor tried to disrupt her flow.

"*Kitty cat in time and space / draws attention to the race / there is the door and there the key / pretty kitty needs to flee.*"

"Celandra!" Sandor was louder this time, poking her gently with a single curved nail. Mandarin orange. Not hard enough to break the skin or get scales caught underneath the cartilage; enough to focus her. I wondered what color dragons bled. Hoped I never found out. "Make sense. Please." He waited until she was looking directly at him. "Why is Dana in danger?"

"Danger danger stranger danger," Celandra muttered, tucking back into her food as though none of her oracular ravings had just happened. Sandor sighed and turned away from her again.

"Sorry," he said. "Girl," turning to me, "we need to find a way to keep you safe already."

"No kidding." Because no argument there.

"There's room at the house," Sam said, glancing at Anshell until he gave his approval nod. "Safest place for someone with Pack affiliations."

"I never said I'd join." Even shaken, I could still think ahead.

"True," Anshell said. "And you do have to prove you can change form on demand. Full moon is almost here. We can give you a line of credit on that protection until then."

"And if I don't shift? By the last night of the full moon?"

"Then you're on your own," Anshell said.

THERE WAS STILL one last thing to deal with before we left.

"Dana, can I speak with you a moment?" No point in avoiding the conversation. I nodded and beckoned Jon into the depths of the darkened, blood-splattered bar, where I pulled up a chair and sat.

"So," Jon said, spinning the double-looped wooden chair back opposite me before settling into it. He crossed his arms, leaning against the top of the chair with his legs spread, one foot planted on either side. "Decided to even the score?"

I met his eyes—blue-green ice—but lost my words as my chest clenched and I swallowed down a pain that might otherwise have been tears. *Fuck.* What could I say? Why should I have to say anything? I managed a noncommittal grunt.

"Be straight with me," he said. "I deserve that much." Jon's voice was level, any visible emotion drained away through a sieve of self-control.

I looked down. Didn't want to see what was in his eyes. Was surprised by the compassion I found there when I stopped being a chicken shit and looked back up.

"Okay fine," I said to the understanding that greeted me. "Yes, I slept with Sam. I'd say I'm sorry, but I'm not sure I have anything to apologize for." Still, I had to look away before I could say those next words. So softly, maybe only someone with super-sensitive hearing might catch them. "Do you hate me now?"

Only the briefest of hesitations before responding.

"I've lived a long time," he said. "Done a lot of things, some of them to you. Am I happy about the situation? No. But do I have any right to be upset after what I've put you through? Probably not. I deserved it."

"You think I fucked Sam to get back at you?" My laugh felt harsh on a throat still rough from smoke inhalation. "Ego much?"

Jon fixed me with those gorgeous eyes and I swam in the depths of them. Longing. Loss. Waves of melancholy squeezing my chest tight with unshed tears. How could I lie to him? I wanted him, I needed him, I hated him—just a bit—for making me share. So, yes, he had to share as well.

"You did deserve it," I said finally. "But that's not why it happened. I don't know what you and I are to each other at this point. Sam is…interesting. The whole shifter thing is different than what you and I have." I sighed. "You know how I feel about you."

"And I you." He leaned forward to envelop the heat of my hands between the chill of his.

"But," I said, distracted by the sensation of his skin on mine. "But we're obviously not 100 percent physically committed to each other, right?" Jon nodded. "So where does that leave us? Can you play nice and share?"

"I don't know," he admitted reluctantly. At least he took a whole ten seconds to think about it. Yes. I counted.

"Then can you tell me you'll be with me and only me for as long as we're together? Exclusively?"

This one Jon thought about even longer, maybe a full minute, before responding. "I don't know about that either."

"Then we're at an impasse," I said.

"So it would appear," he replied.

TWENTY

"YOU SLEPT WITH SAM?" Lynna was lying on her stomach, propped up on her elbows, looking up at me expectantly. Me, I'd curled up in the overstuffed armchair occupying the corner of the room we'd be sharing for the night. Or at least until I found a place where I could keep myself and the people I cared about from being attacked. "Hot or not?"

I laughed. "Hot. Definitely hot."

Lynna wiggled around a bit, trying to find a more comfortable position for her sore bits. Although her physical condition didn't seem to dampen her interest in the latest gossip relating to my love life. Or sex life.

"So, spill. How does he stack up against Dead Boy?"

"His body temperature's a lot hotter than Jon's," I said slowly, ignoring the jab at the vampire's mortality status. "And there's that whole shifter thing. When I'm near him physically, it feels like my fur—my inner cat—is trying to claw its way past my skin to get to him. It's electricity."

I thought back to earlier that night—was it really the same night?—and my breath hitched at the sense memory. Hot didn't even begin to describe it.

"So, what now?" Lynna looked at me expectantly. "Gonna drop Dead Boy for Mr. Alive and Shifting?"

"Unknown," I replied. "Wish I could have my undead cake and eat this live one too."

Lynna laughed. "C'mon," she said. "You know this thing with Jon can't last. Try it with someone else for a while. Seriously. You never know—you might like it better. Besides," she grinned, her lips twitching as though Sam was stretched out on the bed in front of her in all his muscled, naked glory. "Hot *damn* but Sam is fine. You said so yourself."

"I know," I said. "But it could have just been the one time. We'll see."

Lynna rolled her eyes and finally, thankfully, changed the subject.

BRUNCH WITH MY mother the next day was a bleary affair. Bleary for me at least since I hadn't gotten much sleep after all last night's excitement. But I was famished, and the food was her treat, so bagels and cream cheese and lox with a side order of perfectly crispy, lightly salted fries was the ideal distraction. Plus, the company was good. Until I had to start side-stepping questions about where I was staying and why.

"I know I'm supposed to not ask too many questions," she started, "but do you think you could give me a hint? Because I have to hope that whatever is going on with you—and don't try to pretend there isn't," she said, when I opened my mouth to deny it, "is far better than the horrors I've made up in my head worrying about you."

I paused to crunch on a few more fries while slathering white, full-fat cream cheese on my poppy seed twister bagel. Knowing that each second I delayed in responding only added to her clearly heightened anxiety. But what the hell could I say? Crap.

"My kitchen had a gas leak." I skirted the bigger issues for a moment as I speared a slice of oily lox and gently layered it on top of the dairy goodness. "So I'm staying with a friend for a few days. I kind of dropped my phone as I was running out the door and I haven't gotten around to replacing it yet. No drugs, and I'm fine for money." A lie, but a white one.

She seemed unconvinced, but didn't press the matter further. Well, much further.

"If you say so," she replied. "But you know I'm here if you change your mind and want to tell me the truth, okay?"

I grunted noncommittally as I bit into my bagel.

"By the way," she continued, allowing the subject to drop, "Ezra Gerbrecht was trying to get in touch with you. Your old professor? The one who used to work with your father?"

I paused, food halfway to my mouth for another bite, and stared at her. "Huh?"

"Yes," she said. "His assistant called trying to track you down. Said it was important. She left a number if you want it."

"Huh," I repeated. Very profound. "That's weird. Did she say what it was regarding?"

"No," Mum replied. "Seemed very hush hush. I do hope you're not planning to get involved with all of that cloak and dagger stuff again."

Mum knew I'd been working for the government, like my father before me, before I left it all behind for the glamorous world of bartending. Worst few years of her life, she always said. My father died in the line of duty; she was always afraid the same thing would happen to me. Best day of her life, after her wedding and the day I was born, was the day I became a civilian again.

"Not exactly," I said. "I dropped by Ezra's office a couple of days ago with some questions about my vaccines, how long they were good for, but that's about it. He was acting pretty weird though. Spacey. I wonder if he's okay." I thought about it a moment. "Even if he's not, I'm not sure why his assistant would be looking for me. Did you tell her where to find me?"

Mum looked pretty pleased with herself, biting back on a Cheshire Cat grin while trying to look innocent. On a woman of sixty-four, with clear skin and grey hair swept up in a loose bun, it was both disturbing and hard to believe.

"I said I hadn't spoken with you in a few days and that your phone seemed to be out of service, but if she did manage to track you down to please ask you to check in with your mother."

I let out a low whistle of appreciation. "Ma, you're good. Are you sure *you* never worked for the Service?"

That netted me a real smile. "I picked up a few things over the years with your father. Rule number one: never assume that someone who is hard to reach wants to be found."

"Good call," I said.

"What's going on with you has something to do with your vaccines?" Damn, she really wasn't letting it go easily. Was it fair to keep her completely unaware? Ignorance wasn't necessarily bliss.

"Yes." Cracking open the can of worms I'd been doing so well at ignoring. "I was scratched by a were-cat a few days ago, and I've started having some, um, *shifting* issues since then. It didn't make any sense to me because I was supposed to have been vaccinated against all of that when I worked with Ezra. So I dropped by the office to make sure I hadn't missed a booster shot or anything like that. Ezra was kind of spaced, but he said the shots should still have been good."

My mother had gone very pale while I spoke. She started picking apart her napkin at my words.

"Uh, Mum?" Silence. "Is there something *you* want to share here?"

She didn't look me in the eye. Just took a sip of cold coffee, cream congealed along the sides of her cup. Until she found the words she was looking for.

"Your father was a shifter," she said. I gaped at her.

"What? And I didn't know this why exactly?"

"There was no reason to tell you," she replied. "Stuart and I agreed to wait and see. He figured that if you had the gene, it would present itself at puberty and we'd know—we'd deal with it then. And you never showed any signs. So we thought maybe it had ended with you, or maybe it would show up in one of your kids." She smiled at me, but she looked sad. "I miss your father so much," she said, sighing. "He would know what to do."

I thought furiously for a moment, trying to piece together the various fragments of these new facts.

"So let me see if I'm understanding you here," I said. "My father was a shifter." Mum nodded. "And he worked for the government." Another nod. Okay, I already knew that part. "So I'm probably carrying the shifter gene from him, right?" Nod. "In which case?"

"In which case the vaccine wouldn't have done you any good," Mum said, finishing my sentence. "Speaking of which," she continued, "how exactly did you get scratched?"

I looked away with a half-smile quirked on the side of my mouth. "I'm going to have to plead the Fifth on that one, 'kay, Mum?"

She huffed a bit but let it drop after reminding me that the Fifth Amendment only worked in the United States, not here in Canada.

IT WAS MY last day before I shifted fully. Anshell's theory, not mine. He thought the power of the full moon might be enough to pull the shift out of me.

I felt like my entire life had just shifted. More than losing my home, more than losing my safety—I'd found out my father wasn't what I'd thought he was, and that consequently, I wasn't what I'd thought I was. Anshell had offered to teach me about shifting but I'd procrastinated, and now I was running out of time. Tomorrow night I was probably going to change for real, and nothing I had learned up to this point could prepare me for the experience.

Meanwhile, it was time for work. I suspected I'd be taking some time off for the full moon, so until then I wanted to get in as many paid hours as I could. Sandor had managed to get the Swan Song repaired and cleaned up surprisingly fast—something about a special waiver in his insurance policy covering acts of "impending full moon" vandalism—and he'd left a message at Anshell's that I should show up for my 3:00 p.m. shift.

Enough time for a quick shopping trip—black and red anyone?—then a pit stop at Anshell's to take a shower before heading back out. I'd just stepped out of said shower and was toweling off when there was a knock at the bathroom door.

"Someone in here," I called out. "Try the bathroom downstairs if you're desperate."

"Dana, it's me," Sam said. "Can I come in?"

I gulped, my heart pounding in my ears, and suddenly I was damp between my thighs. Crap.

"Dana," he repeated. "Knock knock, pussycat. Please let me in."

I wrapped the towel around me as tightly as possible and unlocked the door. Watched the handle turn as I edged away. Sam's bulk filled the entryway as he took in my tousled hair, the moisture on my shoulders and the steam billowing around me. A low growl rumbled in his throat as he stepped in, pulling the door shut behind him and locking it. Oh boy.

"Sam," I started, unsure of what to say next. "I..."

He reached over, wrapped an arm around my waist and pulled me towards him, meeting my lips with his. So soft. So warm. So unlike Jon. There was no question, as he pressed up against me, that parts of him were *very* happy to see me.

"Ssshh," Sam said. "No talking." He kissed me again. "Just this." He kissed my neck, lips trailing down behind my ear. "And this." He gently pulled my towel loose and dropped it to the floor as he went down on his knees and alternated between my breasts with his hands, nails and teeth. I grabbed his hair and arched my back, leaning against the basin sink.

Whoa.

His mouth nibbled lower, tonguing my belly button, pulling ever so gently on the ring I had there. I groaned. He went even lower, teasing me, his lips whispering against my abdomen, lower still, burying his mouth and tongue between my thighs. *Fuck.* I gripped his shoulders, nails digging into his shirt, as I came, hard. I yanked him up by his hair, my juices still on his mouth, as I scrambled to unbuckle his belt, undo his pants. There was too much clothing between us.

It was all I could do to pull his hardness out in time. Three tries to tear the condom wrapper with my teeth and roll it on without getting anything caught in his zipper. Fully clothed, poking out from his jeans, Sam clasped my ass and lifted me up to the edge of the sink, spreading me, pulling me forward and onto him in one smooth thrust. Face to face. So fucking intimate. The basin shook with our pounding; the tiles could have been falling down around us and I wouldn't have noticed.

All that existed was us; our bodies, our sweat, sensation. And then, finally, release.

TWENTY-ONE

I WAS ABOUT twenty minutes late for my shift. Couldn't stop grinning. Sandor raised two of his three eyebrows at me when I rolled in with my perma-smile and sidled up behind the bar. I shrugged and started setting up the glasses, making sure we had enough ice for the after-work rush.

Afternoon delight indeed.

The post-sex glow lasted into the evening, drifting over cranky customers and netting me surprisingly good tips regardless—as though my super-juiced endorphins were sprinkling happy dust on the patrons around me. People laughed and touched and drank and ate. No weeping tonight, and surprisingly few fights for the night before the full moon. Last call came quickly, and soon we were eyeing the doors and waiting for the last few straggling customers to settle their tabs and leave so we could close up.

Good time for a bathroom break. I wondered whether Sam would be around when I got back to Anshell's place. Whether we might pick up where we left off earlier. I was still a little sore but, *gyah*, I could be convinced to go for another round. Couldn't stop grinning as I ran cold water and soap over my hands, splashing a few drops onto my face as well.

I stepped out the door to the bathroom and directly

into Demon Chick. Cybele. The one from the other night; the one from Ezra Gerbrecht's office. *Huh.*

"Hi, Dana." She smiled at me. "I've been trying to get a hold of you."

"Oh?" Wary. "How come?"

She stepped in closer, breathing into my personal space. I could smell cranberry juice and vodka on her breath. Closer, and her lips brushed against mine. Damn. What was in the water around here tonight?

I tried to edge away even as Cybele bumped me up against the wall with her torso, pinning me in place, a hand on either side of my shoulders. She peered into my eyes, reflecting black with glints of gold back at me. I pushed back and tried to duck out and away to the side, but she followed. Okay, this wasn't fun anymore. I tried to call out for Sandor but she slapped her hand across my mouth and pushed me against the wall again, harder. I glared at her from behind her hand.

"Play nice," Cybele said. "This will all be over soon."

Over her shoulder, a shadow and the smell of something chemical and strong. A cloth covered my nose. *Can't. Breathe.*

Darkness.

I WOKE UP, slowly, and couldn't move. Strapped to yet another hospital bed. No shriveled roses this time, though. No pumpkin orange on black carpet. Instead there was a flickering blue-green fluorescent bulb above my head, snot-green walls and brown/beige pebbles of color on the institutional-style linoleum floor. Round patches with wires coming out of them stuck on my arms, abdomen and legs.

I remembered rooms like these. I revisited them on a regular basis in my nightmares.

This was *so* not good.

How had they gotten me out of the Swan without Sandor knowing? What if he'd seen something and was in trouble? What if he'd seen it go down and did nothing?

My mouth felt like cotton wool; an aftereffect of the drugs, I was guessing. The subjects of our experiments had often complained of thirst when they first woke up. Later, they would forget their thirst in a haze of pain and fear. I hadn't been responsible for the pain, but I couldn't absolve myself fully either.

The door opened and Ezra strolled through. He had a glassy sheen to his eyes, and didn't seem to recognize me at first. Until he picked up the chart. Hawkish, he focused first on the paper then back up at me.

"Dana? Is that you?"

"Hey Ezra," I replied, going for casual. "What's shaking?"

"Not you, apparently," he said. No smiles now. "What brings you to us in this fashion?"

"You tell me," I said. "Can you give a girl a hand, get me out of here?"

"No can do," he replied, shaking his head. "You've been messing with some bad stuff, my dear. Poking your nose in things you shouldn't be."

"I…what?"

"We've heard you've been hanging out with a bad crowd," he said. "Shifters and vampires. Helping to free an offering who should have been left to die."

I processed this. Offering. Was he talking about Mr. Gothy from the other night? I tested my theory.

"Uh, who? Offering?" Didn't have to fake my befuddlement. Much. "What are you talking about?"

Ezra pulled up a squeaking pleather armchair in cheese-from-a-can orange, settling into it and propping up his feet before continuing.

"Now, Dana," he said, moving around to get more comfortable and pouring himself a glass of water from the side table. "You know how this works. In this case, you're operating at a disadvantage. As a human, you won't be able to last as long as some of the abominations can. Make this easy on all of us and tell me what we want to know."

Interesting. My new potential—okay, probably likely—shifter status wasn't common knowledge yet. Keeping that information to myself might be a good thing.

"I hear asking nicely works too," I commented dryly. Ezra smiled mirthlessly at that.

"Fair enough," he said. "How about this. I'll ask you questions, *nicely*, and you tell me the first thing that comes to your mind. If I think you're telling the truth, we're good. If I think you're lying, you'll feel this," he said, pressing a button on the arm of the chair. My entire body lit up with pain and I arched and writhed on the bed. After about five seconds, it stopped when Ezra depressed the button.

"Holy fuck," I spit out, panting. "What the fuck, Ezra?"

"Now, now, Dana, that's not polite. I wouldn't want to have to shock you again before we've even begun. Would you?" He peered down at me through his wire-framed reading glasses.

I bit my lower lip to keep from swearing at him a

second time. He took my silence as assent and continued.

"Good girl," he said. "Okay, first question." I nodded to confirm my readiness. "Is your real name Dana Markovitz?"

I looked at him blankly. "Of course it is," I said. "You know that. You did the background search on me before I joined the Agency, remember?"

Ezra jotted something down on his clipboard. "Quite right, quite right," he said. "Next question. Are you, or have you ever been, a member of the Moon with Seven Faces Pack?"

Another blank stare. *Fake it till you make it.*

"The huh of what? What are you talking about?" Ezra watched me, closely, and pressed the button. Another five seconds of pure agony.

"Jesus fuck, Ezra, what's your damage? What the fuck are the Moonie Faces Pack?" *Poker pain face poker pain face poker pain face.*

Ezra made another notation before moving on. "Next question," he said. I sighed. Truth or lies made no difference at this point; I lay back and waited for the pain. "Have you ever met a man named Anshell Williams?"

I narrowed my eyes. "Yes," I said.

"What is your relationship with him?"

I thought about that a moment, too long, and saw Ezra reaching for the pain point. "Hang on! Hang on," I said. "I was just thinking about that. Anshell Williams is a friend. A new friend. Kind of an acquaintance, but maybe a friend. Is that what you were looking for?" Ezra made more notes.

"How did you meet him?"

"I, uh..." Ezra didn't hesitate to push the pain again. "Fuck, Ezra! Fuck. I can't think when you keep jolting me. Give me a sec here."

"Answer the question and I won't have to hurt you." He smiled. "Much." Edges of evil. He was enjoying this. *Fucker.*

"I repeat, how did you meet Anshell Williams?"

"He came into the bar, the Swan Song," I said with just the barest hesitation, eyeing the source of my pain. "Tried to buy me a drink, ask me out. I turned him down, but he left me his card in case I changed my mind." I knew Demon Chick had seen him give me his card that night, so I had to keep the story plausible. Plus, guys were always asking me out. The allure of the bartender, I guess.

"And you are staying at his house why?"

Oh shit. They had better intel than I thought. But, poker face—I kept that revelation from showing.

"I changed my mind," I said. As though maybe Ezra was going to contradict me. "Would you like to know the details of the positions we tried? How many times he made me come? Whether or not he enjoyed me going down on him?" I pictured Sam in my head to make my words more believable. The Ezra I'd known had had a prudish streak and avoided wanting to know too many details about my sex life. I was gambling that he hadn't changed so much in such a short time. The twitch in his left eye answered my question. *Score.* Point for Dana. Finally.

"Next question," he said. "Was your father part of the Agency?"

"You tell me," I replied, bolder now. "You did the background check. Didn't he work for your side?"

"Quite right, quite right," Ezra said. More scribbling. To remember something he already knew? "So," he said, "on the night in question, why did you intrude on the Feed?"

"What do you mean?"

"The night. The Feed." I didn't respond immediately, processing. Ezra smiled happily and shocked me again.

"You were outnumbered," he continued, as though I wasn't lying there trying to remember how to breathe. "You're human. I trained you well, but how could you possibly have known you would survive against all those blood-crazed vampires?"

"I didn't," I replied through gritted teeth. "But I couldn't leave someone there to die." I caught his eye and tried to reach the Ezra I'd known with a look. "You trained us to always fight for truth and protect those who needed it. The guy, the sacrifice, needed my help. I couldn't walk away."

"How did you survive?" I had him now.

"I don't know," I said, honestly. "There was someone else, a homeless guy, who wandered by. I think he helped me."

"Name?"

"I don't know," I said, my voice rising a notch in frustration, convincing myself of the truth of my words so I could sell it. "He helped me load the guy into my truck and then took off." I stared at Ezra, daring him to disbelieve me.

He seemed to wilt slightly under my gaze. If I could just snap Ezra out of his compulsion…and then he pressed the button again. Oh. My. *God.* I couldn't breathe, pain stabbing in on me from all sides. It felt like it went on forever this time, even though it was maybe only ten seconds. I was panting helplessly when it was over.

"Ezra," I said, striving for calm, "why did you do that?"

His voice shook. "I don't know," he muttered. "I don't know."

"Mr. Gerbrecht," a voice of mellifluous liquid butter intoned from the doorway, "how is our conversation with our guest going in here? Have we learned anything of use?"

"N-n-no," Ezra stammered, flustered, pulling his glasses off his nose and cleaning them to cover his unease. "Alina, I don't think she knows anything."

Alina? A.k.a. Cybele, a.k.a. Demon Chick? What exactly had I done to piss any of them off so much?

"I'll be the judge of that," whoever she was replied.

Oh goodie.

Alina stepped into the room and gave me a moment to understand the craptastic magnitude of my current situation. Fan-*freaking*-tastic. I was bolted to a bed, pain diodes stuck all over me, with a couple of loony-toons who got off on torturing me. Nobody knew where I was, and apparently these freaks thought I knew something I just didn't.

The lights flickered. Alina's eyes narrowed in irritation. "Storm blowing in," she said, in response to my unasked question. "The wiring in this place is abysmal. Ezra, did you free the mice to nibble on the wiring?"

Ezra looked down and pretended not to hear her.

Alina laughed; it was chilling and chocolate fondue fountain sensual at the same disturbing time. "Maybe our friend Dana here would like us to let the mice loose on her. Or, hmm, perhaps snakes would be more to your liking?"

She gave me a lascivious smile and said a single word: "*Serpentia*."

And I was covered with writhing, hissing snakes of green and red and brown. *Oooohhhh shit!*

I'm a city girl. Were these snakes poisonous? Was I about to die a venomous death? Was it a hallucination? That scaled skin whispering over mine as it wound through my arms and legs and around my throat felt awfully, inexplicably, real. Oh gods. This was it. I was going to die and they would throw my body into an incinerator and scatter my ashes across Lake Ontario.

My teeth started chattering. I couldn't stop them. I didn't want to die.

Alina grinned wider, showing fangs. Her horns curved upwards a bit more and started to glow. "*Excrucia clavica,*" she said.

The bones in my neck started to crack and snap. *Pain.* Was she trying to break my neck from the inside out?

"*Argentia piedi,*" she said, cackling gleefully.

I couldn't feel my feet. It started with my toes, a creeping numbness that started traveling up. When it hit my ankles I could see: she was turning me silver. Sadistic fuck.

"Enough," said Ezra. He sounded tired. "Enough, Alina. You've had your fun."

She turned slightly to raise an eyebrow at him. "Do you want to join in the fun, Ezra? You know you're always welcome."

"No thanks," he replied dryly. "But a bar of silver

snakes can't tell us anything. Remember what happened the last time?"

Alina pouted.

"Come now, Alina. Turn the girl back," he said.

Alina sighed, more dramatically this time, and waved her hand in my general direction. "Fine," she said. "*Retirnatai.*"

And then I was myself once more, lying in a puddle of my own excrement. But whole, and alive. Stench and dignity aside, I was going to chalk this one up as a win in the Dana column.

Until the lights went out.

TWENTY-TWO

WET SUCKING SOUNDS. It felt like the sprinkler had gone off, but if so, the falling liquid was something thicker than water. I smelled Ezra's mildewy paper scent standing over me and felt my bindings loosen. My right wrist was almost free when the figure standing over me was yanked back and away. Chewing sounds, a thud against the far side of the room, sticky, gloppy footsteps padding across the floor. I frantically scrabbled at the last of the bindings with my wet fingers. Too slow. *Focus, Dana.*

It was hard with all of the slithering, slaughtering sounds around me. I concentrated on my right hand first, willing the fur to come out and the claws to sprout. If ever a time to shift there was, this was it.

Nothing happened.

I clamped down on an overwhelming urge to growl and resisted—but only just. No way did I want whatever was snickering its way around the room to focus on me in any way. I felt bathed in viscous slime. I had to get out of here. I needed to shift. Now.

I closed my eyes and inhaled through my mouth. Slowed my breathing. Thought about pleasant things—licking an ice cream cone, Madagascar vanilla on a sugary waffle base; climbing into my parents' bed on a Sunday morning. Nothing. I thought about Jon, our tenuous relationship that seemed to be more and more of the past than the future. A tingle, a cool breeze like the faintest of kisses on my lips, but then—too soon—nothing. I was running out of time. The snuffling and snorting was getting closer. I wanted to see Sam again. *Sam.* The memory of him had my nerves tingling, and the edges of my fingers vibrated with that now-familiar itch. I followed the feeling, inhaling what I remembered of Sam's scent, willing myself to Change.

Both my arms now ended in paws, sharply curved claws where my fingertips should be.

I yanked the bindings on my right wrist, hard. My right hand sprang free. I used the sudden freedom to slash down on my left side. Still couldn't see anything but had to risk it. I sat up, undid my legs and looped my knees over one another to sit cross-legged on the bed for a moment. Had to get sensation back before attempting movement. I swiveled my head from one side to the other trying to make out shapes, sounds—anything to pinpoint the location of whatever was in the room with me.

Silence.

I twitched my whiskers and wrinkled my nose, opening my mouth slightly to inhale. All I smelled was myself.

The lights came back on.

I was alone in the room. Covered in blood that wasn't my own. There, in the corner, was the source of the *thud* I'd heard just moments earlier. Ezra's severed head, his eyes glazed and forever open. His body lay on the floor like a skinned bear rug, arms splayed out, legs akimbo.

I leaned over the bed and vomited all over his back.

My, wasn't I a vision of glory and cleanliness.

Maybe I'd head out and hit the town after this. Had to be someone out there willing to hang with a urine—and blood—and bile-soaked girlie, right?

Most excellent. Now I was teasing myself. Had to get out of here. Now.

I swung my legs over the side of the bed, trying to avoid puke and body parts. I needn't have bothered—the entire floor was bathed in blood. With a plop, I landed on the floor, swishing in the liquid as I flattened myself against the wall and headed for the door.

The hallway, institutional though it was, looked familiar to me. If its layout was the same as the place I remembered, there would be an employee shower around the next corner with clean scrubs in the closet beside it. All of these Agency buildings used a similar blueprint. My feet sploshed loudly, bloody footprints in an airless hallway. Head buzzing, I numbly pushed my way forward. Couldn't give in to the shock. Had to keep going. One foot then another. I could do this.

Around the corner I found a supply cabinet but no shower. There *was* a mop and a pail and, wow, some of those paper footie things you might find at a spa. Incongruous, given the surroundings, but I'd go with what I could take at this point. I swiped a rag of questionable cleanliness and wiped myself down, throwing the bloody cloth into the bucket when I was as good as I was going to get. Grabbed a jug of bleach and poured it into the pail, stirring everything around with a mop. Two booties on my feet and another stack under my arm, and I was ready to go back out there. Well, almost.

First I backtracked, mopping up my footprints to the door of blood; couldn't force myself to go back in. Then I retraced my steps, drawing on memories long buried to find my way out. I passed headless bodies, entrails slung like party decorations on walls, eviscerated corpses splayed helplessly where they had fallen. Some mouths still gaped open in surprise. I swallowed thickly and forced myself to breathe through my mouth.

At some point I'd shifted back to human, so I had to be careful about fingerprints. Even though Toronto's finest men and women in blue were unlikely to ever find this place, I didn't want anyone to know I'd been here. Too many questions. Too many nightmares.

The corridors wound up and around in a seemingly endless twist and turn of institutional wizardry. But I knew they had been designed and built by non-magic-wielding humans, and I knew there was an exit. The blueprints were still emblazoned in my head. It was part of our training to know these halls—how to get in and how to get out. Always a chance that something would go wrong. Always had to know how to escape if it did.

My training kicked back in as if it had never left, prodding me in the back, not letting me stop. Hours, days, minutes, seconds—it all passed by as I carefully picked my way through the carnage towards the sweet possibility of freedom.

Finally, the last door. Using my T-shirt to shield my fingers, I pressed in the override code and prayed it still worked.

But luck was a bitch and she chose this moment to spit in my eye.

"No!" I couldn't bite back the frustration and I gave in, just for a moment, planting a solid kick at the door. The door barely even shuddered on the recoil.

I took a deep breath and tried the code once more. Still nothing.

I was locked in a morgue of decomposing bodies with a sea of cooling congealed blood, and at this rate I was going to be joining them. I clamped down the near-hysterical giggles pushing their way up and out of me, nowhere to go but out; too dangerous to be free and roaming the halls. Shadows darting in and out of shadows. Were they sweat-soaked memories or something else? No way to tell, remembering how to breathe, trying to separate the now from then.

A door slammed. And another, farther along the corridor. I paused for a moment then started sliding in the direction of the sound. Might be the source of my own death; might also be my source of salvation. Either way, I had to see whether there was anyone or anything else still alive down here. If I was really lucky, it was someone with sufficient access privileges to get us out.

I had to trust my thinning instincts. Nothing else to go on. My heart was pounding so hard I could feel it reverberating in my throat. I swallowed thickly, around the lump, and pressed on. Five doors. Ten. Eleven. Playing counting games in my head. By the twenty-fifth, I could hear the sound of someone breathing, air rattling wetly. I gambled and pushed open the door.

On the far side of the room, a man was propped against a wall. In the moonlight streaming in through the barred window above him I could see he was young, acne scars still fresh along the sides of his cheeks. His red hair was curly and matted with blood dripping down along his ear from where his skull had caved in. No way to fix that. He looked at me, helplessly, begging me to save him with his eyes. I opened my mouth but no sound came out. As I watched, those eyes dimmed and went out.

From the hallway, beyond the closed door, the snuffling snorting chewing sounds started up again.

No time to grieve, no time to think. I looked down at the corpse and saw a pass card clipped to a cord around his neck. I looked up and saw sweet freedom taunting me from beyond the window. Three steps and I had the security necklace. Five steps and I was on the vent ledge, shaking the grill bolted to the wall. *Fuck.* In human form, I couldn't wrench it out; but cat form would have been worse, even if I could have managed the Change again so soon.

The shaking rattled my new necklace and I realized that, along with the pass card, there were keys. I held them up to the light with red-stained fingers, begging Lady Luck for one more chance. This time she kissed my cheek and handed me a key with an edge that fit exactly into the bolts in the wall. I screwed out the last metal bits between me and beyond.

Claws screeched against the metal door separating me from my nightmare.

My luck held and the window opened.

I dove out and clanged the grill down behind me. Lady Luck must have been feeling guilty for torturing me earlier, because I was only three stories up and a drain pipe was within reach. I grabbed it and shimmied down, my underwear clammy and solidifying quickly in the sub-zero temperatures. Paper booties were useless for gripping but at least my damp fear didn't freeze my skin to the metal pipe as I descended.

Finally, with a plop, I crunched down onto a pile of black-edged snow.

No alarms, no men with guns and Kevlar vests to greet me. Only the cold slap of icy hoar ringing the sides of satellite dishes, encircled by a five-foot-high chain-link fence. The same one that lay just blocks from where I worked. My prison a replica of the fluorescent-twisted corridors of my nightmares existing adjacent to my life without me seeing it. Could I have been held and tortured so close to the bar? Without anyone knowing?

Too many sounds, too many shadows; nothing but paper and a thin sheet between me and anything out there that might want a taste. My lower jaw shook and I clamped down to keep my teeth from clacking together. No luck—the adrenaline and cold pushed my chattering into the involuntary zone. I flattened my tongue and shoved what I could of it between my teeth, muffling the sounds. Each twitch tasting blood as my teeth jerked against my tongue.

I ran. Stumbled. Tried to breathe. Realized, heart racing faster than I could, the necessity of deceleration before I passed out. *Don't think about it don't think about Ezra and Alina leaving you dead or dying or dismembered in a Dumpster or alley don't don't don't.*

I slowed my ice-leadened limbs as much as I dared, keeping the circulation moving while still pushing myself past my limits, hoping that shifter blood would protect me from frostbite. It wasn't that cold out, right? Reaching the snow tunnel walls of the packed ice embankment where so much had begun; the white brick road pathway to my truck.

The light went on inside the cab as I pulled open the door. *Shit!*

I closed the door, making sure it locked, and the

light went off again. Tried to remember how to breathe. Oh yeah. It's that in and out thing involving oxygen. *Right.* At the periphery of my vision, shadows thickened and the drifts of snow stilled. Because tonight hadn't been enough fun already, right? Sure, why not. Throw in some more creatures.

I hummed "How Do You Solve a Problem Like Maria" from *The Sound of Music* under my breath, using the tune to clear my head and let my cold-numbed fingers work their wire-sparking magic to start my engine, keys or no keys. By the time I hit the final aria, darkness was a handful of feet from my front bumper and I was running out of adrenaline. Almost ready to give up and call it a life.

Then the engine coughed and caught. I revved the gas, only once to be sure it would respond, then shoved the truck into gear and slammed my nearly bare foot on the gas pedal.

I WENT TO the one place nobody would look for me. Jon's.

After a shower so hot it bled to cold, after a change from paper to full-on fabric attire, after I was wrapped in blankets and settled into the guest room with a hot mug of chai tea in hand, only then did Jon lean back beside me, waving his hand as if to say "speak." Given that I'd arrived on his doorstep reeking of blood and guts—and other scents he considerately chose not to identify for me—he'd been remarkably patient.

So I told him. Everything I knew, and even a few guesses at what I didn't.

"Dawn is coming soon," Jon said. "Will you spend

the day here? I can't protect you, but maybe my home will be safe enough for you even while I'm dead."

I wanted to go home. But home couldn't be home to me, Lynna was at Anshell's and I couldn't risk going to my mum's place and possibly putting her in danger. I didn't feel safe at the Swan Song, and I wasn't completely certain I trusted Anshell enough to be at the Pack house right now either. Hiding sounded good; if I was going to hide, Jon's place was as good a place as any to do it in.

Plus, Jon's guest room—first time I'd ever seen it—felt like the perfect antithesis to a blood bath. A poufy duvet and down-filled pillows covered the surface of a four-poster canopy bed complete with lacy dust ruffles, sheer curtains and sheets of no less than a 600-thread count of finely spun Egyptian cotton.

All white. It was strikingly feminine, raising more questions than answers. Still, tonight we were trading secrets for safety, so I didn't ask, allowing him instead to tuck me in with a chaste kiss on my forehead before he vanished down the long, narrow hallway to his own daytime rest.

TWENTY-THREE

I FELT SOMEONE'S weight sink down on the bed. Strong, hairy arms pinned mine to the mattress above my head as whiskers tickled my face. I found myself straddled by a snarling partially shifted were-cat, very male, very not happy to see me. He sniffed behind my ears and hissed, spittle barely missing my open mouth and landing instead on my cheek.

I guess Jon's someone-that-I-used-to-know had keys to his place.

"Bitch," he hissed. It came out sounding more like *beeettsshh*. "You need to die already."

I twisted sharply to my left and used the momentum to keep him going until he landed, ass-first, on the floor beside the bed.

"Not today," I said, peering down at him. My head was still sleep-fogged, but the adrenaline kick of yet another attack was chasing that back. "What the hell is your *damage*? Wasn't scratching me enough fun for one lifetime?"

"You," Claude said, swallowing a very un-manly yowl as he overcame his tossed-over-by-a-female humiliation by arcing back onto his padded feet. "Every time I turn tail, there you are. In his gallery. In his car. In his home, and now in his bed."

Sir Hiss-A-Lot clawed the sheer tulle surrounding the bed, leaving shredded ribbons of fabric. So much for Jon's midwinter night's dream of girlish innocence. Claude's fur spiked around his neck, puffed up to make him seem even bigger than he already was. Half feline, half man, one hundred percent the stereotype of the green-eyed jealous cat.

"Yeah," I said, pointing out what should have been the obvious. "His guest bed. Not *his* bed. Guest. Not that it's any of your damned business."

Claude sniffed daintily but said nothing, opting instead to curl his paw into a fist and punch a hole into the wall in front of me.

"I know you're fucking each other," he said, turning to stalk from one end of the room to the other. "I caught you, remember?"

"I remember, asshole," I replied. "What does that tell you?"

Claude growled and leaned forward onto the bed, the pushing of his paws causing the frame to groan in protest.

"It means you're on my territory, bitch," he said. I snarled back this time, allowing my own claws, my own fur to sprout, going up onto all fours in front of him, nose to nose. Claude's eyes widened and he shrank back, just a bit.

"No," I said. "It means your territory is up for grabs. Besides, if you hadn't scratched me," I continued, "none of this would be happening. You turn *my* life to shit and then you have the balls to come in here and tell me *I* won't die and that I'm in *your* way? Seriously?" I practically spit my frustration at the tom.

"The vampire is mine," Claude said, only fractionally calmer. "Not yours." Even furry, I could tell he was hanging on to his calm by a fractional thread.

"Jon belongs to Jon," I said. "You want to kill off everyone he sleeps with? You'll have blood on your paws from here to Nunavut and back pretty soon, because I don't get the sense the man does monogamy. Make it easier on yourself and the rest of us and give it a rest."

I leaned back into my pillows and picked up my mug of tea, now cold, and took a sip as I retracted my own fur and claws with the barest of twitchy itches. McHissy deflated and sank into the far corner of the bed, leaning his back up against one of the four grooved cherrywood posts, watching me through narrowed eyes. I returned the favor for a full three minutes before sighing. I gave an inch. Okay, maybe it was a centimeter.

"You know you have to stop doing this."

"Fuck you," he replied with a huff.

"Whatever," I said. The eye roll part was involuntary. Really. "If you're going to be an ass, you can get out of my room. Now."

"Bitch, this ain't your room," he said. "Get *your* tired ass out of here and maybe I'll be a bit nicer to you."

"Ooh, you mean we can be friends? Best buds? Oh yes, I'd do anything for that privilege." My sarcasm was duly noted with a flare of his nostrils and a narrowing of his eyes. "Besides, every time I set foot out there, something bad happens. So if it's okay with you, and frankly even if it's not, I'm going to hang here for a bit longer. If you want me to move faster, go make me coffee."

"Leave," Claude growled at me, hair starting to rise up along the back of his neck, staring me down anew.

"No," I said.

Jon found us that way a few minutes later, locked in a glaring standoff. He leaned against the doorway, hair tousled with sleep, and stared blearily back and forth between Claude and me before shaking his head and going to get coffee. He returned with two mugs—one for each of us. Claude's was in a travel mug with a big yellow smiley face on the side.

"Claude," Jon said firmly, holding the cat's gaze in his. "It's time for you to go."

Claude's mouth gaped open and shut. Jon leaned forward to whisper something in Claude's ear that made the cat's yellow eyes flash to brilliant moor-kissed emerald and then back again before he turned tail and stomped out of the room.

A couple of minutes later the front door slammed; I wondered whether Claude had taken his key.

Jon slid his palm over the night table. Question answered. He looked from the key to me, raised his eyebrows, then left the room. I heard the door to his bedroom open and close.

Right. One question answered. Only to be replaced by another, more significant one.

Awesome.

I was getting out of here before things got any weirder.

I PARKED MY truck down by the lake and walked past families and children playing, past sand and garbage and ships. Ghosts echoed in my head, chasing me down the path I walked, taking me farther away from the city I knew and the reality I thought I knew.

Ezra was dead. My relationship with Jon was possibly over, possibly shared with a crazy cat named Claude. My life as a norm living only on the fringed edges of the supe community—gone, and replaced with the ability to shift into feline form of some kind. Oh yeah. And I had new knowledge of a father I'd barely known, who'd apparently had the shifter gene and neglected to mention it to me before his untimely departure.

The positives? New allies with the possibility of being new friends. Celandra, the dragon. Sam, the feline. Anshell—still wanted to know what he was. And Jon, who apparently planned to look out for me as long as he could regardless of our relationship status.

I still didn't know why this was happening to me. Or what was I up against. Either way, it involved that crazy demon chick—Alina or Cybele or whatever her real name was. Icy smoke demons kept coming after me. My kitchen was melted goo. There had to be a connection—but what? The best key I had to the lockbox of clues, my mentor from my previous life, was decomposing in a pool of his own cooled blood. And the great unanswered question: How did they get to me in the Swan Song?

My breath came in gusts of icy steam; I walked faster. Not paying attention. I'd looped around and was heading back to my truck. And? What would I do once I got there? I couldn't go home. I wasn't going to go back to Jon's. I couldn't go to my mother's. Lynna wasn't at her place and besides, I was thinking getting kidnapped by a big blue demon was a pretty good indicator of the lack of security around her apartment.

I was out of time and out of options.

THE DOOR TO Anshell's place swung open with a bang. Someone was a little twitchy. I didn't recognize the woman who let me in, all muscle and winding leaf-pattern tattoos, but she'd apparently figured out who I was. She stepped back only enough to let me past before slamming the door shut and barricading re-entry with a series of serious-looking metal locks and fasteners.

"Anika," she said with a nod, and then, "Wait here." My new friend Anika shot me a look that conveyed the potential for serious ramifications should I choose to move from my spot. I matched her look, staring her down just long enough to prove it was *my* decision to acquiesce—I sure as hell wasn't taking orders from a complete stranger.

Tattoo girl didn't seem to care much. "Suit yourself, chickie," she said with a shrug before slinking up the stairs. I noticed she hadn't asked my name, even for show. Exactly how many people knew about me? I was starting to think I didn't want to know.

It was maybe thirty seconds before I heard another bang and then the sound of footsteps, heavy, steady, heading down towards me. I couldn't help leaning back, just a bit, into the shadows of the doorway. Pretty sure I was safe here, or should be, but just in case...

"Dana."

I let out a breath I'd forgotten I was holding and stepped out into the light. With a slight incline of his head, Anshell nudged me towards the kitchen. I sat. He put a pot of coffee on to brew, and slid into the stool across from me.

"Tell me."

"No," I replied. The bowl in front of me, filled with cubes of raw sugar, was suddenly intensely interesting.

Anshell honored my silence for the amount of time it took to make the coffee before trying again.

"Where have you been for the last twenty-four hours?"

There had to be words. My not wanting to say them didn't mean they didn't need to be said. So I forced myself back into that nightmare so that Anshell would know.

"I was kidnapped last night from inside the Swan Song. Tortured. Asked a bunch of stupid questions which I survived purely because something bigger and badder and meaner than me came along and slaughtered everything it came into contact with other than me." I was starting to babble, my eyes suspiciously wet. Anshell looked like he was physically biting the inside of his cheek to keep from interrupting me. "I escaped. Don't ask me how because I'm not so sure I know. Then I ran from the place, nearly naked and covered in blood, wearing these stupid paper booties that did nothing, and managed to make it to my truck. Which I had to hotwire, by the way. Then I went to Jon's, still covered in blood and stinking like raw sewage. Yeah, I've been out having all kinds of fun."

Anshell grimaced. I took a sip of coffee before going on.

"Tell me again how the Pack protects its own. How you didn't know anything about it. You or Sam. Or maybe you did and you're putting on a good show here." I glared at Anshell, who shook his head. "Something is after me. Or someone. It doesn't matter where I go anymore; nowhere feels safe. Even at Jon's, after I showered and burned my clothes, his idiot boyfriend found me. Fucker woke me up to give me shit. Like it's my fault that Jon swings both ways. I mean, really?" Deep, heavy sigh. "I can't go home because my kitchen is melted. Lynna is here, so I can't go to her place. I don't want to put my mother in danger. And even work isn't safe anymore."

"Isn't the Swan Song supposed to be a neutral zone?"

I nodded.

"So then how did whoever snagged you pull it off? Why didn't it trip any alarms? Something's hinky," he said.

I thought about it. "Did Sandor call you? Was he worried about me in any way?"

"I haven't heard from him," Anshell replied, mulling over the words as he said them.

"Let me try." I called Sandor's cell, and the office line at the Swan. Both went straight to voice mail after the first ring.

I wasn't liking where this was going. Because if Sandor hadn't called looking for me, then it was probably because he wasn't worried. And the only way Sandor wouldn't be worried about me vanishing in the middle of my shift was if he was in on it—or something had happened to him as well. Either way, not good.

Anshell had clearly followed the same train of thought because he picked up the phone, punched in a couple of numbers and asked whoever answered to track down Sandor Slodvizik. Unintelligible response, but the voice at the other end of the line must have answered in the affirmative because Anshell said "thanks" before disconnecting.

"Thanks," I echoed.

"Don't worry about it," he said. "Listen, I know you're not sure where to go or who to trust. And I don't blame you. The fact is that we do not know where the leak is, and until we do, we're better off not trusting anyone."

"How do I know I can trust *you*?"

Anshell chose to ignore my question. "You said you told Jon everything?" he asked instead.

I nodded.

"What did he say?"

"It's not him," I replied. "He was angry and protective and told me not to trust anyone as well. He was worried about me coming to your place, which is why I crashed in his guest room—until I was so charmingly woken up."

"Okay," said Anshell.

We sat in silence a moment, sipping our cooling drinks. I didn't know what Anshell was thinking about, but I was casting my brain back to that room with the electrodes. What had Ezra asked me? About the pack, and about Anshell? I was missing something, something important. It danced on the edges of my consciousness but I couldn't touch it. I grunted my frustration; Anshell looked at me.

"What?" He raised an eyebrow to punctuate his question.

"Ezra," I replied. "He wanted to know about the Moonie Toones pack. Moon Face pack. Face of the Three Moons pack? Something like that," I finished lamely. The name was there, in my brain, if only I could access it.

"The *Moon with Seven Faces*," Anshell said slowly,

correcting me. "The pack whose protection you are currently under. What did you tell him?"

"I believe I said something to the effect of 'huh' and then 'Ezra, stop shooting pain at me,'" I replied acerbically.

"Indeed," said Anshell. "Anything else?"

"Well, they wanted to know about *Seven Faces.* But they also wanted information about our personal relationship," I said. "Obviously, I couldn't admit to knowing anything about the pack so I wasn't much help there. Instead I played like we were fucking each other to tweak Ezra's inner prude and get him to stop asking me questions about you."

"You pretended we were sleeping together to forestall further questions? Interesting tactic," Anshell said, lips twitching in a grin that reached all the way to his eyes.

"I would have said just about anything to get him to stop making those electrodes jump," I replied, no trace of a smile on my lips, wiping the mirth from Anshell's and replacing it with sympathy. "It was weird," I said. "They knew we knew each other, but they thought we were physically involved as well and that I was staying here. And they knew about that *incident* after hours outside the bar the other night, the night when Sam and I met."

"That is indeed curious," Anshell concurred. "And it does help us narrow down the list a bit. Who else knew about what happened?"

I thought about it a moment, forming the beginnings of a checklist in my head.

"Sam, because he was there," I said, holding up

one finger. "Jon. You. Sandor. And I might have mentioned it to Lynna."

Anshell gave me a level look, waiting for me to put the pieces together. Welcome to my lightbulb moment.

"Oh shit," I said. He'd been unconscious the whole time, so I hadn't even thought of him. "Goth Guy."

TWENTY-FOUR

IT WAS WEIRD even thinking it. We'd rescued him from a bloody death. Right? So why would he help Alina, or Ezra, or whoever? Was this an enemy of my enemy is my friend deal, or was it something else?

Sam took that moment to pad downstairs, wearing nothing but a pair of drawstring pants and looking delicious. Damn, how did he do that? His chest was far from hairless, but it *was* strategically sleek, drawing my eyes down the shaded path to what lay just beyond the waistband of those stubbornly slung pants. His hair was messy, one side sticking up more than the other, and his eyes were still bleary with sleep. The grin he flashed me, though, was pure mischief.

"What are we talking about down here?" Sam schooled his face into poker straightness when he looked at Anshell.

"We were talking about the fact that Dana was snatched from the Swan Song during her shift last night," Anshell replied. The shift in Sam's stance was barely perceptible, but he pulled up and back just a bit, waiting for more information.

"Her abductors were particularly interested in our clan," Anshell continued, "and knew that Dana had stayed here. She encouraged their assumption that she and I were an item."

"So their intel is inaccurate at best," Sam pointed

out, crossing his arms over that amazing chest as he leaned a muscled shoulder against the door frame.

"*Kaynahorah*," I muttered.

"Right," Anshell said. "But that doesn't necessarily change things. Not only did they know of Dana's connection to us, but her abductors were quite curious as to how she'd survived that gathering you two interrupted the other night. They referred to it as 'The Feed.'"

"Also, Goth Boy may be the leak," I said. "Have you talked to him yet?"

Anshell and Sam exchanged a look.

"What?"

Sam shrugged. Anshell cleared his throat, running long fingers over his closely cropped hair as he stared out the window into the glare of his own reflection.

"He isn't here," Anshell said, without turning around.

"Okay," I said. "So, where is he?"

"We don't know," said Sam.

"Wait. You mean you lost him?" Poker voice was not my forte. "How is that even possible? The guy was unconscious, almost completely drained of blood. It's not like he could get up and walk out on his own."

"Morgenlark's a supe," Sam pointed out. "He heals faster than humans. The guy was gone by the time we came down to check on him."

"Gone?" I couldn't believe it. "How do you lose a patient? Don't you guys have guards or something?"

"He was not a prisoner," Anshell pointed out. "Patients are free to come and go as long as they can do it without substantial assistance. Which, it appears, Joseph Morgenlark was capable of doing." He gripped the counter so hard I thought it was going to crack.

"We do have cameras in certain rooms for monitoring purposes, and we pulled the footage from that night."

"Morgenlark woke up after about three hours of sleep and transfusions," Sam said, glancing at Anshell for the okay to continue. "He yanked out his tubes, made some kind of sign that we couldn't see and then, *boom*, he was up and out the window."

I shook my head. This made no sense. Supe or no supe, nobody recovers that fast.

"What about Demon Blue? Do you still have him?" Both Sam and Anshell nodded. "If this Feed is the coincidence-not-a-coincidence here, maybe he knows even more than you've managed to yank out of him so far."

"Worth an ask," Anshell said, launching himself off the edge of the counter and heading down the basement stairs before that last consonant tongue-touched the roof of his mouth. Sam followed close behind, scooping up a faded grey T-shirt off the back of a chair and pulling it over his head. Damn those guys moved fast. I trailed along behind them, slowing my pace to almost-normal human speed.

"What the fuck do you guys want now?" Blue sat in the corner, his lower lip trailing on the floor before he scooped it up with a single taloned claw and tucked it back into his mouth. Diamonds still twinkled in his flesh, but their light was noticeably dimmer than before. His right arm hung at an awkward angle, even as I watched the flesh and muscle and bone trying to knit itself back together.

"Glad to see you've regained your composure," drawled Sam. "Tell us about Joseph Morgenlark, Gus."

"Never heard of the asshole." Gus picked a loose

diamond from up his left nostril and flicked it at the far wall, where it landed with a sharp *clink* and stuck. Talk about otherworldly snot glue.

"Oh, sure you have," I said, stepping forward out of the shadows. Couldn't let others fight my fights forever. "He's the guy who pulled himself out the supe hospital window only hours after he got there. You know, the shifter who should have died. The one your mistress was particularly interested in, and the reason she put out that hit on me—*after* I saved his sorry ass."

Lazzuri chortled. "Nice security system you dick-wads have here," he said, running his forked tongue along his very blue lips. "Please, by all means give me a room with that kind of view next time, will ya?"

Anshell had the door unlocked in a flash. He threw Lazzuri across the room so hard his back scales embedded themselves in the wall before he fell to the concrete floor with a heavy *thud crackle thud thud* as the demon bounced and rolled.

"Enough," Anshell growled, reaching back to pull the cell door shut behind him before plucking Gus Lazzuri off the floor and holding him by his second throat several feet up against that same indented wall. Anshell was breathing hard, nostrils flaring. "Enough! Who. Is. Morgenlark?"

"I," coughed Gus, "ain't," *cough*, "got nothing," *cough cough*, "to say to you assholes," he finally managed to spit out with a gulp of breath. Sam cleared his throat to get Anshell's attention. Must have worked because Anshell shook himself off and dropped Lazzuri to the floor, taking a step away from his prisoner. I saw ebony fur flowing up over Anshell's shoulders and out the sleeves of his T-shirt, down his biceps; then receding, hair inhaled into flesh again, leaving smooth milk chocolate skin in its wake. Talk about self-control.

What the hell was he?

No time to get a response; suddenly it was Anshell's face pressed up against the bars. I could see the whites of his eyes as they darted around, looking for an out that didn't exist.

Shit.

I had to do something.

"Hey, shithead," I called out. "Drop the guy or you're going to die."

Lazzuri laughed and whacked Anshell against the bars a second time. To the credit of whoever had installed the security down here, the bars didn't budge.

"Girlie," he said, "I'm dead anyways. And this guy and me, we have some unfinished business. So why don't you go upstairs, maybe have your nails done, take a coffee break. By the time you come back, we'll be all done down here. Maybe there'll be some blood to clean up. Asshole shifter blood. But who cares about that anyway, right? Not like being a supe means anything to you."

I didn't have to see Anshell's look of warning to know how to play this one.

"Yeah," I said, schooling my eyes to stay on my target, no sideways glances. I could feel Sam behind me, shadowing; my guess was he was looking for an opening while I provided distraction. "Whatever. But you see," I continued, leaning back and pulling out a kitchen knife I'd grabbed on my way downstairs, "I really hate self-important pricks fucking with my friends, especially in their own homes."

Lazzuri laughed in my face, spraying green spit in

a wide arc that only just missed me. My knife, however, which was out and winging its way towards him, did not miss. As Demon Blue tried to reach the blade sticking out of his skull and pinning him to the wall, Sam had the cell door unlocked and open in a flash. Together, he and Anshell yanked the still-quivering weapon out of DB's skull, sliding the blade across the floor to me before slamming the demon against the wall and banging his head a few times to make their point. Not sure what, exactly, that point was, but I suspected it was something along the lines of "don't mess with us or we'll bang your skull on a hard surface repeatedly." Just a guess.

I cleared my throat to get their attention. I was hoping that supersonic hearing would trump the high levels of testosterone in the basement right about now. "Um, guys?" No response, just more grunting and banging. "If you scramble his brains, he won't be able to tell us anything—even if he's smart enough to change his mind and try." All reason, that's me.

I counted five full seconds of silence before, with a last grunt and bang, Anshell and Sam stepped back and let Lazzuri drop to the floor yet again, oozing green from his head. Funny—Lazzuri didn't seem remotely more cooperative than he had been ten minutes earlier. If he knew anything, he wasn't telling us. Frick. I had no idea what else could motivate him to spill, but obviously violence wasn't it.

Maybe a different approach. I squatted down to a crouch, between all the manly men legs, and caught Gus's eyes as he glared at me.

"Okay, we get it," I said. Attempting temporary amnesia over last week's attempt to kill me. "You don't give a shit about us or what we're trying to do, and you're only out to save your own scaly-ass hide."

Gus narrowed his eyes at me, blue cheek trailing green slime on the concrete floor.

"You believe that these guys—" I indicated to Anshell and Sam with my chin "—plan to ultimately end your sorry existence no matter what you say. Right? So why should you bother helping any of us out, because at least this way you won't go down as a chicken-ass snitch. How am I doing so far?"

Lazzuri slowly nodded, watching me without saying a word, although he did take that moment to let out a globby ball of spit possibly containing a tooth into the corner of the cell. I noticed he was careful to avoid hitting me and the guys this time. Smart.

"I think," I continued, catching the attention of one of his eyes and holding it, "that you know more about this guy Morgenlark than you're choosing to share. Which is, of course, your prerogative. But I also think maybe you're not quite down with the overall plan here. You're out your money for the contract hit on me, and you're stuck in this concrete cell—you can't do anything when this all goes down. No alternate dimensions for you to escape what's coming, and you know that what's coming is probably a lot worse than anything we could do to you. That golden parachute you'd planned to buy with a portion of your cut? Gone." I leaned forward. "How am I doing?"

Lazzuri nodded once more, not bothering to look away now.

"So here's what I can offer you," I said. "Tell us what you know. Help us out even, if we can all find a way to trust each other. If we can stop whatever ball is rolling down that hill—preferably together—then I think the boys here might be inclined to let you go on your merry way. Assuming we all survive."

Lazzuri managed to convey skepticism without opening his mouth. Which might have had something to do with the large boot wedged between his teeth. Somehow he still pulled off a nod, though.

"Guys?" Sam and Anshell exchanged a long look, some kind of communication to which us word-reliant ones were not immediately privy. "Can I get your commitment on this?" It took a moment before they nodded, the air around them shimmering with meaning. *Okay then.*

"Gus Lazzuri? Will you step up and save your ass while saving ours as well? Swear on whatever it is you hold dear, even if it *is* your own hide?"

There was a long pause; I think we all held our breaths for his answer. Finally Lazzuri spoke, although his reluctance was clear.

"Fine," he said. "Assholes. Tell me what you need."

TWENTY-FIVE

FOUR HOURS LATER I stood alone, bathing in the moonlight. Trying to feel the energy of the howling and yowling beasts around me, just past the circle of the fire, flames shooting up from the safe confines of the stone circle. I was the outsider. The norm, welcomed but only just, into the inner workings of the pack for the night. Courtesy for the traveler, or something like that—I admit I wasn't paying super close attention when Anshell went through the ceremonial drama of it all.

Maybe I should have been.

What I did know was that if I full-on shifted, I was in. Open arms, or paws, or something like that. *No pressure.* Automatic privileges available from the moment I said "I do" supported by a sworn pack member witnessing of "I did."

Sam had tried to describe the sensation of the complete change to me, but I was still confused—how do you show cerulean blue to a person blind from birth? There was something about an itch and a pull and a push, but after my third wiseass sexual innuendo, he'd given up.

"You'll figure it out," Sam had huffed, equal parts cryptic and annoyed. I guess I deserved that.

Either way, I was now naked from the waist up, and working on the rest, but it was so damned cold I was having trouble convincing my body to obey. All those old horror movies with the pants ripping as the shift hits. I'd rather not be walking naked in the middle of winter back to the rest of my clothes with a bunch of were-people I'd only just met. Removing the clothes seemed like a good idea when I started. Now, maybe not so much; my breath was hanging on the air, an illusion of warmth surrounded by a mist of pure cutting *ouch*.

I'd thought I'd feel the energy of it all, the spirit and rush of being something larger than myself. Instead, standing at the edge of a snowy field next to a barren copse, I felt like an idiot losing sensation in her extremities.

What the hell was I thinking? Stupid Dana getting caught up in the lunacy of a life I thought I'd left behind. There was a reason I'd quit Ezra's team. Same reason I'd dropped out of grad school, dropped out of my old life, lost touch with my friends from back then and taken up the rewarding career path of bartending. I didn't want to deal with this existence bordering on reality. I didn't want the violence. Maybe I wasn't looking for that white picket fence in the suburbs—in fact, I was pretty sure I wasn't—but at least I could have bits and pieces of the kind of life other people had. That one where you can get up in the morning and have a cup of coffee and not worry about getting jumped by creatures with names so alien you can't pronounce the vowels with your human tongue. Where shopping meant buying shoes or jeans or maybe a new jacket because you liked the fabric or the fit—and not having to think of how you might access a knife or *shuriken* or crossbow while wearing them.

You know. *Normal.*

I didn't know how much time had passed since the pack had taken off, but I could have sworn the moon had nudged position in the sky by at least a foot. Or an inch. Maybe it was a cosmic mile. Either way, I hadn't shifted yet and could no longer feel my fingers. The beasts slinking around my periphery only highlighted my own failings; Anshell wasn't sure I could defend myself, so he'd left proxies with claws behind.

Stupid Dana. Expecting life to tie itself up so neatly with a bow on top.

Nothing was ever that simple.

Except for the clear fact that it was cold out here, so very cold, and I was not wearing fur of my own making. If I didn't either shift or get dressed, I was going to lose something to frostbite.

Screw it.

I bent down to retrieve my red flannel plaid shirt and white tee. Layering up, I pulled on my hat and gloves before digging around for the heavy down jacket Sam had so considerately loaned me—just in case. I wrapped myself in a blanket too, heading for the clump of trucks and cars and SUVs by the road. My keys were out and ready for plan B.

I heard sounds, off to my far right but getting closer. Unlike the rustlings of my shadow guards, who I could no longer sense. A snuffling and snorting. Something shuffling and growling in a distinctly un-feline-like manner. I stilled my breathing, carefully wrapping my scarf up and over my nose and mouth to keep from puffing steam out into the air and advertising my position.

Quietly I slid the rest of my keychain into my sheepskin gloves, leaving out just the one key I really needed. The snow crunched beneath my feet as I edged closer to my truck. Cursing under my breath. Then praying I would make it to the truck without dying.

No, I don't believe in God. And even if he/she/it exists, I'm sure they don't care what I believe as long as I'm as good a person as I can be. But that doesn't stop me from saying please right now. *Please please please.* I don't want to die. I don't want to meet the same fate as so many of the people I used to know. *Pleaseplease-pleasepleaseplease...*

And then my skin itched. That now-familiar feeling just underneath the surface, racing energy, sparks up and down my nerves. My gloves split at the fingertips, claws poking though. The partial shift. Oh shit no, not now *notnownotnownotnow...*

I forced myself to pause, to breathe. *Think.* The plan tonight was to shift. Bond with the pack and figure out how to live in this new body by testing its strengths and assessing its weaknesses. To win you had to know how to lose. I didn't know how to do either yet, not once I shifted. I didn't know if I could survive in a fight as a cat. Even a big cat. I didn't know enough about what was tracking me and how to defend myself as a non-human if it cornered me and I had to fight.

My body knew how to fight as a human. Arms, legs, fingers; boots, weapons and non-bestial muscle memory. The shift might make me stronger, but the me who had trained every day to live to that next day knew how to survive. It's why I was still here when so many weren't anymore. This new me might not be so lucky.

I had to make a call.

With an effort so hard my teeth broke through my

lower lip, blood dripping down onto my chin, I forced the claws back into my skin, forcing the shift to go no further. The snuffling was closer, louder, and had taken to humming "Sympathy for the Devil" by the Rolling Stones. Shit. This thing was sentient, and was heading my way fully aware of itself and me.

So *very* not good.

Its next words were a confirmation.

"Oh, Dana? Where are you, my pretty? I can smell you. Drops of your blood are leading me to you. Sweat and steam and lust and sex and fur. All the best things in life." It chuckled, voice deeply masculine, but I couldn't be sure. Didn't want to get close enough to find out. Certainty in life was overrated. And I was babbling in my own head. I bit down on my poor abused lip, harder now, trying to keep my teeth from chattering in cold and fear.

Because I recognized that voice.

It was the voice of the thing, the creature, the *it* that had severed Ezra's head from his body and left him lying in a pool of his own blood.

That thing knew my name, who I was, probably what I was. Maybe it knew me better than I knew my-self. But I wasn't going to give it that kind of power. *No.* There had to be a way out. Had to be.

"Oh, Dana? Tell me, how does kitty stew sound? I hear that once you skin a cat and use its fur for boots, the meat itself is quite succulent." It chuckled, all warmth and seeping ooze that curdled my blood and chilled me in places I'd rather not visit. Shouldn't visit. From before, from then. "You know I can do it. You've seen the results of my wrath. Shall we do it together?

Do you want to be responsible for the deaths of all of your new friends?"

I didn't answer, hoping silence was enough of a response. I calculated the distances between me, the voice and my truck.

Maybe.

The snow crunched directly to my left, just a few feet away. Now or never. I counted the distance under my breath as I ran. *One* Mississippi...*two* Mississippi... on *three* Mississippi my keys were in the door and unlocking it. On *four* Mississippi I was in with the door slammed shut behind me. *Five* Mississippi smashed the lock in place with my elbow as I turned my key in the ignition.

Nothing happened.

No! *C'mon c'mon c'mon.* I was muttering under my breath like a madwoman now but I didn't care. This creature was after me. All of the slaughter, the pools of blood, was on me. All my fault.

No. Couldn't be. Why? Come *on*, stupid engine, turn over. Turn on. I jammed my foot onto the gas pedal, careful not to flood the engine, just enough to give it the push it needed, and tried one more time.

Success. The engine revved.

I shifted into reverse and floored it. Heard a satisfying thud as I backed into what I thought—hoped—was the slurpy creature with a thing for the Stones. Then I put the truck into drive and steered, hard, out of the spot. Heard another thud, but this was in the back bed of the truck, scrabbling at the rear window.

I veered, hard, shifting to the right this time. I could hear its chuckle behind me; feel its hot breath against the back of my ear. An illusion. The glass held. I resisted the urge to stare at the rearview mirror.

Something else dangled in front of me. A man-sized cat, draped over the passenger portion of my windshield, eviscerated. The trail left by its intestines smeared along my passenger side window with a *flop flop flop* as I bounced over the uneven ground. I couldn't allow myself to get distracted here. I was almost absolutely positive it wasn't Anshell or Sam, but also almost just as certain I couldn't be certain, and muttered another small prayer to whomever or whatever to get me out of here. There was way too much blood on my hands.

Shit.

Anshell had told me something about a signal, something the pack let loose when they hit danger. In this case, I was going to go with my hunch that dangling eviscerated feline equaled a need for a quadruple paws up that Bad Stuff was here and having a bit of fun at the clan's expense. But I couldn't remember what I was supposed to do or say.

I knew it was goading me. Didn't matter. The blood smears and bits of steaming excrement on my windshield had the desired effect, elevating this scary asshole from nuisance to Big Bad To Be Taken Seriously.

Right now, I had to seriously get it off my truck. I swerved sharply to the right and then to the left again, but the strange beast-like thing kept on laughing and *tap tap tapping* at my back window.

There was a screech as a large pile of fur shot over the edge of the truck bed. I braked, hard. Hadn't even seen the cat coming. I looked around to find my truck surrounded by sleekly furred creatures, some feline, some...*other*. Fluidity of fur and feathers and patchy scales flowing into and around each other. I spared a moment to wonder what kind of pack the Moon with Seven Faces was. And another to wonder how they had gotten here so fast. And then I was out of time.

The same moonlight that had mocked me so viciously earlier tonight now illuminated rivulets and rivers of viscous juices. One nasty creature against so many shifters. And the cackling thing was still going, laughing and dancing and swaying in one of the scariest dances I think I've ever seen. Wherever it touched, blood spurted. Never mind that it was outnumbered. I could see the shifters were going to lose. It was time to run. Those cats and whatever else was out there fighting—they didn't deserve to die for me.

I eased open the driver's side door, keeping my feet inside until the last possible moment, when I swung up and over onto the hood. I yelled "Hey!" and was roundly ignored by everyone out there who was now fighting for his or her life. I reached back around, ass in the air, and whacked my horn once, twice, three times. Still nobody bothered to quirk more than a partial ear in my direction. I was going to have to do better than that.

Back behind the wheel, I checked the rearview mirror for friendly obstacles before reversing. Then I floored it. That got the rest of the pack's attention as they dove out of the way to escape my spinning tires. I bore down on the killing machine directly in my path. Sure, maybe this was suicidal. But if I was going, I was taking this thing with me.

Five. Four. I made myself count down what were likely my last few seconds of life. *Three.* I hoped my mother would be able to recover from the loss of both her husband and her daughter. *Two.* Considered that dying might get me out of ever having to choose between Jon and Sam. *One.* Time to say goodbye world. *Oh shiiiit...*

Blinding white light, like the moon had suddenly exploded. I expected to hit something. Expected to hit *It.* Instead, the light, and then I just kept going until I ended up embedded in a snowbank.

I think I passed out. Or blacked out. Or whited out. In between clicks of in/out consciousness, I saw blood. Heard screams. The sounds of a fight that got farther away, fragments of conversation. Words like: *it's gone* and *I don't know if it's dead* and *what the fuck was that anyway?*

I opened my eyes to one of the sweetest sights I think I've ever seen. Naked Sam, flanked by Naked Anshell, opening the side door and leaning in to make sure I was still breathing. I knew these men were no angels, but damned if they didn't feel like my own personal guardian variant of celestial beings right about now.

I felt Sam's mouth on my lips. Checking for breath? Anshell's hand was on Sam's shoulder, squeezing slightly. Damsel in distress yet again.

My head came up so quickly it whacked Sam on the chin, clacking his teeth together and eliciting a groan from my sometime lover.

"WHAT THE HELL?" I blinked furiously, squinting into the darkness beyond the white, trying to find the Big Nasty who had been making entrails jam out of our pack mates just moments before. Or *was* it moments?

Nobody seemed to be fighting anymore. And from the gathering around my truck, it looked like there were survivors as well. "Did I pass out? How long? What did I miss?"

"I think she's fine," Sam called back to Anshell over his shoulder, wry half-smile twisting his lips. But attempted humor didn't soften the tension around his eyes. "You can walk, right? Lean on me," he said, holding out his arm for me to use, a stabilizing force as I extracted myself from behind the steering wheel. "Try not to show weakness," he whispered in my ear, the concerned lover to anyone watching from farther away. "They'll be watching for that. I'll explain later."

I nodded, once, almost imperceptibly. Time to put on a show.

I inhaled and willed myself to stand. Scanning the crowd of wet-fur-smelling people, I saw lots of blood but couldn't tell how bad the body count was. Wasn't sure I wanted to know. All of this was happening because of me.

If only I knew why.

In the meantime, I had to pretend to be worthy of the pack's attention. With effort, I shoved down all the thoughts that distracted me and made me weak. Like the claws I'd forced back into my skin because I willed it to be so. Like the past I thought I'd left behind, had moved beyond, until it insisted on catching up with me.

Too bad Ezra was dead. Otherwise, I'd have a few urgent questions for him.

A hush fell over the crowd as we stepped away from the truck. Sam's nakedness glowed in the moonlight, a contrast to my fully clothed self, wearing a red-and-orange-striped toque with a multi-colored pom-pom that bobbed with each step I took. We were all lucky I hadn't gone with my green Kermit the Frog toque, or maybe the one with the cherry-chewing toucan. What can I say? The way I look at it is this—if you've got to wear a hat, you may as well have some fun with it.

Besides, red and orange hid the bloodstains better. Who knew I'd have to start planning ahead like this. Again.

I looked out over the crowd, huddled together in clusters of flesh and fur. Some had shifted back to human; others were in the form they'd started the night in, unable or unwilling to end the fun early no matter what happened.

"Uh, thanks," I said to the assembled many. "I appreciate you saving my butt tonight. I'm pretty sure I couldn't have survived much longer without you back there."

There was some general shuffling of feet, nodding. A couple of people I didn't know smiled encouragingly.

"You are very lucky to be part of such a fierce pack," I said, hoping it was true, hoping it was the appropriate thing to say. Where did I put that etiquette book on oration politesse following a bloodbath with a Monster of Unspecified Origin and a collection of adrenaline-pumped shifters who'd lost a number of their own in order to save you? There was a flower arrangement for that. Right?

Anshell rescued me. Again. This time, he stepped up beside me, then in front of me, shielding me with his body. For a change, I didn't think it was such a bad thing that Anshell wanted to put himself between all that anger and emotion and me. Human me, as far as we could tell, albeit a human who could sprout claws.

Anshell was doing something now that involved sweeping his arm across the gathered masses—okay, sparsely clumped gathered shifters—his palm upturned as though holding a goblet of crystal-encased liquid. On anyone else it would look ridiculous. Anshell somehow made it seem majestic. Naked butt quiver and all. Maybe I was the only one looking at his butt. Maybe I should stop. Someone was trying to get my attention. Definitely time to look elsewhere.

Sam. Also naked. On my arm. Yeah, that worked for the throat-catching alternatives. Especially since it covered the reality that said arm was the only thing holding me upright. Truly, I appreciated the fact that my butt was not firmly wedged in the snow given that I lacked the strength to continue standing much longer without Sam's support.

I focused on my Knight in Shining Now.

"Ever seen anything like Mr. Big Bad and Blood Smeary before?" I angled my head to Sam's ear, hoping he could hear my voice rustling the quiet of his hair. Inhaling his scent; his earlobe close enough to leave its salty-sweet aftertaste on my tongue. I resisted the urge to climb into his lap.

"No," Sam said. Anshell continued with his rousing oration.

"What about you?" I directed the question this time at Vine Tattoo Girl.

"Nope, never seen nothing like that," she said, shaking her head. "That thing was nasty." She pronounced it *nay-stay*. Sam tightened his grip on my arm and eased me back to sit on the embankment. Apparently the need for projected strength had passed now that Anshell had taken the oratorical floor.

I couldn't help it. The sound of Anshell's voice washed over me, ebbing away all the tension and negativity hovering over me since the last night I spent in the dark and the blood—the night Ezra's head had rolled from his body in a building I hoped never to return to. The last time Sir Beast of the Nasty and I met up.

Ezra. His assistant Cybele and her alter-ego Alina. The Monster Who Refused To Stay Under The Bed. It couldn't be coincidence that they'd been in the same place and time at least once before. Right?

There was something I was missing here. Time to figure it out.

TWENTY-SIX

I WOKE UP in Sam's bed.

His scent wrapped itself around me the way Anshell's voice had the night before, but instead of being soothing it was the sandpaper-rough touch of a cat's lick, brushing against my skin. I could still taste him mixed with me on my tongue. That lingering ache, deep inside. A man who'd seen me naked, who I'd seen naked.

A man who I'd never realized slept with a blanket covered in teeny-tiny hand-embroidered purple and yellow cornflowers, on a bed of similarly-patterned floral printed sheets complete with dust ruffle and matching armchair. No wonder he'd found ways until now to wake up with me elsewhere.

The arms of the chair were almost completely worn through, and the blanket looked aged into discoloration. I'm not sure what I was expecting—maybe the rough ruggedness of a scratchy grey-with-red-stripe army-issue wool blanket, or even just a comforter in a faded denim color.

Either way this bed of whimsy, accompanied by canary-yellow lace doily on the side table, was definitely not it.

"Good morning," Sam said, leaning against the door frame. Shirtless, top button of his jeans open, a mug of steaming cinnamon something in his hand. I wanted to drink him from here. His eyes twinkled. *Damn.* He'd figured out the effect he had on me already.

Who was I kidding. Sam had probably realized the effect he had on women by the time he'd hit puberty.

"'Morning," I managed.

His grin widened as the sight of him sent a message of wetness low into my gut. Damn, that's right—heightened shifter senses. He could smell exactly the effect he was having. But then his eyes swept over me, nestled into his bed, and they seemed to crumple a bit around the edges.

"What's wrong?"

He shook his head, schooling his face into the expression I'd expected rather than the one I knew now lurked beneath that surface. Somehow, faked enthusiasm wasn't quite the turn-on you'd think it might be. Go figure.

Sam sighed heavily as he realized I wasn't buying his act and came over to the bed. The mattress was so soft that when he sat on the edge I had to lean against the bars of the headboard to keep from sliding into him. For some reason, that kind of intimate touching felt like too much now, like an invasion of his personal space.

And then I knew.

"Who was she?"

Sam's jaw clenched and he looked away for a moment, eyes shiny. I laid my hand on his arm. "It's okay. If you don't want to tell me," I said.

He paused so long I thought he wasn't going to say anything. Or that he'd changed his mind.

"She was my wife," Sam said finally, meeting my gaze; he spoke so softly I almost missed it.

"I'm so sorry," I said, meaning it.

Sam gave me a half-smile, weak but determined. This was not a new pain. I wondered how long it had been.

"Five years," he replied. Had I asked out loud? "It's been more than five years since..." His voice faltered.

I gave him a moment to try and compose himself.

"The flowers, the doilies, the armchair...?"

"All hers," he replied. "I couldn't bear to get rid of it. Even now." More quietly. "I can still smell her. A bit. But not like before."

"Why did you bring me here?" I sat up and started looking for the clothes I wasn't currently wearing. I had on an oversized white T-shirt that smelled of Sam, but the scent of him and us was closing in around me, suffocating, too much emotion and not enough space to escape it. What was Sam looking for from me? A replacement wife? A little something something to pass the time?

"Why wouldn't I?" If Sam noticed my sudden agitation, he chose to ignore it. "I live here. I like you. You're temporarily homeless. Where else would we go?"

"I don't know." Because I didn't.

Crap. This was all getting way more complicated than I wanted to deal with. What happened to a good old no-strings-attached fuck anyway? *There are always strings,* a traitorous voice whispered in my head.

Why did I even care about Sam's past? We both had them.

I'd come to rely on this man, just a bit, over the last few days and now that he was showing a bit of vulnerability, look at me, I couldn't get out of there fast enough.

What was wrong with me?

More than one way to take that question. I sat down. Too tired to move, too tired to run. Who was I to complain about a little vulnerability in a guy? I didn't even know *what* I was at this point. And here I was, trying to run away from the one place, the one group of people who might have a hope in hell in figuring it out, giving me a place to call home. Oh gods, I was losing my mind.

"So what did you decide," Sam's deep voice rumbled from the edge of the bed. "Are you running or are you going to stick around for a bit?"

I sighed heavily. So much for stealthy poker face Dana. In the keeping-emotions-from-showing-on-face department, I suspected I'd failed mightily.

"Honestly?"

"That's usually preferable," Sam commented dryly, the man I'd met between the snowbanks flitting briefly across his face as he watched me.

"I'm worried about what you might want from me—or not want from me," I blurted out in a surprising—to me—burst of truth-serum-like honesty. "I'm worried about what I might be. I don't know how you're going to feel about me once we figure all this stuff out."

Sam grabbed a couple of pillows and leaned back into the bed, propped up against the backdrop of the wrought-iron bars.

"Who knows anything for sure? Stop worrying," he said. "Just because I told you something personal, don't go thinking I've turned all chick flick on you. I'm still me and you're still you. Personally, I'm going with shifter if that makes a difference here at all."

"And if I'm not?"

"Then you're not," Sam replied.

I mulled that over a moment, watching the man stretched across an improbably feminine bed. Damn. There he was, lying there, all delicious and...and I wasn't supposed to look at him like that now, because he was vulnerable, and sad, and missing his wife from five years ago.

"Stop it," he said, eyes closed. "Just come here. Close the door first."

I closed the door, but stood at the edge of the bed.

"Come on," he said. "Get naked with me."

Still I hesitated.

"And your wife?"

"She's gone," he replied, stretching out his hand to touch mine. Warmth radiating from his touch as he pulled me towards him. "We're still alive."

I managed to extricate myself for a moment, just out of reach as I pulled Sam's T-shirt over my head and tossed it onto the chair. His eyes burned. I reached down, fingering the elastic of my underwear, and Sam was up, fast, standing behind me, hands running down the sides of my hips. Then he was kneeling behind me. Kissing the small of my back. Dipping his tongue into the top of the crevice, right *there*, teasing then pulling out again. Spinning me around to face him. My eyes closed, and then it was all I could do to throw back my head and remember how to breathe.

His tongue. God. The roughness of sandpaper was working its way across me, soft and hard at the same time, and my nails started shifting back and forth between human and Other. *Fuck*. I grabbed Sam's hair and pulled his head back and away. Too much sensation. He resisted, hands cupping my ass, but I used gravity to sink down to his level on the floor. I pushed him back then crouched, cat-like, on my haunches and crept along the floor. My ass swayed as I tracked my prey. He watched me as I crept closer and closer. Shoulders down, I nosed in between his legs. Too much clothing; he was still wearing his jeans. I growled deep in my throat. Sam just chuckled and waited to see what I would do, how badly I wanted it.

Bad.

I reached forward with a single claw, hooked the eye of the zipper and pulled. Slowly. Watching Sam's face. His breath caught as I reached forward and gripped him through his boxers. Royal blue. And then they were gone, torn apart by my claws.

I engulfed his length in my mouth with one full stroke. The temperature in the room ratcheted up with each ragged breath, each stroke, each drop of delicious salty goodness. And then everything was a blur of fire and fur.

His clothes were gone and we'd just managed to get that condom on before he was inside me, who knows who was on top, who knows who got what and when and how. We rolled around on the floor, arching and moaning. If I was going to hell, gods, this was the way to get there. We ground together and back until there was no more past, only this, now, falling away into each other's arms.

TWENTY-SEVEN

I WOKE UP with the faint scent of dusty roses tickling my nose. Another woman's scent from another time. The weight of Sam's careless touch as he slept, trusting me. Trust that could lead to need.

It hadn't worked out so well before. Relying on other people was a mistake I'd made—and paid for. Whoever said love conquers all wasn't paying attention.

What was I doing here?

If Sam started relying on me, and I fell into old patterns? What then? Hadn't he been through enough pain already?

Away. I had to put distance between us. *Now.*

Gently, I moved Sam's arm from across my chest and quickly, quietly gathered up my clothes and my bag. I thought I'd wake him up when I grabbed my keys, but he kept snoring, his head resting on a pillow grabbed from the bed, curled up on the plush rug on the floor.

Yeah. We never quite made it to the bed.

The thought of the wife and the bed made me move even quicker. Shit. I was going to hell in a hand basket and eating chips and dip on the way down. My hand hovered over my shoes. Deep breaths. I reminded myself that I did not force Sam into anything; what we'd done had clearly been consensual. Beating myself up was a waste of time. I needed to find out what I was before the second night of the full moon tonight.

And to do that, it would probably be good for me to get out of this room and have a conversation with someone who might actually be able to help me.

ANSHELL WAS SITTING at the dining room table, reading the newspaper and drinking coffee—milk, three sugars. Never mind how I knew. He looked up, taking me in with an almost imperceptible nostril flare, and nodded an otherwise silent greeting.

I reminded myself that there was no shame in what I'd just done. Pushed down the sensation of moral filth, of having rolled in the sandy grit of someone else's misery. Even though I knew. Intellectually, logically, I knew—nobody forced Sam to do anything, and being with me was probably a good thing.

So how come I was feeling a bit dirty, and not in a good way?

When in moral doubt, defer and deflect. I poured myself a bowl of cereal, killing another couple of minutes, before plopping down in the chair across from Anshell. Watching as he folded his paper in half before placing it under the edge of his saucer. Yes, the big tough alpha shifter used a plate under his coffee cup. Someone's mama trained him well.

The thought of Anshell with a mama paused the treadmill of anxiety my brain was currently circulating through. Was she a shifter? It was hard to picture Anshell as a child. I got the sense that Anshell was alone in the world, aside from Sam and his pack, but maybe I was wrong. The way I'd been wrong about supes before I started working at the Swan Song.

My spoon clattered out of my hand onto the grooved and scratched tabletop.

"Sandor," I said, then stopped. My friend. My boss. *Shit.*

"Sandor..." I began again, got about as far again.

The edges of Anshell's eyes softened, wrinkles smoothing a bit in sympathy. "We haven't located him yet," he said. "Why don't you and Sam head to the Swan, take a look around?"

I nodded. Blinking back the tears that swelled my throat, making it too hard to swallow. No longer hungry, I put my bowl on the floor for the cat doing figure eights around my ankles. It purred its thanks.

Wait.

Cat?

I looked. Jun, the furry bundle of sarcasm I'd relegated to drug-addled hallucination status, grinned up at me from my milk leftovers.

"Greetings," he drawled. "Miss me?"

"Jun makes a great foot warmer on long cold nights," Anshell commented.

The cat growled a bit from his position on the floor where he was now doing the feline version of a face wash. "I'm nobody's footie," he said with a throaty rumble.

"Sure, you keep telling yourself that," I muttered. Both Anshell and Jun raised an eyebrow at me. Really. You'd have to see Jun try it to believe it.

Funny how the mind goes in rambling circles when irrefutably faced with a reality that seems impossible.

Jun jumped up onto one of the chairs, then up once more onto the table to lie down directly on top of Anshell's newspaper. Typical cat.

"So." Said cat yawned. "What's the plan here?"

"I'm figuring shower, then Swan," Sam said, appearing suddenly and heading over to the kitchen cupboard to snag himself a mug, pouring some coffee and cream and sugar into it before joining us in the dining room. He pulled out the chair next to me with his ankle and sank into it without sparing me a glance. Hmm. Someone was feeling testy about my good afternoon kiss-off.

"Any backup? If something could take down Sandor," I said, "we might need a bit more than just the two of us."

"Don't worry," said Anshell. "You'll be fine. I'll have someone meet you there." He lifted Jun with one hand as he pulled out the folded paper the cat had been using as a butt pad with the other. It was clear we'd been dismissed.

Have I ever mentioned how much I love that feeling?

I TOOK MY time in the shower, washing off the scents of Sam and blood and fur and salt and sweat. If only I was religious, I could believe that the water was washing away my sins, cleansing me, my conscience; Dana reborn. But I knew it wasn't true. I was me and I did the things I had done and now, when the water stopped running, I would face the demons.

I HUNG OUT with Lynna in her room while Sam took his turn in the bathroom. He'd nodded to me in the hallway but was otherwise distant. As though what had happened hours before hadn't happened. Never mind that that's how I'd been playing it, planning to play it. Never mind that I could think of a million reasons why maybe I shouldn't/couldn't/wouldn't get further involved with Sam.

Maybe I was overthinking this. Maybe he was just preoccupied.

"Let me guess," said Lynna, shaking her head. "This morning. After. You ran?"

"What do *you* think?"

"Do you even know what you want?" Lynna pretended to study a spot on the wall for a moment, just below the framed poster of a vaguely melancholy Renoir rip-off hanging over the bedside table. "*Who* you want?"

"That would be too easy," I replied. "What are *you* still doing here?"

"I have nowhere else to go," she said simply. "Until you get your shit together, everyone who knows you is a target. And that includes me."

"I'm sorry," I started, but Lynna cut me off.

"It's okay," she said. "It's not your fault. I understand. We both know I have absolutely zero way to defend myself against this kind of thing. *Zero.* Anshell has kindly offered me a room, a place to stay until whenever, and I've accepted his offer. But when this is all over," Lynna said, almost an under-her-breath afterthought, "I think maybe it's time to take a self-defense course and actually pay attention to something other than the instructor's abs."

I snorted. "That'll be the day."

TWENTY-EIGHT

GRAVEL AND ICE and snow ground crisply underneath our feet as we wound our way to the side door of the Swan. Foot and hoof and claw prints crisscrossed the pathways outside the snot-green, peeling aluminum siding that lined and reinforced the structure.

My key was out but I didn't need it; the employee entrance at the side was open, the blackened door flapping and banging in the wind.

Sandor never left that door unlocked, even during business hours. Never know what might choose to slither in uninvited, he'd say. Made me wonder. Like maybe whatever had happened had been invited. Or at least had access to the code.

I said as much to Sam. He grunted in response.

Fine. Play it like that.

I eased in through the door, back against the frame, carefully skirting the edge and into the inky blackness of the Swan. On the far wall, green effervescent light cast a thin web of luminescence. Sam's warm bulk flanked me from behind; a partner in battle.

I ignored the whispering voices in my ear, in my head. Words that said Sandor was no friend, that he had sold me out. Words that said he was a true friend but was going to die because of me. Voices telling me I was an ungrateful wretch. That I deserved to die. So many good thoughts to wrap around myself like a living scarf that weaves tighter and tighter, cutting off light and hope and air.

I gulped back a choking breath and crept forward once more. Behind me, I heard rather than saw Sam choking as well, gasping for breath. I turned around, took both of his hands in mine, and looked into his eyes until I saw their churning depths calm, until the Sam I recognized was staring back at me again.

Physical contact seemed to help.

This feeling of hopelessness, of fatigue, of blinking fruitlessly at tears that forced their way out regardless of what I wanted; I'd felt it before. A déjà vu moment. Saw Sam struggling with the same.

"Fuck," he said.

Was this emotional warfare the weapon used to take Sandor? Or was it an aftereffect, a lingering scent of magic like a signature at the bottom of a masterpiece, daring those who came into contact with it to press on further? The fear certainly didn't make it easy.

I wondered whether it worked as well on demons as it did on humans. Wondered if Sandor was still alive. Wondered if maybe I might be better off not wondering so much.

"Something happened over here." Sam pointed to the entrance to Sandor's office. I slipped my hand into Sam's and held on, willing us both the sanity we needed to move forward, deeper into the melancholy gloom.

I wondered where everyone was. How did they know not to come into work? Their apartments hadn't blown up and their cell phones hadn't been melted by an ice demon.

Dialed Janey on my new gas-station-special prepaid

mobile. Amazingly, after a series of pops and clicks (lousy reception at the Swan), the line connected.

"Yeah?"

"Hey, it's me," I said. Formal introductions were unnecessary between us, even if she didn't recognize the number.

"Mmm hmm," she said. "Where you been, girl?"

"I'm at the Swan now." I almost didn't tell her. The silence of her response suggested my hesitation was justified.

"Girl, that place has some bad *juju* going on," Janey said, her lazy drawl now tightly clipped in what felt like fear. *Mmm, delicious.* A voice, not my own, was muttering in my ear. Oh, this just kept getting better.

"What happened here? Where's Sandor?" My voice rose.

"Gone," she said. "He met some guy in the back corner—you know, the one with all that red velvet and the privacy spell. There was this blue fog, and a screech, then this wailing like nothing you'd ever heard before. Well," she amended, "I ain't never. The supes neither—it was like they couldn't even hear it. Didn't so much as lift a snout to check things out."

"And then what?" I turned back to Sam, who was now a puff of empty space. *Shit.*

"Sandor wasn't there no more," Janey replied. "Then, next morning, we all get this weird recording saying don't come into work for a few days. Sounds like Boss Man. Something about fumigating the place." She stopped, realizing what she'd said.

I turned around, slowly, and squinted my eyes. Thanks to Claude's scratch, I could now see in the dark almost as well as I could see in the light. Too bad I would rather *not* be seeing what I was currently looking at.

"Know of any cockroaches or mice stupid enough to set tentacle or whisker in the Swan, considering what we put into our drinks?" A rhetorical question.

Sandor's face was protruding from the wall, covered in a sheen of frost so opaque it could have just as easily been plastic, scratched and scored and even chipped in spots around the edges. Eyes wide, all three of them, but the one at the very top was still twitching. Was that even possible? What exactly was the physiology of Sandor's species—could a single eye operate independently of the whole, or was it just a post-mortem spasm?

"Yeah, I'll let you know if I find anything out." I said the words, knowing they were a lie. Kind of like Janey and I agreeing to stay in touch, knowing that we probably would not.

Okay. I was going to go with twitching eye meant Sandor was still alive. So, rescue mission versus body retrieval mission. Check.

But there was no sign of Sam or of the promised backup team. Just me, a frozen bar owner, and whatever put him in that ice-olated state. Ha ha.

Then I felt it. A shadow. Behind me.

Deep, indigo purple. Beside me.

Behind me.

I reached out and grabbed a handful of the purple-lit gloom. It whispered in my ear. "Dana, let me go."

A voice I knew from the dark. Blindfolds and bindings and cravings with complications. *Jon.* Then I opened my mouth and caught the scent of another shifter, not Sam, but *other.*

"Claude," I said tonelessly.

"Princess," he replied, mocking. He may as well have been saying *Bitch-Goddess-who-I-hope-dies-for-what-she-did-to-me.*

"Ass," I muttered.

Jon narrowed his eyes at me in warning. Those beautiful, almond-shaped, green-blue eyes that made places deep within me ache with loss, emptiness. *Shit.* I blinked and looked away.

"What are you guys doing here?" Seemed the obvious question. Jon's shrugged response and Claude's smirk were not exactly what I'd call an answer. "No, seriously. Did Anshell call you in?"

"Do you know what happened?" Apparently it was change the subject day in Jon's world.

"He froze," I said, eyeing my boss statue. Forcing down the bile that threatened to spew every time I looked at Sandor's immobile form. "Do you think he's still alive?"

"Nope," said Claude, earning himself one of Jon's pointed looks this time.

"I don't smell much other than frost demon," Jon said. "I don't feed on Sandor's species, though, so I might not be able to pick up on his lifeblood as strongly as I do yours or Claude's—someone who could nourish me." A faint eye-flick to indicate that Jon's ironic phrasing was intentional. I ignored the barb. Why couldn't life be simple?

There were questions I needed to ask, sounds I'd suddenly forgotten how to form. I shook my head to clear it and looked over my shoulder for Sam. Still not there. And so I found the needed words.

"Jon," I said, "where is Sam?"

Jon flinched.

Claude smirked.

Tension made the space between my shoulder blades twitch. Sexual and emotional ambivalence aside, I was responsible for keeping an eye on my recon partner—and so far, I was not doing a great job. On all fronts.

I took a step forward and Jon stepped between me and his supposed ex. His hand on my shoulder. I opened my mouth to speak, to say I don't know what.

"Dana, I'm fine." Sam's deep baritone came from behind me. I was acutely aware of my proximity to two of my lovers. Could almost smell the spike in testosterone as they both realized the same thing.

A growl from my left brought my attention back to the situation at hand. Again, I wondered—what the hell was this firecracker of unexploded jealous Claude potential doing here? Jon had sworn they were finished, but here they both were—together? I shoved those feelings down deep as I turned around to Sam. Took a deep breath; held it a moment before letting it out. He looked fine.

Okay. I shook my head to clear it. We had a Sandor to defrost.

The last time we needed to defrost someone, we had a dragon to help us out. But Celandra was nowhere to be found—even if I knew where to look in the first place—so we had to come up with plan B. Which in this case, we decided, would involve putting the industrial oven in the kitchen on the highest setting with the handle pulled all the way open so that the heat blasted at Sandor. An oversized exhaust fan angled just *so* made sure the air flow went where we needed it to go.

Turns out melting by open oven is a slow and messy

process. I made a mental note to thank Sandor for putting in such a good drainage system.

Wait.

If we were pouring all the demon ice down the drain, weren't we destroying any evidence we might have of who had created the prison in the first place?

Claude was pacing back and forth alongside the blue-tinged Sandor statue. Every so often he would lean forward and touch his nose to the edge of the dripping puddle before the seeping liquid could descend into the murky depths of the drain. Once or twice I caught him with his tongue out and the sides of his mouth pulled back into a grimace as if tasting the air itself. Maybe he was.

Hmm. Maybe if I was a cat, I could do that as well. I pulled my own lips back into a tentative grimace, inhaling through the sides of my forced smile. A bit of drool as I sucked back, but not hard enough. Yuck. Something familiar? Claude noticed what I was doing and shook his head, a microcosm of a smile twitching at his mouth.

"Give it up," he said. "You will never be the cat you want to be. You are nothing but a bastard blood. A plaything to be toyed with and then tossed aside. I'm pack and you are this week's charity case. You think either of these fine men care about you beyond a quick fuck? You think you have a future with them?" Claude shook his head, an evil glint to his eyes, and licked his lips. "You don't. *I* do. I give my man all the blood he needs. *Wants*. That's how I know, long term, you do not matter. And I will be here, waiting, when you are no more." He rolled the *rrrr* on his tongue, very French, almost a purr of pleasure.

Ass.

Jon and Sam were out of earshot, unfortunately for me. They were over in the corner, speaking in tones so low that even with my newly enhanced hearing I couldn't make out what they were saying. Didn't look like they were planning to fight each other to the death though, so I couldn't complain. Much.

I shifted my attention back to the glacial heat wave progress, if only to tune out Claude's words and the implication behind them. Oh sure, he had self-interest written all over him; I knew which way he swung and where he hoped to lay his head tonight—or should I say between whose thighs. The fact that I knew exactly how those thighs tasted was the problem.

For both of us.

I sighed heavily, the weight of our complications hanging between myself and the jealous cat. But Claude was the maker of his current confines. He'd come here with Jon—and I still hadn't gotten a straight answer on the *why* or *how* of it. Either way, it wasn't my fault that Jon was not monogamous when it came to partners; it *was* Claude's responsibility to accept that he continued to hang around a situation that made him miserable. You know what they say—if you can't take the heat and all that.

Claude kept laying the blame directly at my feet. As though, if I wasn't a factor, he would become the focus of all of Jon's attentions. Not bloody likely. Pun intended.

"You don't seriously think that if I wasn't here, you'd have Jon all to yourself, do you?" So very tired. "You wouldn't because that's not who he is. You can't keep torturing yourself—and anyone else who comes on the scene to steal a piece of Jon's attention. It's not going to happen. He's not that guy."

Claude stared at me a moment, venom in his half-lidded gaze, before he spun on the balls of his feet to stalk out the side door. Fine by me.

MY MIND WAS churning as I went to find out how the defrost-my-boss project was going. First me, then Sam, then Sandor. There had to be a connection.

Sam was linked to both the Swan and to me the night of the Feed, either because he was helping me—or, given what Claude had said, possibly because Goth Boy had at one point been pack. Pack was the connection between Sam and Anshell. Anshell and Sandor knew each other, and Sandor was the Swan. The Feed was linked to the Swan by geography; it had also tied Sam's fate and mine together. Or the Swan and all of us to whatever summoning Sam and I had interrupted.

What if we hadn't crashed the party early enough?

Worse—what if the common denominator in all this was me?

TWENTY-NINE

IT TOOK THE better part of the next few hours to fully defrost Sandor, and even then the tips of his claws and the upper bits of his several ears were still tinged an unhealthy shade of blue. I hovered, pacing back and forth, as the massive chunk of ice dripped down the drain.

Jun hadn't been able to ascertain from taste or smell who had been behind the creation of the Sandor Popsicle. Score one for the other team. But it seemed, by the twitching of his left nostril and the fact that we might have just heard him grunt, my friend and boss might actually be alive. So maybe the score was evening out a bit for us as well.

"What the frakking corpse-hole of a scaling drakking baby's arse happened?" Sandor spit out the words with the last of the spewed frost demon liquid. In fairness, the liquid made it sound more like "*Oot desh frasshken cofs-hll eff eh sshklig drkeg bbsharsh hippned?*" But his meaning was clear.

"You tell us," I said.

Sandor let out another string of curses. I was pretty sure some of them were in another language. Finally he paused for breath and I got in his face, eye to eyes. I even grasped his double chin with part of one hand and flicked its underside with an overly long index fingernail. That got his attention and earned me a growl of my own until Sandor realized who he was directing it at and sent it off under cover of a fake cough.

"So, *nu*? Well?" Every so often I got my Yiddish on. Especially since politeness and patience had their limits and I was stretched past the edges of mine for both. "What happened to you? More to the point, *who* happened to you?"

"Same thing that's about to happen to you, bitch," said Claude. Seconds slowing and stretching. Frost all around me, suddenly, my nose hairs sticking together as the air closed in. Ice like bullet-proof glass. A glacial see-through barrier between me and those who would see me safe. Then, closer: the crack of a gunshot, a flare of blue light eclipsed by a searing pain in my shoulder.

And everything went black. Again.

HEAVY BREATHING, NOT FAR from my ear. It would be great to stop waking up like this.

The light shone down through the bars of the small window above my head, illuminating my cellmate, a.k.a. Heavy Breather Guy. A man, reedy and dressed in black, lay on his back on a cot against the far wall.

"I recognize you," I said.

"How nice for you," Joseph Morgenlark replied.

I rolled my head slightly to the left, then the right, making note of the sore spot on the back of my skull, the throbbing pain that was my shoulder blade. Had Claude shot me *and* whacked me on the back of the head? *And* gotten Frost Demon help? Talk about overkill.

Then again, he'd somehow managed to do it from right inside the Swan Song. A handful of feet from everyone else. Either the Swan's security system wasn't as good as we'd thought, or whoever had breached it was stronger.

I looked around the cell one more time. It didn't look familiar.

"So, any idea what we're doing here? Or at least what I'm doing here?"

"You must have really pissed someone off," Morgenlark said. I couldn't read him from the distance of the room and the gloom of the shadows, but I got the feeling his eyes were closed.

"I piss off people for dinner," I replied. "Any idea whose skin in particular I managed to crawl under this time?"

He seemed to think about that a moment. "If I had to guess," he said, "I would go with someone who either hates the Moon with Seven Faces pack or has some connection with Ezra Gerbrecht."

My breath caught at the name.

"Of course," Morgenlark continued, "it may have nothing to do with any of that. Could be a grudge match."

"Why? Because we rescued you from bleeding out?"

A shrug from my cell mate. I believed in many things, but coincidence wasn't one of them.

"How do you know Ezra?" A sideways approach. I still couldn't believe I was saying those words to a person who hadn't been part of the old team. A team that would be just as likely to turn me into an electrode-protruding test-tube-spurting science experiment as they would to welcome me back into the fold. If they knew.

They couldn't know.

"He's the asshole who helped out at the pack house," said Morgenlark.

I chuffed my surprise.

"How did you think I got out of there?" He gave a small laugh. "Anshell and Sam and the rest of them, they weren't about to let me go so easily. I made a deal with the..." Morgenlark was about to say devil, I just knew it, "with Ezra," he finished lamely.

The room tilted precariously and I felt like upchucking the contents of my last meal. Cereal and milk? How long had it been? Based on the timing, counting back the days, there was no way Ezra could have personally helped out Joseph Morgenlark in his escape from Anshell's. Right? I saw his head severed from his body. Right? At least twelve to twenty-four hours before he was miraculously present for Goth Boy's escape.

It couldn't be.

"How, exactly, did Ezra help you out?" I tried not to let this relative stranger know just how much I needed the answer. But if Ezra was alive, I had to know.

Clicking, clacking. A red light tracking in the dark. Suddenly, I realized that all of this was being recorded via camera in the far corner.

"He reached out a hand and showed me the way," said Morgenlark, without a trace of irony.

"Seriously?" I echoed my last thought out loud, the words escaping tone intact before I had a chance to properly filter them. "Ezra literally reached down and extended a hand to you and poof, you were free?"

"Pretty much," Goth Boy replied. "But he used his proxy. Big blue demon. You're in tight with Ezra—maybe you've heard of him. Gus Lazzuri?"

My turn to swear, long and hard and in several languages both from this dimension and beyond. Granted, this would put Lazzuri's help of the enemy to just before he was caught, captured and made a deal with us. Still. It was all a little too convenient for my taste.

Speaking of, my mouth tasted like gritted sand. The only water I saw came from a stainless-steel dog bowl on the floor. Didn't mean I had to bend down and slurp it up, right?

"Want some?" I held out the bowl to Morgenlark. After all, it wasn't me he'd sold out. Not yet anyway.

Goth Boy glanced over at the bowl I held out and mutely shook his head.

"You probably shouldn't have from that," he commented. "I have a feeling they've spiked it with something."

I growled frustration and put the bowl back. Felt around in my pockets and found a hard candy only somewhat covered in lint. I picked off what I could and popped it into my mouth. I offered to share the next semi-wrapped candy I found with Morgenlark, but he graciously declined.

"I think you're going to need that more than me," he said.

"How do you figure?"

"It's a full moon," he replied. "You're new. How good are you at controlling your shifts?"

I snorted. "What shifts?"

But I caught myself before I shared last night's abortive—and rather bloody—debacle. Some things you wanted to keep private just between you and your nearest and dearest hundred or so pack members.

Morgenlark caught none of my inner dialogue, waiting patiently for me to go on. When I didn't immediately fill the pregnant pause in our conversation, he gave me a verbal nudge.

"Your shifts?"

Ever aware of being on closed-circuit television, I thought for another moment about how to respond. Admit to being a shifter, and I could become either a pawn or a science experiment gone wrong in the power struggle going on between factions unknown but clearly having something to do with Ezra. Deny being a shifter, and perhaps I would be seen as expendable—but maybe less of a threat. Plan C? There had to be a plan C.

"So, if you're so cozy with Ezra," I asked, trying to poke a rise out of Morgenlark instead, "how did you end up here locked up in the same cell as me?"

Yep, when in doubt, defer and deflect.

If he caught my move, he didn't let on.

"I'm bait," he replied simply.

"For who?"

No reply. Only the whirring of the video camera as it swung back and forth, recording our entire conversation for posterity or hilarity or, really, who the hell knew.

THE MOON ROSE higher in the sky. Morgenlark had closed his eyes again and, based on the shallowness of his breathing, seemed to have fallen asleep. Apparently shifting wasn't much of either a fear or a need for him.

I had lots of time to wonder why as boredom and fear warred for my attention. Me being identified as a supe of any kind could make me a target; the Agency had no love for the non-norm humans. Unless the Agency or its agents weren't behind this. Hell, with the exception of the video camera's blinking red eye and the presence of a bowl of water which may or may not have been laced with substances, I had no actual empirical proof that there was *anyone* else out there.

I twitched with adrenaline that seemed to build with each passing moment I remained a caged animal.

I started pacing. Back and forth. I counted seven strides from the bars to the window; six from where I'd been to where Morgenlark lay, muttering softly now in his sleep. Couldn't make out anything useful from his mumblings. Pity, that. I suspected if I lay on my back and started walking up the wall I'd have about another seven strides to the cinderblock ceiling that rained down flecks of peeling *something* onto us every so often. Like something even heavier was pacing atop our box, or maybe a giant stone toddler having a hop, skip and a jump above our heads.

Then again, maybe I was just going crazy.

My eyes tracked the moon as I paced, measuring out the dimensions of our enclosure again and again. In case I'd missed something. In case my count was off. Tried not to recognize the pattern in my bipedal hamster wheel, the similarity to how all those big cats in the zoo got after a while, stalking back and forth.

Captivity was not my friend.

My upper lip prickled. I felt what had to be phantom whiskers, twitching in the light of the moon which was now a smidge away from being full-on high noon in the middle of the otherwise dark sky.

I reached up to touch my lip and came away with fingers pricked by bristles, sharp enough to draw a single drop of blood. Redness reflected in the eyes of another. I realized, with a start that had my heart pounding in my throat, that Morgenlark had stopped snoring and was tracking me with those unearthly eyes.

His nose and jaw had elongated slightly, and his ears had furry tufts on top. His whiskers were fully in. From what I could tell, his hands were still just that but maybe a bit longer, a bit hairier. But it was his pink tongue, hanging out as if to scent the wind between perfectly formed fangs, that was really freaking me out. I knew I should sit tight, not move, not draw any more attention to myself; I did *not* want to be locked in this room with a predatory cat for whom I could suddenly become a midnight snack.

But I couldn't stop myself.

Morgenlark opened his impossibly wide mouth into a yawn, licked his now darkened and thinning lips.

"Hey," Goth Boy said. "I never thanked you for the other night."

Given the change in his face, I was surprised I could understand him at all. I reached up to touch my ears to check that they hadn't morphed into pointed tufts. Still human.

"Thanked me for what?"

"You know," he replied. "When you saved my sorry ass from turning into a vampire barbecue. How'd you do that anyway?"

I shrugged. It all kept coming back to that night.

The question was why.

"So tell me," I said, picking at nonexistent dirt beneath my fingernails. Because I had Morgenlark when Anshell and Sam had lost him. "How did you end up at the wrong end of the straw of that ritualistic milkshake anyway?"

"Fucked if I know," Morgenlark muttered through

a face that was looking more like a tiger and less like a pussycat with every passing minute. "I remember picking a fight with Anshell over my clan membership. All the rules and responsibilities were pissing me off. Except now I have no idea why I felt that way."

"Hmm," I said, as much to make him feel as though he'd been heard as it was a reflection of my, well, reflection on the situation. "What happened next?"

"I remember this gorgeous demon hitting on me—fuck, she was hot; I couldn't wait to get in her pants. Sorry," he muttered, an afterthought as he realized there was another female in the room who might get pissed at his directness.

"No worries," I replied, shrugging it off. I had a sneaking suspicion about the identity of that "hot" demon, and I gulped back a recollected moment of my own. "Then what?"

"We were making out in that hallway, you know—the one that says 'employees only'? That one."

"Employees only" indeed.

"One hand was up her shirt, the other one down her pants. I'm thinking, shit, I'm going to get *sooo* lucky tonight," Morgenlark said. "Then, blank. Nothing. I come to feeling like I'm being sucked. For a moment I think I'm getting the blow job of my life. Except I'm not." He shuddered.

"You were chained and being slurped on by bloodsuckers," I said, to save him from going there himself.

"Yeah," he grunted, reddening slightly. "Yeah."

Lightbulb moment.

"It's okay, you know," I commented. "They had you in their thrall. You must know about the power of the bite. It's not your fault you got turned on."

Morgenlark made a sound that was a cross between a chirp and a growl. I felt for him, I really did. And I was very *very* fortunate that Jon wasn't the kind of guy to turn my head around like that. At least I hoped so.

Plus, there was my tattoo and the vaccine and… crap. Clearly all of which had been so effective when that idiot Claude had scratched me.

It's not paranoia if people are actually out to get you, right?

"So, how does Ezra fit into all of this?" It was the question at the crux of the lunacy that seemed to have become my life.

"He's the guy sitting upstairs, probably enjoying his brandy and a cigar, laughing his ass off at the show we're putting on for him down here." Morgenlark's words ended with a sigh. "You're supposed to shift so he can catch it on tape, prove that you are what you pretend you are not. But I guess he's got it wrong, eh?"

"How's that?"

"If you were a shifter, you would have turned by now," he replied. "Look at me. I've been what I am since I turned thirteen and even I can't keep it together at high moon time. But that's okay. Maybe he'll stick with me and leave you alone after this. I mean, if you're not a shifter, then you can go."

I didn't want to burst his idealistic bubble. I didn't know why I was suddenly so important to everyone, but no way Ezra was going to let me go regardless of which side of the fence my genetic pattern fell on. I shook free some more white powder that had fallen down from above us, dusting the floor with a dandruff not my own. What the hell was going on up there anyway?

Every few seconds there would be a thud, then a puff of ceiling falling. I tried to ignore it. Just as I tried to ignore the tug of fur beneath my skin, straining to erupt for real.

Morgenlark cleared his throat, indicating the camera with his chin. "Isn't the moon beautiful? You can get such a clear view of it," he said, moving from the cot to the curtainless bars-over-glass window. He made a show of running his tongue over his teeth and up, even farther, until he was licking his nose with a darting pink tongue.

Oh.

I sunk back into the shadows, the gloom just beyond what the camera could capture, and touched my face again. Or at least what was left of it. I felt like I needed a shave, like everything was covered with a fine baby fuzz of fur that hadn't been there before. *Crap.*

Morgenlark had noticed and was trying to distract our captors from my unintentional changes. But defer and deflect would only work for so long, after which point I would have to come out of the proverbial cat litter box and greet the world—with whiskers and pointy ears.

THIRTY

I REALIZED WE were no longer alone.

"Hi, Dana."

Ezra's voice was more gravelly than I remembered it. And less dead.

"Ezra," I replied. "You're looking well." I paused, choosing my words carefully. Visualizing puffy clouds drifting across a robin's-egg-blue horizon; anxiety would only trigger another shift. "Better than expected. Weren't you a head separated from a body in a puddle of cooling blood the last time we saw each other?"

Ezra inclined his head slightly as though listening to words, instructions, from a frequency I wasn't tuned into. Then he focused back in on me, pushing sincerity behind those brilliant blue eyes.

"That wasn't me," he replied simply.

"If you say so," I said, shrugging. We both knew it had been him. But I was starting to wonder if maybe, just maybe, there was more than one version of the Ezra I knew.

Sometimes reality was more surreal than fiction.

Morgenlark cleared his throat to get our attention.

"So can I go now?" The moonlight was glinting off the reds in his fur. "I did what you asked," Morgenlark continued. "Tempted her into the shift and you can see how well that worked. But the moon is up now and it's time for me to be out and about."

Ezra nodded, once, and reached out to open the door. He had the keys in one hand and a cattle prod in the other. As the keys inched their way towards the door, the prod was angled in my direction in case I got any bright ideas. Like whacking Ezra over the head with the prod and making a run for it. But what would Morgenlark do if I did that? Was he a traitor or was he an ally?

I realized I couldn't count on the were-tiger's allegiances. Instead, I tracked his movements towards the door of the cell as it opened. He crossed the threshold as Ezra held out the prod in brandishing readiness to use it. On me. I watched and counted, ticking off the seconds. Morgenlark cleared the pathway with a swish of tail that distracted Ezra's attention for just a moment, an eye-blink max. It was all I needed to leap forward, smash down the prod with the palm of my left hand and thrust down and away.

Ezra, caught off-balance, stumbled back and reached out to the wall behind him. I grabbed the handle of the prod and used my foot to sweep his feet out from under him. Ezra's head snapped back and banged on the cinderblock wall with a satisfying *thunk*. Morgenlark turned to me and winked before vanishing out the double-plated glass and metal doors at the end of the hallway.

So. No more help from Gothy Tiger Guy, but no hindrance either. Okay. Good to know.

I shoved Ezra with a strength and speed I didn't realize I had, remembering at the last possible second to snag his keys from his white lab coat before slamming the door shut. His watery eyes peered back now from the other side of the cell bars, slightly unfocused but trained on me.

"Dana?" Ezra's voice was weaker and querulous. "What are you doing here?"

I stared.

"Uh, you tell me," I replied. "Isn't this your party?"

"What party? What am I doing in here?" Gerbrecht's confusion was palpable as his eyes darted up and around the confines of his current space. What I couldn't tell was whether or not it was real. "Dana, what's going on?"

I took a breath and held it a moment before releasing to the count of five. Although the pressure had lifted; with Ezra behind bars, my urge to spontaneously shift had weakened. Opened my mouth, thought better of it, then repeated my breathing exercise one more time before trying again.

"Ezra, when is the last time you remember seeing me?"

Ezra's eyes tracked up and around as though trying to sequence the scattered images scrawled on the uneven walls of his mind into some kind of logical pattern.

"Did you come to visit me at my office earlier this week?" His voice, so hopeful, I almost believed him. Wanted to believe him.

"You know I did," I replied. "What else do you remember?"

"I remember getting called away by my assistant. And...you were gone when I got back? Or did you have to go to work?" Ezra rubbed his eyes and I noticed that his knuckles were chapped red and lined with tiny white-scaled diamond patterns, wizened and wrinkled beyond his sixty-odd years. As though he was aging before my eyes. But how was that possible?

It wasn't, I reminded myself. And yet the evidence was there, sitting on the floor not ten feet away.

How do you reconcile the person you trusted for so many years with the person who was willing to cause you pain and suffering an eye-blink later?

You don't, I realized. All you can do is deal with what you have in front of you.

I crouched, rocking back on my heels as I watched Ezra try to sort through his thoughts. I leaned back against the wall and waited for some kind of sign that would cause any of this to make sense. But there was nothing. No lightbulb, no flashing neon sign pointing to the next step.

Just a big chunk of ceiling that came down with a crash a few inches from Ezra's head, encircling him with a kind of luminescent halo I knew damned well he no longer deserved, if he ever had. A head ducked down and looked around, familiar and flaked with plaster.

"Dana?"

"Over here, Sam," I called, waving my hand to get his attention.

"What are you doing there?" Sam peered down at the cell, then at the enclosure beyond where I sat.

"Getting ready to interrogate the prisoner," I replied. "What are you doing here?"

"Rescuing you?" Sam no longer sounded so sure of himself. "Or maybe," he said, glancing over at Ezra, "given the circumstances, you'd prefer me to help with the interrogation?"

I heard the clacking of scrabbling nails circling

around above; scented shadows reeking of recently oiled metal. Gargantuan mice with swords? Maybe I was starting to lose it.

"You called in reinforcements, eh?" I forced nonchalance to dance over the faint smile on my lips.

"Uh, yeah," he replied. The sound of an explosion had him looking up and over his shoulder. "Hang on," Sam said, pulling his head back up. "Let me check on something here."

Another crash, then silence. I watched Ezra through the bars of the cell as he watched me, trusting that my backup team could take care of themselves.

"Ezra," I said. "What's really going on here?"

"You wouldn't believe me if I told you," he said. Awareness and focus seemed to flit back and forth across his features like wisps of taffy clouds stretched thin and drifting across a clear blue sky. His face shifted as well, planes and shadows forming and reforming in waves. Could be the passing light from the moon playing tricks. Could be.

"Why don't you try me," I said. "Let's keep it simple, start with the basics. Are you actually Ezra Gerbrecht?"

His smile was faint, hovering on lips whose very movements, whether upwards in approval or downwards in disappointment, had impacted me so strongly for so very long. So very long ago.

"I both am and am not Ezra," he said. "I am he that was and is but will be unlike that which came before."

"Okay, nice riddles, sensei master," I said when he didn't elaborate. "Let's try this again. Am I currently speaking with Ezra Gerbrecht, the man who recruited me out of university?"

"Yes and no," he said. "Ezra is still a part of me, and yet not. We are one but also many. We remember you, the gosling that became the swan, the one we watched and waited for. Who left us. Who is here before us once more at the time and place of the key alignments in the sky and here on the ground."

Ezra stopped, like a robotic recording that had run its preset message and now had fulfilled its duties. He didn't close his eyes, exactly, but he did do a single long blink. It was unnerving.

Focus, Dana.

"What does Alina, or Cybele, or whatever her name is, want?"

"Alina has a portal issue," Ezra replied. Oh hello, return of the cryptic. "She needs one opened, and thinks you can help with that."

"How?" But Ezra was done with the sharing if not the caring on that subject, his lips pressed together and his eyes wandering.

"Why do you care about the Moon with Seven Faces pack?" I tried a different line of questioning. Since I had him here and all.

"They are the key," Ezra replied, zoning back in on me.

"To...?"

Ezra refused to elaborate, shaking his head and biting ever so gently on his lower lip as though needing that tang of blood to ballast his resolve. I decided to switch up the path of my questions.

"Tell me about the Moon with Seven Faces pack," I said. "I hardly know anything about them. Help me out here." I mentally crossed my fingers and kept going. "What's the deal there? Can I trust them?"

Ezra gave a laugh; short and sharp.

"Trust is something we should never give away lightly," he said, an abrupt shift back to the Ezra I recognized. "You must *kukn mit di aoygn.* Look with the eyes. Everyone has an agenda, everyone has something they want to achieve. If you're a key player in someone else's scenario, then you can never fully trust them—they will always put their own priorities above yours when the ultimate goal is on the line."

"So you're saying I *shouldn't* trust them?" Shaking my head at myself; I cared what Ezra thought why exactly?

"Use your own judgment, Dana," Ezra said, eyes closing in apparent weariness. "You don't need me to tell you what to do."

My mouth gaped open. That voice…

"Dad?"

Ezra quirked his head at me, tilted to the side. With an impish grin that lifted the corners of his mouth up and over, his skin peeled back like a well-greased zipper. All that remained of Ezra was a pile of skin and a ball of green sparkling dust which came together and then exploded outwards, shooting streaks of glitter that quickly vanished into nothingness.

SAM FOUND ME like that, sitting on the floor, staring into the space which had been Ezra a couple of minutes earlier. This time he'd come down the corridor leading to the outside. He looked through the bars at what wasn't there, then down at me, assessing.

"Dana?"

"Mmph." About all I could get out. I knew I should

be surprised that Sam was there, and I was, but I was running low on shock and awe at this point.

Sam surreptitiously looked me over, nostrils flaring, checking for any signs of blood or other damage. Finding none, he lowered himself on his haunches and then eased back to sit beside me against the wall.

"What are we looking at here?" Sam nudged me with his shoulder, trying to snap me out of whatever reverie I was in.

"Ezra," I said.

Sam looked pointedly at the empty cell in front of us, then at me.

"What about Ezra, Dana? Where is he?"

"He's gone," I managed to choke out. "Dust."

"Hmm?" Sam looked at me, nonplussed.

"Ezra turned into dust and vanished. Or he took off his skin. Or..." I zoned back in again as I noticed the camera on the wall once more tracking us back and forth and back and forth again. "Shit," I muttered, then touched Sam on the knee and indicated the video camera's red eye on the far wall. I felt him jump, startled, before making a big show about helping me stand up.

"We should probably take a look around in there," he commented. "Do you happen to have a way in?"

I handed him the keys. The door swung open and Sam strolled in, looking up and around and away from the camera until he was right beside it and out of view. *Crack.* Camera out and in his hands. No more remote spying on us; at least not using that particular methodology.

"Well, that was easy," I said. But I was forgetting something. Oh yeah. "Wait. How did you find me?"

"Jon," he said. *Huh?*

"I'll fill you in on the way."

"So Claude shot me with some kind of tranq gun," I said, rubbing my shoulder. "Then he said some kind of incantation. Claude *knew* an incantation to mutter?"

Sam nodded.

"And it threw up a wall of ice."

"Yeah," he said. "Ice pellets everywhere. We could see you, but we couldn't get to you. And then you were gone."

I digested that.

"And how did I go from gone to found?"

"Jon," Sam said. "He picked a side. *Yours*. He hunted down Claude and got answers."

I pressed for more details, but Sam got vague on me. Who did what to whom, who cleaned up afterwards, where Jon was now. Guess share time was over.

That Jon and Claude were definitively no longer together was a developmental factoid not lost on me. Fun times to be sorted out at a later date. Here's hoping it was a timeline of my choosing.

The moon was still up and the night only into its early adolescence when we arrived back at the lakeside house in Cherry Beach, flanked by a white cube van, an orange VW van and a single black Suburban. Subtle.

My partially shifted features had reverted to human on the ride over. So much for the group impact effect on my ability to fully shift into something other than what I was currently.

Sam, on the other hand, suffered from no such limitations. Once safely deposited at a safe house on the shores of Cherry Beach with a full reconnoitering of the layout and provisions (blanket—*check*; hot chocolate—*check check*), I was left to my own puttering with a quick peck on the cheek. Apparently still not quite solid, Sam and I. Too bad.

I wrapped myself in a worn duvet covered in bold but faded red orchids, pulled on some warm fuzzy socks and took my steaming mug of cocoa to the second-floor veranda to look up, leaning over the solid wood railing.

Full moon. Only one more night until the climax of the cycle. Until the lunar power was at its strongest, and one of us would prevail.

THIRTY-ONE

I LEANED MY elbows over the railing, watching the tiny waves as they nibbled, toothless slurps, against the edged shelf of ice that made up the shoreline. In the moonlight the feathered expanse of gulls, ducks and swans flanked the snowy embankment like a pebbled path of bobbing stones.

Strange that no one noticed this beautiful house, as big as any Rosedale Valley mansion, overlooking such a prime Cherry Beach piece of Lake Ontario. Sam had tried to explain to me about the glamour surrounding the place—how anyone who didn't know it existed saw a ramshackle, abandoned old lifeguard hut. But he got a bit tongue-tied in the middle. Part of the effects of the spell, I guess.

The pack had left me alone in this house on the water while they went out and about to frolic in the magic of the night. Nobody was expecting me to shift again at this point. At least not tonight.

"Money for a crazy old lady?"

It took me a moment to place the voice.

"Hi, Celandra," I said.

She was below and in front of me, white hair framing her face. Glowing.

One two three, one *two* three. Celandra's feet beat out a rhythm, keeping time with the slapping of the waves. On the up beat, she spread her hands palms-up in supplication; on the down beat she would bring both back in again to her chest with a clap.

"How is Sandor?"

Celandra had a funny way of knowing things. Everyone else had shuffled their feet and cleared their throats and looked away when I asked about him. Likewise for Claude, now that I thought about it. Not that I cared what happened to that bastard at this point.

Celandra slowed her dance slightly, bobbing her head to a tune only she could hear. Then: "Your friends have him," she replied. "He himself is safe for now. But your friends do not trust him." Celandra started singing to herself.

"*Sandor is as Sandor does*

/ With cats around he's all abuzz

/ One claw out, the other back

/ Prepare yourself for the next attack."

This time, the clapping of her hands cracked through the air like gunshots. Snow spun and glittered, and for a moment I thought she had magicked herself away in a puff of icy faery dust.

But no. Celandra had simply seized that moment to escape from the conversation altogether in order to join the growling, howling felines as they played and pounced through the trees nearby. I sighed, longing to follow. It looked like fun, and I wouldn't have said no to a bit of company after my last few hours.

Instead I turned around and went back inside to wait for dawn.

I WAS TOO restless to sleep. Two mugs of cocoa, half a canister of whipped cream, untold handfuls of marshmallows and a hell of a sugar rush later, I was still wandering around the urban chalet listening to the chirping growling whistling sounds of the wind. Alone.

Knock knock knock.

The banging on the door had me jumping almost out of my skin. A healthy dose of self-preservation had me hovering, slinking into shadows. Who knew I was here?

There was no good answer. My heart hammered a staccato *thud thud thwackity thud* in response to whoever or whatever was waiting.

The door handle rattled, and the knocking resumed. There were prickles of sweat on my upper lip. I was back there again. Heart pounding. I couldn't breathe. No, I had to breathe. This was now, not then. And this door was solid. Wasn't it? The pack wouldn't have gone to the trouble of rescuing me only to leave me vulnerable to attack while they went all shift-happy. Right?

"Dana, open the door."

I knew that voice. Streaked to the door and flung it open so fast I was surprised there was no trail of fire in the wake of my path. I leapt into his arms, my legs wrapped around his waist as Jon nuzzled into the crevice between my neck and my jaw, stroking my back and murmuring soft nothings. Holding me. Kissing the top of my head. "Come in," I whispered. Kicking the door shut behind him, releasing one hand to fasten all the locks back in place.

His mouth found mine. I felt the tips of his fangs against my bottom lips, slight pressure, not enough to break skin. I'd had enough of danger for a while. Hadn't I?

But. *Wait.* There were questions. I couldn't think; too close, Jon's scent pushing out the whys and hows and rational explanations needed. Because timing. Because how. Because Claude.

My hand firm against his chest as I pushed away. *Space.* Things needing to be said, understood, explained. My feet touching the floor again even as every other part of me wanted more.

"What is it?" Jon didn't resist, but he didn't back up either. Two steps to the opposite side of the entranceway, where he leaned up against the exposed red and orange brick of the wall. I mirrored his motions and did the same. Trying to avoid his eyes. Just in case.

"How'd you know I'd be here?" A reasonable question to start.

"It's a full moon," Jon replied. "Where else would you be?"

I could think of any number of other places I'd been on any number of other full moon nights that didn't involve the pack house at Cherry Beach.

"And the Swan? When we found Sandor? How did you know to come there? And what were you doing with Claude?"

"What's with all the questions?" Jon tried to catch my eye even as I avoided his, looking at that spot just past his shoulder. Just in case.

"Things change," I said.

"Some things can't," Jon said, shrugging. "Either you trust me or you don't."

"You could trust *me* enough to share." I tried to keep the bitterness from digging in its thorny claws.

"Can't," he said again. This time there was a sigh. "Not my secret to share." Jon took one step towards me, lifted my hand. Gentle. And kissed the tips of each finger. *Electricity.* I stopped thinking altogether for a moment. No. Wait. I was forgetting something, something important.

"Claude?" Yeah. That was it.

"Pack justice." Cryptic. Jon's eyes went distant before returning to my face. Kissing my palm, then the inside of my wrist. "It's up to them."

Jon wasn't giving me a straight answer, not tonight. His lips trailed higher, to the inside of my arm, the bend of my elbow where the skin was softest. I tried to concentrate. To remember why answers were important. Why Jon wasn't a good idea. But he was close, then closer still, and my back was up against the wall. My legs winding around him with barely a thought. Reflex action. I couldn't let go even if I wanted to. Did I want to? *Dana.* My name, his hands; on the back of my head, in my hair, gripping my arms.

One arm snaked up, inside my shirt, cool against the fuzzy warmth of the lumberjack plaid flannel. I returned the favor, dipping my hand down, lower. Belt buckles, jeans, none of it mattered; my hand, insistent, found that warm crevice between his cheeks and squeezed.

Jon groaned and pushed up against me with his hips. The wall didn't move; all I could do was accept the pressure, the heat building within me. Then I was frantically pulling at fastenings and fabrics and everything standing in the way of skin on skin contact.

Fire.

He slid into me with almost no warning; a slight shift of our bodies, and he lifted me up to settle down along his length. One arm wrapped around my waist, the other tangled in my hair, he pulled my head back and pressed down with his lips as he angled up and in.

Just the tip, then out again; a little bit more in and then a bit more out. Inch after less-than-agonizing inch. No jack rabbit pounding this; instead, it was slow, languorous, rising in intensity with each thrust.

Jon let go of my hair and leaned in to brush his mouth over my ear. "Put your hands on my shoulders," he said. He held me in place with his cock while his hands lifted my breasts, one in each hand, together to his mouth. And bit down.

Oh.

My.

God.

I arched as best as I could with the wall at my back, trying to choke off a scream, failing utterly.

With my nipples firmly wedged in his mouth—what, like they had somewhere else they'd rather be right now?—Jon's hands traveled south again to cup my ass. Firmly in hand, I was lifted and lowered again and again as I arched and moaned. Jon did some moaning of his own, vibrating with a sensation that traveled down into my core and had me clamping down on him, hard. Pressure built deep within me, bubbling up, sparkles of energy until we both erupted in a shower of endorphins, panting. Not quite spent.

The front door banged open behind us and I jumped. Jon made a sound, low in his throat, a cross between a grunt and a growl. I felt him, still inside me, shrinking by the second as he gently put me down onto the floor and retrieved my shirt, which fortunately hadn't fallen all that far from where we'd ended up. Eyes down, I accepted his offering and shrugged back into something a little more presentable. He did the same with his jeans. Cleared his throat.

There, standing in front of us having just come back from his shift, was Sam. With his arm around Vine Tattoo Girl's shoulders. They were both about as naked as Jon and I had been when they came in. *So.* Sam met my eyes, a cool stare that went a touch cooler as his nostrils flared and he realized what we'd been doing. As far as I could smell, though, they'd been up to pretty much the same thing. I stared back defiantly.

Anshell saved me from the unbearably awkward moment. Although I wasn't sure it had anything to do with me. His silhouette filled the doorway, the porch light covering his frame. It was a strange contradiction—the man of light who chose that intersection of time to pause, eyes sweeping the room, and clear his throat. Even he wasn't alone though, it turned out. Anshell reached one arm back and gently drew in a woman, maybe a bit older than he was, into the room. I didn't recognize her.

Well. Weren't we just a post-coital group of buddies, hanging out all together in the Big House. Not awkward at all.

Tattoo Vine Girl stepped forward, breaking her contact with Sam, and held out her hand to me.

"Anika," she said, grasping my hand and shaking it. Firm; this was no shy and retiring flower of a frail female here. "We've met."

"Of course," I said. "Dana. Hi."

Nope. Not awkward. Not even a bit.

I heard more voices coming closer from outside. The rest of the group was heading back; too cold in the middle of winter to risk falling asleep in the snow and shifting back to human in minus twenty degrees Celsius. Shifter body temps ran high, but even so, there were certain body bits you didn't want to risk losing to frostbite.

A wisp of breath, air brushing aside as Jon was behind me, arms wrapped around my waist, chin on my head.

"Are you able to offer hospitality?" I felt my hair move ever so slightly at Jon's words to Anshell. *Right. Sunlight.*

Anshell glanced briefly at Sam before replying. Sam's eyes narrowed, tightness making the laugh lines at the outer edges of his eyes seem darker, deeper. But then the moment was gone and he was nodding as though it had never occurred to him to let Jon fry in the oily vat of his jealousy.

"We have a place," Anshell replied, taking his eyes off Sam and focusing in on Jon. "We will offer you hospitality for the day. But we can't stay here with you," he continued. "You won't be safe if someone comes upon you in repose."

"I want to get back anyway," I said, covering my anxiety at leaving anyone I cared about unattended and unable to defend themselves for even a short while. "It's only about 4:30 a.m. Should be enough time."

THE SNOW HIT soon after.

Flakes upon flakes, dancing and swirling, building bit by bit in iridescent drifts of twinkling light. It wasn't supposed to snow like this, not tonight at least, and yet. Clearly someone had missed the memo, opting instead to shake his snowy, itchy scalp all over us.

A chill blew through the open door; even the shifters and somewhat dead guy felt it, with shivers starting up and spreading through the gathered few in undulating waves.

Anshell bumped the door shut with his hip. I tried not to notice the trails of his curling brown hair that huddled in strategically shadowed places: tailbone, hip, just below the underside of his almost nonexistently rounded belly. His pinkish-brown nipples, peaked and hardened by the cold.

I forced my eyes down and away, hoping no one else had noticed me checking out what was right in front of me. Then looked up again and saw Jon, eyebrow raised, a teasing twinkle in his eye. Unthreatened and similarly appreciative of the view. *Huh.*

Lucky for me, Sam hadn't noticed anything at all—which, all things considered, was probably for the best.

A loud knock and then Celandra floated in, spreading frozen melted droplets in her wake. One look at the assembled group before she swept past us for the kitchen, chuckling. I trailed after her. Sure, you could say I was running away from a situation that screamed *awkward.* And? Your point being?

Jon drifted in, wrapping one arm around me from behind and gently pulling me towards him, leaning us against the countertop. Celandra was piling the island high with an assortment of foodstuffs that made sense to her and her alone.

Unsliced ham lay next to a single peeled banana, two jars of pickled artichokes, scattered walnuts still in the shell, and a bowl of something that looked suspiciously like eyeballs but I suspected were actually peeled lychees. Oh yeah. And raw, still-pulsating entrails from some creature who was probably pulsating less without them.

I had an urge to reach forward and plunge my fingers into its steaming, twitching depths. Tasting from the fruits of war, licking the remains of my foe from the tops of my bloody fingertips. Scraping out bits from my claws with pointed teeth.

Wait, what?

"Dana?" Jon's voice echoing through a hollow metal tube. He cared? Then what about Claude, that jealous asshole of a cat who had started this entire chain of fucked-up events?

The moment broken, I turned away from the offal and poked a verbal stick at that furred beast of a subject we'd all been avoiding.

"Claude," I said.

Jon pulled back. What was he afraid of?

"Kitty cat went pitter patter splat," said Celandra in a sing-song voice.

I raised an eyebrow and turned to face Jon. "Is that true?"

Jon didn't reply; instead he turned towards the sink. His hands flexed open then clenched into fists.

Gee, it's not like Jon had anything to regret when it came to me. Right? It wasn't as though his choice in lovers hadn't come around to bite me in the soon-to-be-(theoretically)-furry ass. Right?

But we'd been over that already, he and I. I glanced at him once more, his hunched posture, the angular lines of his shoulders as his neck muscles clenched in sync with his jaw. No, there was more to it now.

I reached up and laid my hand on his shoulder.

"Claude," I said. "What happened to him?"

His throat, gulping, bobbing.

"Claude," Jon said, finally. "Was skinned alive and left out in the frost to die."

Amazing how easy it is sometimes to take catastrophic news in stride.

I couldn't say I was sorry to see the back of his furry little ass gone. But I imagined being skinned alive would hurt. A lot.

I opened my mouth to say I don't know what, something comforting maybe, when Sam interjected.

"Claude's not dead," he said.

Jon spun around so fast I barely caught the blur of motion before he had Sam braced up against the far wall. Almost as fast, Sam had his claws out and he swiped Jon across the cheek, once, just to get his attention.

"You're going to play it like this," Sam growled, "here, in our territory? With dawn so close?"

I moved in then, pushing them apart. Again, I had that flare of sensation I'd had days earlier. Heat, rushing through me from where my skin made contact with Sam; heat met with coolness, grounding me, forcing my focus back and centered on my core as I touched Jon. My nipples hardened from the chill even as my insides melted with molten need.

Gods.

Both men felt it, of course—no chance at dignity for Dana. Two sets of eyes tracked me as I moved to wedge myself between them, Sam in front and Jon behind.

Anshell, standing in the doorway, cleared his throat. We broke apart, my breath still ragged.

Thankfully, Anshell had seen fit to put on some clothes. Small mercies. Sam was smiling that small, possessive, self-satisfied smile that said he knew the effect his proximity was having on me.

Glad someone was enjoying themselves.

Jon, in contrast, was looking anywhere but at me, distractedly running long fingers through his already rumpled hair.

"Is it true?" Jon aimed the question at Anshell and over my head.

Anshell didn't bother pretending. "Yes," he said. "Your *other* lover is still alive."

"Where?" Jon's eyes held Anshell's. *Ugh.* Sam caught my train of thought in the motion of my eyes and smirked. Awesome. Very mature.

"He's safe," Anshell said. "Fast healer."

Jon stared at him a moment, then gave a brief nod.

"I have to go," said Jon. He spun me around quickly and gave me a long deep kiss I suspected was as much for Sam and Anshell's benefit as it was for mine.

It tasted of guilt and sadness and endings.

THIRTY-TWO

THE SNOW GOT more intense, hitting like a wall and spitting flakes of white fury. In the heartbeat between Jon leaving my arms and streaking for the door, Anshell had his arm out, barring the way.

A snarl unlike any sound I'd ever heard from Jon vibrated deep in his throat. Anshell stretched out his other arm to fill the remaining space with his bulk.

I held my breath. In the stillness, the *tap tap tap* of snow pellets hitting the wooden frame of the outer deck beat an asynchronously timed metronome of sound.

"It might be helpful to know where he is, no?" Anshell's casual words belied the strain it was taking to keep Jon from dashing out into the pre-dawn storm.

Jon stilled.

"Tell me," he said. That bit of fang peeking out told me better than any words the extent to which he was on that edge between control and *other*. Something dark and dangerous and bloody. For Claude. The cat who had changed and possibly ruined my life.

"You know he tried to kill her," Anshell said. Jon's eyes flicked to me, then away.

"Are you sure?"

"We're sure," said Sam, padding across the floor to stand with me. When did he put on those pajama bottoms? Damn. *Focus, Dana.*

"You already know he was the one who shot Dana

with a tranq gun so the crew could snatch her from the Swan." Jon nodded. "We're pretty sure he's the one who set off the explosives in her apartment as well."

"Wait," I said. "What?"

Sam turned to look at me this time, reaching out his hand to lightly stroke the back of my neck. Soothing. Not at all like he was coaxing my nerves into a reluctant purr. Nope.

Jon's eyes flicked back and forth between Sam and me. Narrowed. But what could he say with one foot out the door in pursuit of his *other* lover?

My, what a tangled web we weave when to more than one lover we choose to cleave.

My words or Celandra's? Where had that dragon lady gone anyway?

Impatient, I brushed Sam's hand away.

"You knew," I said, slowly, turning back to keep all three of the men in view. "You knew that Claude was dangerous. But he was—is—a member of your pack." Anshell nodded shortly in reply. "And he was—is—your lover," I continued, gaze settling on Jon this time.

"I didn't know," Jon said. "But..."

"But?" I raised my eyebrows, prompting him to continue.

"I should have," he finished, lamely.

"And you," I said, spinning around to catch first Sam then Anshell in a glare. "You knew that green-eyed cat was a danger to me and you didn't warn me."

"It was pretty obvious," Sam pointed out reasonably.

"Oh, sure, I knew he hated me," I replied, my voice rising. "But it's a pretty major jump from 'stay away from my boyfriend' to setting off explosives in my kitchen and shooting me."

"We had your back," Anshell said. "One of us was around you at all times. But we had to be sure."

"We couldn't accuse a pack mate of treason and sabotage without proof," Sam continued. "We had to know absolutely."

"So, what," I said, voice increasingly clipped. "I was *bait*?"

Sam and Anshell exchanged glances, so quick I might have missed it if I hadn't been watching for it.

"We had to be certain," Anshell said. "Considering the punishment."

"And what about me?" My hands balled at my sides. I wasn't sure what I was about to do, but I suspected it was neither pretty nor dainty.

"What about you?" Sam's voice was mild. "What did you expect us to do, exactly?"

"Give me a heads up maybe?" My words plunged forward. "Or was I just a convenient fuck?"

Everyone looked away then, twitchy with the discomfort of too much sharing.

Sam stepped forward, invading my personal space, so close I could taste the salt and vinegar chips he'd had hours earlier on his breath. He took my hands, smoothing my fists into palmed flatness.

When had my life gotten so complicated?

"Excuse us," Sam said to the room in general. Anshell shrugged, but Jon wasn't going to let me be dragged off against my will.

"Dana?" Jon's voice, questioning.

"It's okay," I said. "Sam and I need to talk."

I ALLOWED MYSELF to be led outside, onto the veranda where the chill wind was blocked only slightly by the wicker blinds that slapped against the solid wood beams. I was still amazed at how the glamour held, as I watched two straggling parka-wearing partiers trundle past, oblivious to our presence.

As soon as they were out of earshot, I turned to Sam. "So? Was there something specific you wanted to talk about?"

"I'm sorry," he said, leaning against the wooden railing, "for using you as bait to draw that tom out. Our reasoning made sense, and it still makes sense, but..."

"Sucks to be me, eh?" I turned away from him to rest my forearms on the railing, looking out at the water so I wouldn't have to look at him. "Tell me something," I said. "The sex. Was that part of the full Dana protection package too?"

"Hardly," Sam said, waiting until he could see my eyes. "Being with you, like that, was definitely *not* part of the plan. Any of the plans," he muttered under his breath. Forgetting for the moment that my hearing was almost as good as his now.

I reached out and touched his index finger, gently, drawing a line from knuckle to nail. He gave a little shudder, eyelids fluttering in response, but didn't move. Instead, he closed his eyes before continuing.

"We did use you," he said. I withdrew my hand; Sam reached out and sandwiched it between his. "Up to a point. Weird shit kept following you around, and for the safety of the city, of the Pack and of our supe community, we had to know what was going on. Plus, you hadn't committed. To the Pack. With Claude clawing for you...if you'd become a liability, we might have let him have you."

"Really?"

"Okay, maybe not," Sam said. "But he *is* Pack and you're not yet. Or weren't. Be glad Anshell didn't have to make that call."

"So where does this leave us?" I knew I shouldn't be asking the question if I wasn't prepared to hear the answer. But I pressed the sore spot anyway.

"I don't know," he admitted. "I don't like to share."

"But it's not like you aren't sleeping elsewhere yourself," I pointed out. Sam shrugged.

"Never said it was logical," he replied.

"So tell me," I said, changing the subject, "what exactly happened to Claude?"

"He's alive," Sam acknowledged, letting the subjects of fidelity and fealty drop for the moment.

Seems Claude had taken things one claw too far when he sold out Morgenlark and then me to Ezra's crew. The proof was in some of the recorded footage taken from the compound where I'd been held.

Still, some questions remained open.

How had Claude and Ezra's crew found each other? How had they determined they had a common interest in me? Why did Ezra's crew want to spear me like a bug caught on a thumbtack under a microscope? Or maybe I was wrong—maybe Claude and Ezra had no connection, and their shared focus on me was a coincidence.

And who *was* Ezra at this point? The mentor I'd known, or just a skin being passed around from entity to entity?

Sam was holding my hand in his now, unconsciously strumming my palm with his thumb. My breath caught as he slid a single fingernail up along the inner crease. Whatever he'd been doing before, he was suddenly quite aware of the effect his actions were having on me—and by the grin hovering on the sides of his lips, those actions were deliberate.

Gods. Goddess.

Were Sam and Jon going to try and make me choose between them?

THIRTY-THREE

I HAD TO get away.

Jon left to go after Claude, so Sam gave me a ride to my truck, still parked outside the Swan. Then he followed me home to make sure I made it this time.

Not to my apartment—that was still surrounded by bright yellow "police scene—do not cross—exercise caution" tape. Nope. When the world comes crashing into pieces around you, sometimes you need to spend some time communing with your Aerosmith posters and that single bed with the faded pink dust ruffle.

You know the one. It's a little ripped in that spot where it caught on the rear spike of those biker boots you used to have. Before you lost them in an overly optimistic retrieval mission in Regent Park. A burn mark, carefully hidden, from where you dropped some ash smoking a joint with that guy in grade 11. The hot one with red hair in dreadlocks who didn't say much with words but made fluent use of language with his hands on your body. You know who I'm talking about. That guy.

I hesitated at the threshold of my childhood home. The stairs were concrete slabs forced uneven by the years of crazy hot and cold (often in the same day) Toronto weather. The hand railings had been painted black by yours truly after my father died. Seemed like a good idea at the time but now, as I looked at the peeling formerly white paint rolling off and away from the beveled edges of the arched entranceway, I thought maybe it was time to redo the entire area in something cheerier. Possibly yellow. Or maybe green.

Or maybe I was procrastinating.

I grabbed hold of the bars, careful to avoid the rusted patches underneath; not careful enough as my heel slid on the second step and I had to grip harder to avoid falling on my ass. The metal decay had grown teeth of ice that punctured my wool gloves and embedded themselves in my index finger. I swore as I pulled off a glove and popped my bloodied finger in my mouth.

With my other hand, I quietly jiggled my key in the lock. *There.* I turned to wave at Sam, who waited in his idling vehicle until I was actually inside without anything exploding before driving off.

Should I have invited him in?

The light was on in the kitchen. Maybe Mum had had a premonition I'd be coming by—wouldn't be the first time. Or maybe she never turned out all the lights at night anymore.

I paused for another moment at the threshold, my hand hovering over the beige plastic light switch plate. What had it been like for Mum, alone all of these years since Dad's death? I'd left so soon afterwards—so wrapped up in my own wants, needs and desires—that I hadn't stopped to think about how lonely my mother must have been.

A flash of guilt, a lump in my throat. I swallowed hard a couple of times before crossing the floor, first to fill up the red plastic kettle and then to turn it on. I drifted around the kitchen, poking in cabinets until I found something suitable to add to the hot water. A hardened packet of instant hot chocolate and an unopened bag of multi-colored marshmallows. I shoved a handful of the mini-marshmallows in my mouth and moved my search to the fridge.

Aaahhhhhh. I let out a breath I hadn't even realized I was holding when I saw the canister of aerated, homemade whipped cream. Mum's secret stash; her culinary kryptonite. And there was still at least half left.

The briefest streak of silver in my peripheral vision had me ducking out of the way of the baseball bat whistling past the place where my head had just been to connect with the fridge door. There was a clanging *thud.*

"Dana? Is that you? Oh God, are you okay?"

"Lynna?" I peered up at my friend from my crouched position on the beige linoleum floor. The friend I'd thought was staying with Anshell. "What are you doing here?"

"Tell me you're okay. Are you okay?" Lynna pushed a clump of dark hair streaked with red up and away from her eyes with the hand not currently clenching the bat.

"I'm fine," I said. "Seriously. But why are you here? Does my mum know you're here?"

"Of course I do," my mother said, coming out from the other doorway, twirling her own bat like a Victorian sun parasol. "You think I don't know when your best friend is sleeping at my house? I put her in the guest room."

"Normally I sleep in your room," Lynna interjected. "But your mom had a feeling you'd be stopping by soon so this time she put me down the hall instead."

"You had a feeling, eh?" I straightened up and walked over to my mum before reaching out to pull her into a bear hug. "Good call on the whipped cream."

My mother quirked me a small grin, strangely very much like my own.

I WASN'T KIDDING about the Aerosmith posters. There was a small shrine to Steven Tyler in the corner of my old bedroom where ticket stubs, sweaty concert T-shirts and even the boots I'd worn the last time I saw him play were spread about in a semicircle.

Mentally shelving my teenage obsession with the big-lipped rocker a moment, I took a sip of my marshmallow-filled mug—three parts marshmallows, one part hot chocolate—and rolled the steaming liquid perfection around my mouth. I still had a change of clothes here for the odd time I stayed over due to snowstorms or laziness, although the selection was somewhat limited. Digging through my drawers yielded a pair of cotton candy–pink "cat's meow" flannel pajama bottoms and a matching pink rhinestone-edged kitten "Yowza" tank top. I kid you not.

I finished off the outfit with a terry cloth hoodie—pink, what else?—and fuzzy bunny slippers. You can guess the color.

Dawn was breaking in pinks and blues over the grey-tinged backyard. And yet, despite it all, I was nowhere near ready for sleep. Too restless. Go figure.

I lay on the bed anyway, mattress still molding to my body perfectly, and felt my blood rush and beat its way through me. As the sun nudged its way up along its arc of sky, the throbbing intensified until it filled my ears and threatened to spurt out of my nose. I brushed the back of my hand against my face and it came away wet and red.

Lovely.

Red sky at night, sailor's delight / Red sky at dawn, sailors be warned. The old saying echoing in my head.

I could feel the light tickle of blood as one drop, then another, paused on the edge of my upper lip. I touched the tip of my tongue to the salty cleft where the drop hung, just for a moment, before rolling down to coat the back of my throat. Bangles of gold, rings of light, encircling my wrists and neck and head and ankles.

The fuck?

I tried to sit up but couldn't. I was pinned to the bed by these bands of my own creation. I tried to speak but all that came out was a croak.

Not here. *No.*

My mother and Lynna were both unprotected. Whatever was doing this to me would get them next and I couldn't warn them. Couldn't stop it.

Ironic how being pinned down this time wasn't so fun. Might be a while before Jon and I played another one of those games. *If you ever get to see him again*, said a traitorous voice, taunting me in my head.

I looked around the room for a clue. For anything to tell me why this was happening.

Nothing.

I arched my back, shook my shoulders, wiggled my toes and twisted my neck, rolling from side to side. Releasing my panic with each labored exhalation of breath.

And then. I blinked.

The sun was a little higher and I could feel its warmth on my legs. The strange glowing restraints were gone. The pink Hello Kitty clock beside the bed told me an hour and a half had passed. It was 6:30 a.m.

Was I having blackouts now? Was this some nifty new way for the Big Bad to let me know they could get to me whenever, wherever I was? Or was there something here, in this house, affecting me? I sat up with a groan, too jittery now to risk closing my eyes.

I tried to take a sip from my mug, but all that met my lips were the gelatinous remains of chocolate-soaked marshmallows.

I needed coffee.

The kitchen felt too far away and I didn't want to wake up my mother or Lynna. Then again, after that trippy interlude I just had, I couldn't *not* at least check on them. A quick trip down the hall confirmed both still were safely tucked into their beds, snoring peacefully.

I used the bathroom while the coffee brewed, marveling at the random lavender velveteen-edged hearts on the wallpaper. When did my mother develop this whimsical side? Since when did she start putting it into her home decorating practice?

For that matter, when did we start taking trinket-focused pride in our home generally?

Too weird. The way this week had been going, maybe Ezra had swapped out my mom for someone else entirely. Unless the Ezra skin was my father. In which case…

And what *had* just happened? Everything had gone strange as soon as I tasted blood. No, wait—I'd spilled it first. But that had never happened before, that reaction, and I'd bled lots of times. Was there something special about here? This house?

I tested the theory. Coffee in hand, I walked towards the front door and tried to sense a difference in the area's energy. Nothing. Back to the kitchen. The living room, the den, the dining room. Still nothing. *Pffft.* Yeah, I was losing it.

Shook my head at myself as I took my coffee upstairs to stand in front of the French beveled-glass doors to my closet. Maybe I still had something worth wearing here.

And then I felt it. A thrumming *something* from the other side of those doors. What *was* that?

MY BEDROOM CLOSET was definitely more packed with stuff than I remembered.

The source of whatever was pinging off my nerves was there, I could feel it, but where? I scanned the area but saw nothing obvious. Stronger at the back of my neck; a more powerful prickling crowning my scalp.

I looked up.

Huh.

I dragged my pink sateen-covered dressing table chair to just inside the frame of the archway to get a better look. Climbed onto the chair with one foot out to test my weight, the other foot following cautiously behind as I hoped the decades-old faux-antique-circa-1989 stuffing would hold. I held on to the door frame as well. Just in case.

On top of the inside wooden wainscoting, hidden under a flap of loose wallpaper made looser with a bit of help, I found a long-forgotten joint.

I remembered the night I'd put it up there. It was late, maybe 3:00 a.m., and I'd just snuck in from a party—well past the curfew we pretended I still had. I'd made it to my room safely without waking anyone up. I thought. I was so sure I'd pulled it off. There I was, joint in hand, ready to hang out my window and smoke it…when the light went on in the hallway.

Busted.

But not quite. I found the spot in the closet and then dove into bed, fast, fully clothed.

Too late. My mother was standing in the hallway, arms crossed, foot tapping.

So very busted.

Although maybe not as thoroughly as I'd thought when I was fifteen, given that my contraband was still there. *Score.* Okay, sure, it was now a dried-out pile of vaguely THC-enhanced dust with just the faintest aftertaste of wallpaper glue. But it was a symbolic reminder of a time before complications, before I'd developed the urge to scratch then shave then scratch again at the backs of the palms of my hands.

I reached up once more to that same spot, fiddling with the crispy paper to see if any further hidden treasures lurked. Nope. Behind the paper was the wall, and nothing seemed particularly different about that. Paper, wooden slat, grooved seam between slat and wall. A nail. And, oh, *ow!*

For the second time in as many hours, I was sucking on a part of me as it bled, nicked by something unexpectedly serrated. At this rate I was going to need a tetanus booster.

I was feeling a bit lazy at this point what with the tiredness and bad waking dreams and not sleeping.

Maybe I didn't staunch the blood as thoroughly as I could have. Perhaps a bandage would have been advisable.

Either way, when I reached up to put the shriveled joint back where I'd found it, I left a smear of blood on the paper. I could smell it, and the taste echoed from my tongue to my nose in a bouquet of coppery dust.

Blood singing to blood. Something calling me. There was light streaking from the tips of my fingers as I waved them in front of my eyes.

Psychedelic. And I wasn't even stoned.

From inside the closet there was a glow—golden, warm, like the sun so ready to rise just beyond the horizon of my window. It was getting stronger and brighter, but with no light source I could see.

I was cautious. After the last few days, I understood anything could happen. Still better to know, I hoped, than to shut the door and back away, always wondering about the glow monster in the closet.

I took a step forward. No good—too far away to see anything yet. Another step. Heart thudding in my chest. I raised my hand, held it forward, reaching out to touch or maybe ward off whatever it was in that closet.

Three drops of my blood pointed the way to the neatly labeled and stacked, glowing abyss.

I followed the trail, feeling very much like Dorothy on the yellow brick road, hoping I didn't come across anyone's heart, head or some other appendage that might pass for courage along the way.

Another step and I was inside, looking up, where the light outlined the square window-sized, board-covered pathway to the attic. Huh.

The pink sateen throwback to another life became my ladder yet again. I balanced and then reached up to gently push open the aperture.

THIRTY-FOUR

THE FIRST THING I felt were crumbled bits of what I hoped were non-asbestos-based insulation—as opposed to dried squirrel excrement or some other form of potentially noxious droppings. Whatever it was crumbled to the touch, dry powder with a sticky resin tightening the skin on my fingertips. Reminded me of the glue we used in grade school—the kind that went on white and was all kinds of fun to peel off afterwards.

I resisted the urge to peel, but just barely.

Instead, using the boxes to wedge my feet with each wobbling step, I pushed and pulled myself up and through the hold. Nothing fell as I passed. Bonus marks for stealth.

The space was filled with books. White wisps of clouds drifted lazily across the early morning sky, so blue, passing in and out of view from several skylights placed at seemingly random intervals. The rafters were lined and sealed and lined again between the blue—no wonder I never remembered our roof leaking as I was growing up.

Light drifted in from a window on the far side, overlooking the front door of the house. Except I'd never noticed a window from the attic. Or an attic of this size. Or, really, any attic at all beyond a slight incline of roof over the top of the bathroom and bedrooms. Not that I spent much time thinking about it when I lived at home, but a whole extra floor was something you'd think I'd have noticed. Right?

I turned around, slowly, to make sure I was seeing everything I needed to see here. Books. Windows. *Okay...*

So where was that glow coming from?

Although the room was filled with a thin light, blue and yellow on dust, my eye tracked to the call of a different light source: the pulsating heartbeat of gold, *there,* towards the back. A cardboard box marked simply: "Books and other miscellanea." Wedged up high, on top of a stack of other boxes on top of a bookcase that couldn't possibly, logically, exist.

And yet. My father's handwriting. There, on the outside.

I reached for it but couldn't. My hands touched air. Even though when I took a step back, I could see it.

After a few abortive attempts, I paused. Sank back onto my haunches in a deep squat—my old yoga teacher would be proud—and looked for clues, neon arrows saying "go here," anything that might be useful. I even muttered *abracadabra* with a general waving of my arms in a vaguely (so I thought) Merlinesque sort of way. Nada.

Frustrated, I started absently flicking the tips of my fingers back and forth as I reviewed the facts. *Flick.* I was in a place that shouldn't exist. *Flick.* Something kept glowing at me, trying to get my attention, but wouldn't let me near it. *Flick.* Appearances could be deceiving. *Flick.* What was the deal with the Ezra skin and—*flick*—what was the connection between Ezra and my father? Did Ezra have anything to do with his death—*flick flick*—or, in light of my recently weird conversations with Ezra, should I be saying "disappearance" instead?

This time my *flick* pushed something loose in the well-seasoned floorboards as a finely pointed chunklet of said floor was now embedded in my index finger.

I groaned frustration. Sure, it was a fluke, but it still felt like the room had given me the finger.

A quick pluck between two surprisingly sharp fingernails and the offending wooden bit was out. I held it between my thumb and forefinger in the unnatural light, strangely fascinated by the drop of blood glistening as it hung, balanced, on the tip. The dust around me chose that moment to go up my nose for a tickle and I sneezed, blood drops scattering.

It was the third time I'd bled in as many hours. What next—torture by paper cut? I sighed. But what the hell. One more try and then I was done. Really.

I reached up towards the glow. This time, I closed my eyes and felt rather than looked for its source. My index finger stung a bit where the dust had gotten into my wound, but the potential success dancing ever closer to my reach kept me going.

There.

I grabbed the box with both hands and pulled it down before it had a chance to change its mind.

Lifting the lid displaced a cloud of dust that had me sneezing seven times in succession. My imagination, or did things get even brighter?

But it was all worth it when I saw the note—a stack of lined papers actually—with the words "Dear Dana" at the top in the unmistakable penmanship of my father. I sank to the floor and started reading.

Dear Dana,
I wish we'd been able to have this conversation in person. Unfortunately, you're probably reading this because I'm not here to tell you myself.

You have very special blood. Protect it. There will be people who want to get close to you in order to make use of you for that blood. Trust only with care.

You are descended on my side from a powerful genetic line. We can take matter—ours or those of others—and mutate it. As a result of that ability, we can strengthen the power of any group.

Don't mix blood with anyone. If another supernatural entity's blood comes into contact with yours, yours could adapt to absorb some of its properties. It won't kill you—probably—but it could make your life very confusing.

No kidding, I thought to myself.

This isn't my only letter for you. But it's enough for now.

If you want to come back to this place, in case you haven't figured it out yet, you'll need to spill blood thrice. Seven sneezes pays the price.
Love always,
Dad

I re-read the letter twice, making sure I'd gotten it all, that I hadn't missed some pertinent detail in the blur of tears I kept swiping at with the back of my hand. I probably looked like a raccoon with all the grit

I was smearing on my face but I just couldn't make myself care.

I tucked the sheaf of papers into the waistband of my drawstring/elastic combo pajama bottoms.

Focus.

I stood in front of the ever-expanding bookcase of serendipitous surprises and wondered, knowing that answers to the mystery of why Ezra and Cybele (a.k.a. Alina) and maybe even a handful of vengeful others wanted me was probably there. All I had to do was figure out what I was looking at and what it all meant.

SOON THE THREE of us stood there—Mum, Lynna and myself—and stared at that bookcase in the room which should not exist.

"I had no idea," my mother said, her eyes tracing the edges of the room.

"Don't look at me," said Lynna. "I spent lots of time in your closet, but it's not like I ever saw anything weird."

"So Dad never said anything about this? No hints or clues?" I couldn't help prodding, even as my mother winced at the reminder her long-dead husband was capable of keeping such a huge secret under the roof they'd shared.

Mum shook her head.

No words.

Lynna looked back and forth between us.

"You'd better tell her," Lynna said.

I LEFT OUT the part about what I'd been doing when I got scratched and who I'd been doing it with.

But my mother isn't stupid.

"What aren't you telling me?" Mum glanced at Lynna, who looked down and away.

"A lot," I admitted.

My mother looked around until she found a dust-covered, burnt-yellow crushed velvet easy chair, and sat. She reclined back, pretending this was all normal. As if.

"Tell me," she said. "And this time, please fill in those blanks you think the person who gave birth to you wouldn't want to hear."

So I did.

And in return, my mother told me about my father, what he had shared with her about his research.

"If Dad had been tampering with his own blood," I said, "wouldn't that have passed on through him to me? He was with the Agency before you got married, wasn't he?"

"He was a junior scientist back then," she acknowledged. "But I can't believe he would have put either of us at risk that way."

"We don't know he did," Lynna said. "Not on purpose anyway. All we've got is that he worked for the same super-secret government group Dana did. We know he prepared this secret room for her."

"And we know he didn't tell me anything about it," Mum said.

I reached over to give my mother a hug. Whichever ring of hell she was currently circling, I was pretty sure it sucked.

"Oh, *Danyankele*," she said, kissing the back of my hand.

The floor shook and the bookcases rattled against the walls. I stared.

"Ma, say that again."

"What? *Danyankele?*"

The cases, walls and floor shook again.

"One more time?"

"*Danyankele.*"

The panes of glass in the windows chattered like teeth. The bookcases rocked from side to side, edging farther and farther apart until I was looking at a large wall filled with notations and drawings. Its dimensions defied the confines of the house, never mind the attic space that should not be.

There was a series of circles and lines, drawn and joined, in a pattern that reminded me of an air hockey table. Oblong for sure. A circle at the top and a circle at the bottom, with several pairs of circles stacked atop each other. Familiar, but from where?

I took a picture with my phone. Then did an image search for anything that might match it. Had to stand near the window to get more than a single bar of reception, but the results finally started to load.

Not that the results made me any less confused.

There were the etchings of da Vinci's *Vitruvian Man* side by side with the garish reds, oranges and more muted blues of a tarot card spread. Maps of constellations, drawings of chakras, and a recurring image of the yogic Kundalini snake. Also hopscotch, although I doubted a children's game had anything to do with it.

Neither Mum nor Lynna were any help either, although the pattern felt familiar to them too.

Too bad Dad hadn't included a cryptic-to-real-life translator.

"KEEP ME POSTED." Mum kissed my cheek once I'd gathered up my stuff to go and gave me a hug that seemed to go on for ages but didn't last long enough.

"I'll meet up with you in a few hours," Lynna said. "At the house."

Anshell's, of course.

I nodded to them both and left with a mystery for another day. One I'd hopefully live long enough to see.

THIRTY-FIVE

ON MY WAY, I stopped by the supe hospital to check on Sandor.

He looked so frail, if that was possible, his normal shade of vibrant green paling out into an unhealthy blue sheen. Even his snout had lost the edges of its definition, softened and flaccid, almost blurry.

I rubbed my eyes and looked again. Still a bit smudged.

Another blink and everything came into focus.

My boss was lying on his back, looking more blue than green. His IV drip had a bluish tinge to it as well, and tiny multi-faceted crystals seemed to twinkle as they shifted around in the bag.

Sandor was talking in his sleep. I couldn't bring myself to wake him.

"Gustav, no," Sandor mumbled. "No! Don't go. It doesn't have to be like that." He muttered a few words I couldn't make out. Something about tomato sauce, popcorn and breaded eyeballs.

"Dana!"

"I'm right here," I said.

The sound of my voice nudged Sandor's somnolence. He opened his eyes, all of them, and blinked rapidly before realizing I was there beside the bed and not part of an argument in his head with someone named Gustav.

"Dana," he repeated, but this time he knew he was talking to me.

"Hey," I said, smiling my relief at seeing Sandor alive and awake. Reached over to squeeze his hand, then let go, remembering with a belated *whoops* that maybe our relationship wasn't the touchy feely kind.

"Hey yourself," Sandor replied, ignoring the awkward moment. He didn't seem unhappy to see me, not exactly, but he was doing this nervous scratching at something behind his ear that flicked flecks of skin and several bright and shiny somethings onto the bed as though he couldn't stop himself.

"Sand? Everything okay?" The hell with status quo PDA. I touched his forearm to focus his attention, make him stop.

Sandor stared at my hand, then at his own. Realizing what he was doing. I pulled mine back and he slid his under the top sheet; whether for protection or distance I couldn't tell.

"Sand, who was that guy you met with before you got frozen? Janey said she saw you."

"My brother," he replied.

"You've never mentioned a brother," I said. "What's his name?"

"Gustav." Sandor met my eyes this time, a brief glance, before looking away again. As though he didn't want to see what my reciprocal gaze might say. "Gus."

"Gus." Okay, so Sandor had a brother and his name was Gus. And? Sandor raised his eyebrows and waited for me to make the connection. *Ahhh crap.*

"Gus? As in *Lazzuri*? The blue fucker who tried to end me?" I stared at my boss, my friend, the one I'd trusted as a norm in the midst of *other*.

Sandor nodded and started picking at some invisible thread, under his claws this time. Or maybe the plan was to pull one out. Either way, his silence was just as well given that I was now sitting there with my mouth hanging down to my knees.

I forced myself to breathe and looked, actually looked, around the room and at Sandor. The bluish tinge to his skin. The crystals in his IV drip.

Psycho nurse Gwen swept into the room as I was rearranging the scattered blocks of my previously held worldview. The one in which life made sense, Sandor was my friend, and nobody ever tried to kill me. Yeah. That one.

"So, how is our patient today?" Her hair was tied back so tight it seemed to yank her chipper smile into a rictus grin.

"Fine," he said, watching me. What was the correct response when asked such a rhetorical question by a mentally unstable nurse with access to hypodermic needles filled with liquid that could take down a large, human-sized cat?

"Fine," I echoed automatically. Because I was, or would be, and either way this woman freaked me the hell out.

Gwen shook her head at me indulgently, as though she could read my thoughts and found me to be an amusing child.

The way the last week or two had been going, maybe Gwen *could* read my mind. She raised an eyebrow at me then and smiled a wide, toothy, very un-nurse-like grin and winked.

I blinked.

When I reopened my eyes, all was as it had been

moments before, with Gwen hovering over Sandor and checking on his various attachments.

Huh.

"Explain it to me," I said, after Gwen left again.

"I tried to talk him out of taking the contract," said Sandor. "I told him about you. How you were under my protection. That we were friends."

"And yet...?"

"He's family," Sandor said. "Blood. I can't *make* him do anything. But I thought I'd convinced him to take a pass."

"It never occurred to you to, oh I don't know, *warn* me there was a contract out on me?"

"Didn't get the chance," he pointed out. "Frost attack. Then you were snatched."

Maybe he was being reasonable. But I didn't care. Sandor had found out his brother the assassin was planning to kill me—and hadn't given me the heads up I needed to avoid the whole thing.

I could tell Sandor wanted things to be okay between us. Like before. I nodded and smiled but my thoughts were anything but okay.

I left soon after. I didn't know what I would have said to him if he'd pushed the conversation further before I'd been able to escape. *So, stab anyone good in the back lately?*

THE SUN HUNG low in the sky with that heavy, midwinter feel when the edges are bright but there's a pit of cold so deep your skin goes numb regardless of how many layers you're wearing. At least it wasn't snowing.

I turned my cell phone back on to discover I'd

missed several calls and texts from Anshell. He left me detailed directions on where to meet him.

It was good to be behind the wheel of my truck again. I felt pathetically grateful. It was bad enough I had to rely on the kindness of others until I could get back into my place; at least this way I didn't have to beg a ride too.

Anshell had arranged to have it fixed—not as good as new, but at least as good as it had been before. I tried to take it for what it was. Anshell was being a good guy, and this was proof of the kind of treatment I'd get as a member of the Pack. Tried *not* to think of it as guilt money for having been used as bait.

So I sang along with the default retro rock station, whacking the steering wheel to the beat, as I poked along in traffic going 30 km/hour in what should have been a 70 km/hour zone.

I didn't make it up this way often, and as I stopped and started and stopped again, I tried the area on like a spring jacket in a designer outlet store. You know it's not really your style, or your color, but the buttons are kind of nice and isn't it time you made a change?

But the rows and strips of big-box stores and warehouse outlets did little to spice up the greenery lining the pseudo highway. The food was burgers and fries, the restaurants either chain-processed deli meat establishments, sports bars or all-you-can-eat MSG-laden Chinese buffets. I swallowed thickly at the fumes. No cafes or bookstores or screen-printed T-shirt places. No health food eateries or micro-batch bakeries. The houses had me humming that song about little boxes made of ticky-tacky that all looked just the same. Aside from the random clumps of Canadian Geese flocking together, this was *not* my place. Not my people.

Yeah, okay. I'm a bit of a city snob.

Then I saw the sign for the park and water reservoir area. I checked the text on my phone against the map I'd sketched out on a napkin. Anshell wanted me to meet him in a park?

A few of the oversized grey, black and white birds stared as I passed, turning to hiss as they caught my scent. I stared them down, swiping my tongue across my lips; they backed off with a startled chorus of honks. Predator and prey. Maybe they were supes too—magic and otherness were hardly exclusive inner city phenomena. Might be time to start paying closer attention to my surroundings.

I followed the road, lined with white-painted rocks that seemed due for a fresh coat, and bumped over the speed rods covered with asphalt.

The winding ribbon of pavement gave way after a couple of turns to a gravel road and then, finally, snow-packed tracks with bits of dirt and brown grass mixed into the white. At the second cracked wooden post, I turned right. A raven, black and shiny with a streak of robin's egg blue on its wing, watched me pass.

I was hoping there was nothing Hitchcockian about its presence. Or the fact that I couldn't see it in my rear-view mirror when I looked back to check.

But then it landed on the hood of my truck with a squawk and I almost jumped out of my skin. I slapped my door as I got out, hoping to scare it away even as my stomach growled and I had a sudden craving for chicken. Go figure.

I scented Anshell before I saw him and followed the

trail of overly large boot prints to a house. Despite its incongruous placement in the middle of what I'd assumed to be a city-owned park, it looked like a completely normal house. One of those 1950s ranch-style bungalows found in the suburbs before the invasion of pre-fab monster homes. With painted white shutters, a yellow front door and flower bed pots under the main floor windows, it felt like a piece of idyllia left over from another place and time. The blackened pit with a grill still drifting the vague aroma of recently charred beef did nothing to dispel it.

My stomach was growling again.

I found Anshell around the side of the house, leaning against a large metal gate, his black leather glove-encased hands clasped together.

I was struck by the coiled energy twined around him. Even in the semi-wilds of the outer city, Anshell was a heartbeat away from being muscle in action if the situation changed. One of those things that made him a good pack leader, I realized.

I had to pause for a moment to admire his clean, lean lines. Just because my plate is full doesn't mean I can't eye dessert, right?

"Like what you see?" I could hear the grin in his voice.

I grunted. Anshell took the sound as an affirmation and chuckled.

High ground, Dana. Find the high ground here.

"So I'm guessing you didn't call me all the way up here to check out your ass," I said. *Whoops.*

"No, I did not," Anshell replied. "I wanted to show you something," he said, motioning for me to come closer. I couldn't see what he was watching from my current vantage point so I moved beside him.

On the other side of the gate was a pasture. Bounded by snow at the edges, the wooden fence posts lined with wire and log splits marked the border between Toronto in February and someplace else, where brilliant emerald-green grass was being nibbled on by some of the most beautiful horses I'd ever seen. They were magnificent, all shining fur, rippled muscles, solid-looking forelocks and…big shit-eating grins.

Okay, I know enough to recognize what I don't know, but were horses supposed to do that? I don't recall reading about *that* in *Black Beauty.*

"There's something you need to know," Anshell said.

"That you're full of manure?" I know. I couldn't resist.

Anshell shook his head. What, no smile?

"Old joke," he said. "If you're quite done?"

I nodded, barely controlling my urge to keep going with the puns. The more tense I get, the weirder my sense of humor gets. *Hoof in mouth disease, anyone? A problem I need to rein in?* Forced myself to look around again instead: hello grass, trees and horses. Suburban nature.

"So," I finally managed. "Why did you want me to meet you here?"

"Well," Anshell said. "You've been targeted—we know that. But why?"

I shrugged, waiting for him to go on.

"Exactly," he said.

"I'm not the only one," I pointed out, joining Anshell in his leaning-on-the-gate activity. "Your pack name keeps coming up every time I get imprisoned, especially if torture is involved. And I haven't even officially joined. What's up with that?"

"That seems to be one of the questions we need to answer in a fairly immediate manner," Anshell said. Then stopped again.

Was he waiting for me to fill in that auditory space with something?

I tried to oblige. I watched the horses cantering about and chewing on grass, hoping the patterns of brindle, ebony, chocolate and grey would somehow shift the clues around in my head and reflect a pattern of clarity back to me.

"Yeah, I've got nothing," I said finally. "You're going to have to tell me."

"Let your mind go," Anshell said, the sound of his voice a rumble. "Don't try to force it. What do you see?"

I scented the cooling grill mixed with the sick-sweet smell of manure and the sharp tickling tang of grass, too green and too fresh for this time of year. I rubbed my eyes to look again, but the smells hit me again instead. A pressure on my chest as I drew in the sweet, heavy smoke.

I looked around but the scene wasn't one I recognized. Clouds rolled in and there was mist at ground level. The horses were still there, chewing, seemingly unconcerned by the sudden shift in my worldview.

"Let it go." Anshell's voice, a breath in my ear. "What do you see? What are your senses telling you?"

"I see horses," I said. My voice sounded muffled, the sound penetrating only so far. "Clouds and fog. Summer grass that shouldn't exist in Toronto in February."

"We both know this," Anshell replied. "Relax into it. What do you feel? Sense? Taste?"

I opened my mouth, parting my lips with my tongue, tasting the air. Blood. Salty, coppery, metallic.

"I taste blood," I said.

"Good," Anshell replied. "Keep going. What do you hear?"

I closed my eyes and leaned my head back, mentally angling my ears like antennae—even as I knew, with the small part of my brain that still held logic, what I was doing wasn't possible.

"I hear pain," I said, because I did. "Over the chewing and the horses eating, there's screaming." I opened my eyes. "Why? Who's in pain and why aren't we helping them?"

When I opened my eyes, the screaming stopped. The scene was as it had been before I started reaching outwards with my senses. Normal. Except, of course, for the strangely green grass. I could have sworn it was painted on if not for that smell of July with grasshoppers and cicadas and lying on your back in a field, the pointed shafts prickling the back of your neck and the sun so strong you have to shield your eyes against it.

Anshell was still there as well, looking out at the pasture that shouldn't exist. The only sign he might be at all restless was in the way he rubbed the tip of his nose with his gloved thumb.

"Are you willing to go back in?" He spoke without turning to look at me.

I thought about that a moment. You mean I had a choice?

"You have a choice," Anshell said, echoing my thoughts yet again. "There are some things you need to see, know, and this is one of the only ways to explain. I don't know all the details myself."

I snorted my incredulity, releasing a puff of frosty steam from my nostrils.

"I'm serious," Anshell replied. "I can hold this plane open for you for a bit longer. Perhaps it will help you find some of those answers we all need about you. Now that you've had a taste, you know what to expect next. It's your choice."

"I don't understand," I said, shaking my head. "What did you do?"

Anshell looked away; apparently something was fascinating there on the edge of where the grassy knoll met the snowy embankment.

"Sometimes it's helpful to be able to see things from an alternate vantage point," he said. "The first peoples here, they have a tradition of spirit walks. You've heard of this before?" I nodded. "It's similar to that. Altering perceptions. Accessing memories buried in our synapses. Some people use hypnosis; I prefer this."

"Is it a pack thing? Can everyone do this?"

"No," Anshell replied. "But I can."

"Why me?"

"I believe you have power," he said. "The partial change you do?" I nodded. "It takes most shifters years of practice to master it. Some never do. But you started with it, even though you haven't managed a full shift yet. You can't quite walk, but already you're climbing the stairs backwards wearing a blindfold and balancing a teacup on your head. You're something different."

I shook my head. No words.

"Do you want answers?"

"I don't know," I said.

"You have to know," said Anshell. "Decide. If you want to try to find those answers, I will stretch it open for you once more and we will see what you can find."

I hesitated.

"Decide," Anshell repeated. "I will count to five and then we're done—we'll find another way."

I nodded. Counted in my head even as Anshell spoke the numbers aloud. I let him get to four.

"Okay," I said. "Open up."

THIRTY-SIX

THE SCENE STOLE over me more easily this time. Maybe because I knew what to expect.

This time, what hit me first were the sounds. I closed my eyes to make them stronger, trying to block out my other senses.

Again with the screaming. Many voices, layered one atop the other, threads of pain weaving together in a braid of sound. I followed and found, surprisingly, that I could make out individual differences in those layers.

One voice sounded particularly familiar. Female. Like mine but not like mine.

I was able to make out murmuring as well. Low and soothing, a stream over pebbles. A man's voice, calming. Threads of tension through the bursts of pain.

"Hannah," the voice said. "Ssh. It's okay. Not much longer now."

"Stuart! Easy for you to say." A female voice I knew yet did not know. Panting.

"It's okay," he replied. "You knew it would be like this. It will be over soon." Another grunt, distinctly female. The sounds seemed to be coming on more frequently. Consistently? Definitely closer together.

"How much longer?" The woman's voice, softer now, hoarse. "Soon?" Her voice rose, hopeful.

"The baby's crowning," the voice of the man who answered to the name of Stuart said. "We're almost there. C'mon, Hannah," he said. "When you feel that wave coming on, you have to *push*."

More clouds; the scene changing with the breaths I was taking in and releasing.

"*Danyankele*," said the man. The voice tender. That voice. I recognized it with a shock that made my head jerk and my eyes do a little twitch.

"*Danyankele*," the woman replied, warmth and love like liquid chocolate. I wanted to run my fingers through it and lick off the tips, rolling droplets of sweetness around on my tongue.

And then the scene of my birth was gone, replaced with snap-click precision by scenes from elsewhere in my life.

Swaddler to toddler. My first puppy. A mistake—we never really bonded, no matter how hard I tried. For some reason, Sunshine was always a little bit scared of me. My parents finally gave her away to a nice family with normal children who didn't scare the crap out of the dog.

Gingy the cat was my ninth-birthday present. She was a keeper. She followed me around and we carried on full conversations. She slept with me at night, staying close by me during meals in case something "accidentally" fell from my plate.

Then the funeral. One of the worst days of my life. Numbly standing through all of the kind words, the prayers, the formal military salute, the draped flag. The pomp in no way diminished by the circumstance. My mother, equally numb, nodding at the well-wishers, her hand gripping mine. A man stopped to speak with her—I didn't see his face—and the pain spiked as she squeezed my hand harder. My mother who would never hurt me on purpose. She released me as I gasped, horrified at what she'd done, cupping my face between her hands as tears streaked the dirt I'd rubbed into my cheeks from when I'd thrown a handful on my father's coffin.

More moments, clicking by faster now like a series of slides propelled forward by remote control.

Click. My mother and I, coming home after the funeral, closing the door behind us and locking it, not sure what to do next.

Click. Grade 8 graduation. My mother sitting with her parents on folding plastic chairs in the gym. Me, standing on the podium in my pink pleated skirt, lacy white and pink rose-covered blouse with matching ballet flats, blinking back tears and wishing my father was there to see it.

Click. Him. With the questions that made my stomach clench sickly sweet bile. The touch I needed a shower to get off me. Haunting me. Until. And then.

Click. High school graduation. This time I was dressed in black with a dark pink streak in my hair. My mother sat alone in the auditorium; my grandfather had passed away two years earlier and my grandmother was living in an old age home. I sauntered over to get my diploma and caught my mother's eye. She winked her approval, dabbing at her eyes with a shredded tissue that left flecks of white dotted across the tips of her lashes. I wished my father had been there yet again.

Click. University.

Click. My first class with Ezra.

Click. Recruited by Ezra.

Click click click. It all came whirring to a slow-motion rendition of my admissions process into the Program. Sitting in a chair, trying to ignore my blood filling vial after carefully labeled vial. The cute lab technician I couldn't convince to crack a smile.

Cut to me and the cute lab technician grappling in the laneway out back. Suffice it to say I got him to crack a smile. I had a pretty good time as well. At least until he bit me.

Fluorescent lights. More blood tests. Lab technicians speaking with men in long white coats, conferring. Low-voiced exchanges in the hallway outside my room, words like "infection" and "incubation period" and "strange" and even "quarantine." Drifting in and out of consciousness.

And then there was Ezra.

Everything narrowed in focus and relative time shifted to an approximation of real time, minutes and seconds proceeding at the speed of normal.

"Hello, Dana," he said.

It took me a moment to place this younger version of him. Oh. Right. Preternatural Biology 200-level.

"Hi, Professor Gerbrecht," I replied.

"You're probably wondering why you're here," Ezra said.

"Yeah."

I was back in my body from seven plus years ago. Having the same conversation. I wondered how long Anshell would be able to keep the window open.

At least now, terms like "subcutaneous sanguinicity" and "goreal vissimilitude" barely made me blink.

"Hang on," I said, interrupting a script which had already played itself out. "What do you mean by subcutaneous sanguinicity?"

It was clear from the surprise that blinked behind

Gerbrecht's eyes from one moment to the next my question was unexpected.

"Well," he began...

I was seven years younger and far more innocent the first time we'd had this conversation. This time I needed straight answers to the questions I hadn't known enough to ask.

"Why me?" I pushed myself upright on the layered pillows. "What's your interest in me specifically?"

Ezra himself leaned back this time. Dropping the bullshit veneer and showing me his earnest, I'm-giving-it-to-you-straight face.

"What did we learn last section about the genetic compounds that compromise the human strand integrity of the average shifter's molecular structure?"

"Uhhh..." Hard enough for me seven years ago when the lesson was fresh; now it felt like picking out lint from my belly button using tweezers while blindfolded. I poked around in the cobwebs of my brain until I found something potentially useful. "That shifter DNA looks like human DNA but crossed with something else, like the gene pool of whatever species they change into?"

Ezra nodded. "And what did we learn about the blood composition of magic users?"

"To the naked eye it looks exactly like everyone else's," I parroted, quoting him almost word-for-word from the lecture I'd sat through the week prior. Well, that week plus seven years and change. "But when you get it under the right kind of microscope, it has a glow—each of the molecules has its own kind of aura, and different kinds of magic-users have different molecular glows." I stopped. "But what does this have to do with me?"

Ezra leaned forward, his white lab coat—covered elbows resting gently on the brown corduroy ridges of his pants. "Dana, your blood is special. It's one of the things that showed up on those tests from right before you were attacked, and it's why that blood-sucking lab technician couldn't resist you."

"And here I thought it was my girlish wiles and enticing personality," I commented with a half-smile.

"Not quite," Ezra replied. "Your father was studying this blood, his blood, your blood, when..."

Ezra didn't fill in those blanks. He didn't need to. My father's mysterious disappearance happened on Ezra's watch. Or at least in his general vicinity.

But there was more than one way to go fishing, and I decided to go with the bobbing orange plastic lure of misdirection.

THIRTY-SEVEN

EZRA GOT THERE before I did.

"What do you remember about your father?" Wide-eyed, innocent with guile. The man who scattered seeds of bullshit on the ground around him like a farmer tossing about handfuls of chicken feed to his waiting audience of hungry birds. Ezra—the farmer of birdseed bullshit. "Did he ever talk to you about his work?"

I narrowed my eyes at him, holding the question in my mind and turning it around. "No," I said. "Not really."

I added the "not really" because it was true. I'd been too young when he died for my father to have told me in any great detail what he'd been doing. But he had tried to explain to me in ten-year-old terms how he spent his days.

A chef, he'd said. *Only instead of making food, I'm making science. I'm mixing ingredients together to see what makes people.*

Like salt?

My father had humored my questions. I'd caught him on a good day.

And flour? Hot dogs?

My father had laughed, drawing me in to kiss the top of my head.

Something like that, he'd said. *But maybe not the hot dog part.*

Seven years ago when he'd asked this question, I'd said "no." Because it was, ultimately, true.

My sense of self-preservation was different now, though. What did I know? What could Ezra tell me, the Ezra from back when there was trust?

Still. Thoughts of butterfly wings flapping change through time held my tongue.

"No," I said. Again.

YOUNGER. I COULD feel cloth swaddled around my hips, dampness between my legs. Uncomfortable, because I was wet, but maybe dreaming; bright lights overhead and men in robin's-egg-blue masks with white edges and strings tied behind their matching white and blue cap-covered heads.

That same voice from before—my father? And another I'd heard so much more recently. *Ezra.*

"Don't be a *putz*," he was saying. "They say babies can't even feel pain the way we do."

"Tell that to the boy in the middle of his *bris*," my father muttered. Unconvinced.

"We're not performing female circumcision here," Ezra pointed out. So reasonable. "We're giving her a little something extra, like an investment for later, and then the keys to help her find it."

Conflicting desires warred for supremacy in the brown depths of my father's eyes.

The needle was huge, and I held my baby hands up to touch it. If the men were surprised, they didn't show it.

"Ssh, ssh, *Danyankele*," my father murmured, stroking my head, distracting me from the rubber band being tied tight around my chubby forearm, two fingers tapping lightly to prime a vein before gently inserting the needle tip to extract my blood. Ezra took it from my father's free hand and turned his back to us. When he returned, moments later, the vial was no longer red but rather a blue that swirled. It was the past, and I was powerless to stop either of the men as a new syringe was plunged back into my arm, a different vein, this time filling me with whatever they wanted. No control as I was rolled over onto my stomach and a cream of some kind was slathered onto my back, numbing where it touched. I felt a more precise pressure then, and the whirring of a needle. Was that a tattoo needle? What the…?

I couldn't do anything.

So instead I tried to follow the path of the needle by the pressure I felt.

The first point, at the base of my skull, then several more, spaced wider apart, below. A final singular point at the base on my tailbone. The sequence reminded me of the drawing on my father's wall.

I opened my mouth to cry. To ask. To try and understand.

But I was just a baby.

THE NEXT SCENE was mist and grass, with bits of frozen ice pepper-pricking at my face as I came back to the present. Disoriented. As I blinked and tried to re-focus my eyes, nausea gnawed its way up my throat. Heartburn? Indigestion? A side effect of my inter-dimensional sightseeing excursion? Maybe I was just hungry.

The grill behind me was smoking, and the greasy smells of charred flesh had my stomach growling. I saw Anshell standing over the fire, poking at the glowing bits with a stick. Was that coffee with cinnamon?

"Thanks," I said, when Anshell put a steaming mug of the stuff between my chilled hands. The warmth of the cup jabbed pins of sensation into the nerve endings of my fingers, an accompanying sense memory of the pricks tattooed into my back.

"Hungry?" Anshell did something by the fire I couldn't see, something that caused whatever was cooking to spit grease with a cackle and cough of smoke. I could tell it involved juicy goodness by the scented droplets of grease and fat that hung in the air around us.

"Yeah," I said, flopping down into one of the metallic lawn chair rockers and taking a sip of caffeinated ecstasy.

"Here, take this," Anshell said, turning around and handing me a burger, orange cheese oozing out from between the patty and the bun. Ciabatta, I noted approvingly. Not one of those mass-produced, over-processed buns.

"Mmmm." My moan of culinary pleasure was involuntary but *damn*, the man could make burgers. Also, apparently spirit walks made a person hungry for meat.

"Did you get what you needed?" Anshell settled into the chair across the fire from me. The flames reflected in his eyes, changing them from one moment to the next—first yellow, then brown, then orange and back to brown again.

"How much did you see?" I tried to focus on the shape of Anshell's face, his head, the span between the back of his skull and the tip of his nose. More equine than feline. Lines and edges distorting in the encroaching darkness as the sun dipped into the tree line.

"Nothing," he said. "It takes a lot of energy to keep it open." Anshell shrugged his indifference to the effort he had just expended to help me. Or himself? Those lines were blurring like the edges of his jaw, partially obscured now as a puff of smoke pushed his way.

I didn't hear him cough, but I did see him blink back what I assumed were grit-related tears. A manly man who cries only in the face of campfire smoke, or maybe chopped onions.

I pictured Anshell, bare-chested and well-oiled, beating his breast in an imitation of every King Kong movie ever made, and had to snort back a laugh. Which caused a whole chunk of burger to divert its passage from my throat to an alternate departure point out my nose. My turn to cough until I cried.

Anshell shook his head, a small smile playing on those full, brownish-pink lips. I wondered, again, if he could read my thoughts.

"Sometimes," he said.

Awesome, I thought.

We sat quietly for a few minutes as we chewed our food. Then:

"What happened to Claude?" I asked.

Anshell's eyes widened a moment. "We have him in custody," he said after the briefest hesitation.

"Meaning?" It was just the two of us and I wasn't letting him off the hook this time.

"Meaning," Anshell replied, "our mutual *friend* Claude has been punished and is now recovering from the aftereffects of that punishment."

I opened my mouth to ask but Anshell beat me to it.

"Yes," he said, "Claude will be there tonight if he is up to it."

"And what's to keep him from finishing the job he started and killing me for real this time?"

"Nothing," said Anshell. "But if he tries, we will stop him."

"I feel so reassured," I said. Yes, there were hints of acrid bitterness in my tone. The burger I'd been eating turned to a molten weight in my stomach and Anshell watched as I put the paper plate with the remnants of my uneaten, bun-encased patty down on the ground.

"He is pack," Anshell said, his tone pointed. "You are not."

"Nice. So we're talking underhanded invitation here? Join or we'll take the crazy cat's side over yours?"

"Listen, Dana," Anshell said, leaning forward. "It's obvious there is some kind of connection between us. I shouldn't be able to read your thoughts so clearly—not before you've been through the allegiance oath ceremony."

"I'm not big on ceremony," I commented.

"Be that as it may," Anshell continued, as though I hadn't interrupted. "Our paths do seem to be intertwined somehow."

"I'm so sick of hearing that," I snapped. "Everyone seems to be interested in my *path*, but nobody is telling what that path is or why they care so much about my every move. Or non-move." I slammed my hands down on the arms of my chair, sending a few flakes of rust-encrusted paint up in a puff of blue. "No more bullshit, Anshell. Tell me what you know and I'll share what I know and maybe we can figure out what's supposed to happen tonight."

Anshell stared at me across the fire, leaning back and steepling his fingers as the world around us got darker and darker. Twilight. Still he watched me and I watched him.

"Okay," he said finally. "Your ability to shift is the opposite of what we normally see. Being able to do a partial shift usually takes years of practice, and it's the first thing you've learned to control. Meanwhile you are still struggling to do a full shift. It suggests there's been some kind of mutation in the way your body processed the infection of Claude's scratch."

I'd studied the patterns and behaviors followed by shifter DNA strands against those found in the genetic structure of norms back in my Agency training days at the University of Toronto. A scratch like Claude's enters the bloodstream, attacks the red blood cells, splits the white blood cells and introduces a new Y factor into the mix. That Y factor would replicate at a constant rate, coating and changing the consistency of the white blood cells so they'd become thicker and stronger. The entire sequence was predictable, with results validated enough times to be part of the core curriculum. What Anshell was suggesting didn't make sense.

"Ever seen anything like it before?" Maybe he'd observed variances at the supe hospital.

"Never," Anshell replied. "Because of that, we also have to consider the possibility we may not be able to predict what you'll do under the full moon. Especially on the third night when the lunar power will be at peak strength."

"Well," I said. "That's reassuring. So you think it's my blood then?"

"Not sure," he said. "Maybe. But then there's that

other thing. Have you noticed almost all of this unwanted attention you've been getting traces back, timewise, to the night you and Sam disrupted the Feed ritual outside of the Swan?"

"We dusted anyone without a pulse," I pointed out. "We didn't see anything or anyone else. Plus what about Claude? He had nothing to do with raising Alina. Right?"

"He pled ignorance," said Anshell. "At a time when he would have been motivated to tell truthful details of anything he knew."

I didn't want to think about what that meant. More than one way to skin a cat. *No.* Either way, Claude was a big question mark. I knew what he wanted, and what he'd been caught doing, but I wasn't convinced he was responsible for it all. In fact, I was pretty sure he wasn't.

Besides, if Anshell was correct, I had bigger problems than just Claude.

Whatever had been raised the night of the Feed was demon-style big, bad and chasing down my ass.

And I had one more night to figure out why.

THIRTY-EIGHT

IT WAS ALMOST TIME.

We were at Anshell's house in the poshy-posh Summerhill area again, girding ourselves. Well, his fighters were. Me, I was back at the dining room table channeling my university cram sessions with a large chai soy latte and a stack of books on rituals involving numbers, blood rite patterning along with the philosophical and psycho-preternatural potentialities contained therein. There may have been a history book or two thrown in as well.

I was lucky my presence was not required dark and early. I was also lucky to have reinforcements with me: Mum and Lynna.

Yes, Mum had surreptitiously checked out Sam, glancing over at him while pretending to check email on her phone. He was a gentleman and pretended not to notice. Instead, he turned on the charm and passed by the table every few minutes to get his flirt on. No joke. Although, okay, it *was* kind of amusing to see my mum in a fluster.

But I couldn't blame her. Even my breath caught when he tilted his head just *so* and glanced over at me. Damn it.

I looked away, anywhere but at him, and my eye twigged on a diagram of circles and lines the book referred to as the Tree of Life. The song I'd heard in religious school growing up hummed between my ears:

"*It is a tree of life to those that hold fast to it*
/ and all of its supporters are happy..."

I fought the urge to clap to the beat of my memory. Maybe dance around a little with a tambourine and a hip shimmy.

"It's a tree of life," I said, staring at the picture on the page. That same picture, if I turned it clockwise, that my father had drawn on the wall of his super-secret room. I pulled up the photo on my phone to be sure.

"Huh," said Sam, poking his head over my shoulder. "You've got that same pattern of dots on your back."

I stared at him. Yes, my mouth was open. My mother, for her part, was doing her best to pretend the reason Sam knew the pattern of markings on my back was because the two of us had maybe been to the beach together and I had maybe been wearing a bikini. Never mind that it was the middle of February in Toronto—and that my skin was pasty-ish white even in the middle of July. And that I hadn't owned (or been seen in) a bikini since junior high.

"Take a look at this," Sam said, calling Anshell over. A dishtowel over one shoulder and an oversized clear slurpee cup with sliced lemons and carrots did nothing to diminish Anshell's masculine, alpha presence as he padded into the room. Sam nudged the book toward Anshell, pointing to the top half of the diagram, an area surrounded by six points with a gap in the middle. "What does this remind you of?"

Anshell stared at the page, then at me. Oh yeah. Anshell had seen me naked too. Sam was nodding and smiling.

"Your father said your blood was a kind of amplifier," Sam said. "Right?"

"Dana, you told...?" Mum's tone echoed the note left for me by my father. But what could I do? I had to trust someone at some point, didn't I?

"Yeah," I said.

Mum went back to studying her phone for social media status updates. Pretending not to worry, pretending she wasn't listening to every word.

"Hear me out," Sam was saying. "What if Dana's blood actually is an amplifier? Look at this picture. What does it make you think of?"

Anshell looked at the drawing again.

"It looks like an opening of some kind. A mouth. Or maybe a star." Anshell looked back up at Sam. "You think it could be a portal?"

"A portal," Sam repeated. "Exactly." He pointed his finger to a specific spot in the upper center of the pattern. "What if this is the reason everyone is after Dana? Spill her blood," he tapped the spot for emphasis, "here, and what happens? What happens if we turn the pattern upside down?"

"Reverse it, you mean?" Anshell fiddled with a loose thread on the dishtowel. Considering. "Except they've managed to open at least one other portal without her. The Feed you disrupted. The vampires spoke of raising Alina, and we know she is here now, therefore logic suggests that is also when and where she came through. So maybe Dana isn't critical for the first part. Which then begs the question of why this Alina is interested in her at all." Anshell turned to me. "Dana, when you were captured—"

"Which time?"

"Either," said Anshell, his mind still chasing down Sam's new theory. "They talked about spilling your blood, correct?"

"Yeah." I was trying to process all of this. "But—portals?"

"You work at the Swan." Ivy Vine Girl. *Anika.* At least she was dressed this time—baggy grey open-necked T-shirt, black yoga pants, deep purple hoodie. Easier to focus when I wasn't trying to not stare at her nakedness. Or Sam's arm draped around her. "You must get visitors from dimensions there."

"And?"

"Ever ask how?" Proving Anika was not as familiar with our clientele as she thought.

"That's not happening," I replied. "Don't last long at the Swan by asking questions."

"What about the Agency?" I'd forgotten Lynna was there. "Could you ask them?"

I shook my head. "The less the Agency remembers me, the better," I said. "Plus Ezra is still with them. I think. Anything he knows, there's a good chance they do too."

"If Dana's father's theory was accurate, and her blood is an amplifier, maybe we've been looking at this all wrong," Sam said. "What if they don't need her to open the portal at all? What if they need her as some kind of living, breathing doorstop to hold this inter-dimensional gate ajar while the baddie's friends come over to play?"

"In which case," said Anika, "isn't it possible her blood could be used to close it as well? Assuming what her father wrote her was true."

"Stuart was telling the truth," said Mum. Guess

she'd changed her mind about staying quiet after all. "My daughter's blood *is* an amplifier, and whoever keeps coming after her must have figured it out."

TOGETHER, WE CAME up with a plan.

"BAIT," I SAID. To Sam's crossed arms, my mother's tightly pressed lips, and Lynna's pile of shredded paper towel. Anika gave me the nod, though. "Come on," I continued, turning to Anshell now. "It worked before. You know, that time you *didn't* tell me what you were doing." Sam flinched. "You know it makes sense. It's the best way to find out what's going on, draw them out. They want my blood? Let them come and get it."

"It's a risk," Anshell replied.

"And not a good one," said Sam.

"No," said my mum. "I can't lose you too."

"Look," I said, gentling my tone. "I'm a target anyway. They're coming for me. Isn't it better for me to face them *with* backup? Instead of alone at 3:00 a.m. in a dark alley or parking lot or my own bed?"

"Does that mean you're committing to the pack? Even before your full shift?" Anshell's questions were a formality—we all knew it. It's not like I had a choice. Not anymore.

"Yes," I said, and kept the rest of it to myself. "Can I, though? Without the full shift?"

"It's unusual," Anshell acknowledged, exchanging a glance with Sam. As though my capacity to change relative to pack status was another in an ongoing series of arguments both for and against my membership. I wondered which side Sam came down on. "Your partial shift takes more power than a full shift. In theory, at least." He shrugged. "But tonight would be your last chance this moon cycle. We'd be gambling that you can do it."

"Are we talking calculated risk or long shot?" Always good to know one's odds going in.

"You would have the pack," Anshell said. "And your vampire friend Jon as well, if he is willing. In case." Anshell didn't say in case of what. I didn't push it.

"So, what, your brilliant plan is to use my daughter to draw out these evil creatures?" My mother, ladies and gentlemen. "And then?"

"The bad guys come out to play," said Anika. "And our Alpha and his second come up with a ritual to slam that portal door in their demon-ass faces." She turned to Anshell. "Am I right?"

Anshell nodded.

"And what if..." Lynna trailed off, shook her head and started again. "What happens if the plan fails and the bad guys capture Dana? Use her blood to keep that portal open? What then?"

"Then we have a larger problem," Anshell said. "Let's do what we can to avoid that."

ANSHELL AND SAM drifted off to get ready, leaving Mum and me alone. I reached out and touched her hand. There was a lighter area on her ring finger where her wedding band, stubbornly lodged all these years since Dad's death, was now gone.

Huh. She was mad.

"You were a baby," she said. It felt as though the words were being scraped up and out from deep within my mother's chest, the weight of the guilt and sorrow and time compacting her shame. "I was tired and I had a migraine and you were being fussy. I thought Stuart was being helpful, offering to miss an afternoon of work to take you to your doctor's appointment. It was supposed to be a routine checkup."

"What happened?" I tried to squeeze mom's hand for support but she gently withdrew it. Pulling into herself.

"I don't know exactly," she replied. "I assumed you'd been to the doctor and everything was fine. You were asleep when I got up, and your father didn't say anything.

"It wasn't until I was giving you your bath that night that I noticed the spots. I'm not religious, you know that, and I had no idea what the pattern represented. Until now. But I did ask. Your father was distracted, as always, and said something about allergy tests. That the marks would probably fade over time."

"But they didn't."

"No," she said, "they did not. Your father mentioned something about a reaction to the needles, the possibility of allergies. I was stupid enough," bitterly this time, "to believe him."

I reached over to take hold of her hand. She was so hard on herself, always. How could I blame her for loving and trusting her husband? Why would she not have?

"I don't blame you," I said. She sniffed and blinked back moisture but didn't reply. "I get the feeling Dad had a *lot* of secrets."

"And they killed him," Mum said, as though finishing what she assumed to be my dangling, unsaid thought.

"Maybe," I said. Did she need to know Dad might still be alive but wearing the skin of my former academic advisor? It was still only the beginnings of a theory, and I had no real proof. Given how disturbing the possibility was to me, on so many levels, I definitely didn't want to inflict that emotional spectrum on my mother until I was certain. Maybe ignorance didn't equal bliss, but I doubted *this* knowledge would bring any joy either.

I NEEDED A break from all of the emotional drama, so of course I went to check in on Sandor. No danger of drama there. Nope.

He was napping lightly when I arrived, his snores filling the small, antiseptic room.

I eased myself into the squeaky orange-circa-1973-pleather-slash-vinyl chair. Just me and my hot, decaffeinated rooibos chai tea. Pulled off my hat and gloves, undid the buttons on my coat, and stomped snow and damp off my boots before swinging them up and onto the window ledge.

"Want some?" I knew Sandor was faking me out with that whole snuffle-plus-snore-interruptus combination. Hell, he'd taught me the routine.

"C'mon, Sandor," I said, as he continued the sleep charade. "Enough. We both know you're awake. Be my friend. Stop pretending and talk to me."

Sandor didn't respond immediately. Instead, his third eye—the wart-encrusted crown embedded in the blue-and-green-edged folds of his forehead skin—darted, twitching, feigning REM sleep.

"Fine," I said. "I'm not in any rush. It's only coming down to the third night of the full moon. No big. I'd rather sit here and drink my tea, play games on my phone. It's not like I have some place to be."

Still nothing. Although Sandor did make a teensy tiny snort out of his right nostril and only his right nostril. Don't ask me how he pulled that one off.

"Yup, that's me," I continued, settling in and leaning my head back on the padded headrest.

Gods, I was so tired. I leaned back even farther and shut my eyes. Just for a moment. There might even have been snoring. Maybe.

"Probably should have made that tea a caffeinated one," Sandor's voice, ever wry, cut into my impromptu nap time.

"Indeed," I acknowledged without opening my eyes. "Feeling better?"

"Right as acid rain," he said. I felt a light chill on my cheek, even at this distance, a breath of air expelled with his words.

"Excellent." I opened my eyes to look into his. At least *that* stayed the same—an eye for an eye, even if the surrounding skin glowed a different shade than the one I expected. "How long have you known?"

"Known what?" Sandor snorted, a nasal orifice-sized bubble of cerulean twinkling snot expanding and contracting from his snout. Nifty. "Girl, I knew you were special when you walked into the joint some three-ish years ago. Just didn't realize why, or that everyone and their butler's ass-wiper would be gunning for you. Keeping you safe wasn't easy, no matter how smooth I made it look."

I stared at my boss. Mouth hanging open. "You... what?"

"Kept. You. Safe." Sandor enunciated each word as clearly as he could through sausage-warted lips swollen from the medication or IV drip or whatever. Who knows—maybe that was his real mouth? I certainly hadn't been seeing the real Sandor.

And, apparently, he'd been keeping some pertinent Dana facts from me as well. Sweet.

"Do *you* know why I'm suddenly so fascinating to such a wide array of interested parties?" Regardless of Sandor's answer, the question had to be asked.

He shrugged noncommittally. At least I think it was a shrug—it was a little harder to tell than usual under all that new skin and a hospital gown.

I thought back to the day I'd walked into the Swan Song looking for a job. Fresh from my discharge. Sandor had checked me out, up and down—not in a lascivious, lip-smacking, needing a shower plus hand sanitizer kind of way but more of an are-you-sure-you-can-handle-this-job thing. I'd held his gaze, no problem. After the lives I'd seen and the things I'd done? No way a tusky, warty demon guy was going to scare me off from a good job with off-the-grid income.

But that was then. And since then, no trouble—not from the patrons and not from my former employers either. I should have been curious. I should have wondered why.

Stupid Dana.

And then I started to remember.

The three-headed banana demons with conical skulls that made strange whirring sounds who'd been giving me a hard time about their order, complaining edging towards ugly and a probable lack of tip. And then, something more—that intangible tang of sulfuric danger. I'd smelled it before. And yet… I turned my back on them. Should have known better. When I turned to look again they were gone, steam still rising from the seats they'd embedded their exterior bits into just moments before. And they'd left a tip after all—a nice one.

Coincidence?

That time I'd thought I was being followed from the Swan. I could feel the malevolent presence so close, my hand was reaching for a weapon I'd stopped carrying months earlier. And then. A whistling. A screech. Silence. I ran for my truck and took off so fast I was lucky I hadn't blown out a tire or flipped my vehicle on the icy gravel. I never went completely unarmed again after that.

So many times, so many dangers; so many neck-prickling moments made right again. I still knew how to fight, how to defend myself, but I hadn't had to use those skills as often as I'd thought I would have. Or probably should have.

Sandor watched as realization after realization shutter-clicked its clarity across my face. Until, finally, I closed my eyes against all the things I'd allowed myself *not* to see.

Sandor sat up and reached out to take my hand. Squeezed it. Patted it. Made a few harrumphs and *there there* noises. "Doesn't make you any less of a tough girl," he said.

"Um, thanks?" I didn't know what else to say. Thank you for watching my back against threats I'd been too dangerously oblivious to notice? Thank you for protecting me against entities and elements I might have been safer off knowing about so I could at least have maybe been more cautious?

"What kind of life would that have been for you," Sandor said. "Looking over your shoulder all the time.

Running. Hiding. Scared. I was afraid it would kill that spark that made you *you*—the ballsy girl in combat boots who didn't take shit from anyone."

"I'm still her," I said.

"Yeah," he said. "Now. But you had to get there, and I had to make sure that happened. There are too many ways to kill a human soul—or somewhat human, I guess, in your case, eh?" A brief chuckle before he remembered the situational seriousness. "I couldn't let that happen to you," he said.

I realized I could choose to be pissed. My friend, my boss, had neglected to tell me how much danger I was in because of who I was and what I'd done. Would I have figured it out sooner if he hadn't? Maybe. But somehow I knew everything Sandor had done had been with the best of intentions.

Probably why they say hell is paved with them.

"So tell me," I said. Figured if we were going for the big reveal, we might as well dig in with a spoon and a shovel and maybe even a red-painted tin metal bucket. "Why does your brother Gus—pardon me, Gustav—want me dead?"

"He's not my brother," Sandor said, looking away.

Was he embarrassed?

"He's my half-brother by my father. Charming guy, my dad." Sandor's tone implied otherwise. "My mother looked like the me you're used to seeing. Since I can swing both ways, I figured it would be in my best interests to look different from Gus, seeing as we have different *interests* as well."

"Like not killing me," I said. Best to confirm that one.

"For instance." Sandor nodded to emphasize his point. "You know, he's not a bad guy."

Trying to convince me, or himself?

"The thing about Gus is he only cares about family, himself and money—and not necessarily in that order. Someone offered him a *lot* of money to get you, and profit outranked family this time around."

I leaned forward and my elbows dug into my thighs. "Why me?"

Sandor shrugged, a remarkably fluid motion for his bulk and temporary infirmity.

"Been trying to figure that out as well," he admitted. "From what I can tell, someone told the big bad wolf you're special. Not riding at the front of the bus 'special' but the kind of special that makes you a key ingredient in certain rituals. You've never smelled precisely *right*. Human, but not exactly human."

I digested that a moment.

"Makes sense," I said.

Sandor raised a tufty green and yellow eyebrow at me. The one in the middle of his forehead, of course. The other two were busy looking around at anywhere but me.

"Everyone is interested in me—or almost everyone. It feels like I'm the Holy Grail, a catnip-filled sock toy and an ice cream sundae rolled into one big Dana package. There's always someone or something sniffing at my ass these days."

"Not always a bad thing," commented Sandor.

"Granted," I acknowledged with a head tilt. "Still, it would be nice to get a break from it all. Maybe catch some sleep."

"You can sleep when you're dead," Sandor said. "A state of things I'm hoping you don't have to worry about for a long, long time, if I have any say in it. And," he looked at me pointedly, underlining his words with a big thick Sharpie marker, "I plan to. So don't you go taking on any Big Bads, using up any more of your nine lives, without bringing backup. You read me? Am I being squeaky clean and clear here, girl?"

"Um, yeah."

Sandor reached over and grabbed my hand. Spikes of diamond-dust-blue hairs tickled at my wrist.

"You're the one they need," he said. "You can block passage or blow it wide open. You don't even need to bleed out to do it. It's all in those markings on your back."

"Does everyone know about my tats?" I muttered under my breath.

Sandor continued as though he hadn't heard me, although of course he had—I'd seen his ear tufts twitch.

"Girl," he said, "you're marked for greatness or for infamy. It's up to you which way you swing."

THIRTY-NINE

BACK AT THE HOUSE, I knew the final arrangements were falling into place but I wasn't ready to go back yet. Restless. I still had two more hours to kill until the moon rose in the sky to exactly *that* spot. The one that would unlock whatever needed unlocking.

Currently it was that space between my shoulder blades at the base of my skull.

Sure, taking a nap would be the wise thing to do. But I couldn't just lie down and do nothing, and my mind wouldn't shut up.

I craved the familiar, separate from the pack and the blood and the Feed. Tired of making decisions. I wanted control without control, relative trust without strings and responsibilities and mornings after where I had to be part of something that was else. Even though there were always complications. Even if nothing was simple.

THERE WAS A hand-printed sign on the door saying "Closed for private function. Please leave all deliveries at the back door." I ran my fingers around the edges.

A tall silhouette in shadow on the other side of the barrier; I heard the deadbolt click, saw the door swing inward. Hesitated only briefly before I crossed the threshold into the dusky sanctuary of the gallery.

The door shut behind me.

"Are you sure?" Jon's voice, hesitant, echoing against the exposed brick walls of his exhibition space. "I thought, with Claude—"

"No," I said. Not turning to look. "I don't want to talk, and I don't want to think. Can you do that for me?"

"Yes." Knowing what that meant. A blindfold appearing and then vanishing into black as he tied it over my eyes. Blessed darkness.

For the first time in days, since all of this began, I was able to relinquish control. What happened next was out of my hands and in Jon's. Sam and I didn't know each other well enough yet for these games. With Jon it was different; I didn't have to explain. It was worth pretending Claude didn't exist for a little while. Even if all of our problems would still be there when we were done.

Jon's long fingers drifting down to deftly undo the buttons on my coat, pull off my sweater, lift my T-shirt over my head. My bra still on. I suspected not for long.

In my mind it could have been anyone or anything circling around me as I stood, half-naked, in a gallery on Queen Street West with the door unlocked against February's evening cold.

A streetcar went by then, rattling the windows and shaking the floor enough that I could feel my inner thighs quiver at the passing vibrations. A gust of chill air as the door blew open a crack. Firm footsteps on the wooden floor, a small creak with each *thud*, then the clear *click* of the deadbolt sliding into place.

I could feel the tips of his fingers working their way around the underside of my breasts between my rib cage and the edges of my bra. Oh *yes*. The tips of coolness reaching, then peaking; nipples straining to meet his ever-elusive touch. A scrape of fingernail and I shuddered.

Gods.

I tried to reach back, to touch, but all I felt was empty air where moments before I knew he had been. Was I sure it was Jon? Really?

Breath hitched in my throat at the thought that this was a stranger I had allowed to touch me, to partially disrobe me. The fantasy. Opened my mouth, to speak, to say—what? My mouth covered first by two fingers, then by cool dry lips tasting copper-salty with an after-hint of caramel. Then, too quickly for me to protest, more fabric over my mouth. I could breathe. But this, this game was new.

Without my sight or the power to speak, I stood there. Waiting.

Cool fingertips in front of me now, fumbling with the button on my jeans, easing down the zipper while leaving my pants on. Reaching around to trail along my waist from tailbone to belly. All thoughts of what I had done earlier in the day were banished by the thread of energy tracing along my nerve endings.

I tasted cloves and cinnamon and I licked my lips.

"I'm leaving your hands free," he said. "You can't speak a safe word, so you'll have to show me."

I grunted softly, the sound muffled.

Jon chuckled low in his chest and I felt the vibrations echo somewhere lower in me. "Be creative," he said.

And then he was in front of me again, his tongue inside my belly button, his hands reaching in and around to cup my ass. Urgency unbound. My pants now down around my knees, held in place by the heavy boots I still wore.

I couldn't see, couldn't speak, couldn't run.

This is how it all started, a traitorous voice whispered in my ear.

And then Jon fastened his teeth on my nipple, sucking, drinking me in without drinking from me, and all other thought was gone, focused on that fine point that was the hardened nub of me and the sharp pain that was his mouth on me.

He was in control.

But this was release. Relinquishing control; just for a while, knowing I could.

I trusted Jon—enough. Enough to do this with me. Enough for him to know that this release was what I needed.

Oh.

Oh Gods.

My hands, gripping Jon's now bare shoulders—when had that happened? Drinking me in. Going lower. Along my belly, *there*, teasing as he dropped to my inner thigh. Teeth on flesh; an imprint that didn't break the skin. Nudging my legs open. I kicked my pants down, the boots holding them in place. *More.* His tongue like a cat's, rasping, grooming, faster and slower and then even faster. Darkness honed my awareness of that point, him, *there.* And then.

I would have left imprints on his shoulders had he still been human. As it was, I arched back so far into my first release that it was only Jon's strength, his arms wrapped around me, that kept me upright. More or less.

I sank to the floor, reaching for him, and felt his belt buckle. A barrier. It felt flat, etched with ridges and vales that left an imprint when I pressed too hard.

I yanked.

The buckle resisted, even as the man behind it did not. If anything, the hardness pressing against the fly of his pants took up the space I needed to wriggle my way in. The denim felt rough against my skin.

I gave up then and thrust my hands down the front of his pants. So smooth. So cold. I wanted to hold it in my mouth and suck it like a Popsicle.

Jon took my wrists in one hand and placed them behind my back while he deftly unhooked his belt, unclasped the top button of his pants.

Frustration caught in my throat; if Jon gave any response, I didn't process it. Instead, I was struck by my current state: naked, my wrists held in place, my mouth covered so I couldn't speak and my eyes covered so I couldn't see.

And now, silence.

I wanted to scream, just to hear something. I struggled in his grasp unable to get free. Started to panic. Couldn't breathe. Couldn't move, couldn't speak the word I needed to make it stop.

"Ssh," Jon whispered in my ear, letting my wrists go, putting his hands to good albeit distracting use, feathering them up and down my sides. A wet finger trailed from my throat, down between my breasts, lower still to that place where heat meets wet.

I could breathe again, and it was good.

I reached out and grabbed the one thing I could—him—and pulled. Hard.

At that, he groaned. Blessed sound. I did things I knew would make him groan more, and he rewarded me with a hum deep in his throat. Maybe it was more of a growl.

You'd be surprised at what you can accomplish with just a fingernail and a thumb. Really.

Finally, Jon grasped my wrists and extricated my hands. Not wanting to end things prematurely? I heard the *whirr* of a zipper being pulled down—not my own this time—and my hands were free to reach out and touch at will.

A brief brush of flesh before it danced tantalizingly out of reach.

"No," he said.

I made a questioning sound in my throat.

"My turn," he said. And slid his hands from my waist up my sides to cup my breasts once more before sliding his hands back around to lift me up. I could feel his hardness between my cheeks, then. Even more so when he leaned me over what felt like a cold, flat surface—table? countertop?—and slid in.

My hands slapped down flat, reaching out to find an edge to hold on to. Instead, pressing down, I found myself flat on my stomach with my arms stretched out to nothingness. Jon's hands on mine as he leaned into me, fingers interlaced in mine as he plunged into my folds. The energy of his thrusts, tantalizing slowness interspersed with bursts of intermittent speed increased the friction elsewhere. Breath catching, hitching, until my moans sliced through the buzzing quiet of the room.

We gasped and gripped at each other through our release, and I was free.

FORTY

I STOPPED TO grab a coffee on the way to back to Cherry Beach. A smile whispering across my lips and a warmth, *there,* remembering as I stood in line to pay; muscles stretched and limber.

I PARKED AND went out to meet the night but there was no more time. The moon was rising into the fullness of its final triumvirate and events were already in motion.

I ran.

I wore my boots and my fashion-forward parka and my hat, scarf and gloves. I shouted at the moon, darting back and forth from the lake, trying to disperse the resting birds in the scatter of frozen sparkle dust I kicked up as I passed.

I ran to the trees, to my supposed pack mates, cats and horses most of them, darting tails and paws and hooves in the twisting shadows. Large wings rose up behind me, blacking out the moonlight momentarily before a blast of fire singed the tops of the nearest firs. I could have sworn I heard someone or something singing "Happy Birthday" right before another treetop went up in flames.

"Celandra?" I was panting, my mouth open slightly, tasting scent on the wind. My cheeks tickling, ticklish, twitching.

The dragon behind me was chuckling. Right before she bumped me with her nose.

There was a very large cat beside me with a grin that reminded me of Sam's. It nudged its head up under my hand and started purring, encouraging me to scratch that spot—yeah, *there*—behind its softly tufted ears.

I felt a puff of warm air, saw the steam drift past; smelled hay and saliva and sugar and spring, and turned to find a stallion, deep black swirls in his fur and near his tail. His stance said alpha and the way he looked at me said Anshell. A smile incongruous on a face otherwise equine, like the Cheshire Cat grins of the horses in the meadow that should not have existed.

Still, he bumped a head larger than most medium-sized dogs under my other hand, the one not already full of cat, and whinnied in pleasure as I scratched that spot for him as well.

"Anshell," I said, and he nuzzled my hand.

I became aware of eyes on me, a cool breeze at my back. An intangible sense of longing and loss and re-birth tanged my tongue. I had a brief image of pome-granate seeds, sucked then spit out, bloody drops on the snow.

"Jon." I acknowledged his presence without turn-ing around or releasing my touch on the magnificent beasts.

"Dana," he replied, ghosting up behind me, laying his hands on my shoulders. The gang was all here. Now all I needed was Celandra.

Where had that dragon gone?

She emerged from the trees, naked, her wrinkled breasts and sagging stomach and flaccid-skinned upper arms dancing and jiggling with each springing step.

Celandra came close to me, winking at each of my companions in turn, before reaching out her arms to cup my face with hands smelling vaguely of days-old fish and urine and lemongrass and ginger.

Her touch sent a jolt through me and I arched my back involuntarily, surprised. I was wet and sweating and couldn't quite catch my breath. But not in a bad way. Then, not in a good way.

Bones stretching. Fur sprouting. I tried to cry out but instead all I could hear was a yowl. Of pain, of frustration—no time to analyze before a spear of no-question-about-it pain slammed into me. Hard.

And still Celandra held my face, all laughter gone, staring me down. Gods, how was it possible to survive this kind of pain?

I slammed on the brakes, mentally forcing every joint, every nerve ending, every spike of tufted fur back from whence it came. Visualized my skin smooth and whole and unmarred by anything other than the fine downy fuzz found on all normal humans.

It didn't work.

All those times before when I'd tried to shift and couldn't. Two nights of frustration and now this. Pain. Oh gods, the pain.

I was on my stomach now with no awareness of how I'd gotten here. Swiss cheese holes of consciousness. I suspected the pain was causing me to black out. Also the pressure. I could feel someone or something's weight on my back, resting against my tailbone.

Pressure. And hardness between my cheeks. Teeth, longer than any human's had a right to be, holding my neck in place. The scent was familiar, almost my own but not quite. I tried to swipe my paw backwards to push whoever or whatever it was off me but couldn't quite reach. I kept overshooting and underestimating relative distances and angles, not used to my new shape yet. Panting. Panic shooting out through my ears as fangs sprang from my teeth. I nicked my tongue and tasted blood.

My hair had fallen over my eyes and everything I saw was through the drifting ivy snakes curling down from my scalp, shadows in my vision. Puffs of flame, spurting free, told me Celandra was close by.

A cool hand on my forehead, stroking. Murmuring soft nothings, words blending together. All I could hear was my name—*Dana Dana Dana*—falling from Jon's lips and dancing in the breeze. What was he doing here again? But the chill of him on my forehead felt so good. So right. A ballast in the midst of all of this mewling, roiling heat.

And then I felt a head of fur bump up against my cheek. It, too, felt so familiar. But it didn't smell at all like me and I tried to raise my head to look at who or what it was.

No such luck as the teeth pressed more firmly against the back of my neck.

Then the screaming started.

I COULDN'T MOVE my head—whoever or whatever was on me kept the jaws of my immobility locked in place. But I could angle my newly pointy ears around, and the sound I picked up from my furry sonar was anything but reassuring.

"Come out, come out, wherever you are." The voice was all kinds of lusty, wrapped in layers of dark chocolate with the hinted promise of a juicy, sweet cherry if you took a bite right *there*.

My nipples tightened at the sound, and I could feel the male pressing down on my back harden a bit in response as well.

The stallion reared up and let out a warning whinny, its front hooves coming down so close to my face that the dirt it kicked up sprayed up towards my eyes and nose. I blinked and sneezed. Which did little to relieve the tightness in my core; if anything, the jerk of my sneeze served to rub further those places I was trying to ignore.

"Let me go," I growled, trying again to buck the male off my back. This time I pushed myself up onto my paw pads and kicked with the balls of my still-human feet.

Still human and still in combat boots.

The guy on top of me grunted in what I hoped was pain, releasing his jaw-hold on my neck and rolling off to lie beside me, nursing his now-sore kidneys.

"Claude?" Even in partial cat form and at a stage whisper, my incredulity was irrepressible. "What the fuck are you doing here?"

"Saving your furry, worthless ass," he grated harshly back. Whispering with that much force must have hurt. Almost as much as my boot. I allowed myself a small, bewhiskered smile. But wait, what? Saving my ass? That same ass he'd tried to separate from the rest of me through a barrage of jealous gunfire?

"Here kitty kitty kitty." That voice of liquid butter spread across perfectly crispy toast called out once more from the opposite end of the beach. "Give us the girl with the map on her back." Mutterings rippled through the scattered pack, questioning sounds layering one over the other. Words like *map* and *back* and *what the fuck?* I wasn't even a full member yet and here they were, trying to help me. "You don't need her. We want her. And what we want is what you want too." The owner of the voice, female, was dressed in poured-on fire-truck-red PVC and platform toe point shoes as she oozed her surety at the sanctity, the rightness of her position. *Any position you want*, her voice seemed to promise without ever uttering the words. *I can stretch in ways you can only imagine. All for you, only for you. Unless you want to share. I can do that too.*

"Just give me what I want," she said, aloud.

Nobody answered.

The shrieking started up again, or maybe it had never stopped.

"Why the hell would you want to save my ass *now*?" The words tickled where the tenderness of new teeth poked through previously unbroken gums, whistling through the spaces.

"Reparations," Claude bit out. I wondered if that hurt as well. "Either I protect you like my life depends on it, or I'm out of the pack."

I think my laughter surprised us both. Human emotion pushing through a jowl unsuited for the expression; the sound more of a snarling lisp that frothed my lips. "Ironic justice," I finally managed.

"Yes," Claude replied, voice tight. Maybe he wasn't appreciating the humor of the situation like I was. Then again, maybe I'd be pretty pissed as well if the *not*-me that my lover was sleeping with became a do-it-or-else protection scenario.

Still, I wondered whether the stick had enough of a hold over the carrot to make this new relationship work.

I wasn't betting on it.

More screams. I sat up and looked around.

Twigs scattered and pressed into the snow as though ground in place by large boulders, or maybe boulder-sized footprints. Beyond the scatter and grind were rings of glowing red lights evenly spaced in pairs. I couldn't tell from this distance whether they were Seven Moon eyes or those of the oily-voiced siren who called to us even now from the darkness. I felt exposed, and I caught Claude's wandering eye, motioning him to follow my lead and edge farther away from the light.

"She's here," he called out to the darkness. "Just over there." Claude stayed where he was sitting but motioned to a clump of trees down the beach.

"What are you *doing*?" My hiss followed his, threads of sound in the darkness.

"Saving your ass," he hissed back. "Remember?"

"We have her." Anshell's voice rang out, all bass and timbre, rumbling in his chest. No longer at my head but away from me and closer to those trees.

"You have nothing." Ezra's voice. It boomed and bounced along the *slap slap slap* of water sloshing through a crack in the ice. He was somewhere off to my right—and not as far off as I would have liked. "What you have is a dream, a promise of what might be. It is a fairy tale."

Anshell's answering smile was tight. I squinted eyes that could make out detail in dark that even an hour earlier I was sure I'd have missed; thought maybe I was seeing the shadowed outline of a great cat pacing around and beside him. Sam?

"If she's just a dream," Anshell called back to him, "then why do you keep trying to catch her in your net?"

"I'm not," replied Ezra.

"I am," called out the female who had laughed while Ezra had tortured me. A voice I wouldn't soon forget. "Give her up or your pack dies. Anshell Williams, leader of the Seven Moons pack, will be leader of nothing but bloodless corpses. King of bloodless bones!"

She laughed at her own macabre joke. Then she clapped her hands together and the pairs of glowing eyes stepped forward, each with their hands—claws, I corrected myself—wrapped around the neck of a clan mate.

I could smell the salty-coppery scent mixed with wet fur from here. Also the fear, as the Vine Tattoo Girl—Anika—was thrust forward. Above the tendrils etched into her skin was a trail of beaded blood, pearl drops of red. A necklace of life cut short.

In a flash she was flanked by two vampires, ghouls with long slavering tongues that lapped at the blood seeping from her jugular. I couldn't move. And even if I could, there was nothing that I could do to stop this scene, this series of actions already in motion.

Nothing, whispered the wind. *Nothing. Just wait.*

From behind the vamps, two blue ice demons glided forward. They swept their bows to all of us, their waiting audience, ostensibly to be sure they had our collectively rapt attention. I couldn't speak for anyone else just then, but I sure as hell wasn't looking elsewhere. Male and female? One was definitely larger than the other, with the stereotypically burly-broad shoulders of a linebacker—inter-dimensional or otherwise—while the other was smaller, more rounded, fractionally more delicate. I was as surprised as anyone, maybe, when the smaller one let out a deep guttural groan and stepped forward to lay a hand on the bleeding woman. The larger one, with a whistling, higher-pitched squeak, lay its hand across the seeping throat and fused the gash in place with a swathe of twinkling blue frost.

Then they opened their palms and raised up their hands as though in supplication to the ripe moon. Tendrils of wispy blue frosted smoke seeped out of their slack-lipped mouths. The shimmering ice-tinged particles wrapped themselves around the woman, curling and swirling faster and faster. Her eyes were wide despite her clenched fists of bravado.

"Stop," said Anshell. "She is not part of this."

"If they stop now, she will bleed out before you can get to her," Alina said. "Frost is the only thing holding her life in place. Would you deny her that life? For someone who doesn't even belong to you?"

Anshell didn't answer immediately, scanning the shadows of the trees for any sign of his crew. Alina took his silence as an opportunity to show a bit more of her hand. Pressing her luscious cherry-red lips together and whistling. Once, twice.

We followed her gaze to where at least a dozen clan shifters, in various states of animal to naked human form, were being held by their throats by twice that number of vampires and flanked by twice that number again of glittering blue frost demons.

We were well and truly screwed.

Anshell continued as though he hadn't noticed.

"You are in contravention of the Inter-Species, Multi-Dimensional Accord of Non-Interference," he called out. *The Accord of what now?*

"This act is one of unprovoked aggression and will be punishable by the Council Forces if you don't release mine forthwith."

Alina laughed a mirthless bark. It was the first nonsexual thing I'd seen her do all evening. Unless maybe someone was into that barking thing.

"You think those fools will help you?" Alina made a show of slow-motion head shaking and *tsk-tsking.* "Who do you think whispers the sweetest of sweet nothings in their many, many, many pointed ears?" She licked her lips, leaving a trailing sheen of saliva behind. "As luscious as you are," she continued, "and *mmm*, but you are a prize specimen, you've got nothing on me and mine. You are outnumbered. Plus, you care what happens to your minions, which makes you weaker than me."

Anshell said nothing. The great mystical leader in whom I'd put my trust, and all he could say was nothing? Where was his plan B?

Anshell looked across the gloom directly at me. Oh yeah. He could read my thoughts. *Damn.*

He blinked. Once, twice. And then he vanished, taking Sam along with him. At least I thought it was Sam.

"Be cool," Sam whispered in my ear. I jumped involuntarily anyway. He was behind me, naked, the bristle from his unshaven face rough against my cheek. I felt his hands on my upper arms, rubbing up and down, whether warming himself or me I wasn't sure. Sparks shot from my nerve endings everywhere he touched. I was no longer cold.

I realized I was human again. From one blink to the next. No wonder Sam was reminding me to chill.

As if it was possible to be cool around him. The

man was heat incarnate, his nearness distracting even as he wrapped me in a blanket of protective comfort.

"I'm fine," I said instead. As though I wasn't freaking out at my loss of control, at the potential of my impending doom.

He nodded, breath warm in my ear, and then he was gone.

THERE WAS A flash as lightning brightened the sky and the scene in all its desperate beauty. White and grey and red and blue. Thunder rumbled so hard it felt like the earth shook a moment in response. But it was Toronto, and winter, and while snow-smothered thunder and lightning storms were rare, frost quakes were rarer still.

I was alone—arms outstretched, standing as the rain and snow came down, dotting my arms with moisture. Another flash and I saw silhouettes of others, but they seemed tiny, far away from my vantage point, like cockroaches scuttling beneath rocks and leaves. Never mind that there were no leaves right now, only layers of packed-down death and decay moldering, semi-frozen, in the frosted earth below. Never mind that just moments, minutes, hours before I had been thrashing around on the ground in the painful throes of my first almost completely full shift.

Now I was naked from the waist up, partially clothed from the waist down, and drenched fully in moisture as rivulets of semi-frozen liquid drew a pattern of veins and living writhing snakes through the curls of my hair and down along my shoulders and sides and in between my breasts. I raised my arms and felt pinpricks of cold on my fingertips. Paws with needle-sharp claws. Then

I was fully human again. Did I do that? Recognizing my bits and ends and expectations and limitations.

Plus I was naked on the beach without feeling cold. Nifty.

Another flash, another bang of thunder. No time to ponder my belly button as fighting broke out all around me again. I had a feeling it had been going on before that as well. Could I have been that distracted? But then I ducked out of the way as a blue crystal-encrusted warty fist headed towards my ear.

It was as though no time had passed, and I was immersed in another one of Anshell's full taste-touch-feel hallucinations. Except my now was actually *now*—and had the power to end my current timeline and existence for real.

Through the fray, a pattern was shaping and reshaping itself. I felt rather than saw Anshell and Sam heading towards me. There was a rush of cool air, the lightest feather touch, and the cold storm of heat that was Jon fanned out behind me.

We were untouched, even by the spray of scattered blood and crystals highlighted by the moon. Protection magic of some kind? Everyone else was fighting and screeching and dying.

For me? In spite of me? I hoped I was worth it.

"Here," Jon said, handing me a T-shirt and sweater. I had no idea where my bra had gone or what shape it was in now. Again? This was getting to be a thing around Jon. "Ritual doesn't require you to be frozen."

I shrugged on the layers and felt immediately better.

"Where to?" The flow of blood and crystals and fur and nails was distracting. I didn't want anyone else dying for me. Seriously, how was it that none of the fray was touching us? It felt as though we were wrapped in a protective bubble that pulled and distorted in spots but never let any of the bad through.

Still, I was grateful—I knew the pack was providing a necessary distraction for what we were going to try to do. Me, Anshell and Claude with Sam and Jon watching our backs.

It would work. Right?

TEN MINUTES LATER found us away from the battle.

I was trying not to shiver.

Thanks to whatever weirdness was going on with my blood and that whole semi-shifter ability I seemed to have developed over the last few days, it's not like I was feeling the cold for real. I knew intellectually that it was cold out, could feel my nose hairs stick to themselves as a reminder that the temperature was not exactly suntan, sunscreen and umbrella-on-the-beach weather. It was a different kind of chill I was feeling. That sinking, snaking, crawling prick of fear rippling along my spine telling me to be anywhere but here where I was now. Clearly I was leaning more towards the flight aspect of this whole potential scenario here.

"What are you thinking, girl?"

I shook my head at Anshell's words.

Didn't want to think. Didn't want to feel either.

"It's okay," Sam said, coming up beside me. "The fighting isn't here." I scented him and he smelled like pack. Familiar, and yet different from me. He was wearing a shirt, pale blue denim, which was open and hanging loose against his skin. I wanted to push aside the fabric and nuzzle into the crook of his neck, taste that spot behind his ear. A faint smile wisped the edge of his mouth as though he knew what I was thinking. Maybe he did. "The pack will hold off the others for as long as they can. As long as it takes."

"What takes?" I shook my head to clear it. Sort of worked. I had a curious gnawing feeling in my gut, a hamster on a spinning wheel, a hunger for...for what? Popcorn? I shook my head again.

Guess my skull was thicker than I'd realized. Either that or it was muffled by the fur that had been sucked back into my pores. Science and everything I knew about biology could not adequately explain the metaphysical conundrum that had pounds of fluffy full-body-coverage fur vanish into nothingness when shifting back to human. I didn't put on fur weight—even though logically speaking I should be at least ten to twenty pounds more. Did it dissolve? Or did something else happen to it?

All of which had nothing to do with what was going on in the here and now. Plus, Anshell had been speaking while I'd been spacing. I wondered if it was important, what he'd been saying.

"So you understand," Anshell said. "You know what comes next? Do you consent? Remember—you need to say the word."

"Huh?" Very eloquent, Dana. But it did convey my I-have-no-idea-what-you're-talking-about response to Anshell's request for verbal affirmation. Even though I did. *Focus, Dana.*

"Do you understand what comes next?" It seemed as though Anshell was having a hard time with patience. His voice was tight and his features kept blurring, and I didn't think it was my eyes this time.

Just in case, I rubbed them. Nope. Anshell was still smudged. I turned around to see more.

Sam was cat and man, layers of feline superimposed onto human. The man was muscles and an orange glow with light that seemed to burn from within, some kind of large fiery feline mixed with what could have been a snow leopard. White with spots. Beneath it all was man.

Before me were rings of fire. Rocks and pebbles scattered in a symbol of infinity. The flames burned blue and red and green; within each center spun a strangely tear-shaped vortex of light and dark and shadow.

Anshell extended his hand to me across the fire. His arms came into focus, patterns of hair in flèches pointing towards the ends of his fingers. Sparks poking out from where he ended and the air around us began. Intermingled energies.

What had they called me? A prism?

"You know what needs to be done," he said.

"Yes," I replied. Even my voice sounded strange to me, as though wrapped in layers of different atmospheric pressure zones. My back was prickling.

"May I?" Jon touched the inside of my wrist with two fingers, lightly.

I had to shed a few drops of blood. *Right.* And of course Jon would be the logical one to help with that. Because vampire. Among other things. Even though we'd never truly shared blood before, and it still kind of grossed me out. Did he usually brush his teeth afterwards? Was that even a thing? *Focus.* Would it hurt? *Think about something else.* Fuck. Okay. If I was going to spill my blood this one time, Jon may as well get some pleasure out of it because I sure as hell wasn't. I glanced at Sam; got the chin bob of approval before I looked away.

Deep breath. I could do this.

"Okay," I said.

Jon nodded, and the hint of fang in his smile highlighted the predator I knew he was capable of being. I braced myself for the pain, sharpness puncturing skin; instead I felt the brush of lips, a feathering tickle and a surge of something other than hurt. And in that moment there was only Jon and me and *oh!* and nothing else mattered.

It wasn't our physical relationship that was complicated.

I didn't even feel him bite me, as high as I was on the wave of Jon-induced endorphins I was riding. *Wow.* Only vaguely aware as he wrapped his fingers loose around my wrist and shook a few drops of blood from it, gentle, on to the ground in front of us before licking the tiny wounds closed.

"Take off your sweater and shirt," Anshell said.

"Um, no, I don't think so." Even as I became aware, again, of the pain scattering once more across the back I couldn't see. My voice now hollow, reverberating sound along a long spiral plastic tube. Still. It was cold out—at least the last time I'd checked—and the logical part of my brain banged its fists against the doorway of my sanity, pointing out reasonably that removing my shirt in such temperatures on the say-so of some guy I couldn't even keep in focus was not something I wanted to be doing.

My back was really starting to prickle now, with the

fabric of my shirt sticking to points on my skin. It was the strangest sensation.

It burned.

"Dana, take off your sweater and shirt," Anshell repeated. Maybe he had something there. I was starting to feel the cotton melt like bubbling wax against places that should have been ice. In fewer seconds than I had fingers on my hand, my T-shirt was off and thrown to the side.

My skin still burned. I felt Sam slinking up behind me, felt his warmth drawing out an answering fire from my back as he leaned in to look closer.

"It's your spots," he said. Breath hot against my spine, drawing goose bumps. "They're glowing."

Anshell came over to take a look and whistled through the space between his teeth.

I was getting a bad feeling about all of this.

"Tell me again—"

The tension I'd been holding in my breath exhaled just a bit as I recognized the husky melody of Jon's voice.

"Why are you *really* interested in her?"

"She's kind of cute," said Sam. "And a damned good fighter."

I rolled my eyes. Sam was baiting Jon. Fortunately, Jon had had a lot more years to get in touch with his inner Buddha and wasn't grabbing this worm.

"Anshell?" Jon turned to catch the pack leader in his gaze, dismissing Sam.

"It has already begun," said Anshell.

"*The time for dancing has begun / upon her back has cast the sun / all aglow in misty purpose / as the Evil calls to its service.*" Celandra did a hip shimmy and slid out from the shadows towards the fire. "*There below the midnight moon / twice before has shone its doom / calls to home its errant daughter / all her foes now meant for slaughter.*" Celandra raised her hands up towards the light of the moon and clapped, twice. Drama queen. "*Then there is but one who can / stand before her to a man / on her back will point the way / to the worlds must be kept at bay.*"

"Celandra," I said. "Could you possibly be a little less cryptic?"

She leveled her smoky-grey gaze to mine and raised a bony finger to point. At me. I closed my mouth. There was something in her eyes that slithered up my spine and froze the words against my tongue.

"*Unless the fire horse spins its wheel / until the Glormath hears the appeal / all will be lost and there for naught / so many great warriors will be caught.*" Celandra spun and spun until I felt dizzy, but I could not look away. Her eerie words spun in my head along with her hair. "*Light and dark begin anew / fire and ice and fur there too / but the one who bears the blood...*"

"*Is marked for life to block the flood,*" Anshell finished. The great leader was looking a little shocky himself. Celandra nodded her approval.

"Were you taught how it ends?"

Anshell shook his head at the dragon's question. "Only that the one who bears the marks will burn with the path of the bridge between this world and the next," he said. "But I always thought it was a children's song. Do you think...?" Anshell's words trailed but his eyes were on me, flicking back and forth to Celandra for confirmation. That I was some kind of lynchpin for a prophecy uttered by a dragon woman a few brimstone crumbs short of a full and fiery loaf of sanity.

Celandra said nothing but arched a single bushy, tufted eyebrow at Anshell. I could have sworn I saw something crawling along one of the curled hairs. *Ick.* Anshell sighed and nodded.

"Um hello? Semi-naked girl standing here waiting for information, please?" I tapped my booted foot in a show of demonstrable impatience. Jon touched my shoulder, possibly in a show of support, and…oh, wow. The burning in my back felt cooler. Less painful. *Relief.*

"Thanks," I said.

"Don't mention it," Jon replied with a mock-gallant tilt of his head.

"So…we're thinking now that Alina is preparing a ritual to open the door between the first and second worlds?" Sam stepped forward, motioning to the infinity fire pit and I moved in closer to look. To my right was a circle of lights and flaring points of blue and green weaving around what could have been Alina in the middle. To my left was the infinity flame loop replicated in miniature—was that Anshell, Sam, Celandra, Jon and myself there? *What the…?*

"Your back maps out where the worlds start, end and join together. Where you scatter your blood within that pattern affects whether you're opening or sealing that link. Assuming the stories are correct," said Anshell.

"Not looking to take a blood bath today, thanks," I muttered. "What do you need me to do to make this stop?"

"This," Anshell said, stepping forward and laying his hand on my shoulder blade.

"And this," Sam said, laying his hand on my other shoulder blade. Fire seared the veins and points on my back. Where had Jon gone?

"And this," said Celandra, laying a dry palm on my forehead. It smelled surprisingly of rosemary and mint and sage. My back curved forward into her embrace.

A coolness started from the base of my spine and branched outwards in a web of counter-balancing ice. *There.* Jon's hands spreading blessed relief up from my waist, along my hips, curling out to touch the points of fire sparked by Anshell and Sam and Celandra. I heard Sam's whistled wonder as the area around us lit up with an eerie glow of blue flame.

"No!" I could hear Alina's screech of frustration even from this distance. Whatever we were doing here must be working. I craned my neck in the direction of the sound; saw an answering blue and orange glow from the other end of the beach. There was a winding snake of light twisting up into the darkness above, the shadowy reflection bouncing off the atmosphere around the moon. Twisted shapes tumbled down from the coiled life form above, down from dimensions unknown, creatures sounding of nails on metal sheets, screeching out their pain and hunger and lust for life consumed. They wanted to consume us, humans, humanoids, they were all of evil, all of desire. I could feel each and every one as they dropped from the hells above.

From behind me I could hear Anshell's voice, low, chanting. I smelled burning herbs mixed with something worse, something dead. Sam's voice joined in. We were going to have to have a conversation after this was all done, Sam and I. Assuming we lived through the night of course.

Then Sam and Anshell were both within the range of my sight. Hands clasped around each other's forearms; another joined the circle. Claude. *Awesome.* And so my night was complete. I could feel Jon's dry kiss on my hip, distracting me momentarily. Saw Claude's answering glower before he stripped down and clasped arm to forearm with his pack mates. Felt it as Claude's shift was yanked from within by the call of the moon above.

Where was Celandra?

As the chanting continued below, I felt the rush of wind and heard the sound of beating wings, up and up and up again. I could hear her cackling laughter, her shriek of joy as she ascended into the darkened heavens or hells above towards the door. Celandra seemed to grow, perhaps a trick of light or shadow, filling the sky with her presence. And then her mouth unhinged from its fastenings and dropped open.

Wind inside me now. The pumping of my blood matching the tempo of her flight. Separate strands of energy weaving together into a glowing net with six points. I pushed against resistance I could not see, my will, my power versus whatever was out there. A moment when I thought maybe I wouldn't be enough. My legs anchored by a suctioning vacuum of movement; then lightness as gravity gave way and the mouth of the portal boomed shut.

This time I wasn't imagining the cries of pain and frustration and death as the dragon ate the creatures that fell. Celandra didn't catch all of the crawlies—many had fallen before. But as I watched through the bleary haze of my watering eyes, I saw her fly higher and higher until she reached the last creature to make it through, closest to the gate itself.

And ate it.

FORTY-ONE

AN EERIE SILENCE FELL. *One, two*...on *three* the yells and yowls of pack erupted and the sounds of slaughter started up.

The entire beach, from what I could see at this distance, had begun to glow with that strange twilight-esque hum of blue that etches out a line in the sky, delineating the border between air and sand. I hoped it meant those frost demons were meeting a messy and somewhat violent demise—I'd rather not spend the rest of my life looking over my shoulder wondering if me or someone I cared about was about to be turned into a large chunk of ice.

Sam was there and then he was not, vanishing into a spin of snow and fur and leaping towards the sounds of battle. He tried to squeeze my shoulder as he passed, but it was part of the transition from man to cat and instead I narrowly escaped being scratched for the second time in a week by a Seven Moons pack member. Anshell didn't even bother to say goodbye, whinnying as he flew over me in a spray of snow and stones towards those who looked to him to lead.

I was not, as it turned out, one of those who followed well.

My back was still burning, and tiredness spread like gasoline on a trail of spark and singe. So I sat. Crystalline layers beneath me crunched as my denim-covered ass compacted what was below. Bonus—my jeans acted as a solid barrier so the cold didn't seep through right away. Better, though, was its proximity to my back. So weird, those prickles of heat where the rest of my anterior surface felt numb with chill. Everyone else was taking care of business, right? Alina had been defeated? I could take a moment to lie down?

"You left me for this? A girl so lazy she would let others die for her while she takes a little nap?"

"Claude." Jon's voice carried a warning unmistakable in its saturation of threat. "Isn't there someplace you need to be?"

"Like, for example," I said from my now prone spot on the ground, eyes fluttering, "talking less shit about me and more getting off your own ass to back up your pack?"

Claude growled before glaring at Jon and stalking off towards the fight. Like Sam and Anshell before him, he glided gracefully between forms—one moment man, the next he was cat. I wondered if I'd ever get used to that. Or be able to do it myself.

And then we were alone, Jon and I. I allowed myself to relax just a tiny bit more and lean back until my pain was numbed by the chill of the ground below.

"Comfortable?" Jon's voice pierced the fog of my perceptions.

"Yeah," I said. My eyes were still closed.

"Planning to get up and help out?" Was Jon laughing at me?

"Eventually," I said.

"Good," said a new voice. *Alina.*

"Immortalis factus est immobile faciunt illud alibi,"

she said, and suddenly I could no longer sense Jon. "We have much to discuss, you and I."

CRAP. WHERE WAS JON?

I felt a hand displace the air on its way towards my face; a hand attached to a man.

I allowed Ezra to pull me up to a standing position. On the way, I scooped up the rest of my clothing. If I had to meet my untimely death, I preferred to do it wearing more rather than less.

"Dana," he said, inclining his head towards me in greeting.

I nodded in reply. Wary. "I'd say it was a pleasure to see you, Ezra," I said, "but we both know that would be a lie."

If I'd hurt his feelings, he didn't show it.

"That's too bad," he replied with a flash of surprisingly white teeth for a man of his apparent age. "I'm always happy to see you."

"The prodigal student returned to sprawl at the feet of her master?"

"Has a nice sound to it, you at my feet looking up at me adoringly," he said. "But we both know that's not you. Unless forced." His voice rose hopefully. "Are you going to fight back so we can do a bit of forcing? It was so much fun the last time." Ezra's voice had taken on that sing-song edge of childlike insanity again.

"As you can tell," Alina interjected, "your old friend Ezra would very much like to play with you a while before we skin you alive." *Oh crap.*

"We only need your blood; the skin bit is a bonus, because I want to make what remains of your life extremely painful for all the nuisance you've caused us."

"Sorry?" It seemed like the right thing to say at the time.

"Sorry indeed," Alina replied. If I looked directly at her, would I turn to stone? Or was that a nightmare from some other fairy tale? "First you interrupt our summoning of me, and co-opt one of my willing minions into becoming less than fully behind our cause. Then you split my friend Ezra's attention when he should be keeping his eye on the ball: me. And now, on what should be my magnificent day of door opening and souls awakening, what do you do? You team up with those furry imbeciles and get in the way of my day. My *big* day. The one where I get what I want, and all of you suffer and, with any luck, die. But did I get what I wanted? Hmm?" Alina looked at me as though asking for a response.

I opted to oblige. What can I say—even I have my moments of conviviality. Seemed prudent when dealing with what I was assuming was a demon, particularly one who was threatening to carve me up for fun. "I'm going to go with…um…no?" I raised my eyebrows and tried to push the corners of my mouth into something approximating a helpful, nonthreatening smile. I suspect it came out looking more like a rictus grin.

"She's going to blow!" Ezra clapped his hands in glee and bounced up and down on the balls of his feet. There may have been humming.

"Charming," I said, turning to address her royal evilness. "Truth?"

"More like a dare," she replied. The great Alina joked? Who knew she had it in her? "Keep pushing and you'll find out."

"Come on," I said, dropping the *little innocent me*

act. "We both know there's nothing I can say to make this situation any better than it is. You want me for something. I want to be nowhere near you for whatever that something is. Nothing changes the fact that you need me, and I'm not going to enjoy helping you."

"*Clickety-clack she's headed for the rack!*" Ezra's giggling was bordering on maniacal. I wondered whether I should introduce him to Celandra; at the rate he was going into sing-song land, they'd probably get along. Had to believe I'd get through this sufficiently to facilitate such an improbable introduction. To think anything else would mean it was over, and it didn't feel over. Not yet. Not while my skin still hummed with power and my back pricked with heat.

"Indeed," Alina replied with a smile that likely glued cockroaches to the spot, then pinned them with thumbtacks to watch them squirm. I tried to comfort myself with the knowledge that cockroaches theoretically could survive a nuclear winter. But since I was not a cockroach—didn't even particularly like them, really—the whole self-soothing in the face of danger thing wasn't very effective.

Okay, maybe my mind was skittering and scuttling around like one.

Crazy mentor, crazy demon, a whole lot of fighting and nobody at my back. Again.

Assuming I got through all of this, I was thinking maybe it might be time to update my self-defense skills. Until then, I was going to have to improvise with a little game of Let's Pretend.

"Let's pretend, for a moment, I have no idea what you're talking about," I said.

Alina raised a perfectly manicured eyebrow in response.

"Pretend?" She smiled slowly, languorously. "I can pretend we're pretending."

"Whatever," I replied. Apparently I'd managed the whole ball of confusion look better than I'd anticipated. Cool. "Didn't you say I needed to consent? How can I consent if you've skinned me and I can't shape the words to say 'yes'?" I took a deep breath, then another. Trying not to scream at the thought of becoming a skinless pulpy mass of blood and flesh. *Focus, Dana.*

"Continue," Alina said.

"What is it exactly about my skin, my back, that is so important to you?"

"Now you are being foolish," she replied. "You know more than you say. I will let you proceed because I am curious; life is long and offers so few real surprises. Anymore. But do not test my patience. You know why your skin is important."

"Okay, then let's look at this a different way," I conceded without explicitly accepting her words as truth. Two could play at this game. "We live in a digital age. Couldn't you just take a picture and be done with it?"

Alina started laughing at that, so hard that tears ran down her face. Ezra too.

That worried me. When Ezra found something amusing, it had a tendency to result either in pain for me or imprisonment for someone I cared about.

Finally: "No," she said, wiping the frozen tears from her cheeks with the back of her sparkly hand. "There needs to be actual skin involved. And blood. And why am I telling you this again?"

"So basically," I said, "it's me specifically."

"*Yuppy yuppy you're the guppy!*" Ezra was too damned cheerful.

Alina glared at him. Ezra subsided somewhat, but I could hear him continuing to mutter under his breath.

"It matters not," she said, reaching out to pick me up by my throat. She started shaking me around like a sock monkey in the jaws of a puppy. I couldn't have stopped her even if I'd tried. Instead I saw spots with black around the edges of my vision and wondered if this was it for me. My consent would become moot within the next breathless sixty seconds or so. "Even though you and yours managed to block the door—and slammed it in my face—I am no longer alone on this side of things. There are others who managed to make it through. Who, even now, are leaving this place to gather in wait for the next door to open."

"So you're good then," I managed to choke out, struggling with the need for air and trying to calm the panic banging its ineffectual fists against the inside of my chest.

"Not quite," she replied. With the hand not wrapped around my throat, Alina pressed her fore and index finger against my forehead.

The beach vanished, the night was gone, and we were alone.

MORE TO THE POINT, I was. Alone. In a cell consisting of ice and wool and a steaming pot of what appeared to be hot water. At least I could breathe again. An assortment of tea bags, herbal and otherwise, were arranged in a random yet strangely organized pattern. Cubes of sugar, stacked in perfectly symmetrical rows into a pyramid of crystalline brown, sat on a plate to the side of the pot. Two cups with saucers and teaspoons lay waiting.

I knew I should be worried. And I was, somewhere inside, somewhere below the numbing familiarity of waking up in a strange place alone with no discernible escape path. At least this time there was herbal tea. I reached out to rummage around, hoping for something chai-like.

FROM ONE BLINK to the next I had company. Again? Or had I simply not noticed?

I reached out with a strength of mind and purpose I hadn't realized I had until that moment. Touched Alina's cheek. Above the bone, the pronounced line that cast hollows and shadows below. Resisted—but only just—the urge to trace that line, that darkness, to those lips of cherry-red sweetness.

She burned with chill and I gasped and pulled away.

"You are such a child," she said, *tsk-tsking* me. I noticed she didn't touch my hands though.

"Tell me," I said. "Again. I missed it the first time." I felt as though my words were very far away, and I had trouble hearing myself through the rushing *whoosh* of air between my ears where my brain was supposed to be. "Tell me why. Why you need me since the door has already opened and shut. Since you have an army rising even as your minions are being slaughtered." Alina growled a bit at that. Ezra merely giggled.

"Because," she bit out.

I tried not to linger on the points of her teeth, on those things I knew from recent memory that sharp edges could bring forth. *Where was Jon?* I tried not to wonder where he'd gone so suddenly, and why, and how. What that might mean.

When had Claude scratched me? Had it only been seven days ago? When had Sam and I interrupted Alina's sacrificial calling? *Six days.* Only six days ago. I thought about that a moment. Sam and I *had* interrupted the calling ceremony. And yet, here she was, in front of me as though the summoning ritual had been completed. And yet, she'd already been ensconced in Ezra's office as his assistant—not a newbie but one who had been there long enough to assume control and engender his trust in her competence. Six days—even six days like the last ones had been—did not logically add up to that.

So either Alina had been there before the summoning ritual, or she had shown up about a week ago as a result of it all and found a way to take over. Which meant the individual sharing this space with me was wearing a skin—the skin of Cybele, Ezra's grad student assistant.

And what about Ezra? I'd seen sides of him over the last few days I'd never thought would be aimed at me. Never mind the whole potential father-speak coming from his mouth at odd times. I'd seen evidence of potentially three separate personalities in one with him. Schizophrenic delusions? Maybe. Or maybe the human I'd known as Ezra was just a skin too.

The last week's worth of days, hours, minutes and seconds shutter-clicked across my consciousness, dragging each momentary image into stark dissimilitude. Contrast and sameness. I wondered if this was my life—my new life—flashing before my open eyes before I died. I wondered why there were no images of my life before now. As though I did not exist before what I was now.

Well that was a first. A voice in my head not mine. "*Come on, girl. Snap out of it.*" Anshell? "*Look around so you can tell us where you are, where they have you now.*"

I looked around but saw only bare white walls. A window covered with bars above; through it, the full moon. Pulsating almost. But cold, so cold. I didn't think it would help me.

"Where am I?" I asked Alina instead. It distracted me from her teeth, and from the skin on my back, still burning.

"Does it matter? Would it help you to know how close you are to home, and yet so far that the geographic closeness won't help you? Nobody knows about this place."

And then, somehow, I plucked the image from her mind. *Huh. That's new.* The lighthouse past the beachfront area of the dog park—a cylindrical cone of white-painted aluminum siding with a largish beacon of light and three flèches of red striped lines. It rose up into the trees which shielded it from both direct moonlight and obvious view. Unless the light was strobing, it was completely invisible from the beach. I chose not to wonder too hard, at that moment, why a lighthouse would be hidden. Why the space where I was, within, did not match the remembered area without.

Instead, since I hoped what I saw was real, I focused on the image of that place and prayed to that which did not want to be named for Anshell to find me.

"*It won't help, you know.*" Ezra was suddenly lucid in front of me. His lips had not moved and he spoke to me in a voice both familiar and not. "*Even if you escape, she will find you.*"

I watched his lips gape open and shut, a fish gulping at water for air. Thought maybe this would be a good time to lose my mind, just a little. I closed my eyes, a deliberately long blink, then opened them again. Leaned back in my chair and allowed my eyes to roll up and back into my head. My stomach lurched. I swallowed, throat thick with acrid bile.

In my moment of madness, I knew what to do.

ALINA LEANED FORWARD; so close that I could smell ginger and clove and if I reached out my tongue, I was sure I'd taste lemon with the faintest after-bite of meringue.

My hair had fallen partly forward into my face as I shielded my gaze. I could feign shyness, hesitation. It was only an act. I could feel the fur under my skin, my blood through the rivers of my veins.

Alina unfurled a clenched fist, long fingers with purple and black-striped nails and blue tips. A bastardized, demon version of the conventional human French manicure. Carefully, with just an edge of blue, she separated a single curl from the rest of my hair that lay across my cheek. My breathing stilled as I tried not to broadcast my fear, my hesitation; my acid reflux.

Not quite the reaction she had expected, apparently, her eyes widening just a bit but not enough to throw her off. I pushed my face to blankness, eyes downcast still, as I thought furiously back to that night outside the Swan. What had they said, those vamps in the midst of their summoning? Calling forth Alina, great mistress of…?

Blank. I was drawing a blank.

I did remember the puff of dancing dust Sam and I had made of the ritual-focused vampires, mindless in their desire to help their mistress rise from whatever pit I wished she'd return to. And in a small corner of my brain where thought and discomfort lurked, a tiny whisper of a voice pointed out to me that maybe I wasn't ready for her to go just yet. Because I needed answers.

Alina placed her palm against the flatness of my breastbone.

That slight bit of pressure did it. My palm became a paw, my nails—suddenly claws; I drew five jagged lines of blood down the side of her neck. Mixing hers with mine. Feeling what she felt.

Too much.

I leaned forward and emptied the contents of my stomach on my captors. Both of them.

They gaped at me, stunned by the sickly sweet bile I'd covered them with. I widened my eyes in horror, and this time I sold it.

I don't think Alina cared much about my horror though, because she let out a high-pitched shriek that probably would have shattered standard-issue glass had there been any around. I allowed my eyes to check out the windows through the fringes of my bile-spattered hair, but no luck.

A drop of my own spittle fell from the end of a strand of hair and plopped onto the end of my nose. Yuck.

I almost puked again right there but this time I resisted. Okay, the resistance was what you might call "barely" and there was retching involved, but still. I think it might have bought me a couple more milliseconds of sympathy from my captors than I'd had before. Maybe.

Alina was clawing at the spittle dripping down her eyelids as if it burned. Maybe it did. I wasn't sure she'd noticed the blood dripping underneath. Ezra looked stunned but otherwise had made no move yet to clean himself off.

"Get it off me!" Alina continued to shriek. "Make it stop!" She reached out blindly to grab at Ezra, who leaned back just out of reach and watched her like a bug squirming on its back with its wings and legs pinned down under a microscope. There was utter clarity behind eyes which had been rheumy with age and confusion moments before. Was Alina loosening her hold on Ezra in her moment of freaked-out meltdown? *Interesting.*

I glanced over at Ezra, checking to confirm my suspicions, but he wasn't paying any attention to me. I rose from my chair, graceful with feline speed and softness, and edged carefully, quietly, to the door I could now see etched in darkness on the far wall.

I was almost completely behind Ezra when he spoke.

"I wouldn't do that, Dana," he said. Perfect lucidity. "You're only putting off the inevitable."

"I'm good with that," I replied, raising the chair and smacking him over the back of the head with it. "Good thing you're not me," I muttered under my breath, stepping over his prone body.

Only then did I notice Alina had vanished. I could have sworn her voice still lingered, shrill, on the air.

I opened the door; Anshell, Sam and Jon almost fell

on top of me in their haste to get through. The looks of shared surprise on their faces were priceless.

"So," I said. "Did we win?"

FORTY-TWO

IT *WAS* ONLY for now. We all realized it. Alina had escaped, Ezra had vanished (apparently temporary unconsciousness wasn't enough to keep him down), and there were reports almost daily of otherworldly nasties lurking about and stirring up trouble. We weren't sure about the aftereffects of mixing Alina's blood with mine either.

Plus there was that thing where Ezra talked like my father, came back from the dead, and could drape the Ezra he used to be around his shoulders as easily as he could shed it in a puddle of discarded evaporating flesh. Because *that* was normal.

Normal was a word I could no longer apply to any area of my life. I had a target on my back, something weird in my blood and a scary-ass demon after me. More questions than answers, and a lifetime of hints and half-truths to unravel.

MY PERSONAL LIFE was no less simple. Even though my ability to do a partial shift put me in a select club of near-alpha-level power in the supe community, I couldn't be a full pack member until I managed to control my shift completely. So for now I was considered a Friend of Pack, which was something like an affiliate or associate member without the voting privileges. Shifter version of a learner's permit.

I still saw Sam, although we weren't labeling things. Jon too, occasionally. But with his loyalty to Claude, after everything that had happened, I suspected it wouldn't last much longer. Jon had made himself pretty scarce since that night on the beach.

Still, I wasn't ready to choose. Neither one seemed inclined to make me, either.

Not yet, anyway.

THERE WAS A knock at my apartment door. It felt good to be home—not begging for favors, not couch surfing.

It was late. I opened the door and saw Sam first. Smiled. Then I saw Jon and my smile widened before wavering, hesitant. Both of them? Here? At the same time?

So many ways this could go, so few of them good.

* * * * *

Dana's story continues in
BETRAYED BY BLOOD,
the next book in the MARK OF THE MOON *series*
by Beth Dranoff.
Don't miss it!

ACKNOWLEDGMENTS

FIRST BOOKS TAKE a village, and *Mark of the Moon* was no exception. Gratitude to my very first beta readers, without whom I'd have had no idea this story was worth finishing: Opher Caspi, Sandy Alexopoulos Jones and Melanie Fishbane.

To Kelley Armstrong, herself an accomplished author and the first person to tell me my story was publishable.

To all the people who gave me edits, feedback and productive encouragement along the way, including: Angela Fleury, Caitlin Sweet, Melanie Fishbane, Leigh Elliott, Katy Came, Chris Szego, Doug Schmidt and Marc Bissonnette.

A huge shout-out to my full-manuscript beta readers for their time, patience, feedback and appreciation for my words: Galya Braggio, Angela Fleury and Judy Silver.

So much respect and gratitude to my amazing agent, Rena Bunder Rossner, who gambled on a story she loved. And then polished my book to land the miracle three-book deal. Her instincts, support and encouragement have been invaluable and are so appreciated.

Thank you to Kerri Buckley of Carina Press for taking a chance on me. And for choosing Stephanie Doig, an editor who possesses the awe-inspiring ability to protect my voice while coaxing my words and plots into something so much better. All writers need a good editor and I'm no exception.

Thank you to Jack Marmer for being there when he didn't have to be, and for loving when it was a choice and not a requirement.

A special thank you to Judy Silver for her support, friendship and love above and beyond.

An overwhelming thank you to my mother, Linda Silver Dranoff, for a lifetime of love and support—even when you didn't understand what the hell I was writing! You've led by example. You were the first to teach me *show, don't tell,* and I know you've always got my back.

So much love and gratitude to Zak Dranoff-Caspi. For his patience and ingenuity in talking me through the plot walls I hit along the way, for helping to keep my fight scenes realistic and for his enduring enthusiasm for my stories.

And finally for Opher Caspi—my best friend, partner and the love of my life—for supporting me no matter what, even when I couldn't see that pinpoint of light at the end of this writing tunnel. You believed I could do this and here I am.

AUTHOR'S NOTE

WHILE THIS STORY is set in Toronto, Canada, it is a work of fiction. Some of the specific locations exist in real life and some don't; the characters themselves exist only in my mind. And now on these pages. If they remind you of someone you know, or you think I know, that's great—it means I did my job! But I promise you I made it all up.

ABOUT THE AUTHOR

Beth Dranoff tends to follow her interests. She co-founded and ran her own boutique digital agency during the dot-com boom, has produced and written for everything from websites to webisodes to children's television, has managed hundreds of online and offline projects from agency to IT to broadcast, and has handled clients of all company sizes. She has even worked in social media marketing, online community management and event promotion. Dranoff's actual degrees are in political science (University of Toronto) and broadcast journalism (Ryerson University). When not writing, Dranoff can generally be found working some kind of managerial role in either digital production or marketing communications. She lives in Toronto, Canada, with her family, her dog and more books than she can count.

Find her online at:
Facebook— www.Facebook.com/BethDranoff
Twitter— www.Twitter.com/randomlybibi
Instagram— www.Instagram.com/randomlybibi
Web— www.BethDranoff.com